ZERO DAYS LEFT

Chris Lamkin

www.zerodaysleft.com

This is a work of fiction. Names, characters, organizations, places, events, and incidents are either products of the author's imagination or are used fictitiously.

ISBN: 978-1523701728

*To my wife, my best friend
and my companion for life*

CHAPTER

1

EXPLOSIONS OF THUNDER ring out as Calvin Johnston fumbles for the directions he wrote down earlier in the day. "Where are they?" he mutters while taking a quick look around the car. He slides his hand between the seat and the console, taking his eyes off of the road only for a second. It's a tight fit and his hand feels squeezed—the corner of the paper taunting him. He wiggles his fingers back and forth against the cool, dark leather, inching his hand forward a little at a time. "Come on," he says, wishing he had taken the time to learn how to use his navigation system. "Just a little more...almost there...got it!" In one fluid motion he pulls up the wrinkled and partially torn directions to a therapist recommended by a coworker.

A flicker of light catches the corner of his eye and he turns toward the passenger seat where he sees an image of his wife, Janice. Her body is stiff and her expression dull. The faint smell of her perfume makes his hands shake as he reaches toward her, knowing she isn't real. She mouths, "I love you," then vanishes the moment they are about to touch.

Within an instant, the rain changes from moderate to a torrential downpour. Cars become increasingly hard to see as the rain pounds against the new sporty Audi A6 Sedan he'd purchased earlier in the week. The clatter of oversized raindrops striking the windshield echoes throughout the car. The sky lights up with streaks of purple and white as branches of lightning suspend in midair for several seconds before being swallowed up by darkness. Trees and bushes are pushed and pulled as the wind carries pieces of trash high into the air before depositing them along the highway.

Calvin reaches down and turns off the radio, realizing he should focus on the road. The reflection of the clock against the passenger-side window shows a backwards 6:43 p.m. Water that has vaporized into a thick smoke-like mist is churned out from the tires of other cars, making it difficult to see. Calvin eases up on the gas, doing his best to keep distance between himself and the vehicles in front of him, using only the tiny red dots from their glowing taillights as his gauge. Lights passing in the opposite direction become half-second blurs as they travel down US 75. The barely visible green road sign ahead shows that Parker Road Exit 31 is in three-quarters of a mile.

In the distance, he spots a diesel heading toward him on the opposite side of the highway. The truck's headlights are flashing on and off as if to send some kind of Morse code message. Intrigued, Calvin watches the flickering lights become more rapid the closer they get. He adjusts the wipers to a faster setting, hoping to get a better look. He constantly checks the road ahead, but his eyes inadvertently end up fixated back on the truck. The trailer is being thrashed around by the wind and seems to be having difficulty staying in one lane. I'm glad there is a divider wall separating us.

Suddenly, the rain slows and his vision of the diesel becomes clear. The cab of the truck is painted white, with a large red lightning bolt stretching down the side. There is something familiar about it, but Calvin is unable to figure out what and dismisses it from his mind.

Calvin drives onward, unaware there is a large puddle of standing water hiding on the other side of the concrete barrier. The diesel, which is heading straight for it, continues to build up speed, until it hits the water full force, sending it soaring into the air and over the wall, creating a tsunami-like wave over ten feet high. Before Calvin has a chance to react, the water comes crashing down like a dirty, wet blanket covering everything in its path. His windshield wipers, struggling to keep up, are not able to clear off the muddy water fast enough, forcing him into panic mode.

Without thinking, he locks up his brakes, sending his car into a spin. Doing his best to regain control, he frantically steers in the opposite direction without any luck. The tires slide on the wet pavement as he pushes the brake pedal with both feet, applying as much pressure as his legs will allow. His car spins out of control as multicolored tracers drown out everything visible and turn them into nothing but smears of colored lights. A loud crash rings out as his car slams into the median wall, throwing his body forward and smashing his chest into the steering wheel. His arms and shoulders continue to move forward, while his ribs nearly collapse from the force.

The car bounces back into oncoming traffic before finally coming to a stop. This is it. He feels powerless against whatever fate must have in store for him. With his body rigid and his eyes tightly closed, he waits for the unavoidable impact. Instead, several bursts of light and fading car horns are the setting in this dismal reality, until they fade into near silence. His head begins to throb softly at first, until all at once he feels an enormous amount of pressure, as if someone were wrapping their fingers around his brain and squeezing. He fights with every ounce of energy his body has left but is too exhausted and easily falls into a trance-like state. His face turns pale white and loses all expression. His eyes glaze over as he mumbles, "Peux-tu m'entendre?" very slowly, pausing a few seconds between each syllable. Without making any other movements, he repeats the phrase several more times before finishing with the words "Du gehörst mir."

The whooshing of the windshield wipers on high speed wakes him from his dreamlike state. Feeling the slow release of the formidable grip, he gradually raises his head and notices the rain has stopped, the sun is shining brightly, and the highway is now completely empty. The entire area is disturbingly quiet and devoid of any traces of the storm.

He clutches the steering wheel, then slowly releases his grip before reaching over, with a trembling hand, and turning off the wipers. He eases his feet off of the brake pedal, trying to make sense out of what just happened. I need to pull over and get my head on straight.

He looks around in a daze. Where are all of the cars, and why isn't the road wet anymore? Both sides of the highway are vacant, and the entire area has turned into a ghost town within a matter of seconds. Unable to make sense of anything, he begins to drive again, veering to the right toward Exit 31. From the exit ramp, he sees a Shell gas station a little ways down the service road.

Pulling into the parking lot, he immediately drives toward the back by the air and water machine. There is sign with "Truth or Ignorance" handwritten in blue permanent marker duct-taped across the center of the machine. He glances around the empty parking lot, searching for additional clues and feeling uneasy. He looks up, hoping for any sign that life exists and is distraught that not one solitary bird is flying overhead. Pushing these concerns out of his mind, he parks and gets out to inspect the damage. Dreading the future repair bills, he reluctantly walks toward the front of his car and stares in disbelief. He stands in the same spot without any sound or movement.

Finally, he musters enough energy for a single phrase: "What is going on?" The front of his car is as clean and spotless as it was when he first drove it off the lot. There is not a scratch or even as much as a single drop of water. "I don't understand," he mumbles, replaying the entire scene over in his mind. I hit the divider wall hard. So hard it threw me forward and I almost hit my…. Stopping in mid-thought, he glances toward the windshield. All of the airbags are still loaded. As hard as I hit the wall, at least one of them should have deployed. Reaching up to feel his chest, he presses from one place to another, wondering why he is not hurt. What is happening to me?

He lifts both arms over his head, interlaces his fingers behind his neck, and walks around his entire car several times, hoping to find some shred of proof of the accident he is beginning to understand didn't happen. Instead of feeling excitement at the thought of an undamaged car, he is deflated by the realization that there is some truth to the idea that he needs a therapist.

He gets back into his car and slumps in his seat with his head hanging low, feeling a strong sense of disappointment and confusion. Unable to motivate himself to continue, he decides to just sit there for several minutes. With his face in his hands, he mutters, "I refuse to turn into my father."

He thinks of Janice and wonders why he saw her image earlier. His thoughts are scattered and his will is broken.

Am I really losing my mind? Is this how my father felt for all of those years? Am I destined to repeat his…. Calvin stops mid-thought, unwilling to relive any painful memories. Instead, he focuses his attention back on his family. He imagines Janice playing with their three-year-old son, Daniel, on the steps in the shallow end of their pool. He envisions them both laughing and focuses on her smile. He loves the way her eyes always seem to sparkle whenever she smiles that big, gorgeous smile. He can picture Daniel wearing his blow-up arm floats, slapping at the water and watching the rippling waves as they slowly move away.

"This is the moment where I either lose my life completely or I gain it back," he states with authority, as if someone else were there to benefit from his long-overdue pep talk. He feels a calming sensation as he recognizes that his family is his strength and, as long as he has them, he can face whatever challenge life has in store.

He removes his hands from his face, straightens his shoulders, and sticks out his chest. He takes several long, deep, calming breaths until the stress and anxiety slowly slip away. Looking in his rearview mirror, he first notices his thick, dark brown hair parted in the middle, leaving the center of his forehead exposed. His high cheekbones compliment his square chin, but his light brown eyes are surrounded by dark circles. Wow, these last few months are really taking their toll on me. He notices several red veins in each of his eyes. I really need to get some rest.

He glances over at the gas prices for regular unleaded and shakes his head in disgust. "Every summer like clockwork," he grumbles.

Putting on his seatbelt, he discovers that everything appears to be normal again. He sees several large, black grackles sitting on the phone lines above the street and can hear the humming of the cars as they drive along the highway. He is relieved to no longer be alone, but at the same time fears he is losing his grip on reality. He recognizes that he is in serious need of a therapist and decides to head to his appointment.

Before he pulls out, he is distracted by an older farmer walking toward the convenience store. His skin has been overexposed and appears leathery. He is wearing blue overalls, a dirty white undershirt, and a red bandanna is sticking out of his back pocket. Heading away from his red Ford pickup, the farmer steps onto the curb and walks past a tan Jaguar parked directly in front of the double doors of the store. Calvin notices that the tailgate of the pickup truck is down, revealing several deep dents and extensive scratches along the inside of the bed. The back window is decorated with a number of farming stickers, but it's the "Little Elm, Texas, Farming Association" outlined with bright red lettering that catches his eye.

As he looks away from the pickup, he is startled by an older woman pumping gas who looks to be staring directly at him. Her gray hair is tucked very neatly underneath a light green hat with a dragonfly pin on the front. She is nicely dressed in a long, green, lacy skirt, but the clothes are outdated and look to be a little worn. He remembers today is Wednesday and wonders where she has been. Judging from the look on her face, there appears to be quite a bit on her mind. It becomes apparent that she is staring slightly over his head rather than directly at him. Her fierce attention is focused toward the group of trees located past the parking lot, in some undeveloped acreage about fifty feet out. He looks in the same direction and sees several white lights in the shadow of a large oak tree. As he watches, the lights disappear one at a time until all have vanished. Her grandson, who isn't much older than five, is sitting in the backseat, his attention centered on a toy. The parking lot is now busy with cars driving in and pulling away. All Calvin can think about is speaking to the older woman. About what, he is uncertain, but it doesn't seem like he has much of a choice.

The handle of the gas pump clicks backwards as the pump automatically switches off, indicating that her tank is full. She remains standing next to the pump with her hands down by her sides, still staring into the distance, unaware that the gas is no longer pumping. He continues to watch, a little bothered by the nozzle sticking out of her yellow Honda Accord, but he decides to mind his own business and says nothing. There is a bumper sticker on the back of her car that states, "Making the right decision can open the right doors," with a picture of a white door with a large, red lightning bolt. He is instantly reminded of the diesel and thinks, Okay. That's a little odd.

He opens his car door and gets out, closing it behind him gently until it latches. He kicks away some leaves that have collected against the curb and decides to lean against his hood, refusing to take his eyes off of her. She slowly turns her head until their eyes lock. The hairs stand up on the back of his neck and a chill runs down his spine. Without hesitating, he jumps to his feet and says, "Yep, I'm done," feeling completely creeped out as he swiftly makes his way back into his car. Driving away, he notices that the handwritten sign has disappeared.

Coming off the ramp for US 75 and still headed north, he approaches a green and white highway sign that reads "Spring Creek Parkway Next Exit." He spots a shadow of some sort, but it is impossible to make out. It resembles a figure leaning against the sign, eerily watching him. The harder he stares, the more blurred the figure becomes, yet the sign is still clear. Driving past, he notices something glowing on the right ankle of the dark shadow. After passing it, he constantly checks his rearview mirror, uncertain if the image is real or another mental "episode." His hands tremble as he considers the possibility that he may be going crazy.

CHAPTER

2

INCAPABLE OF CLEARING out of his head the image of whatever was leaning against the sign, Calvin tries to focus on the radio. He switches between several stations before giving up and turning it off. Already four minutes late to his therapist appointment, he drives down Spring Creek Parkway while briefly scanning the directions for the street address. Looking up, he sees a large Medical Plaza sign outlined in red brick with the number 1811 printed on it.

"That's it," he says, switching from the middle to the right lane, relieved he hasn't missed it yet. There are three rows of freshly planted pink begonias on each side of the sign, surrounded by dark brown mulch several layers thick.

He turns into the parking lot, concentrating on the suite numbers as he slowly drives alongside the one-story building. He is amazed that there are at least fifteen different businesses on this side alone. As he drives, he sees a sign for diabetes care and another for spinal professionals before nearing the office of psychiatry. *Suite 109; this must be the place.*

He pulls into one of the many open parking spots located in front. The time on the clock changes to 7:09 p.m. and, as he is getting out of his car, he notices that most of the other businesses along the plaza are already closed. The building is made of red bricks and, judging from the dullness of color, he guesses it's about fifteen to twenty years old.

The door to the doctor's office is solid glass with a dark tint and displays the name "Dr. Rachael Livingston" in white italic letters with her office phone number listed directly underneath. Walking in, he hears a buzzer sound in the back section, behind a closed wooden door, indicating that someone has just entered.

As he makes his way to the front window, he is surprised to see it shut. He pulls a blue pen out of a cylinder containing an assortment of different colors, prints his name on the sign-in sheet attached to a clipboard, and is startled when the glass window abruptly slides open with a loud scraping noise. An overweight woman in her late fifties with short, curly, black hair is sitting behind the glass, glaring back at him. "What is your name?" she asks, using an offensive tone.

Stunned by her rude display, and not in the mood to be cordial either, he looks down at the sheet where he has just written his name and says nothing. A little put out, she grabs the clipboard and scribbles her initials in a blank box on the same row as his name before placing it back on the counter. He turns around and heads toward a U-shaped row of armless black leather chairs surrounding a table filled with popular magazines. He glances over and considers picking one up, but decides against it. *I would rather just stare at the unfriendly woman, hoping to annoy her.* All seats are empty so he strategically chooses one next to the window, where the blinds are half open, and he is able to see his car. He is admiring the metallic gray color when the doctor opens the door and says, "Mr. Johnston."

He quickly jumps to his feet. "Yes, I'm Calvin Johnston."

His first impression of her is that she is unbelievably attractive and probably in her late thirties. A light-skinned African American with thick, dark, wavy hair cut just above her shoulders. She appears to be about five foot eleven and is very slim, reminding him of a runner. He can tell she has expensive taste in clothes, judging from her long-sleeved silk top complemented by black, silky dress pants. Walking up to her, he notices there's only a few inches height difference between them. Looking up to make eye contact with him, she shakes his hand and introduces herself as Dr. Livingston.

She asks him to follow as she heads down a short hallway with tan Berber carpet. She passes a restroom on her left before turning right into her office. On her way to her chair, she grabs a coffee mug from the coaster on top of her mahogany sculpted desk. The entire place is limited to a waiting room, a short hallway, a bathroom, and one office, but so far seems to be more than enough space for her practice. He scans the room and sees a couple of stacks of papers, along with a few manila folders, sitting on top of the desk next to her stylish, red reading glasses. There is also a new notepad of paper with an expensive-looking ballpoint pen lying on top. The white, textured walls are mainly covered with a mixture of original oil paintings and framed diplomas, but nothing to indicate she has any kind of life outside of this office.

"Did the receptionist offer you anything to drink?" she asks, before taking a couple of sips of her coffee.

He laughs and responds, "What, Mrs. Personality over there? I got the impression the only thing she wanted to offer me was the door."

"I would like to apologize for Judy's behavior," she says in a soothing voice. "We've been working quite a lot of late nights recently, and I can tell it's beginning to take its toll on her. So far, I've received two complaints this week, and I'm planning on talking to her about it later tonight, if I have time."

Only two complaints this week? "No worries," he says, trying to be sympathetic and understanding now why she's drinking coffee at 7:15 at night.

"Would you care for bottled water, coffee, or Coke?"

"No, thanks. I'm good," he says, still a little on edge and ready to get this session started.

There's only one chair in the room, other than the one occupied by Dr. Livingston. He walks up to it and rubs his hand over the dimples in the maroon leather. He figures it's going to be stiff and uncomfortable. Sitting down, he sinks into the cushion and is shocked at how well it conforms to his body.

He has waited long enough to tell his story and is relieved that the day is finally here. Therapy is a far cry from his usual behavior of keeping his personal life bottled up and separate from everything else. Doubts start to seep in, and he wonders if he should really tell all or be a little more conservative. The more he thinks about it, the more he realizes he should probably stick to his instincts, which are telling him to be discreet. *Otherwise, she might think I'm crazy.*

"I would like for you to tell me what brings you to my office."

Ignoring his own advice, he states, "I have been having weird things happen to me over the last few months."

"Can you describe these weird things?"

"Well, I'm not really sure where to begin." He places his hand on his head and runs his fingers through his dark brown hair. He's immediately distracted by the several strands that have broken loose and watches as they fall from his fingers.

Dr. Livingston senses his loss of focus and calmingly says, "Please feel free to take your time."

"Thanks," he responds, diverting his attention back to her. "I think I will start with the first experience and work my way to some of the others. This should give you a general idea of what I have been living with over the last few months." He clears his throat a couple of times before continuing. "It began when I was having dinner with my wife, Janice, and my son, Daniel, roughly three months ago. I was sitting across the table from her and my three-year-old son was in his booster seat to my left. We often sit around the table in this order, since my wife is right-handed and she finds it easier to help him with his food. Anyway, I can't recall what we were talking about at the time, but I do vividly remember seeing a shadow of some sort as it passed by the kitchen and headed down the hall toward the bedrooms. Luckily, my wife's back was to the hall, but it scared me half to death. I jumped up right in the middle of our conversation. My first instinct was to grab a weapon of some kind, but something inside my head was telling me it wasn't necessary." Calvin stops and begins to massage his temples in a circular motion, hoping to relieve a slight headache he feels coming on.

"What happened next?"

"I ran over and immediately searched the master bedroom before heading across the hall to my son's room. I thoroughly checked every possible hiding spot and called out several times to whoever was in the house. I tried my best to reason with the intruder so that we could avoid anyone being hurt. The weird thing is I never found evidence of a break-in or any proof that someone was ever in our house that night. The more I thought about it over the next few days, the more specific characteristics of the figure reminded me of my wife. The shape of the person, and certain movements in particular, but it never made any sense. She was directly in front of me when it happened."

Dr. Livingston picks up her glasses and puts them on. She then grabs one of the pads of paper, opens to the second page, and scribbles some notes.

"Since then, I would hear whispers sometimes at home, and other times at work, but I could never make out what was being said." He pauses and takes a few deep breaths. "I wasn't planning on saying anything, but two separate incidents happened on the way here today."

Stunned, Dr. Livingston glances up at Calvin briefly. "Are you okay?"

"Honestly, I'm not sure. I saw an image of my wife in the car. She looked very real. In fact, I could even smell her perfume."

"What was she doing?"

"Nothing, just sitting in the passenger seat and staring at me."

"Did she say anything?"

"Yes. She told me she loved me as if she were saying good-bye."

Dr. Livingston scribbles a quick note before asking, "Have you called to check in?"

Embarrassed, Calvin looks away briefly before making eye contact again. "No. I was afraid she would hear the uncertainty in my voice. She already worries enough about me. I didn't want to add to it. Besides, she's probably giving Daniel a bath right at this moment."

Sensing she should move on, Dr. Livingston clears her throat before speaking. "You mentioned there were two incidents on the way here. Do you mind discussing the second?"

Calvin begins talking faster and gesturing with his hands. "I know I wrecked my car, but when I got out to survey the damage nothing was wrong with it."

She chimes in, intrigued by what he is saying, and trying to calm him down. "Describe in detail exactly what you were doing at the time of the disappearing car accident."

The words "disappearing car accident" ring in his ears, reminding him of the earlier ghost town. He anxiously blurts out, "I forgot to tell you that all of the people, including their vehicles, disappeared and stayed gone for several minutes immediately following my car accident."

She can tell he is beginning to get a little too excited and worries she's losing control of the conversation. She switches tactics to help separate him from his emotional side.

"You're doing really well. Usually on a first visit we talk about past history, bad relationships, and generally speaking most people are overly cautious and afraid to open up until their third or fourth session. I have to be honest in telling you that so far I'm impressed. However, I'm also a little concerned we may be moving a little too fast. Before we continue, I would like to have a better understanding of your background. We can start with, how long have you been married to Janice?"

Calvin takes a deep breath and holds it for several seconds, fighting the urge to continue on without her approval, desperately in need of answers. He studies her mannerisms and softens slightly as she smiles at him, attempting to make him feel more comfortable. He realizes this is a necessary step in removing the anxiety overtaking his emotions and decides for the next few moments to let down his guard. He scoots back in his chair before releasing his breath, unaware he had been biting the inside of his lip.

"We've been married a little over thirteen years."

"How would you describe your marriage? Any current strains?"

"No. Not really. My marriage seems to be going quite well. Janice has been extremely supportive under the circumstances. I couldn't imagine going through any of this without her by my side."

"You mentioned you have a son named Daniel."

"Yes. That's correct."

"Please tell me a little about him."

"Fortunately, he takes after my wife's good looks from his jet-black hair to his pale, white skin." Calvin's shoulders lower as he starts to feel his frustrations weaken a little. "He turned three on April 21."

"The challenging threes," she says, smiling.

"Sometimes," he says, laughing. "He's home all day with Janice, so they have formed a really strong bond."

"That's nice. I bet he really enjoys the quality time. Sounds like you have a very stable family life."

"I do. So far we've been very fortunate."

"I noticed you are wearing a college ring. Which school did you graduate from?"

"I received my undergrad from Texas A&M and have a master's in business from Baylor University."

"That's impressive. Have you always lived in Texas?"

"Yes. All of my life."

"How long have you lived in North Texas?"

"About ten years. We were living farther south, down by Houston, until I received a job offer from a major soft drink company headquartered just a few minutes from here."

"What do you do? Specifically, what's your job title?"

"I was promoted back in January to regional vice-president of sales."

"Congratulations. Sounds impressive. Do you mind giving me a quick overview of your day-to-day responsibilities?"

Without hesitation, Calvin sputters out a well-rehearsed job description that he has used in various company and departmental meetings. "My primary roles are to meet or exceed sales revenue, budgetary objectives, and sales profitability, coupled with anticipating and reacting to trends or shifts in the industry."

"Wow. That's a mouthful."

Calvin pauses momentarily, ignoring her comment. He's suddenly feeling overwhelmed and incapable of escaping the apprehension that's quickly building in the pit of his stomach.

His eyes lose focus, and his jaw clinches. "Or at least those were my responsibilities until Monday of this week."

"What do you mean? What happened on Monday?"

"I have taken a personal leave of absence until I can figure out what's going on inside my head. There have been too many close calls with uncontrollable outbursts caused by…" Calvin stops, becoming paranoid, and looks around the room before muttering the word "fear."

Dr. Livingston senses that his stress is returning and decides to switch subjects. "How about your parents? How would you describe your relationship with your mother and father?"

"Pretty strong. We usually speak at least once a week." Calvin's eye twitches as the untruth rolls off his tongue. He envisions his father's lifeless body lying face down on beige-colored carpet and immediately dismisses the image, refusing to let it go any further. *Tell her! I can't, it's way too early.*

Calvin musters up a fake smile, hoping to mask the reality that afflicts him. His pulse is racing as he struggles to contain the unnerving feeling that is lingering on. He shifts in his chair, desperately trying to reduce the agitation as it builds with each passing moment.

Dr. Livingston flips another page over and continues jotting down notes. "I get the impression from your body language that you're holding something back. Is there anything you would like to tell me? Or maybe discuss in greater detail?"

He starts to speak and freezes, feeling powerless as unrecognizable screams fill his head. Unable to focus on anything else, he stares into her dark brown eyes, incapable of speaking a single word. His face loses color, turning pale white as the last of his sanity is pushed out by the darkness slowly creeping in. He glances up and sees her lips moving but is unable to hear any sound as each word escapes her mouth.

"I'm sorry," he interrupts, trying to contain his anxiety. "You can't help me…no one can."

CHAPTER

3

DR. LIVINGSTON STOPS in midsentence, overcome with shock and irritation by Calvin's disruption. "I missed what you just said. Would you mind repeating it please?" she asks, using a slightly agitated tone.

Calvin's demeanor is showing symptoms of defeat. His broad shoulders are slumped and curved inward, while the desperation in his eyes pleads that he wants to be left alone. His behavior reveals signs of surrender as he lowers his head and fixates on one specific area of the floor. Refusing to look up, he mumbles, "It's not important."

She stands abruptly, pushing her chair against the back wall before swiftly sliding her coffee cup to the side, out of the way. She leans over her desk as far as she can, positioning her hands until they are less than two feet from his head. She claps hard and loud three times, hoping to break the trance he has inadvertently fallen under. A stinging sensation instantly shoots through both of her palms and each finger, leaving her stunned as the sound echoes off of the walls before fading away.

Calvin is startled by the noise and looks up, instantly making eye contact.

"Yes, it is important," she replies firmly. "Do not give up on me and, more importantly, do not give up on yourself. You mentioned you had everything going for you leading up to three months ago, and from what I gathered, your life was nearly perfect. Is this correct?" she asks, trying to engage him in conversation once again.

"Yes."

"Then give me the benefit of the doubt, and I promise I will do everything within my power to make sure we figure out specifically what is going on with you. I will dedicate all of my resources..." Dr. Livingston's voice trails off and she giggles nervously, realizing she had lost herself in the moment. She rubs her hands together, hoping to ease some of the discomfort, while still maintaining eye contact. "My apologies for the outburst. It appears the late nights are having an impact on me as well. I'll understand if you choose to end this evening's session early. I would even be willing to refer you to another doctor as a replacement. I know several in the area who I would recommend."

Calvin blinks twice, still stunned by her display. He chuckles a little at first, before losing control and bursting into full-blown laughter. He's unable to stop for several moments, feeling the weight of his concerns slowly being lifted. He reaches up and wipes away a tear while trying to catch his breath.

"Are you kidding?" he says, feeling refreshed. "This is the best I've felt in several months. I didn't realize how bad I needed to laugh."

Dr. Livingston removes her glasses and places them on the corner of her desk, purposely avoiding eye contact.

"I believe it's my turn to be honest with you. I rarely lower my guard as much as I have since entering your office, but I don't feel I have anything to lose. I'm willing to put my trust completely in you, and your unorthodox methods, as well as your surprisingly loud hands," he says, then grins widely.

She reciprocates the smile, then gives him a look of severe concentration. "Then let's begin with a slightly more challenging approach. I want you to clear your mind. Try not to think about anything except the sound of my voice. Now tell me your first thought."

He closes his eyes and focuses on her soft, soothing tone. He can feel his anxiety fade as he holds each word in his mind before speaking. "I'm sitting on a park bench at lunchtime roughly three months ago."

"Please be detailed," she interjects. "Start from the beginning."

"Sure," he says, feeling like her interruption was unwarranted. "I was sitting at my desk reviewing my department's budget when I experienced whispers in my head for the first time at work."

"When did this happen?"

"Sometime around the second week of March."

"What did they say?"

"I don't know. It was all jumbled together, and I couldn't make out any of the words." The image of his father returns, but Calvin quickly pushes it out of his mind. "I thought maybe the strain of the new position was already getting to me. I wasn't really sure what was happening, but I knew I needed to leave before anyone found out. Luckily, it was almost lunchtime so I decided to go somewhere peaceful to clear my head. I had brought a lunch, which consisted of a ham and cheese sandwich with Lay's Potato Chips." He stops, feeling a little irritated. "Is it completely necessary for me to mention every detail?"

"Yes. I'm a true believer in it. When trying to figure out the surrounding problems, it's always a good idea to concentrate on the specifics. Some of my most skeptical patients are surprised to find out that the simplest details can help them uncover the root problem. There aren't any guarantees that it will work for you but, based on my experience, I have found it to be good practice and I would like to stay with what I know works."

"Yes, ma'am," he says, feeling like he has just been scolded. "My lunch consisted of a ham and cheese sandwich with Lay's Potato Chips," he repeats. "I figured I would drive to a park—correction, Lakeside Park—a few blocks away from my work. It has a beautiful pond with several varieties of ducks and a wooded area. I discovered its location a few years ago and made a promise to myself to frequent it at least once a month, if possible."

"That's a great idea. I bet it helps break up the monotony of your day."

"Exactly." Calvin stands, removes the wallet from his back pocket, and places it in his lap before sitting back down. "Sorry. It's been digging into me and driving me crazy." He laughs as he hears the word "crazy" leave his lips and wonders if maybe it was a poor choice, given his current situation.

"Please continue," she states, pretending not to notice.

"I parked in the empty, gravel lot. I was sitting at one of the picnic tables facing the pond, relaxing and watching the ducks. When, out of nowhere, a diesel appeared and pulled in behind my car. He not only took up every spot, but blocked me in as well. I wasn't planning on leaving anytime soon, so it wasn't a big deal, but it bothered me on principle. I remember looking at the cab of the truck. It was all white with a red lightning bolt down the side." Calvin's face loses expression, and he begins fidgeting in his chair. "You were right about having me list every detail," he says, his voice fading and his eyes fixating on her.

"Are you okay?"

"No, I'm not sure that I am." Unwilling to stop at this point, however, he says, "I remember noticing the truck driver was extremely overweight, but I can't seem to picture his face. He stood at the front of his cab, watching me with barely any movement. He eventually made his way over to the Porta-Potty and was gone for several minutes. I also remember feeling relieved as I saw him driving away. I'm pretty sure I saw him again on the way here. I believe he's the one that caused my car accident that didn't really happen. He kept flashing his lights as if he knew it was me. I wonder if he's the one that mind-controlled me to say those phrases."

"What? What phrases?" she asks.

"How could that even be possible?" he continues.

"What phrases?" she asks again, a little louder this time.

Calvin is able to remember each word as if someone had etched it into his memory. "The first phrase was '*Peux-tu m'entendre?*'" he says with certainty. She scribbles it down and impatiently awaits the rest. "The second was '*Du gehörst mir.*'"

She jots this down as well before asking, "Do you know what either means?"

"I have no idea, but I keep envisioning the word 'gotcha.'"

"Well, I believe the first phrase is French and the second sounds like German. We can look them up on the Internet to know for sure." She flips the first page of her notepad over, guarding every word. She places the covered notepad on her desk, along with the pen, and opens the middle drawer to retrieve her iPad.

This is too real for me. He stands and slowly paces around the room, hoping to clear his mind. Looking at one of the oil paintings, he admires the blue waters of a canal lined with beautiful white stone cottages. His attention shifts to a framed doctorate degree in psychology from the University of California at Berkeley, and he is more impressed than surprised.

As he passes a mirror, he glances at his reflection and stops instantly. He can hear Dr. Livingston talking in the background, but isn't listening to what she's saying. He's unable to take his eyes off his reflection as he sees a much older version of himself, in the vicinity of mid-to-late eighties. His hair is completely gray, his entire reflection old. A long, faded scar stretches down the left side of his face. Both cheeks are drooping, with wrinkle stacked upon wrinkle. He lifts his right hand and places it on the center of his cheek. He's mortified by the excess of skin that he's able to move as he pushes the wad up, well past his eye, only to release and watch as gravity swiftly pulls it back down. He hears Dr. Livingston in the background saying, "You belong to me," breaking his concentration.

"What?" he asks, turning to face her.

"I was saying the first phrase is French and translates to, 'Can you hear me?' While the second is German and means, 'You belong to me.'"

His body starts to shake uncontrollably as he visualizes every single translated word, and he becomes nauseated as each rattles around inside his head.

"I belong to whom?" he mumbles, refusing to let terror devour him. He glances toward the mirror again, only to find that his normal reflection has returned.

Spooked beyond belief, he shouts, "I gotta go!" and rushes toward the door. He shoves his wallet back into his pocket with trembling hands. His chest tightens, and he is unable to stop his mind from racing, leaving him unsure of everything except the need to get out of there.

"Sorry, Doc, I guess now you'll have time to talk to you know who," he calls back, pointing in the direction of the front desk.

Calvin leaves the office and hurries down the hall, making his way through the waiting room before exiting the building, refusing to look back.

He smashes the unlock button on his key chain and his parking lights flash twice, illuminating the sky. He quickly opens the door and jumps into the driver's seat. His hand bumps against the steering wheel, knocking his key onto the floor. He immediately reaches down, fumbling blindly. "Come on!" he yells as his frustrations build. Jumbled whispers fill his head the second his fingers grip the key. Ignoring them, he pushes his key into the ignition and starts his car, slamming the shifter into reverse. His console screen displays the view of everything behind him as he hurriedly backs up before driving away. He half expects the doctor to come rushing out, but remembers that he had prepaid for the session when he scheduled the appointment. *I have to calm down.*

"C-a-l-v-i-n," is whispered from the backseat, softly but distinctly, the moment he pulls onto Spring Creek Parkway. He can feel warm air pressing against his neck. His muscles twinge, forcing the hairs on his body to stand on end. His voice cracks as he says with hesitation, "Hello. Who's there?"

Sensing his fear is getting out of control, he nervously looks behind him. *Please go away.* He takes several more quick looks back and is unable to see anything out of the ordinary. Chills run down his spine as "C-a-l-v-i-n" is whispered again, this time up against his left ear. His reflexes take over, and he throws his left arm up as if to swat a fly, but only makes contact with the dark gray leather of the headrest. Searching frantically, he turns his upper body to the right, more than halfway around in his seat, but is unable to find anyone. He checks for cars before yanking the wheel to the right and turning down a side street. His tires squeal as his car comes to an abrupt stop. He slams the gearshift into park, rips off his seatbelt, and jumps out. Standing next to the side of his car with his right hand clenched into a fist, ready to fight, he leans over and stares in disbelief at an empty backseat.

Fed up to the point of breaking, he screams angrily, "Show yourself now!"

He's distracted by flickers of light that are escaping from closed curtains in the window of a house across the street. A shadow moves from side to side. *Someone is watching me.*

He leans against his vehicle for several minutes, unsure what to do next. He imagines the curious onlooker contacting the police to report a lunatic yelling in the middle of the street. Images of the Shell station consume his thoughts as he desperately fights to push them away. He opens his car door and, while settling in behind the wheel, calls out, "What do you want from me?"

CHAPTER

4

CALVIN GLANCES ACROSS the street at the shadow of the curious onlooker one last time before pulling up to the stop sign. His mind is heavy and confused by the experience of hearing his name whispered and feeling the warmth of someone's breath against his neck. Without warning, he imagines the long narrow hallway of the house where he grew up. He sees an image of his father sluggishly walking past, muttering jumbled words. Calvin cringes at the memory of the worst day of his life. *I can't do this right now.* But his mind is unwilling to let the memory fade. He sees his father disappear through the doorway of the spare bedroom and waits, with his jaw clenched, for what is certain to follow.

Calvin is suddenly snapped out of his daydream by the honking of a car behind him. He gives a quick wave and turns onto the main road while trying his best to clear his mind. He glances into his rearview mirror and takes in the beauty of the orange fiery glow of the setting sun illuminating the lower half of the sky behind him. Only twenty minutes have passed since his session ended abruptly with Dr. Livingston, but already he's wishing he had stayed longer. His interest quickly fades as thoughts of the gas station return, drowning out any false expectations of heading straight home. Doubt rushes through him the moment he passes under the overpass for US 75. He heads north onto the service road, in the opposite direction of home, which leaves him feeling uneasy and guarded.

The closer the glowing yellow sign comes, perched high in the air, the further he falls under its enticing spell. The rhythmic clicking of the right blinker replaces the eerie silence as he sluggishly turns into the parking lot and makes his way along the left side of the store. He approaches the first of two double pumps and sees a black convertible BMW with tan leather interior displaying a "Plano West Lacrosse" sticker on the center of the bumper. The yellow Honda Accord belonging to the older woman is directly across, the nozzle of the gas pump still attached to the car. He is overcome with a sense of panic as he notices that the area is completely vacant and that he is all alone. *This is bad. Maybe I should leave and come back another day.*

His unsteady hands change position on the steering wheel, gripping it tightly, unsure if he should continue. He glances toward the second set of double pumps, located on the other side of the parking lot, next to a small sign stating "Entrance/Exit." He sees a completely restored 1973 Harley-Davidson Low Rider with Kansas license plates and has already stereotyped its owner. He drives over to the familiar water and air machine before stopping by the curb.

His heart rate increases as he spots a crowd of nine people gathered together in the field about fifty feet out. They are facing away from Calvin, directing all of their attention to the same undeveloped wooded area that the older woman was staring at earlier in the afternoon. There is a rickety barbed-wire fence surrounding the several acres of property with three-foot wooden posts sticking out of the ground. The gate is made out of steel pipes covered with orange rust. He scans the perimeter and notices overgrown weeds along the fence line branching out from behind the posts. The field is blanketed with tiny pink and yellow flowers, thick green grass, and scattered clumps of dirt.

All nine people are motionless, standing roughly two feet apart from each other, concentrating on a large oak, front and center, in the cluster of trees. Calvin places the gearshift in park, turns off his engine and slowly makes his way out. Everyone appears to be completely oblivious to him. He purposely slams his door, hoping to get a reaction, but to no avail. He steps onto the curb and follows a worn dirt path up to the gate, but decides against entering for now.

Scanning the crowd, he chooses to concentrate more on the people closest to the trees and spots the older woman and her grandson holding hands. A few feet over to their right is the farmer from earlier. His red bandanna is still sticking out of the back pocket of his overalls and flapping gently in the breeze.

To the right of the farmer are several teenagers, roughly eighteen years old, huddled closely together. All three are female, and all three are slim and attractive. The first is African American, with long black hair, wearing a blue-jean miniskirt, and a spaghetti-strap white top. Calvin shifts his attention to the girl to her right and watches as her strawberry-blond hair is blown into her face. Her pale, white skin stands out against her black shirt. Her body is stiff and rigid. The last of the three girls has cropped blond hair and a perfectly shaded bronze tan, complemented by her khaki shorts and a light pink shirt.

A strong gust of wind blows, causing the larger branches of the oak trees to sway. Suddenly, the wind stops as quickly as it had started, and the wooded area becomes calm once again. A bright glow radiates from the right ankle of the blurred figure standing on one of the larger branches high above the ground.

No, this can't be. Calvin, unable to turn away, concentrates intensely, but is disappointed to see nothing more than the same outline he saw earlier. The longer he stares, the more blurred the figure becomes. *It's almost time* rushes into Calvin's thoughts repeatedly, and all he can do is lean against the gate and stare, mesmerized by what he can't explain.

The fluorescent streetlamps turning on makes him snap his head around, shocked by the unexpected change. He glances back to the oak tree, uncertain how to process what he's seeing. *Just a big blur of nothing.*

It's almost time… It's almost time … It's almost time.

It's almost time for what, you coward? Why don't you stop hiding and show yourself?

The farmer turns around and faces Calvin, then takes several steps in his direction before stopping abruptly, twenty feet away.

Okay. That's spooky. He feels a sudden connection with the farmer and is shocked by the man's lack of emotion and expression. Only an empty shell of the man appears to be standing there, staring back blankly, slightly hunched from age and hard work.

"What do you want with me?" Calvin shouts.

The farmer stands motionless, unaffected by his words for several minutes before finally speaking. "You are going to kill me."

Baffled by his words, Calvin starts to speak but stops as he notices an outline of the number one forming in the center of the farmer's forehead. Calvin immediately looks away, confused by what he is seeing, and then he hears the whisper, "One day left." Unsure how to process this, he watches in silence as the farmer gradually turns around and walks back to the same spot a few feet over from the older woman and her grandson.

Calvin scans the crowd again and this time focuses on a hippie with a long, black braid resting more than midway down the center of his back. He's wearing a black leather strap wrapped around his head, blue jeans, a black leather jacket, and black boots. Confused by the jacket, Calvin mumbles, "It's June 10th in Texas, you moron," but quickly realizes his misguided anger is being fueled by his lack of sleep and growing concern for his mental state.

He glances to his right and sees a man roughly six feet tall with wavy brown hair wearing a navy blue designer suit. To his right, completing the count of nine, a slightly balding man stands at an angle, allowing Calvin to see him from the side. He is morbidly obese, with his green Mountain Dew T-shirt riding up in front, partially exposing his belly fat. Calvin instantly turns away. *I would rather get creeped out by the old lady.*

All of a sudden, images of his father return, despite his desperate attempts to clear his mind. The harder he tries to banish them, the deeper the images burrow in, haunting and tormenting him. The gibberish spoken earlier becomes clear, concise words making him cringe as he hears his father say repeatedly, "I can't fight them any longer."

Calvin is paralyzed with terror as each flash of memory reveals another detail he has tried for almost three decades to erase. "Please stop," he mutters, his chin shaking uncontrollably while he fights to hold back tears. The image only deepens as he pictures his father disappearing through the doorway of the spare bedroom. "Stop!" he yells, feeling the force of his anger freeing him from his trance.

He looks up with tears streaming down his face and fixates on the glowing right ankle, refusing to look away. *Were you the one he used to speak of? Or, more importantly, are you responsible for his death?* Inundated by suppressed memories of his childhood, Calvin struggles to contain his emotions, hoping for some sort of resolution. Instead, his questions are met with silence, causing his anger and frustration to build.

"I'm not afraid of you," he screams, wiping away the last of his tears.

CHAPTER

5

CALVIN CONTINUES TO stare as hundreds of flashes of white lights, roughly the size of half dollars, appear out of nowhere and begin fluttering next to the branch and the unidentifiable figure. They shuffle around hurriedly, lining up one on top of another as if each has a specific role to play with only minimal time to do so.

Calvin's eyes grow larger as the last of the lights settles in. They shake violently before changing to red and disappearing, each leaving behind a fingernail-sized white light twinkling wildly. Within seconds the twinkling lights have faded, leaving no trace that they ever existed.

Calvin pulls out his iPhone and immediately switches to the camera function, upset for not thinking of this sooner. He holds his phone out, hoping to get a picture of the whole scene, but knows he's already too late. He quickly snaps several of the trees, the area the figure once occupied, the hippie, the older woman and her grandson, and several also of the man in the suit.

One by one, each person turns and gradually heads toward the gate in single-file, led by the man in the Mountain Dew T-shirt. Their movements are slow and lacking energy. Calvin slides his phone into his front pocket and swiftly retreats to his car. He watches as seven of the nine members of this cult-like group approach the gate. Unsure what to do, Calvin locks his doors and sighs with relief as they pass by without incident. The man in the suit unlocks the Jaguar with the click of a button before opening his door. The three teenagers head for the BMW as the old man shuts the tailgate of his truck.

Where's the guy in the Mountain Dew shirt? Calvin searches the parking lot only to find him opening the door to his Volkswagen Jetta.

The older woman and her grandson are the last to turn around. Still holding hands, they walk in unison, eventually making their way through the gate. Their pace is slow, and their focus is on the ground. *Something about that woman really does creep me out.*

Relieved that the Honda is parked at the front pumps, Calvin waits for them to change direction away from him toward their car. *Why are they still heading this way? That doesn't make sense. Why would they intentionally go out of their...* An uneasy feeling consumes him, interrupting his train of thought. *They're walking to me, not their car.*

He nervously moves his foot to the brake and starts his engine, then gently slides the gearshift into drive. He can feel his heart beating faster the closer they come. Both are still looking down at the ground and not giving any indication that they are aware of his presence. The older woman is mumbling something, but the words are too soft to hear.

Incapable of stifling his curiosity any longer, Calvin rolls down the driver-side window a little more than half an inch, hoping to catch a few words. Once she is less than three feet away he listens carefully and cringes as he hears her say, "Calvin...Johnston."

How does she know my name?

His chest tightens as she says, "Trust your mind and listen to what it tells you, Calvin Johnston." They walk to the front of his car and stop. Wild scenarios play out in his mind forcing his heart rate to increase as he envisions a possible ambush from the others. Paranoid and afraid, he frantically looks around, imagining an onslaught from the remaining seven, charging his vehicle, screaming, "Die, Calvin! Die!" But the parking lot is empty, with the exception of the older woman's yellow Honda Accord.

He turns around to find her and her grandson still standing at the front of his car, staring at the ground. Intrigued and fearful of the older woman, Calvin watches her closely as she gradually raises her head until he's able to see the dull gray color of her eyes. He winces as she whispers, "You are becoming your father." A brief flash of his father lying face down on beige carpet, with trickles of blood in the corners of his mouth. A partial smile forms on the left side of the woman's mouth as she stares, unwilling to break their connection.

Calvin lets out a surprised cry and throws the gearshift into reverse, punching the gas without a second thought. The tires squeal, and his car zooms backwards before the rearview camera has a chance to turn on. After achieving some distance between them, he slams on his brakes. Looking up he sees the older woman and grandson have lost interest but continues to watch as they walk toward their Honda.

The older woman returns the pump to its holder and screws on her gas cap. Giving in to his paranoia, Calvin scans the parking lot one last time, hearing her engine start in the background and sees her driving away. He slips the gear into drive, debating whether or not to follow as they turn right onto the service road, heading north.

"Maybe next time," he mutters, wishing this day were over. "Something's telling me I need to be with my family."

On the drive home, Calvin is relieved that nothing else bizarre happens and he feels a calming sensation as he approaches his house at the end of the cul-de-sac. He clicks the garage door opener and pulls into the garage. He thinks about how exhausting his day has been, but it all seems to fade away the second he sees his wife leaning against the frame of the open door leading from the garage to the kitchen.

He watches her display one of her biggest smiles yet. She's wearing his long-sleeved, button-down plaid shirt and looks truly amazing. Normally he would joke about her needing a tan, but tonight, seeing the long curls of her jet-black hair against her light complexion is nothing short of awe-inspiring. He looks down only for a moment and takes his key out of the ignition. Looking back up, he notices his wife is no longer there and the door is shut. *She's up to something.*

A little confused, he calls for her before stepping out of his car. *I'm really not in the mood for games tonight.* He walks up the two steps leading to the kitchen, opens the door, and calls out again. The house is pitch black and dead silent.

"What's going on?" he mutters, concerned she hasn't responded. He flicks on the kitchen light and heads toward the living room. He notices that the family portrait that is normally above the fireplace is missing. Afraid of waking Daniel, he decides to quietly patrol one area of the house at a time, starting with the master bedroom. He turns on the light switch, then makes his way down the hall and stops at the doorway. He's puzzled to see that their bed is made and Janice is nowhere to be found. He looks around and discovers the room is void of all pictures, including the photos from their wedding and the day their son was born. He scans the top of the dresser and is surprised to see only a paperback turned upside down, the remote for their plasma television, and the red glow of the alarm clock revealing that it is already 9:45 p.m.

Dizziness strikes hard. He hunches slightly before reaching up with his left hand, bracing himself against the lightly textured, cream-colored walls. Shallow breaths, resembling those of a panting dog, are the only noises he's capable of making for the next few moments. Regaining his composure, he takes a couple of steps toward the dresser and runs his index finger along the top, revealing a thick layer of dust. He looks down at the bronze-colored handles on the front of each of the drawers and opens the drawer he knows contains her socks. Empty.

Consumed with panic, he grabs the second handle, and in one swift motion pulls the drawer all the way out of the dresser. He watches as it falls to the floor. *This one is empty too. Why is this happening? None of this makes any sense.*

He kicks the drawer to the side and shuffles around one of the light-brown bedposts before rushing over to their closet. Thrusting open the door, he's relieved to find that the suitcases are still stacked in the corner, but is riddled with doubt once he realizes none of her clothes are occupying this space either. *Did she leave me?*

He makes his way to the door and hurries across the hall to Daniel's room while dialing her cell phone, only to discover her number is no longer in service. Standing in the middle of his son's room, he's unable to locate any evidence of the boy. The room is set up as a guest bedroom. Piled on top of a queen-sized bed are dusty boxes with the word "blankets" written with red permanent marker in his own handwriting.

"There is something seriously wrong with me," he mutters, understanding that his exhaustion is both mental and physical. He tries his wife's cell one last time before screaming her name. Feeling like the wind has been knocked out of him, he slowly makes his way back down the hall, glancing up at the empty walls that were once lined with pictures. He walks to the kitchen and plops himself down onto one of the wooden chairs surrounding the table, unsure what to do next. Remembering what happened earlier, he places his face into his hands, hoping for the same results. He closes his eyes and takes several long, deep, calming breaths, thinking of Janice's smile and Daniel's laugh until the feelings of stress and anxiety slowly begin to slip away. He continues to focus on his breathing while remaining optimistic that this is just another episode and all will be back to normal soon.

His mind wanders back past three months ago. He remembers better times, long before his life had started to unravel, and can feel his tension easing. His thoughts drift outside his realm of comfort and allow an image of the older woman to creep inside. He regurgitates the words "You are becoming your father" and is struck with a restless feeling. He lowers his head onto the kitchen table, begging and pleading with whoever is listening to please end this now, but all he can focus on is the emptiness that radiated from the dull gray of the older woman's eyes.

A soft hand caresses his shoulder before slowly moving up the nape of his neck and onto his head. He feels the light scratching of fingernails against the surface of his scalp and hears his name being whispered. Suddenly, his reflexes kick in and he is shrieking and throwing his hands in the air. He jumps to his feet, unaware that he's tangled in the chair, and instantly falls, crashing against the hard ceramic tiles.

Janice, startled by his behavior, lets out a scream and takes several steps backwards. Daniel awakens, afraid of the uproar coming from the kitchen, and calls out "Mommy" with tearful cries. Calvin immediately jumps to his feet, apologizes, and kisses his wife repeatedly, excited to have his family back. He swiftly uprights the chair and pushes it against the table, before kissing her for the fifth time. Her pink polo shirt catches his eye as he flashes back to moments ago, realizing she's no longer in plaid. He quickly dismisses the thought and hurries over to their son, wanting nothing more than to hold Daniel tightly in his arms and never let go.

CHAPTER

6

ALL NIGHT LONG Calvin tosses and turns, unable to sort through the many problems weighing so heavily on his mind. Sleeping lightly, he can hear the noise of a clanking cart with one bad wheel being pushed down a hall in his direction. He can also sense the presence of several people standing over him, discussing the day's activities and schedules.

"Calvin," someone whispers. He can feel the gentle touch of someone tugging on his arm. "It's time to wake up."

Immediately he sits straight up in bed, utterly confused. He notices that Janice is still lying next to him and starting to stir from all the commotion. Looking around the room he is relieved that nothing appears to be out of place.

She's lying on her side, facing toward him, with the covers resting below her neck. All of her facial features except her chin are hiding behind the long, thick, jet-black locks of her hair. He watches the comforter, snug around her body, lift with each deep breath, and continues watching as the hair dangling in front of her face is blown outward with one slow, steady release of air.

He leans over and gives her a little nudge before brushing her hair back with his hand. She opens her eyes barely past a slit, only to close them just as quickly. He nudges her again, this time a little harder. "Good morning, my love."

She smiles and slides her hand out from beneath the sheets until it's on top of his and caressing it softly. "How are you feeling?" she asks, her morning voice cracking.

"I'm okay. Already starting off with a weird dream, but nothing I can't handle. Under the circumstances, I would say I feel pretty good."

"That's great to hear. How did your therapy session go last night? Did she prescribe you any good drugs?" she asks, smiling.

"I think it went really well, up until the part where I ran out of the office after about forty-five minutes, shouting, 'Sorry, Doc.'"

"No, you didn't."

"Actually, yes I did," he says with a chuckle.

"Really, what happened? Are you okay?"

"I'm fine. Long story short, let's just say my little episodes, as you like to call them, don't seem to be going away anytime soon. In fact, they seem to be getting worse."

"What do you mean they're getting worse?" she asks, her tone switching to one of concern.

"There's no need to worry. I'm okay," he says, rubbing her hand for reassurance. His light brown eyes shift away from hers as the thought of the older woman's words leaves traces of doubt in his mind. "I'm going to tell you something, but you have to promise me you won't overreact."

"Why would I overreact?" Panic settles in as she pushes against the headboard. Her arms shake uncontrollably as she struggles to sit up. Realizing she's still weak from last night's sleep, he reaches over and helps her the rest of the way up. He continues watching her, refusing to speak, until she responds.

Reluctantly, she forces the words "I promise" while making eye contact. "What is it?"

Sensing that the tension is thick enough to swim in, he changes his mind and decides to make a stupid joke, hoping to ease the mood. "I'm really your cousin, which makes you a pervert."

Not amused in the slightest, she continues staring at him, focusing on every movement. "Please be serious. I'm really worried about you."

"I swear I'm fine," he says, leaning over and kissing her lips.

A deafening silence looms as Janice hesitates to speak. Finally she says, "Did you mention your dad?"

"No. I wasn't ready. Besides, I was afraid of what she might think."

"You are turning into your father. You shouldn't have to—"

"What did you say?" Calvin interrupts, the words ringing in his ears.

"I said you aren't turning into your father."

He takes a few moments, confused by her comments. "Why would you say that?"

"Because I know you. And I know there hasn't been a day since this began in March that you haven't secretly compared yourself to him." She leans over and kisses his lips softly while rubbing his unshaven face. "Having occasional issues caused by stress isn't the same thing as what he went through."

His voice turns shaky. "I'm not so sure about that."

"What do you mean? Please tell me what I know you need to get off of your chest. I'm here for you."

"I know," he says softly.

"I promise, no judgment."

Calvin brushes away several strands of her hair that fell in front of her eyes. "Yesterday, on the way to the therapist's office, I got the distinct impression that something was trying to communicate with me. Two separate phrases kept popping into my head. During my session, I spoke to Dr. Livingston, and she told me the first phrase was French and means 'Can you hear me?' while the second was German, meaning, 'You belong to me.'"

Janice's expression turns stone cold as the insinuation registers in her mind.

Calvin continues speaking, afraid that if he stops he might not have the courage to finish later. "What I can't seem to get out of my head is the fact that I never studied French or German. I took Spanish in high school and college. I have racked my brain and haven't been able to come up with any plausible explanations. I could defend hearing voices by stating basically the same as you, that the additional stress with my promotion and lack of sleep are the culprits. But how do I explain being able to pull up two separate phrases from two separate languages with which I have no familiarity?"

It's immediately evident to Janice that he's right. None of this makes any sense. Her head feels as though it might explode from the overwhelming amount of questions and concerns piling on top of each other. She tries to sort through them, but quickly gives up, realizing she needs to stay focused on him.

"What are you going to do?"

"I'm not sure, but I'm toying with the idea of maybe going to see Dr. Livingston again. It's hard to explain, but during the entire session it felt like I was exactly where I needed to be. Only——"

"Only what?"

"I'm not sure if she'll take me back, since it was pretty rude of me to leave the way I did."

Seeing an opportunity to lighten the mood, she says, "Shouldn't be a problem. Just turn on that charm of yours and show her your cute little dimples." She reaches up to poke his cheek but is blocked by his arm.

He cracks a smile, thinking back on his session. "This is kind of funny."

"What's that?"

"Yesterday I was feeling sorry for myself, and Dr. Livingston got out of her chair, leaned over and clapped three times in my face to get my attention."

"Seriously?" Janice laughs, caught off guard. "That's hilarious."

"Scared the crap out of me."

"I really like this woman. I think you should stick with her," she says, reaching up to clap, but she stops when they hear Daniel calling, "Mommy."

Janice looks over at the clock, which shows 7:45 a.m., and says, "He's up a little early today. I guess we're being too loud. Will you do me a big favor?"

"Maybe," he says sarcastically.

"Would you go get him and bring him in here to me? I feel like cuddling."

"Of course." Heading toward the door, he stops just outside of the frame. He turns back to face her, making an attempt at dry humor. "I'll be back before you can clap in my face three times."

He walks across the hall to Daniel's room and is met at the doorway by a sleepy, dark-haired child rubbing both eyes with bunched-up fists. He's wearing dinosaur pajamas with matching socks. His pale, white skin and natural black curls leave little doubt that he is a direct descendant of his mother.

"Daddy," he whispers, and lifts his arms. Calvin leans over and engulfs the tiny-statured frame with his broad shoulders. His son immediately wraps both arms around his neck and gently lays his head onto his chest. Calvin rises and takes a deep whiff of his son's hair. *This is the best part of my day.*

Heading to the master bedroom, he finds Janice completely submerged under the white down-feathered comforter. He lifts the covers and gently places Daniel's limp body next to hers, then makes his way to the kitchen to fix a pot of coffee.

He calls and leaves a message for Dr. Livingston, apologizing for his quick departure, and asks for the next available slot, if at all possible.

More than forty minutes have passed, and he's finishing up his second cup of coffee, wondering if his wife and son have fallen back to sleep. He's overcome with fear as he flashes back to them vanishing the night before. He rushes to their room, only to discover that both are still in the same position, sleeping soundly. He sneaks into the bathroom, quietly changes into his bathing suit and grabs a towel before heading to the kitchen.

Calvin opens the patio door and tosses his towel into one of the four chairs underneath his covered porch and watches as the clear blue water of the swimming pool sparkles wildly from the sun. He remembers when they first decided on the L shape. It seemed practical for laps, plus the design was different from any of the others they had previously been shown. Still happy with their choice, he walks the length of the sideways L shape and heads toward the deep end next to the diving board. He opens the skimmer and pulls out the thermometer, cleverly disguised as a green and white plastic frog. *Wow. Eight-thirty in the morning and already the pool temp is 92. Gotta love Texas weather.*

Diving into the deep end, he's immediately surrounded by the warmth the water provides. Without wasting any time, he begins to swim the length of the pool, but all he can think about is the farmer. *Why would he be the only one to turn around, and why would he have said that I'm going to kill him? None of this makes any sense.*

With each stroke of his arm, a different word is pounded into his head, until the phrase "It's almost time" has taken over his thoughts. *Yeah, yeah, I've heard it before. It's almost time. Almost time for what?*

To kill echoes throughout his mind almost instantly. Calvin stops mid-stroke and comes up for air, choking on the mouthful of water he has just inhaled.

CHAPTER

7

CALVIN GRADUALLY MAKES his way down the hall, regurgitating the words "to kill" over and over in his mind. Droplets of water fall from his bathing suit and glide down his legs as he makes his way through the open door of the master bedroom. At first glance, it appears Janice is sleeping on the bed alone until he notices a slight movement from their son, who is cocooned against his mother. Her arms wrapped around him tightly, as if to protect him against any unknown dangers. Calvin softly walks toward them, stopping just shy of the headboard, and admires their beautiful faces. *How peaceful they look.*

He's hoping the mind-numbing madness that his life has become will soon end and things will return to normal. His dark brown hair is still sopping wet and the continuous cool air circulating from the vents above causes a wave of chills to run down his body. His well-defined arms, still taut from the laps, dangle alongside his tall, sleek frame.

He leans down and hovers over his wife. A couple of droplets of water descend toward her cheek and explode on impact. She stirs a little as he carefully reaches across Daniel until his hand is gently gliding over her face, brushing the remains of water away. He kisses her forehead and whispers, "I'm sorry."

"Sorry for what?" she whispers back.

"For everything. It doesn't seem fair you have to suffer right along with me."

"In sickness and in health," she says, staring into his light brown eyes. "You're stuck with me until death do us part." The words ring in his ears the second they leave her lips. Words he hasn't heard her speak for over thirteen years. He remembers that chilly Saturday afternoon when he was only twenty-nine and Janice had just turned twenty-seven a month earlier. He recalls the huge fight they'd had the night before, and how both had threatened to call off the wedding. *What a mistake that would have been.*

"Hi, Daddy," a second voice whispers sweetly. Calvin looks down and sees two big, beautiful dark brown eyes wide open and staring attentively at his every move. He notices that Daniel's face and neck are riddled with sleep lines from the crumpled blanket and lightly traces the outline with his index finger. His son's pale, white skin appears to be flawless, as only the skin of a three-year-old can be.

"Hey, sport, how are you feeling today?"

"Sleepy," a groggy voice answers.

Calvin smiles for a moment before having it stripped away by the phrases "until death do us part" and "to kill" rattling around inside his mind. Feeling anxious, he whispers to Janice, "I need to go for a drive and clear my head."

"Okay. Please be careful. Oh, and before I forget, Daniel has a play-date at 10:30 this morning."

Calvin nods and mouths, "I love you."

"Good-bye, Daddy," the tiny voice calls out.

Calvin rubs his fingers through Daniel's hair, thinking how soft it feels, before turning and walking toward the dresser. He changes out of his wet bathing suit and into some khaki shorts, a white polo shirt, and tan sandals. He heads across the room, blows Janice and Daniel a kiss, and closes the bedroom door behind him. On his way to the garage, he glances down at his phone and notices he has one missed call and one new voicemail. He opens the car door and takes his time settling in behind the wheel. He waits until he's backing out before hitting "play," excited to blast it hands-free over his speakers. The message is from Dr. Livingston's office, confirming an 11 a.m. appointment.

Excellent, he thinks, feeling awkward over his excitement at the thought of seeing a therapist. Backing out into the street, he realizes he has no idea where he's going. He looks around at several empty driveways, relieved work isn't on his agenda for today. *Which way should I go?*

Images of the Shell station immediately take over his thoughts. Although he is skeptical at first, his reluctance eventually turns into acceptance knowing answers to his many questions might reside there. *Besides, it's practically on the way to Dr. Livingston's office anyway.*

Forty-five minutes have passed, and Calvin heads down the service road, feeling enchanted by the soft glow of the yellow and red Shell sign. As he pulls into the parking lot, the first car he spots is the Honda Accord, this time sitting in one of the spaces at the front of the store.

"Not again," he mumbles, starting to regret his decision.

All the familiar cars are either at the pumps or parked in various spots scattered along the lot. But just like yesterday, not a soul is in sight. He continues driving down the left side of the building, stops next to the air and water machine, and shuts off his engine. He sees the three teenage girls slowly walking in the field, heading toward all of the same participants as before. *You're a little late to the party.*

He watches their every movement intently, until they make their way back to the same places as last night. Calvin glances toward the left side of the field and is surprised to see the older woman and grandson missing. He scans the crowd and realizes everyone's still wearing the same clothes as before, down to the red bandanna hanging out of the farmer's back pocket.

"Where are you?" he mumbles, eyes flickering from person to person, surveying the entire area.

Movements coming from the green and brown brush lining the front of the undeveloped wooded area catch his attention. He spots the older woman emerging from the seclusion of the trees with her grandson trailing behind. She looks in Calvin's direction and signals for him to come over by lifting her arm and waving, as if she were fanning herself in slow motion. Not willing to take any chances, he slouches down in his seat, knowing full well the tint of his windows should prevent her from being able to see in.

The farmer turns to face Calvin and gestures in the same fashion as the older woman. The three teenagers are next to summon him, followed by the man in the suit, the long-haired hippie, then, finally, the overweight gentleman in long khaki shorts. About sixty seconds pass, and all nine people are now beckoning for him to join their odd array of members.

No, thanks. I'm pretty sure I'll be sitting this one out.

Several branches of the giant oak begin to shake excessively in the same familiar side-to-side motion, as if large gusts of wind once again have chosen to visit only the top portions of the trees.

I know what's coming next, he thinks unable to look away. "And there it is," he says, watching the figure appear right on cue. Disappointment surfaces as Calvin notices that most of the features are still blocked from his sight. Only the white glow radiating off of the right ankle is recognizable.

"Come on," Calvin whispers. "Let me see you."

He stares eagerly, hoping to penetrate whatever defense mechanism is surrounding the figure, but is forced to look away because of the pressure building inside his head. He has an irresistible urge to join the nine members and fights against the intense force pulling at him from the inside out. Ignoring his better judgment, he reaches toward the door and presses the unlock button, feeling compelled by a greater power, as if being willed to do so. He's incapable of imagining anything good coming from this and struggles to resist, but the urge is too strong to overcome. He makes his way out of his vehicle, dragging his feet through the dirt trail, with each step hoping to lengthen the time it takes to reach the gate.

Once he is through, each of the nine people stops motioning for him and begins chanting different phrases. The desperate impulse to turn and run is immediately squashed as he realizes that whatever control he once held has since been relinquished. He passes the teenagers and listens as they quietly murmur, "You must have forgiveness to face your fears."

The farmer approaches and stops directly in front of Calvin. His face is old, weathered, and sunken, with lines of dirt in each of its creases. His eyes are a dull gray, reminding Calvin instantly of the older woman. But all Calvin can do is stare at the number zero etched into the center of the farmer's forehead.

"I know what this means," Calvin mutters. "It's not going to happen. Not with me anyway." He turns his head and cringes with the whispers, "Zero days left."

"Do what has to be done," the farmer's voice bellows, causing Calvin to shriek with surprise.

The man in the navy-blue designer suit positions himself to the left of Calvin before asking, "Do you accept this challenge?"

"I don't understand," he calls out, his voice shaky. "What challenge? To kill?"

The farmer, while repeating his phrase, closes his eyes and places both arms behind his back, clasping his hands together before extending his neck.

The man in the suit reaches over with icy cold fingers and takes hold of Calvin's hands, coaxing them onto the farmer's shoulders. Coldness radiates off both men as Calvin winces at the thought of what must come next. Calvin's broad shoulders and his height of six foot three have him towering over the slender farmer, who is barely five eight and small in frame. Calvin's eyes glaze over, and his face loses all expression. He gradually moves his hands, placing one on each side of the farmer's neck, and squeezes lightly. The chanting becomes louder, and the intensity of the moment builds.

I'm supposed to kill him. I can feel the desire coursing through my body. Wait...how can I take the life of this man? A man I know very little about.

Calvin's focus changes, and his eyes slowly return to normal. The farmer, deprived of any emotions, keeps his eyes closed, by all appearances willing, prepared, and waiting to die as if to serve some greater purpose with his sacrifice.

Calvin's insides start to hurt. He feels as though he has just suffered a great loss, one that will take more than a lifetime to overcome. An image appears inside his mind as his wife consumes his thoughts. She is lying on her back, motionless, bent and broken, the concrete ground beneath her discolored. He's unable to tell where she is, or exactly what is going on. He pictures several people rushing from all directions, doing their best to come to her aid, but they're too late. Her lifeless body lies limp and disfigured, surrounded by a pool of her own blood. Her eyes are open wide but lack vitality.

"Why are you showing me this?" Calvin yells, keeping a firm grip on the farmer. He turns his head to face the branch where the figure is still standing and calls out, "Are you trying to tell me that if I don't kill this man, you're going to kill my wife? Why not take me instead? I'm right here."

The images of Janice disappear, along with the deep sorrowful pain.

Calvin imagines himself lying in a bed alone with no one around him. He doesn't recognize the room but is reminded of a hospital. He looks to be at peace, without any signs of pain, but is unable to tell if he's alive or dead. The images quickly fade as he's snapped back into reality by all of the movement around him.

The chatter from individual chants adds more chaos and continues to grow louder. The farmer remains emotionless, still doing nothing to resist Calvin's grip around his neck. The group has formed a circle surrounding them both, each person yelling and raising their fists in the air, unaware of the hostility that has overcome them.

Calvin's nervousness increases as he realizes the circle is closing in. He takes it as a sign that the final moment is upon them. *This is really happening.*

He feels parts of him slipping away, falling deeper under the hypnotic spell of their chants while surrendering his mind and body wholly. *I could choke the life out of him in a matter of minutes.*

Calvin's anger increases, sweeping through him like poison infecting both his mental and physical state. His heart races, and his hands tremble. He tightens his grip and can feel the muscles in his arms tense from the extreme concentrate of adrenaline flowing rampantly through every extremity. The farmer's face turns red and he gasps for air. Slight gurgles escape from his throat, and strands of saliva run down his chin. Calvin watches tiny spit bubbles form around the farmer's lips.

"I'm sorry...this is for my wife's survival."

CHAPTER

8

DON'T! **CALVIN'S INNER** voice commands. He lets out a deep breath while staring into the eyes of the farmer, hoping for a glimpse of anything other than the already too familiar emptiness, which has plagued him since their first encounter. "Show me some shred of emotion, or you're going to die!" Calvin yells, still gripping him firmly. The farmer's knees buckle and for a split second, Daniel's tiny voice emerges from Calvin's memory, the sweet little words "Good-bye, Daddy" as they were spoken that morning.

The thought of his son, coupled with the image of his wife sleeping peacefully, instantly reminds him of what he could easily destroy in the next few moments if he doesn't regain his control. Without hesitation, he releases the farmer and shouts to the figure and all eight other members, "My wife and son are my strength. I will not kill for you." His anger turns to fury. "Do you hear me?"

With that, he pushes his way through the crowd, while the farmer crawls on his hands and knees, coughing deeply. Calvin stomps off through the field toward his car, feeling like his self-confidence has been fully restored, his head held high, and his posture straight. Approaching the gate, he glances back and discovers that the eight members are still circling the farmer as vultures would circle the dying or already dead. *They don't care that I left.* His shoulders sink. *The whole time I was walking away, it never occurred to me to wonder what would happen to him.*

Fearing for the farmer's safety and overrun with guilt, he lowers his head before muttering shamefully, "Leaving him to die is the same as killing him."

Without any more delay, he runs back toward the crowd, feeling his heart skip a beat as the farmer tries to stand but is brutally knocked back down. The group is showing signs of a mob mentality, screaming and shaking their fists violently. Afraid for the worst, Calvin shouts, "Stop!" but his cry goes unnoticed. He picks up speed, heading straight for them, repeatedly yelling "No!" before stopping abruptly less than five feet away. Breathing heavily, he glances at the farmer and grimaces at the sight of him crouched on the ground with his face in the dirt. He walks over and helps him to his feet, feeling uneasy about turning his back on any of the eight members.

The chanting has stopped, and the entire area is quiet. The group has calmed and now stands motionless with their arms to their sides, watching in silence. Calvin gently takes the farmer by the arm and escorts him safely to his truck, without so much as a word passing between them. Instead, he quietly and without exuding any emotion climbs into his truck and drives away, leaving Calvin with the distinctive feeling they will never see each other again.

One by one, starting with the three teenagers, the group forms a single-file line and continues walking until they are consumed by the dense woods from which the older woman and her grandson had emerged earlier.

Calvin's focus changes as hundreds of flashes of lights appear high in the oak tree and begin shuffling around. He watches in awe as they perform the same routine as earlier and begin to outline the figure. Once in place, they shake violently before changing to red and eventually disappearing, leaving behind small traces of white lights.

Still on edge, Calvin glances over to where the remaining eight people are hiding and shows zero interest in pursuing any of them further. He looks down at his watch and is relieved and happy to see it's nearly 10:30 a.m. *Time for the doc.*

Pulling into the medical plaza, he's surprised by the amount of people and cars in the area. He sees an archway entrance at the front of the building and is curious where it leads. In front of the building, there is a car in every spot, including each of the six handicap spaces.

Driving alongside the building, he notices a sidewalk separating the outside offices and the parking lot. He briefly looks down at his console, displaying 10:48 a.m., before glancing at the overflowing lot to his left and shaking his head in amazement.

"Wow. Maybe I should stick to after-hours appointments."

Off in the distance, he sees a white metal sign with red lettering stating "parking in rear" and continues driving in that direction, hoping for better luck. Turning right, he's disappointed to find that it, too, is mostly full, but is relieved the two back rows are nearly empty. After parking, he walks toward the building and is stunned to see another archway identical to its counterpart in front.

There is an elderly couple with bright gray hair holding hands. A mother in her early thirties pushes a stroller with three small children following behind all in a row, like little ducklings. Everyone seems to be relaxed and in no hurry as they make their way through the entrance.

Knowing he still has ten minutes before his appointment, he thinks *Why not?* and changes direction. The closer the archway entrance comes, the more he's reminded of an oasis covered with thick, lush, green grass. A feeling of normalcy consumes him as he watches several kids running around barefoot, enjoying the cool, soft blades of St. Augustine with every step.

To his left, a koi pond in an S shape stretches from one end of the secluded area to the other. As he stares deeply into the water, every shadow he sees conforms into the figure of the farmer, serving as a constant reminder of his earlier actions. He's astonished by the size of some of the fish within the pond but is more impressed with the carefully detailed signs displaying pictures, names, and a long history of each. He's able to identify the traditional goldfish, koi, golden orfe, and plecostomus by comparing them against the signs, and he marvels at their distinguishing features.

Water trickling down the side of a fountain steals away his attention as he approaches the middle of the pond. He makes his way to the back, searching for an open spot not riddled with children throwing in coins and talking loudly. He sits down sideways on the ledge surrounding the fountain and is almost hypnotized by the relaxing sounds of the water bubbling out the top. He watches the overflowing water splash into a three-foot-deep enclosure and is mesmerized by the ripples revealing a shadowy silhouette. He quickly looks behind him, thinking someone must be walking up, but is disappointed to see no one around. He leans his body to the left, then to the right, but the shadow never moves. The more he studies the outline, the more he realizes that it's reforming into the frame of the farmer.

"Not right now," he mumbles a little louder than he intends. A breeze gently blows, and he swears he hears his name being whispered very faintly. He looks around and notices a few people staring, making it obvious it's time for him to leave—and he does so quickly. He walks around the building and is relieved to spot Suite 109.

Opening the door, he's greeted once again by a buzzing sound, alerting everyone to his presence. He's shocked to see the sliding-glass window wide open and a fresh new face sitting behind it. A young girl in her early twenties with blond, curly locks and bright, clear blue eyes is smiling widely, waiting to assist him.

"How are you today?" she asks in an upbeat way.

"Not too bad. How about yourself?" Calvin responds, walking up to the front.

"I'm good. Thank you for asking. Are you Mr. Johnston?"

"Yes."

"Hi, Mr. Johnston. Don't worry about signing in today. I can go ahead and mark you down. If you would, please have a seat, and Dr. Livingston should be right with you."

"Wow. That's great. Thanks."

He turns around and stares at the U-shaped alignment of chairs. *I guess I'm not going to be able to sit where I can see my car this time.* He glances over at the table in the corner with neatly stacked magazines, but before he has a chance to pick one out, Dr. Livingston opens the door separating the waiting room from the hall. She's wearing a navy blue skirt with a sleeveless white top, revealing her light brown skin. *It is nice to see someone other than me has changed their clothes since yesterday.*

"Mr. Johnston, it's been such a long time since our last session," she says, grinning.

He laughs and shakes her hand. It doesn't appear she's holding a grudge from his quick departure last night.

"Why don't we head down to my office?"

She motions for him to lead this time as she shuts the wooden door behind them. He continues down the hall and passes the bathroom on the left, before hanging a right into her office. He immediately heads for the comfortable maroon chair as Dr. Livingston closes her door. As she passes him, she shoots another smile in his direction, and then settles behind her desk.

"So what do you think of Cindy at the front desk?"

"She seems really sweet. What happened to Mrs. Personality?" he asks.

Dr. Livingston's smile fades. "She's using vacation time for today and tomorrow."

"Oh. That's good. I bet she will enjoy some time off." Calvin looks away, sensing the change in her tone, and feeling partly responsible. He wonders if this was forced time off or a decision mutually agreed upon. He clears his throat and patiently waits for her to look up. "Dr. Livingston, I want to apologize for storming out of your office yesterday. I got rattled, and I shouldn't have left the way I did."

"No problem. Based on what we discussed in our first session, I completely understand. In your position, I might have acted in the same manner. In fact, I was relieved when I heard you wanted to schedule another appointment. We've made great progress on your first visit, and I'm looking forward to seeing what we uncover in this one as well."

"Me too," he says. Something about being in this office really puts me at ease.

"I was going over my notes last night after you left, and I realized you had started telling me about the trucker and the accident, but we ended up getting sidetracked on the two phrases instead. I would like to start there, if that's okay with you."

"Sure. That's fine. I was on my way to Plano for my session with you. I was driving down 75, headed north, when I noticed a diesel on the opposite side of the highway flashing its lights on and off. I'm guessing to get my attention, but I'm not really sure."

She flips back one page and says, "You had mentioned the door of the cab was painted white with a red lightning bolt. Is this correct?"

"Yes."

"Does this pattern mean anything to you?"

"Not really. There was quite a bit of lightning and it was raining pretty hard when I was driving here."

The scratching of her pen on the paper distracts Calvin.

"Please continue."

"The heavy rain was making it difficult to see, and I remember wanting to see the cab of the diesel, but it was impossible to make out until right as it was approaching me."

"What do you mean? Did something change?"

"Yes. The rain stopped, and I was able to get a clear view of the door. It's as if I was meant to see it."

"This is the same truck you believe you saw at Lakeside Park on one of your lunch outings, is this correct?"

"Yes. I'm not really sure what significance it has in all of this, but as we were driving down the highway separated by a barricade, the diesel hit some standing water hidden from my view."

"Perhaps this is what the trucker was trying to signal you about."

"Maybe," Calvin replies, having his doubts. "But if that were true, why wouldn't he have just switched lanes? Of course, I guess there could have been water built up in the middle lane too. Anyway, the next thing I see is a huge wall of water like a tidal wave coming over the cement divider, which hits my car and covers my windshield. Before I knew it, I panicked and locked up my brakes. I know that was stupid, but when you can't see while driving down the highway at sixty-five miles an hour a fierce kind of panic that I can't even begin to explain comes over you."

"I bet it does."

"I remember spinning in circles until I crashed into the wall. I kept expecting to get sideswiped by another vehicle, but after it was all over, no one was around. It's as if everything turned into a ghost town. I couldn't see any water on the road or anywhere for that matter. So I figured I should pull over and inspect the damage. I was afraid to stay on the highway in case everyone came back. The nearest exit was Parker Road, and I was able to find a Shell gas station on the service road."

"I know the place. I've stopped there a few times for gas. You're doing great, by the way," she says with an encouraging look. "How long were the people missing?"

"Ten, maybe fifteen minutes, give or take a few."

"What were you doing right before the people returned?"

"I had put my face in my hands and thought about nothing other than my wife and son. Shortly after, everything was back to normal. It seems most of the instances I've recently experienced usually end up going away as soon as I concentrate on my wife and son." Calvin looks down and notices his hand is shaking. "I'm sorry," he mumbles.

"Sorry for what?"

"I'm starting to freak out again, hearing what I'm saying. Nothing like this has ever happened to me, and I know how it must sound."

"No need to worry. I'm on your side and here to help in any way that I can. I want you to know that we are making great headway, but there are still details I feel I'm missing. I would really like to know what you are experiencing so that I can begin treating you."

"Makes sense."

"You had mentioned in yesterday's session that your wife is not only familiar with your situation, but sympathetic as well."

"Yes. So far everyone has been."

"That's great to hear. You would be surprised how much easier it is to already have the much-needed support. Did anything happen after you left the gas station?"

"I swear I saw something leaning against the highway sign for the Spring Creek Parkway Exit."

"Can you describe what you saw?"

"Not really. It was a figure of some sort, but the image was really hazy, making it difficult to make out. I did notice there was something glowing on the right ankle," he says, before pausing for a moment.

"Please continue."

"Nothing else out of the ordinary happened on the way here. However, while I was in the session with you, I got up to clear my head and saw my reflection in your mirror. Well, a reflection of a much older version of myself anyway."

"Describe what you were feeling at the time of seeing this."

"At first I was freaking out. I was hoping it was all some kind of trick, but it seemed too real to be a joke. At one point I even moved the saggy skin of my cheek up and down, watching it bounce around. It was very disturbing, to say the least."

Dr. Livingston lets out a laugh, caught completely off guard. "I'm sorry. I realize this isn't a laughing matter."

"It's okay," he replies. "I've had some time to let it sink in, and after everything that continues to happen to me, I'm starting to feel numb to it all. Do you mind if I take a look again?" Calvin says, gesturing toward the mirror. "I'm wondering if I'll see the older version of myself or just my normal reflection."

"Please do. I'm curious about that as well."

He stands and takes his time walking to the mirror. "Here goes nothing," he says, leaning over to sneak a peek. "I have a quick question. Would you like for me to tell you everything in sequence or should I skip around and touch the highlights?"

"Let's stay in order for now, if possible. I believe the events are happening in a particular order for a reason and think staying as close to it as possible could be crucial in helping us understand what we are dealing with."

"Okay. Makes no difference to me," he says in a weird tone. "Although I think we may want to jump out of order for the time being."

"Why do you say that?"

"Because the farmer I saved earlier this morning is looking back at me."

CHAPTER

9

DR. LIVINGSTON JUMPS up and hastily makes her way over to the mirror, unsure of what she will find. As she approaches, it's obvious that the only reflection, other than her own, is that of Calvin who is staring deeply into the mirror, engulfed by the appearance of the farmer.

"Is he still there?" she asks.

"Yes. He's mouthing something to me, but I have no idea what. I've tried to read his lips several times, but I can't make out any of the words."

"Is he alone?"

"No. It looks like he's with the figure I talked about earlier who was leaning against the highway sign. Only his leg isn't glowing anymore."

"Are you able to describe the figure?"

"Not really," he says disappointedly. "So far the only words I can come up with are big blur of nothing."

"Any chance you could do a little better?"

"Let's see. Do you watch the news?"

"Yes, every morning."

"Have you ever seen when they interview someone, but don't want you to see their face?"

"Yes. I think I understand now."

"Instead of just the face, it's the entire figure that's blurred. Wait!" Calvin says excitedly, "The farmer has stopped talking and is holding up ten fingers. His hands are shaking severely, and he's standing there staring at..." Calvin looks over at Dr. Livingston.

"What?" she asks.

"He's staring directly at you."

A chill runs through her as she digests what he's saying. Realizing she's too close to this situation, she takes a few steps backwards and, while turning toward her desk, she hears Calvin say, "The blurry figure is coming toward us at a really fast pace."

"What's happening now?" she asks impatiently before turning to face him.

As the words are leaving her lips, the glass suddenly cracks down the center, startling both and leaving them speechless for several moments.

"Did that really just happen?" Calvin looks over at Dr. Livingston standing frozen with her mouth hanging open, enthralled by the jagged line across the glass.

"I guess so," he says, answering his own question.

"I see him," she whispers. "The farmer. He's wearing blue overalls with a dirty white undershirt, and he's pointing at me. Is that what you see?"

"Yes."

"I don't see the blurry figure you were talking about, though."

"I don't see him either anymore. I think he's gone."

Unexpectedly, the reflection changes back and both are now looking at distorted images of themselves. They continue standing in the same spot for a brief period before sluggishly returning to their seats.

"Do you think the glass is really broken or are we both imagining it?" she asks, concerned she may have somehow gotten caught up in his hysteria.

"I don't know. It definitely seemed real to me, and still does. We could ask Cindy, but we may end up looking crazy."

"I have an idea, but I need your help in removing the mirror from the wall."

"Sure," he says, heading over to meet her. They both grab hold of the bronze-colored frame and lift it off the anchor screws.

"Here, try and lean it against the wall at an angle." A few grunts escape as she struggles with the weight and the awkwardness of the shape. They gently lower it to the floor. "Okay. That's great." She pulls loose the left side of the hanging cable from the backing with one solid yank, then straightens it out so that more than three inches of the wire is showing.

"Please have a seat, and I'll be right back."

She hurries out of the office, afraid she's close to losing her composure. After crossing the hall, she heads directly for the bathroom and quickly shuts the door. She turns both handles of the faucet on high for background noise and stands dead still in front of the sink, terrified at the sight of another mirror.

She studies her reflection closely, seeing herself as she truly is at this exact moment—frightened beyond belief. Her body trembles as she feels her self-control slipping away. Her chest tightens and begins to ache. She replays each moment over in her mind, incapable of shaking the fear looming over her like a dark cloud. Fear she is certain is not only for her safety, but for her sanity also, which is now in question.

"I'm not the one who's supposed to be in this situation. I'm the one who's supposed to help people in this situation," she mutters. "Oh my God, I'm talking to myself out loud."

Okay, I need to calm down and try and work this out in my head. What do I know for sure? I know I saw the farmer and even described the clothes he was wearing, with which Calvin agreed. Maybe we were just feeding off each other and suffering under the same delusion. Yes, I bet that's it. Although if the mirror really is cracked, then it's pretty safe to say we are both in way over our heads. Either way, I need to remain professional and not let on to anyone that I'm losing control. She closes her eyes and stretches her neck from side to side, trying to loosen up.

She shuts off the water and takes a couple of deep breaths before making her way over to the reception area. *The moment of truth*, she thinks, peeking around the corner.

"Cindy, would you please bring me a Diet Coke with lime when you have a chance?"

"Yes, ma'am," she replies happily.

Dr. Livingston walks back into her office and closes the door behind her. "I need a favor. I know I was freaking out earlier, and there's no time to explain, but I need you to play along, if that's okay. Just follow my lead."

Before Calvin has a chance to respond, there's a knock at the door. He looks behind him and then back to Dr. Livingston, who is awaiting his response.

"Of course," he replies, a little confused.

"Please come in," she calls out from her chair.

Cindy carries in the Diet Coke with two lime wedges neatly positioned side by side on the rim of the glass. She places the drink on a coaster next to Dr. Livingston's hand.

"Oh man, seven years' bad luck. That's a bummer. Looks like the wire came loose. Do you want me to help you carry it out to the dumpster?"

"No, thanks. I believe I'm going to leave it for now."

"Okay. Let me know if you change your mind. Mr. Johnston, would you like anything to drink? "

"Um, no thank you. Thanks for the offer, though."

"No problem," Cindy says with a smile and closes the door.

"Wow. She really is a sweetheart. I hope you don't mind me saying, but I like her much better than the last person."

"Yes, she has been a blessing so far, and I'm planning on asking her to stay on full-time, starting next week," she says, feeling like she's straying off subject. "Alright, so where were we? Cindy noticed the crack in the mirror, which means we aren't sharing the same delusion. However, it does mean that something else is happening to both of us."

"I understand now," he says, his puzzled look vanishing. "That's why you pulled the wire out to make it look like it came loose and fell. Pretty clever."

"Thanks. Deep down I knew she would be able to see the crack. Although, something I have been wondering is why I didn't see the blurry figure. Why didn't it present itself to me?"

"I have no idea."

"Speaking of which, what do you think about calling the blurry figure something like Figure X, and we can solve to find X. Has a nice ring to it, don't you think?"

Calvin laughs, recognizing that she must have been a math nerd growing up. He shifts in his chair, realizing her mannerisms have changed since the incident. "Are you okay?"

"Yes. I'm sorry. I'm trying to appear as if I have everything under control, but to be truthful I'm still freaking out. I'm not sure how to process what I saw and just need some time. How are you so calm?" she asks, squeezing both limes into her drink, too preoccupied until now to take a sip.

"I'm just glad you saw the farmer. Maybe I'm not nearly as crazy as I originally thought. It feels good to share this burden with someone else for a change. Besides, so much has happened to me over the last few months, I guess I'm pretty much numb to it all, except for the whispering. That still gets me every time."

Dr. Livingston's facial expression changes to concern while she shakes her head no. "Oh, I hope I don't have any of that in my future."

"I hope not too. But if you do, you can always call me, so at least you aren't alone."

"I appreciate that. I know it must be horrible going through this by yourself. I couldn't imagine having to face the challenges you've had."

Calvin starts to speak to what he knows comes next but stops, as common courtesy sets in. *No sense in sending her over the edge on a gut feeling.* Instead, he just smiles and tries to make her feel as comfortable as possible.

"Let's see. It's 11:52. Looks like there are only a few minutes left in this session. Do you have anything going on at noon?"

"No, I'm pretty much free for the entire day."

"That's great. I penciled in an hour for my lunch today. Although, with everything that has just happened, I'm finding myself not nearly as hungry as I would normally be about this time."

"I completely understand."

"Also, I really don't want to end this session. How about we keep going and I won't charge you for the extra time?"

"Sounds good to me."

"However, I do have a new client coming at 1:00 today. We should probably stop somewhere around a quarter till."

Calvin sits quietly, nodding.

"You mentioned you're on leave from work. Is this correct?"

"Yes, until I can get my head right, so to speak."

"Since you are off from work, what are your thoughts regarding daily sessions beginning as early as tomorrow? We can talk about the special low rates for what I call 'emergency meetings' later. For now, I'm more concerned with helping you, which will incidentally work toward my involvement in this matter as well. I feel it's necessary to press this issue until it's either resolved, controlled, or both of us are locked away in a psych ward somewhere."

"Perfect," he says, laughing.

"Good to hear. How about we start where we left off yesterday before you checked your reflection?"

She reaches over and grabs her notebook.

"Sorry to interrupt, but why don't you use your laptop to take notes?"

"I never quite mastered the skill set. Not only am I really slow at typing, I'm also extremely loud. My nails are constantly clicking on the keys while I struggle to keep up. Let's just say I was asked politely by several of my patients to switch back to paper."

Calvin smiles, "Makes sense. It wasn't important. I was just curious."

"No problem. Okay…Getting back to it. I would like to address the two phrases." She takes her index finger and moves it across the page from left to right until she finds what she's searching for. "It says here, the first phrase was French and means 'Can you hear me?' while the second phrase was German and means 'You belong to me.'" She glances up and catches Calvin looking around the room. "You had mentioned you didn't know what they meant. Now that you do, what are your thoughts?"

"I was speaking with my wife about this exact topic this morning. As I explained to her, I took Spanish in high school and college. What I find interesting is that I've never spoken French or German in my life, yet I put together complete sentences for both languages. I can't explain that."

Intrigued, she asks, "Do you ever go to the cinema on French movie night?"

"No. Never. Why would anyone do that on purpose?"

"I guess it's safe to say you never rent them as well," she says, smiling.

"Pretty safe to say," he responds with a chuckle. "I've racked my brain and tried to come up with an explanation, but the only thing I can think of is that maybe those thoughts were planted in my head."

"You say it like you already have someone in mind."

"Not really someone, more of a something. I think the blurry figure is behind it. I'm sorry...I mean Figure X. Although I'm not really sure how, it seems as if he can control my thoughts whenever he's around."

"What exactly do you know about this figure? Do you think it's human?"

"No, I don't. If you had seen some of the things it's capable of, you would agree."

"Like what exactly?" she responds eagerly.

"Well, after my session last night I was on my way home and heard whispers of my name when I was driving. It felt so close. It was as if the breath was tickling my left ear."

Dr. Livingston's body tightens as she imagines this becoming her own fate. "Do you think Figure X is the one behind all of this?"

"Yes, I do."

"What do you think it wants?"

"I have no idea. All I could think about after the whispers was driving to the Shell station as if something really wanted me there. So I did. As I drove up, I noticed all of the vehicles were parked either at the front of the building or at the pumps, but no one was around. It was really strange. I ended up driving down the side of the store, where I saw a group of nine people standing in the field next to the station. Shortly after I arrived, there was a gust of wind that only affected the top portions of a section of oak trees. Then, out of nowhere, Figure X appeared on one of the branches about fifteen to twenty feet above the ground."

"Please describe what you were able to see."

"Basically, I saw a white glow around the right ankle area, but everything else was hidden or better yet blurred out. Later, several white lights formed all around him, changed to a red color and disappeared, taking along Figure X. Like some sort of transport or 'Beam me up, Scotty' kind of way. So I'm pretty sure it's not human, or from this planet anyway."

Dr. Livingston studies her notes, not quite sure where to go next. "It sounds like Figure X has somehow formed a special kind of bond with you and linked into your mind. Can it make you do things?"

Calvin instantly imagines his hands wrapped around the farmer's throat. He pushes the image out of his mind. "No, I don't believe so. So far, it has only been able to control certain thoughts but not my actions." He wants to scream out the word "almost" but knows he would have to explain in more detail.

"Why do you think Figure X has targeted you, and what do you think it wants?"

"I have no idea. I'm just a normal guy."

"I've noticed you sometimes refer to Figure X as a male and other times as an it. Do you think it's male?"

"Honestly, I'm not sure, but if it's responsible for the whispers, then it seems to be male."

"Fair enough. How about we refer to Figure X as a he?"

"Sounds good."

"You mentioned these types of experiences have been happening for only about three months. Have you suffered any traumas or any deaths of close relatives?"

"No."

Calvin's eyes dart around the room as he's flooded with memories of his dad. He looks down at the floor and picks a focal point. *I can't lie to her anymore.* His confidence increases; *now is the time to reveal all.* Glancing up, he notices Dr. Livingston is gone. He takes his time standing, hoping she will return at any moment, gradually makes his way over to her desk and peeks under it, just in case she's being funny or employing another unorthodox method, like last night. While heading toward the hall, he calls out, "Hello…Cindy, are you out here?"

CHAPTER

10

AN EERIE SILENCE has the hairs on Calvin's neck standing on end.

"Why is this happening again?"

He calls for Cindy one more time before stepping into the waiting area. He looks through the open sliding-glass window and spots an empty chair facing him. He walks to the entrance and rests his hands on the handle of the door. He peers through the dark tint of the glass and notices that the parking lot is full of cars but empty of people and activity. *I wonder how long it will last this time.*

He debates whether to stay in or take a chance on discovering what the outside has to offer. *Why not?* Feeling a little closed in, he opens the door and is startled by the familiar buzz announcing his departure. He steps onto the sidewalk and is distracted by the appearance of Janice standing next to the corner of the building roughly thirty feet away.

"Hey. What are you doing here?"

He takes a step toward her but instantly freezes at the sight of the long-sleeved, button-down plaid shirt.

"I saw you last night wearing the exact same shirt before you disappeared. He concentrates harder, his expression switching to doubt. "You're not real, are you?"

Without responding, Janice turns and walks behind the building, disappearing. *She's headed to the back entrance of the courtyard.* He immediately begins jogging and even calls her name several times as he approaches the archway at the entrance, but she's nowhere to be found. A whisper of his name is carried on the wind, forcing him to stop and look up. He sees her image over by the fountain and slowly walks in her direction surprised to see that the koi pond has plenty of water but is absent of fish.

"Janice, are you trying to tell me something? Please...I don't know how much more of this I can take."

He continues toward her, refusing to let her out of his sight, and stops less than three feet away.

"Honey, I love you, but I don't understand. Please help me so that I can get better."

She stares directly at him; her eyes are dull in color. "It's almost time," she whispers. "One will go away soon."

"One what?" he asks, almost ready to give up.

She turns away and heads through the arch. Feeling like she has something else to tell him, he starts toward her, but as he comes closer to the archway she vanishes.

"Seriously? One will go away soon. That's my big clue?" he screams in frustration. "Do you mean you? I see you just went away soon."

He continues walking and passes under the archway to the front entrance. He glances at all the parked cars and wonders why the eight handicapped parking places would be clumped together in one area.

"Who cares?" he mumbles, feeling his frustrations growing.

Calvin slowly turns when he notices the driver-side window of a long, black, four-door sedan glide open about three inches. The sedan is parked in the sixth handicap space to his left. He starts to call out, when he sees a thick smoke ring pushed through the crack of the window. Calvin watches as it floats through the air for a couple of seconds, until it's destroyed by a light wind. *Why haven't you vanished like everyone else?*

The windows are limo tint and make it impossible to see in, as they reflect the sun like a mirror. Through the open space of the window, he sees a pair of lips with a thin light brown mustache launching a second smoke ring. Calvin decides against talking with the stranger, turns around and heads back to Dr. Livingston's office.

After what seems like an eternity, he finally makes his way back to her suite and is pulling the door open when the buzzer sounds again. He laughs and shakes his head, muttering, "I guess if there's anything I would consider 100% reliable, it would be that buzzer."

Calvin is ready for everyone to be back and has a pretty good idea of what needs to be done. He makes his way to Dr. Livingston's office, takes her doctorate degree, and flips it around so that the backing is facing outward. He then carefully picks up the mirror and turns it around so that the glass is facing away from him. He sits down in the maroon chair before placing his head in his hands and floods his mind with as many thoughts and memories of Janice and Daniel as possible. His shoulders start to relax, signaling it's starting to work. Within moments of the first thought, he hears the phone ringing in the background, and at the same time Dr. Livingston is asking him a question about the nine people in the field.

"I'm sorry, Dr. Livingston, for interrupting, but I just had another episode, and everyone disappeared, including you and Cindy."

"Really? I think we just got the break we needed, since it happened while you were here. I have been carrying on our conversation and asking you questions this entire time without losing sight of you once. In fact, you have been extremely responsive in answering every one. So, it sounds like this portion may be only in your mind. If that's the case, how would you feel about having blood work and possibly even a CAT scan? The more we are able to rule out by a process of elimination, hopefully the better chance we have of making the correct diagnosis."

"Sure. Whatever you think is best. I'll pretty much go along with anything at this point."

"Great to hear," she says, relieved.

"You mentioned we had conversations, and I answered questions. Like what, if you don't mind me asking?"

"Of course not," she replies. She scans her notes, flipping back and forth through several pages. "What do you remember last?"

"I had mentioned I thought Figure X was male, based on the whispers. Also, you had asked if I have suffered through any recent traumas."

"Okay. Let's see...the next subject we discussed was the nine people. We even went through descriptions of each, including the pictures you have taken with your iPhone."

"Really?"

"Yes. We were in the middle of talking about how you protected and saved the farmer, before watching him drive away safely. You mentioned you thought he might be from Little Elm, since you had seen the Little Elm, Texas Farming Association sticker on his truck, in case we want to try and find him."

"Red truck?" he asks.

She looks down at her notes before responding. "Yes, a red Ford, to be exact."

"Wow, I've been busy. How long do you think we talked?"

"Well, let's see," she says, looking down at her watch. "My watch says it's twelve thirty-five. About ten minutes before I was hoping to end our extra session."

He stares at his watch and says disappointedly, "That's what I show too. Only I don't remember any of it. Shortly after we began the new session, you disappeared. So, I lost between twenty and twenty-five minutes."

"Seems like it," she says in a soothing tone. "Too bad there isn't proof."

Calvin turns around in his seat and glares behind him. But there is proof," he says excitedly. "Look at your diploma hanging on the wall and the mirror that broke earlier. Notice anything different about them?"

Dr. Livingston's eyes first lock on the diploma and then flicker immediately to the mirror leaning against the wall. "How's that possible? When did you turn them around?" she asks, shocked as the realization sinks in.

"Right after you disappeared the idea came to me. I figured if and when you came back, if they were untouched, then I would know it was all in my head. Looks like I might not be totally crazy," he says with enthusiasm.

"Or we both are," she spouts back, deflated.

"That's true, but either way I won't be alone in this any longer," he says, feeling a sense of relief.

"Maybe we should cut this session a little short. I'm having a difficult time processing all of this new information."

"That's fine. Oh, if you need to talk to someone, please feel free to call me anytime. You should have my cell phone number from the online forms I filled out."

"Thanks. If you hand me your phone, I will program my personal contact information for you as well."

"Perfect," he states.

"So just out of curiosity more than anything else, what did you do for the twenty or so minutes no one was around, besides redecorating my office?" she asks with a smile while handing his phone back to him.

"I went outside."

"Do you mind being more specific?"

"Not at all. I'll try and make this quick, since I know you want to clear your head before preparing for your next patient. Did I tell you that during my disappearance last night Janice and Daniel both went missing?"

"No. You didn't."

"Well, they did. Coincidentally for about twenty to twenty-five minutes. I pulled into my garage last night, and I saw an image of my wife wearing my long-sleeved, button-down plaid shirt. She was waiting for me at the door." Calvin pauses and becomes flustered. "I don't know how to say this next part."

"Just blurt it out. No need to sugarcoat anything anymore."

"Turns out she was only a *version* of my wife, if that makes sense...because it doesn't to me," he mutters.

"I understand. Like a vision or a dream."

"Sort of, I guess. Anyway, when my real wife and son later came back, she was wearing an entirely different outfit. I saw the version of my wife in the plaid shirt again just now."

Dr. Livingston's expression is blank as she looks at Calvin.

"I followed her to the courtyard in the middle of the building, where she had a message for me."

"What's that?"

"It's almost time; one will go away soon."

"Interesting," Dr. Livingston replies. She looks down at her watch. "I think I could spare a few minutes more."

They both take their seats.

"That's great," Calvin says, "because it gets much better. She led me to the front entrance of the arches, where all of the handicapped parking spots are located."

"Yes, I always felt that was a bad design."

"Me too," Calvin agrees, grinning widely. "So I lost Janice, but I noticed something I'm not sure how to take. Apparently I wasn't alone. Janice had led me over to a man in a car for a reason. I get the distinct impression he is somehow involved. Although with the vibe I was getting off of him, I sure hope he's not. He didn't seem to want to be very friendly. He just stayed in his car, blowing smoke rings from his cigarette. At least I think it was a cigarette. I couldn't really tell that either. I did manage to see he had a thin brown mustache, though."

"What else can you tell me about him?"

"Not much. He drives a four-door black sedan, but I didn't get the make or model. The windows must have been limo tint or darker because of the way the sun reflected off of them. I don't know, I guess that's it. I hope I'm wrong about his involvement so I won't have to see him again."

"Yes, hopefully not. Doesn't sound like anyone I would like to interact with either," she says, feeling creeped out. "Well, I guess that's it for now, unless you have anything else to add."

"No. I don't believe so."

With a smile plastered on her face, Dr. Livingston says, "Thanks for coming in. Same time tomorrow?"

"Sure. That sounds great. Oh, did you still want me to get my blood drawn and the CAT scan?"

"Why don't we hold off for now? We can leave it as a possibility for the future, if needed."

They shake hands, and Dr. Livingston walks past Calvin. Before she has a chance to open the door, they hear the buzzing sound echo throughout the back office.

"Sounds like your next patient is here."

"Yes, it does. He's early."

Dr. Livingston escorts Calvin to the waiting area and shakes his hand again before saying good-bye.

She calls out, "Mr. Jergens, I presume."

"You can call me Jeff," he responds from one of the chairs lining the wall. He stands and moves toward her cautiously, refusing to break eye contact.

On his way to the exit, Calvin glances up at the new arrival. He is overcome with a nervous feeling as he recognizes the thin brown mustache and smells the strong stench of stale cigarette smoke reeking from his clothes. Jeff is in his early-to-mid-twenties, and arrogant, judging by the way he struts across the room with his chest sticking out and his arms swinging with each step.

Deciding against leaving right away, Calvin stops just before the door and sits down quickly. He pulls out his phone and starts texting Dr. Livingston, making sure to wait until he can hear her office door clicking shut before sending.

She is on her way to her desk when she hears the vibration of her phone, but she refuses to look at the message, feeling it would be unprofessional.

Calvin stands and heads for the door; his only thought for the moment is getting home. The buzzer sounds, and immediately Cindy calls out "Good-bye, Mr. Johnston" loud enough to warrant a smile and a wave.

CHAPTER

11

DR. LIVINGSTON FOLLOWS her normal routine and takes out a new pad of paper before flipping to the second page.

"How I usually start off the session with a new patient is by asking a series of pretty generic questions. For example, what brings you to my office today?"

"It's simple really. I need help," Jeff says with a thick Southern accent.

"Help from what specifically? Please be as detailed as possible when answering my questions."

"Yes, ma'am. I need help from myself. As you can see, I'm not what you would call handsome or probably even be considered average looking. I'm barely five foot six and was born with bright red hair and freckles that seem to get worse with age," he says, picking at his fingernail. "I've been reminded all my life of my inadequacies. 'Your teeth aren't straight.' 'You're way too skinny.' 'You're so short, you should be a horse jockey.' I believe that one to be my favorite."

"And how would you respond to those tormenting statements?"

"I would prefer not to say it in front of you, ma'am. I'm making a new rule beginning now, that it wouldn't be proper to cuss in front of someone who is trying to help me."

"*Proper*—not really a word I hear very often as a psychiatrist. I would have to say that not only do I agree with your rule, I also appreciate the extra effort. So basically you would defend yourself against those types of verbal attacks using…*creativity*."

"I like that," he says, his Southern twang ringing loudly as his excitement builds. "Has a nice ring to it."

"Says something about your character."

"You bet it does."

"Kids can be extremely cruel at times," Dr. Livingston states, using a sympathetic tone.

"Yes, they can be and often were. Although these tormenting questions, as you called them, didn't come from any kids."

"From someone you know?"

"You're pretty good. I knew you were the right person for me, but I'm not quite ready for this line of questioning right now. So how about I get to that at a later time?"

"That's fine. I'm here to help you. Where would you like to start?"

"How about we begin this session like an AA meeting, since that's as close as I can get to fit my needs? Should make me feel right at home."

"Okay," she says hesitantly, not sure where he is going with this.

"But before we get started, I'm looking for guidance, and I'm hoping it can come from you. So if we both agree you are willing to be my doctor, then I am ready to get started."

"Of course I agree."

"Great," he says while pressing stop on his iPhone recording. "Save that for later, in case I need it. My name is Jeff Jergens. I'm twenty-four years old, and I'm a killer." He pauses for several seconds, waiting for a response. His frustration increases each moment she remains silent. "You didn't say 'Hello, Jeff.' Why didn't you say hello to me, like we're in an AA meeting? You agreed to it as if you were willing to honor it, but never followed through. How am I supposed to tell you what's on my mind if I feel like I'm not welcome here?"

"I'm sorry. I must have missed the cue. It won't happen again," she says, realizing she needs to treat him very delicately.

"I'm just funnin' you," he says with a chuckle. "So I'm ready to get this show on the road. Are you ready?" he says, bright-eyed and rubbing both hands together swiftly.

"Yes," she says reluctantly.

"Okay, here we go. You will be the first person I have told my story to, so forgive me if I seem a little anxious."

"Please take your time," she says in a soothing tone.

"Here goes nothing. I've never killed out of self-defense, and I've never killed out of necessity. I kill for one reason and one reason alone…I kill for pleasure. Well, at least I used to, anyway. I guess you could say it's kinda like my job. But all that's different for me now. And because of this change, I am struggling with some inner demons that I need your help with."

Dr. Livingston stares in amazement, surprised at how forthcoming he has been. "I usually like to start my first session a little slower." She loses her train of thought—the pungent odor of stale cigarettes has found its way over to her. She notices his thin brown mustache and realizes the text was most likely from Calvin, trying to warn her. She thinks back to his session and hears him saying, "I get the impression he's somehow involved." She looks up and stares into his light green eyes. *I'm getting the same feeling.*

Jeff, tired of waiting, says, "Do you want me to keep going?"

"Yes, of course. How about you start from the beginning and work back to what you were talking about?"

"Why not? I was nine when I encountered my first victim. I was walking down Woodsdale Avenue in Atlanta, Georgia, minding my own business, gazing up at the large pine trees, mesmerized by the smell, wondering how something so immaculate ever made it as far as it did."

She stops writing and looks up for a few seconds, caught off guard.

"Immaculate. Yes, I know what it means."

"My apologies. That wasn't what I was thinking. Please continue."

"I must have read it somewhere or another. My guess is I only read it once. The reason I say only once is because every time I read something, whether on purpose or not, it always stays with me."

"Can you give me an example of not being on purpose?"

"I was once in a stall in a rest area on my way to Texas and saw a poem scratched into the inside surface of the door. Let's just say not only did I not read that on purpose, but having a memory like mine isn't always what it's cracked up to be. I still have that darn thing rattling around in my brain."

She laughs, mostly to help put him at ease, but she also does find it a little funny. He laughs back, which seems to ease some of his tension.

"Where was I? Oh yeah, the black raven I stumbled upon in the middle of the red dirt road, squawking and carrying on, kicking up all sorts of dust. The only thing of importance at that very moment was that I walked up when I did. If it had been a few minutes earlier or a few minutes later, the raven and I might not have crossed paths. I told myself that it was my duty to put it out of its misery. If truth be told, I needed this kill to help put my mind at ease, whether or not I knew it at the time.

"Somehow I found a way to justify and make it all right. It's funny how justification seems important to so many people. The fact of the matter is the bird really was hurt and wasn't going to live much longer. The part I am reluctant to say out loud and have never told another soul is that I took my sweet time doing it. I needed to make sure that the life of the bird was taken with my own hands. After several minutes of torture, I finally decided to put an end to its misery. Snap, crackle, and pop can describe many things other than my favorite cereal, or at least it did that day anyway," he says with a snort.

"I apologize for interrupting. Did you say you were nine when this happened?" she asks, already knowing the answer but trying to slow down his momentum while reminding him that she is still in charge.

"Yes, ma'am."

"Thank you. Please continue."

"How many times have you said to yourself out of morbid curiosity, if nothing else, how interesting it would be to actually get a glimpse inside of a real-life killer's head? Feel what the killer feels, and think what the killer thinks."

"Never," she responds immediately. "I've never said or thought anything remotely like that."

"Well, you're gonna have your chance anyway," he says with a smirk. "Has someone ever ticked you off to the point you wanted them dead? How about when a person cuts you off in traffic, or maybe someone who received a promotion over you because he or she was sleeping with the boss? Or simply put, you don't like the person and think they should die. You name it, there is always a reason to kill."

Dr. Livingston continues to take notes without so much as a glance up.

"People never cease to amaze me. They watch their murder shows on TV night after night and don't even realize the real thing could be waiting right around the corner with a knife, gun, or my weapon of choice."

Dr. Livingston stops briefly before asking, "What do you consider—?"

"My hands. My weapon of choice has always been my hands. There's nothing more exciting than feeling the life you're taking cross through your fingertips before spreading throughout your whole body. It is a rush with no equal."

"You say these things as if you are going for shock value."

"Sometimes," he says without emotion. "I like to get a read on people. It's kinda a game I play."

"I'm intrigued. So what's your read on me so far?"

"I can't say just yet. However, I recognized the patient that was in here before me. That guy's a mountain of a man. What is he, six foot three?"

"I'm sorry. I am not willing to divulge any patient information, especially to another patient."

"Not even his height? Seems a little odd."

"You should be able to tell by the tone of my voice the answer to that question. I would never betray the trust of anyone in my care, unless the law required it. But I'm guessing you already knew this. Did I pass your test?"

"I reckon you did. Trust is important to me too. He did seem like a big crybaby, though. I heard him yelling, 'That's my big clue. Do you mean you?' Blah, blah, blah. I don't really know who he was talking to but, man, that guy's a bigger lunatic than me," he says, laughing obnoxiously.

Dr. Livingston shoots him a warning look.

"Okay, I'm sorry. I guess I might have crossed the line a bit. It's good to know you are tight-lipped with patient information. I sure hope you are as quiet for me when the time comes."

She puts her pen down, looks up at him and opens her mouth to say something but then senses this is his lousy way of asking for help.

"You know, not to change the subject, but I once saw the Grand Canyon in person," he says proudly, but then his face loses expression and he mumbles, "I was told I didn't deserve to see something of that magnitude."

"Who would tell you such a horrible thing?" she asks, trying to regain their connection.

Surprised at how good her hearing must be, he answers, but does so without making eye contact. "My father. I was eleven at the time."

Jeff stands and sticks out his right hand. Dr. Livingston also stands, shocked at his gesture.

"Are we calling it a day?" she asks, half kidding.

"Yes, I believe we should. I think we've covered enough for now. However, I'm planning on seeing you again real soon. What if I keep my next week's appointment but add another one much sooner? Would that be okay?" he says, using a strange tone bordering on desperation.

"Yes. You can call the office, and we will try and work you in as quickly as possible. Just to be open and up front with you, unfortunately I don't offer discounts for emergency sessions."

"Wasn't expecting one. See you soon, Doctor," he says, turning to walk away.

"I look forward to it," she says, wanting the last words. *I wonder what I have gotten myself into.*

CHAPTER

12

AS HE'S PULLING into his driveway, Calvin looks down at the console and notices the time is 1:42 p.m. He spots Alicia's white Expedition parked in the street directly in front of their house and is happy to see Daniel's playdate hasn't ended yet.

He parks in the garage, walks into the kitchen and is surprised to see her and Janice sitting at the table, each drinking a glass of wine. He starts to make a joke but notices Alicia's red, swollen eyes, indicating she has been crying, and decides against it.

"Are you okay?" he asks, leaning over and giving her a hug.

"I'm fine. Just trying not to think about it right now."

"Where are Daniel and Brendon?" he asks. "Are they sleeping?"

"No. We gave them both steak knives and sent them into the other room to play."

Calvin's expression changes to a look of surprise from the verbal attack.

"I'm really sorry," she says before he has a chance to comment. "I had a late night. To answer your question, yes, we put the boys down about thirty minutes ago for a nap. Janice and I were just reminiscing.

Did you realize I've known her for twenty-seven years? I think that's right," she says, calculating in her head again.

"Wow. You would think Janice would have picked a different person, especially if she'd known it was going to last this long," he says with a smirk.

"Okay. My turn. You would think Janice would have picked a better husband, regardless of the length of time you've been together."

Janice laughs loudly and is glad all three of them are spending time together again.

"Ouch. I guess you won that round," he says, smiling. "But just to clarify, Janice didn't pick me. I won her in a bet and held her to it."

They both look over at Janice, who is sipping her red wine, and say at the exact same time, "Sucker!"

Janice, caught off guard, laughs and coughs, choking a little. "How did I get dragged into this?"

Alicia stands up and gives him another hug, this time much longer and more meaningful. "I've missed you. It's good to have you back to your normal self."

"Thanks. I'm feeling much better today," he says, releasing his hold. He takes a couple steps backwards and leans against the kitchen wall. "I've met with a therapist over the last two days."

"Yeah, Janice mentioned it to me earlier. Seems like it might be helping."

"So far so good. I'll spare you the details, but we've agreed to meet on a daily basis. She seems pretty competent, and I have a lot of faith in her abilities."

"That's really great to hear. Please let me know if there is anything Dave and I can do for you."

"I will. Speaking of Dave, is the lightweight sleeping next to the kids?"

"This is my cue," Janice pipes in, knowing what's coming next. "I'm going to check on the boys to make sure they're okay. I'll be right back."

Alicia runs her finger across the rim of her wine glass in a slight daze. "You mean 'moron'? He left for New York early this morning. Get this. We were having an argument last night over the fact that the kids and I hardly ever get to see him, since he's always traveling. I'm tired of him being gone so much and want more of a father figure for the boys, not to mention a husband for me. He proceeds to tell me he has no plans of changing any part of his career. Oh, and the best part—this idiot looked right at me and said, 'End of discussion.'"

Calvin laughs, unable to control himself.

"That was at 11:30 last night. Three hours later we were still talking about how that was not the end of the discussion."

Calvin laughs even harder.

"He had to leave this morning at 5:30 to catch his flight. I had originally planned to drop him off at the airport to avoid the parking fees, but too bad for him. And I hope he's tired."

"I can picture him saying that. Was he talking with his hands?"

Alicia laughs. "You know him pretty well." She holds up her glass and shakes the crystal-clear liquid in a swirling motion. "That's why I'm drinking, even though it's early. I thought a glass of wine sounded like a good idea."

Calvin raises his hands in front of his body about shoulder height. "No judgment from me. Although I see you peer-pressured my wife into joining you."

"It was pretty hard to do. I believe it took one 'I don't know' from her and one 'Are you sure?' from me before she gave in."

Janice walks in from the hall with her quarter-full glass of red wine clutched tightly. "Hey, that's not true. I can recall tossing in a 'maybe' at least once or twice before my weakness overthrew my good judgment."

"Way to be strong, honey," Calvin says, giving her two thumbs-up. "I would join you myself, but I was thinking about heading out a little later. Driving around seems to help me clear my head. One quick question," he says, aiming his attention toward Alicia. "I don't want to pry, but doesn't Dave bring home buckets of money? Janice tells me all the time how nice it is for both of you to be able to hang out together during the daytime on weekdays. If he cuts back on hours and trips, would it mean you could have to go back to work?"

"Actually, that's two questions, but since it's you I'll go ahead and answer both. Yes, he does make a lot of money. He brought up the same point, and I told him Brian is going on fifteen in a few months and really needs his father right now. Not to mention he's going to miss Brendon turning five on Saturday. We have plenty in savings and could always downsize if needed. But honestly, I would rather go back to work if that meant having him home more. I'm not sure how much longer I can continue living this way. I miss him, and the kids miss him. Our lives are so much better when he's in them."

Janice walks over to the table, carrying two separate Frisbee-sized platters. The first is beautifully laid with Gouda, Bocconcini, Swiss, and Colby stacked neatly in a circle. The second is filled with buttery crackers, freshly baked bread thinly sliced, and French baguettes. In the center of each tray are thin slivers of apples and nectarines. She places both dishes gently on the table and says, "In case anyone wants a snack."

"I would love one," Alicia says, reaching for the Bocconcini. "This looks so wonderful. I usually only eat these in my salads, but I have never been able to resist mozzarella."

"I know. That's why I added them."

Alicia smiles and tears the small egg-shaped cheese in half, before placing a piece in her mouth. She chews for several moments, introduces several sips of her white wine, and closes her eyes as her palate bursts with well-blended flavors.

"Would you like some oil and vinegar, or maybe some basil?" Calvin asks.

"No, thanks. This is perfect by itself," Alicia responds. "Oh, one last thing before I forget. He made me so mad I was fuming. During our argument last night, he seriously asked me if I was going through menopause at forty. He said it seemed like my hormones were all out of whack."

"Wow. That doesn't really sound like him. Has he recently changed?"

"Not too much. Most of the time he's his usual self, but I think he was overly tired yesterday from all of the travel. Hindsight being twenty-twenty, I'm guessing my timing may have been a little off. However, in my defense, unless I wanted to have the conversation over the phone, yesterday was really my only opportunity until next week." Her demeanor changes as she feels the slight buzz from the wine. "I'm sorry for unloading all of this on you. I'm sure, with everything going on in your life, this is the last thing you need."

Calvin stares into her eyes and says with care, "Please, as long as we have been friends and as good as you and Dave have always been to us, we will be your shoulder anytime you need one."

He can tell by the change in her expression that she is on the verge of crying again and quickly makes his way over to her, calling out with enthusiasm, "End of discussion!"

"Very funny," she says, snapping out of her trance. "I was about to tell you what a sweet man you are."

He smiles, places his hand on her shoulder and massages gently without saying a word.

She pats his hand and says, "Thanks for listening."

"Anytime."

Janice finishes the rest of her red wine and heads for the sink to rinse out her glass. "Okay, I drank my one and a half glasses, and now it's time for me to switch to water. Otherwise, I'll be asleep by three o'clock."

"Lightweight," Calvin says with a wink.

"Funny," she says back. "I invited Alicia for dinner tonight and also reminded her she is always welcome to stay in the guest room if she likes. Brendon could sleep in Daniel's room. I'm sure they would enjoy a sleepover."

"I'm sure they would, but I don't know. It's pretty comfortable here. I'm afraid if I stay the night, you might not be able to get rid of me...ever," she says with a grin. "Although it's over an hour drive back to Oklahoma. Maybe I will, if you're okay with it as well."

"Of course," Calvin replies. "You know you and your family are always welcome here anytime. What about Brian? Will he be home alone?"

"No. He's sleeping over at a friend's house tonight. School ended for us on June 5. Since then, I haven't seen him. I guess the apple doesn't fall too far from the tree."

Calvin's eyebrows arch, and he makes a look of confusion. "Just a suggestion, but you can say no to Brian, right? Or are you getting soft in your menopausal days?"

"Keep it up, funnyman. You should really think about doing stand-up comedy," she states mockingly. "I have already told him he needs to be home on Saturday to celebrate Brendon's birthday."

Calvin looks at Alicia and winks before walking over and turning on the patio ceiling fan. He grunts as he slides open the glass door, forgetting it sticks on occasion.

"Don't say a word," he says, pointing to Alicia before she has a chance to chime in.

She closes her mouth and sits back in her chair, disappointedly realizing she waited too long and missed her perfect opportunity at an old-man joke.

"I'll be out back for a while," he calls to Janice.

The heat pounds on him instantly as he makes his way over to the four beige patio chairs. He sits down in the one directly under the ceiling fan, looks around his backyard, and is tempted to jump into the light blue, clear, crisp water of the L-shaped pool. Beyond the pool, he admires the bright green color of the Bermuda grass stretching across his acre lot to the black wrought-iron fence surrounding the yard.

Looking through this fence, he follows a dirt trail with his eyes until it meets up with a bridge encased in metal with a dark stain on the wooden planks for the walkway. The bridge crosses the creek and leads to an empty field, where he is reminded of the times he used to spend with Daniel, flying kites and giving piggyback rides.

An occasional breeze blows through, minimizing the stifling 102-degree heat only briefly. He closes his eyes, relaxing, and hears the faint cry of a siren in the background. Without warning, the incessant whining of the ambulance becomes unbearably loud, as if it has pulled up next to him and stopped. He hears someone call out, "Do you know your name?" Startled by the sudden interruption, Calvin sits straight up, discovering the noise of the siren is gone and he is alone sitting in his chair. *Did I fall asleep?*

A feeling of panic overwhelms him as he wonders if everyone has vanished again. He jumps out of the chair and, while turning toward the door, notices both women are sitting at the kitchen table. He opens the door and immediately feels a chill from the cold air rushing out to greet him.

"Did ya'll hear the siren?"

They both look at each other before saying, "No."

"Oh, I guess it was pretty faint, now that I mention it."

"Are you okay?" Janice asks, detecting a strange tone in his voice.

"Yes, I'm fine."

Alicia senses something might be wrong and tries to distract him by stretching out her arm in his direction while shaking her cell phone. He's relieved to see the smile on her face and wonders what she's up to.

"Here, I want you to see the e-mail I just got from Dave."

Calvin takes the phone and immediately begins reading.

Sorry, sweetheart. I wish I could say these words directly to you in person, but for the moment this will have to do. I wasn't able to sleep on the plane, knowing how deeply I must have hurt you. I have sat here uncomfortably switching from side to side, weighing the merits of both conversations. After a considerable amount of time, it occurred to me how much of an idiot I've been. Everything I'm working so hard toward means nothing without you, Brian, and Brendon in my life. I would like to sit down with you next week when I'm back in town and work out a compromise.

I have declined my meeting in San Francisco for the following week to make certain I will be home. This is the first step in my commitment to us.
I'll call you tonight once I'm settled.
I love you!
D.

One last thing…I thought you might need a laugh. This is a pretty big campus, so they assigned a guide to me. I have somehow misplaced him. It's like he vanished out of thin air. I turned around and he was gone.

Calvin stops reading briefly, feeling his heart flutter. Sensing Alicia is waiting patiently for him to finish, he pushes the thought out of his mind and resumes reading.

So now I have six minutes to make it to one of the conference rooms by myself and have no idea where I'm supposed to be. Must be karma.
I wish I were with you.

"This is the Dave I remember. Glad he's back," Calvin says, handing her phone back. "Romance at its finest…through an e-mail."

"I'll take it," she says proudly.

Calvin makes his way toward the door and is met by Janice.

"I'm not playing…are you okay? You don't seem like your normal self since you came in from the back porch. Is there anything I can do?"

"No. I'm fine. I swear. I just want to go for a drive and clear my head."

"Please be careful."

"I will. I promise."

Calvin leans over, kisses Janice good-bye and waves to Alicia, then heads out into the garage. As he backs out into the street, only one destination occupies his thoughts.

After roughly forty minutes of driving, he pulls into the parking lot of the Shell station and is stunned to see the black four-door sedan with limo-tinted windows parked at the front pumps. Pulling up, he carefully examines the car, making certain it belongs to the only other person that stayed behind when everyone else disappeared.

"I knew I wasn't finished with you yet," he mumbles. "What could you possibly be doing here?"

Calvin gradually makes his way down the side of the store, taking inventory of all the familiar vehicles, minus the red Ford pickup truck. *Let me guess. Everyone's out in the field picking pretty flowers today.*

Continuing toward the back of the building, he parks next to the air and water machine. Staring in the direction of the group, he notices there are seven members circling around Jeff and the overweight man in the Mountain Dew T-shirt and khaki shorts. Calvin watches as Jeff places both hands on the man's shoulders, gently persuading him to fall to his knees.

"No!" The word bounces off the tightly sealed windows and echoes loudly inside his car.

Jeff rearranges both hands. One is now on top of the man's head, and the other is under his chin for better leverage. Afraid of what's coming next, Calvin pushes open his door with great force and yanks off his seat belt. He jumps out of his car and runs full speed toward the gate. The crowd continues to circle the two while chanting, "Do you accept the challenge?

As Calvin makes his way through the gate, he notices the bright white glow coming from the ankle of the figure standing on the oak branch. He looks back over to the crowd and hears Jeff shouting angrily, "I accept!"

Calvin yells out, "Please don't!" Hoping to make a difference. He stops roughly ten feet away and watches as the group of seven continues to circle their newest prey. An unsettling feeling rushes through him as he realizes that the fate of the man in the Mountain Dew shirt is now in Jeff's unstable hands. The chanting softens, and each person slowly turns, directing all of their attention onto Calvin.

"Your too late, Crybaby," Jeff calls out. "I'm here to do what you were incapable of doing to the farmer."

"What? How do you know about the farmer?" Calvin asks, stunned.

"Because I know everything about you. You're the reason I'm here."

CHAPTER

13

JEFF'S INTENSITY INCREASES as his focus switches to the overweight man. His expression hardens thinking, *It won't be long now.* The man's face reveals no traces of emotion. Only an empty stare filled with an indifference to living or dying radiates from his dull gray eyes.

Jeff tightens his grip. A small trace of a smile forms in the left corner of his mouth.

"This is going to hurt you more than it does me," he says. "And by the way, I hate Mountain Dew."

With that, he moves his hands in opposite directions in one quick, fluent motion, snapping the man's neck and killing him instantly. A loud cracking sound rings out and descends on the crowd, hushing their chants. His lifeless body drops to the ground.

"No!" Calvin screams, rushing to him.

Jeff places his right foot on top of his kill and proudly stares up at the figure in the oak tree, as if presenting an offering. The remaining seven shuffle around and form a human wall, standing shoulder to shoulder in a line of protection for Jeff. Calvin stops a few feet from them and stares, confused by their gesture. He debates crashing through, knowing it would be relatively simple to do, but something inside is telling him to wait. He uses his height to his advantage and stares over the three teenagers. He focuses on the dead man lying on his back and wonders why his life was taken. *What purpose could this possibly serve?* He's distracted by light traces of the number zero forming in the center of the lifeless man's forehead and immediately thinks of the farmer. Calvin looks up at Jeff with curiosity exuding from his eyes, wondering if he's noticed it too, when he hears a voice whisper, "Zero days left."

Calvin looks around anxiously, wondering where the voice is coming from.

Flashes of white lights appear and begin to surround Figure X and the body of the man in the Mountain Dew T-shirt simultaneously. Within moments, the lights begin to shake before turning red and vanishing into thin air, leaving no traces of either. Only a few small twinkling lights are left behind, suspended in midair momentarily before fading away.

Calvin turns in the direction of the parking lot and watches as the man's Volkswagen is consumed in the same manner, only to disappear without any trace seconds later. The small twinkling lights glimmer widely in place of the missing car as Calvin refuses to accept that this is happening. He's filled with a sudden burst of anger, forcing his jaws to tighten and his fists to clench. *I should throw him on the ground. I could place one foot on top of him to see how he likes it.*

He cringes at the thought of calling the police and reporting the murder. *And tell them what exactly? Where's my proof of any wrongdoing other than trespassing?* His rage softens at the realization that there's only one viable option. *Let him get away with it. At least for now anyway.*

Calvin is turning to leave when something diverts his attention. He stares directly into the eyes of the man in the suit and flinches as an outline of a number appears in the center of his forehead. Calvin briefly closes his eyes, hoping it's a mistake, when he hears the whisper, "One day left." He opens his mouth to warn him but sees that only a shell of the man exists, and any words spoken to him would almost certainly be in vain.

The remaining six people head toward the opening in the large, densely wooded area in single file until all have been swallowed up by the trees. Jeff follows behind at a slower pace, and as he's about to enter, Calvin shouts out from pent-up frustration, "You're not going to get away with this." He waits eagerly for some sort of confrontation but is disappointed when Jeff doesn't acknowledge and disappears behind several trees and red-flowered shrubbery.

Calvin quickly makes his way back to his car with only thoughts of his family to keep him company. *I wish I was home.*

He starts his car, still confused by the image of Jeff standing over his kill. As he turns right onto the service road, Jeff surfaces from the shelter of the wooded area and takes a few steps onto the field.

"So long for now, Crybaby. We'll meet again real soon. You can bet your life on it," he says, laughing loudly, and heads back into the trees.

A couple of hours pass before Jeff emerges once again, feeling regenerated and more powerful than before. He heads straight for his car, mumbling something unintelligible. He opens the driver-side door and, before sitting behind the wheel, is distracted by a flash high in the light blue, cloudless sky.

"Hello, old friend," he says, looking up.

The sun is shining brightly, and its rays are shimmering off of the object several hundred feet in the air. There's a familiar glow about it, one he hasn't seen for almost three years, and he welcomes the object's arrival wholeheartedly. It's a mixture of red and silver, hovering in one spot. He tilts his head to the left, and the colors are bright red with little bits of silver tint, instantly reminding him of all the past bloodshed they have shared together. He then tilts his head to the right to see bright silver with a hint of red. The harder he stares, the more the object seems to change, until his mind is consumed by an enormous amount of pressure, forcing him to look away.

This night just got a whole lot better. I sure hope I get to kill me either a cowboy or a cowgirl tonight. His heart rate increases at the thought of the potential jackpot of having both. In a hurry, he opens his car door and quickly settles behind the wheel.

He looks down at the mounted compass on the dashboard and mutters, "Northeast." Looking back up, he concentrates on the shimmering distraction and estimates it's somewhere between fifteen and twenty miles away.

He starts his car, doing his best to keep his excitement down to a bare minimum, before whispering, "The beacon is back." Turning right, he heads north down the service road and notices his clock is showing 6:37 p.m. He enters the northbound ramp of US 75 toward McKinney and eventually makes several turns while keeping his eye on the object. *This never gets old, no matter how many times I've seen it.*

Before long, he's turning into the parking lot of a Baptist church directly in line with the beacon. The sign in the front reads, "Welcome Alcoholics Anonymous Members for Thursday Night Meetings at 7:00 pm."

The entire building is covered with tan siding outlined neatly in white trim. A freshly painted white cross sits high on top of the steeple, outlined with gray and black shingles. Jeff parks in one of the open spaces in front and checks to make sure his gun is still in the glove compartment before turning off his car. He observes strangers deeply absorbed in themselves and their own conversations as they pass by without even so much as a glance in his direction. The first to catch his eye are two women in their early sixties making their way down the sidewalk, talking loudly while heading for the front entrance. At first, Jeff wonders if they're twins, but then he notices that one appears to be a few years older than the other. They both have older-style haircuts and not much concern for fashion or fitness. *Welcome to the country.*

He gleams with excitement as a tall, extremely skinny man wearing a cowboy hat with Wrangler jeans and brown, scuffed boots swaggers past. *This guy looks like a true rancher. So far, he's my favorite. I hope it's him.*

Jeff smokes an entire cigarette, including part of the filter, before opening his door and stepping out to grind the butt onto the asphalt. Looking down, he sees a red stain on the side of his shirt. He's unable to distinguish whether it's ketchup left over from lunch or dried blood. He leans toward it to do a smell test but decides it's too much of an effort, and he really doesn't care either way. *Dirty is dirty regardless, which means I now have to change.* Feeling a little put out, he makes his way to the back of his car and pops the trunk. He leans in and pulls out a dark blue collared shirt still wrapped in clear plastic from the cleaner's. *This should do for now.* He takes off his tainted shirt and tosses it into the bed of an old pickup truck parked next to his car.

Good riddance. I didn't much care for that one anyway. He throws his trash on the ground and shuts the trunk. Within seconds of swinging open the entrance door of the church, he's smacked in the face by the strong aroma of freshly brewed coffee.

"This must be the place," he states out loud, using a Texas accent, getting into character. "Howdy," he says, passing the cowboy, and he is thrilled when he receives a nod and a tip of the hat.

He hears a voice behind him state, "It's a little past 7:00, and we are ready to begin, if everyone would please take a seat."

Jeff hears the announcement but isn't much on authority and figures he'll sit when he's good and ready. He counts a total of fourteen people heading toward the aluminum folding chairs set up in a circle. He watches the group and is reminded of cattle being herded. *We have an excellent range of specimens from short to tall, and thin to fat. I couldn't ask for a better grab-bag assortment. I wonder which one will be my target. Okay, so let's see. Eenie, meenie, miney, mo.*

The man who made the announcement earlier introduces himself as Pastor James Smithers. Jeff turns and isn't surprised that the big booming voice is coming from a larger man with a long, fluffy white beard. He's tempted to yell out "Ho, ho, ho," but refrains, knowing he must stay in character. *I need twang and lots of it tonight. Yee-haw.*

Pastor Smithers steps to the middle of the circle and clears his throat. "I'm glad to see quite a few of the same familiar faces and I welcome all newcomers. I would like this meeting to begin by allowing the opportunity for first-timers to start us off tonight here at Holy Temple Baptist Church. So, if you've never attended one of our weekly meetings in the past and are comfortable enough to take the lead, please feel free."

Now this is worth heading over to my seat. He calls out with a Texas accent as he approaches an empty chair, "This is my first time visiting your church, and I would like to be the one that kicks us off, if that's okay."

"Of course, young man. We would be delighted to hear what you have to say."

"Great," he says enthusiastically. He looks around the room and refuses to sit. "Hi, my name is Jeff, and I'm a killer."

The crowd hushes. He looks around and is met with silence and blank stares from fourteen sets of eyes. A crooked smile crosses his face as he thinks, *Going as planned.*

"Where's my greeting? Shouldn't the correct response be 'Hi, Jeff?'"

A low murmur takes over as each person begins discussing Jeff's introduction. Pastor Smithers shuffles around in his seat and clears his throat several times before leaning forward, preparing to step in.

Jeff stops him by stretching out his arm and holding up one finger. "Please, I'm not finished yet."

Pastor Smithers gives him a disgruntled look, then sits back, allowing him to carry on. Jeff turns his head as far as he can in one direction, stretching out his neck until it cracks. He's caught off guard when an unexpected chuckle escapes as he's reminded of the overweight man in the Mountain Dew T-shirt and khaki shorts.

"Sorry," he calls out. "I'm a little nervous, being my first time here and all. Let me start again. I'm a killer of my own hopes and dreams. By accepting that first drink after I swore I would never do it again, I knew I was destined to walk in the very same footprints of my father, who abandoned me at an early age." He looks around and this time is greeted with several nods of understanding and appreciation. "So I'm going to say again. Hi, my name is Jeff, and I'm a killer."

The words echo off the walls as "Hi, Jeff" comes rushing back from only a small handful willing to participate in one of his favorite schemes. He stops to pretend it's too tough to continue and even places his left hand up to his eyes and rubs gently.

"I feel like some of you can relate and remember back to that first drink. Now, I'm not talking about your first drink ever, but that unforgettable first drink after reaching sobriety for any substantial amount of time. This is the one that causes you to fall off the rapidly moving wagon we all desperately attempt to cling on to. I remember feeling weakened with each drink as I held that bottle in my hand. I knew my control over my own mind and body was only an illusion, and yet I continued. How insignificant I felt the more times I fell prey to the wicked grasp that held me so tightly." He scans the room slowly, making eye contact with each person, before locking eyes with the two sisters he spotted before the meeting began. He smiles as the number zero appears on their foreheads. He looks away and is barely able to control his excitement as he hears the whisper, "Zero days left." *I was hoping for the cowboy but will settle on a two-for-one instead.*

Without losing his place, he continues, "I remember the crimes I committed under the influence of alcohol, and I'll remember each additional crime I'll continue to commit while under the influence of alcohol."

Several people stop nodding, confused by what was just said.

"I'm kidding. It's just a joke, folks," he says, holding both hands in the air. "I wanted to make sure y'all were still payin attention."

He receives some loud laughter and a few shallow claps.

"Why do we drink? I used to think my father drank because of the guilt from all the beatings he'd given me and my mom." A look of disgust crosses his face. "Yeah, right. Who am I kidding? That man's eyes never showed an ounce of remorse, drunk or sober. Which is why I killed him. He was a useless man not worth the dirt he would often pass out on."

A few gasps, followed by a few groans of disbelief, then silence as they await his next words. A dark-haired teenager wearing a sleeveless black "Got Dope?" T-shirt calls out, "Did you really kill him? Or is this another one of your lies?"

Mr. Smithers holds out his hand, signaling to the young man to keep it under control, and asks, "Curtis, what have I told you about wearing that shirt here?"

"Sorry, Pastor Smithers. It was the only one that was clean."

Jeff opens his mouth to answer when a petite, mousy girl with cropped blond hair comes walking in and trips over one of the legs of the dessert table. A loud scraping noise reverberates as the table slides from one place to another, diverting everyone's attention over to her.

"You've got to be kidding me. Who is this person?" Jeff mumbles, feeling his temper rising as she unknowingly steals his thunder. He feels a sense of absolution as he realizes one simple gesture of kindness could be an easy source of temporary revenge.

He points his finger toward her and calls out, "How about we give the incredibly distracting young woman who just walked in a chance to speak?"

Her face turns bright red. She waves him away and quietly finds an open seat, too embarrassed to stop for any of the treats.

"Are you sure?"

Her head immediately lowers, and she slinks down into her chair, trying to hide her humiliation.

Pastor Smithers stands abruptly, coming to her aid. "Thanks, Jeff, for sharing. I think we've heard enough for now. I believe we should move along and maybe give one of our regulars a chance to speak."

Jeff glares back and leaves the circle. *I'm going to kill this man, and I'm going to take my time with him.* His frustrations increase with each step as he heads toward the refreshments table. *That stupid mousy chick threw me off my game.* He heads straight for the desserts, grabs several cookies, licks each of them, and puts them back. He then pours a glass of lemonade, spilling it on purpose, and refuses to clean the mess.

Pastor Smithers continues with the meeting, unscathed by Jeff's behavior. "How about we hear from one of the Kearman sisters? It's been several meetings since either of you have spoken."

With a simple flick of their wrists, they both decline, and Pastor Smithers moves on. "Frank, how about you? Would you like to give it a try?"

In slight recognition, Jeff tilts his head up at the mention of the name. Frank is an African American wearing camouflage pants and matching shirt. Jeff is unsure why he looks familiar and wonders what weaknesses he must possess other than the obvious addiction to alcohol. Frank speaks very slowly and seems to be a shy man with little or no confidence. Jeff looks him up and down several times before thinking, *You got to keep an eye on the shy and quiet ones.* He watches for several moments, studying his mannerisms, before dismissing him from being any kind of real threat.

Frank begins by describing his weekly adversities dealing with the nearly ten years of being sober. Extremely bored, Jeff rolls his eyes and blocks him out, thinking everyone in this room is going to die of old age before he's done speaking. He finishes his lemonade, sets the empty cup next to the trashcan, and heads down toward the men's room. He's curios by the double doors leading to the chapel and opens both quietly to get a peek. There are thirteen rows of seating on each side leading up to the pulpit, which is set up on a stage covered in red carpet. He can smell the strong odor of wood polish and is impressed with how every one of the light blue hymnals is neatly placed in a holder behind each of the pews.

"Okay, I'm still bored," he mumbles.

Directly across the hall is the office with the name "Pastor James Smithers" stenciled on the door. Jeff reaches over and jiggles the knob, disappointed it's locked. He debates picking it but figures that will come in time, if it's in the plan. He wanders around for a while and finally makes it back to his seat inside the meeting room. In total, seven people speak that evening, before the meeting finishes up with the Serenity Prayer, led by Pastor Smithers. As soon as it ends, Jeff is unable to escape Curtis's curious questions.

The mousy girl is pacing nervously, awaiting her opportunity to get even with Jeff. Several minutes pass, each one increasing the intensity of her frustrations, until she becomes completely fed up and storms out to the parking lot.

Curtis, tired of receiving indirect answers, asks in an irritated tone, "So did you really kill your father or not?"

"I did," Jeff responds, "over and over, but it always comes out looking like a car accident."

Feeling like Jeff is only toying with him, Curtis' feels forced to turn and walk away without saying good-bye.

Jeff comes strolling out and walks past the mousy girl, pretending not to notice her.

"Are you kidding me?" she says loudly.

"Who, me?"

"Yes, you. What's your problem?" she asks angrily. "Why did you embarrass me the way you did?"

"My apologies. I was upset because you interrupted my speaking. I was out of line."

"Of course you were out of line. Who does that to someone?"

He reminds himself to stay in control and wait for the target. Frank walks up to the truck parked next to them and asks, "Are you okay, Miss Kathy?"

"I'm fine, Frank. Thanks for asking."

"Just thought I would check," he grumbles, and then starts his truck.

A cloud of black smoke seeps out of the tailpipe as he lets the engine idle momentarily before backing up and driving away.

Take good care of my shirt, Frank.

The metallic streetlamps outlining the parking lot of the church flicker on and off a few times, before casting additional lighting overhead. Within moments a slight grouping of June bugs has already found their way and begun circling.

"It's dusk and should be dark before too much longer," Jeff says, trying to stall long enough for his future victims to walk out of the building.

He studies Kathy's light blue eyes and notices there's something familiar about them. The more he tries to concentrate on where he knows her from, the more his mind is unwilling to reveal any information.

"What?"

"It's dusk and should be dark before too much longer."

"Who cares?" she responds, still agitated. "Is there something wrong with you?"

Jeff ignores her question and watches as the two sisters pass by. They get into an older four-door maroon Oldsmobile and take what feels like an eternity to put on their seat belts.

As soon as the reverse lights appear, Jeff looks at Kathy and says, "Tell you what, I have somewhere to be. I apologize again if I was rude."

"*If* you were rude?" she snaps. "Whatever, dude. You're not worth it."

She turns away and heads toward her car parked on the other side of the parking lot, taking long, quick strides.

The cowboy swaggers out of the building as Pastor Smithers watches Jeff from the entranceway. The two ladies turn right and slowly head down the street. Jeff jumps in his car and immediately pulls his gun from the glove compartment, laying it gently on the seat next to him. He heads out into the street and feels his adrenaline pumping at the thought of what he knows is soon to follow. He stays several car lengths behind them, careful not to follow too closely. After a few minutes, they turn into a rock-covered driveway and head toward a white mobile home set off in the distance. Jeff follows them down the driveway and stops roughly ten feet behind, wondering if they'll even realize he's there. He glances over at the trailer and notices it's older and run-down, with orange rust stains streaking the lower sections. Unkempt shrubbery spills over the walkway and partially blocks the steps leading up to the front door. He curls his fingers around the handle of his revolver and waits, unsure who will be first, his heart pounding with anticipation. The maroon Oldsmobile moves from side to side as they shift around, but neither woman seems to be in a hurry to leave the comforts of the car.

"What are they up to?" Jeff mumbles. "Do they know I'm here?"

He focuses all of his attention on them and is unaware that someone has pulled up and parked at the edge of the property.

The driver-side door of the Oldsmobile opens slowly, and as the older of the two women places her foot onto the gravel, Jeff jumps out of his car and heads straight for her. He pulls the trigger twice without a glimmer of self-doubt, hitting the driver both times in the chest. Her white shirt is instantly consumed by red, and her lifeless body slumps in her seat, restricted from falling to the ground only by the fastened seat belt. Her sister jumps out of the passenger side, screaming, and runs toward the trailer. Jeff tosses the gun inside their car, catches up to her, and jumps onto her back, yelling "Yee-haw," forcing her to collapse to the ground. She's unable to put up much of a fight and weakens after a short struggle. He wrestles around, toying with her, before snapping her neck and putting her out of her misery.

"No cowboy tonight, but I did get to ride a cow," he mumbles with a snort.

Out of breath, he finds the front steps leading up to the trailer and moves several stray branches out of his way before sitting. He stretches out and crosses his legs, soaking in the intense rush flowing over him as he ponders his latest kills with pride.

Within a minute, both of the sisters' bodies and the car are surrounded by white lights, which then disappear, revealing only a forest-green four-door Buick still parked at the edge of the property. He's unable to make out the driver and remembers he threw his gun inside their car. The Buick slowly makes its way toward him and stops roughly fifteen feet away. He gets to his feet, ready to dispose of any loose ends, then notices that Kathy is the driver. She places the car in park, opens her door, and steps out.

"You shouldn't be here," Jeff calls out.

"So you're the one," she says, coming closer.

"One what?"

"I saw the number seven etched into the Kearman sisters' foreheads and heard the whispers of 'Seven days left' at last Thursday's meeting. I wasn't a hundred percent sure what it meant, but I had a pretty good idea. As hateful as these women were to me, I wanted to be present when it happened. They always sat there quietly with their judgmental looks, and I could sometimes see them whispering when I talked. Let's just say I made it a point to be present when they met their demise. Honestly, I thought it might be me to kill them, since I heard the voice and all, but I'm relieved it was you instead."

"Why are you talking so much?"

"Sorry. I talk a lot when I'm nervous or excited."

"Your boyfriend is a lucky man," he says, making his way toward her.

She ignores his comment and takes a few steps backwards, ending up next to her driver-side door. "The second I walked into tonight's meeting, I knew you were the one. I actually tripped over the table because I was captivated by the dark aura surrounding you." She holds up her hand for him to stop, fearing he is getting too close. "I've been watching their trailer off and on all day long, wondering when it was going to happen and who was going to do it. This was exhilarating. I've never seen anything like it. Oh, one last thing, and I'll stop talking."

"Sure. Anything. Just name it."

"Do you see a number on my forehead and hear a voice when you lock eyes with me?"

"No."

"Then I guess I'm safe. What now?"

"I don't know. Why are you bothering me?"

"There's no reason to be rude. It's obvious we're on the same team."

"What team are you talking about, you crazy person?"

She smiles, unaffected by his remarks. "I wasn't really upset with you, by the way. I was only acting so I could stay close. As soon as you wanted to leave after spotting the sisters' reverse lights, that was the clincher for me. There's no way I was going to miss it."

"Well, you didn't. Congratulations."

Frank drives by in his old pickup, and his brakes squeal loudly as he slows down. He stops in the middle of the road, lowers his window with several cranks and calls out, "Are you still okay, Miss Kathy?"

She smiles and waves him on. Jeff doesn't even give him the courtesy of a glance or an acknowledgement of any kind.

As Frank drives off, Jeff states, "That guy is really getting on my nerves. I don't suppose you saw a number on his forehead or heard any whispers on the amount of days left for him, did you?"

"Nope," she says, grinning widely.

"That's a shame."

"How long have you been doing this?"

"Doing what exactly?"

"Killing people."

"A very long time," Jeff answers, his eyebrows arching. "Although a lot of the details are a little hazy."

"Why?" she asks, trying not to let on that she knows.

"I don't know or care," he says in a hateful tone.

She stares at him with a blank look. "I may have gotten in over my head."

Without hesitation, Jeff jumps at the opportunity and says harshly, "Let me get this straight. You drove up to a murder scene and jumped out of the car to meet the murderer. And just now you feel like you may be in over your head. Are you on any medication you might have forgotten to take?"

"No. I don't take any medication. I'm not even an alcoholic. I just go to the meetings every Thursday because it makes me feel like I have a family for that one hour." Kathy looks away, her eyes filling up with tears. "Most everyone in there is always nice to me, except for the Kearman sisters and you."

"Seriously?" he mutters in a low voice, looking around in disbelief as if someone were playing a joke on him.

"I've never told anyone that before. I was always too embarrassed to admit it out loud, but now you know."

Something about this girl has him baffled. "Look, no offense, but I think you should probably leave now. While you still can."

"No. I want to hear more."

"I don't think you understand who I am or what I'm capable of."

"I disagree. I just saw you shoot one sister and ride the other like an animal before snapping her neck. I think I know exactly who and what you are."

"And yet you're still here annoying me instead of running away and minding your own business."

She slowly reaches behind her, pretending to scratch an itch, and feels the butt of her gun nestled in the small of her back. She gives him a slight smile. *I've already killed you once. Shouldn't be any issue to do it again, if need be.*

"I should make it clear to you, I don't have to wait until I hear a whisper or see a number to kill. Do you understand what I'm saying?"

Kathy nods emphatically, signaling she understands the not-so-subtle point he's making. She walks backwards and refuses to so much as blink until she's safely in her car. Backing out of the driveway, she extends her middle finger, smiling widely.

He shakes his head as a smile manages to escape. "This girl's going to be the death of me. I can feel it."

CHAPTER

14

THE CLOCK CHANGING to 6:30 a.m. initiates a soft, subtle beeping noise ringing out from the alarm clock strategically placed on the opposite side of Dr. Rachael Livingston's bed. The hum of the fan easily drowns out the sound, making it impossible for her to hear. Gradually, the beeps become louder, until they have progressed into a more serious, exasperating sound blaring throughout all areas and echoing off the walls of the master bedroom.

"Jack. Please make it stop," she says, her morning voice raspy.

She rolls over to her back before grasping a down pillow and placing it over her ears for temporary relief. She reaches out to nudge her husband but is met with a cold, empty sheet.

"Make it stop."

She stretches out her arm. Her fingertips glide across the nightstand and blindly stumble across the snooze button before pressing it quickly and welcoming the peace and quiet.

The aroma of pancakes wanders in through the crack under the door, drifting over to where she's lying. She can hear laughter from her six-year-old daughter, Sandra, and the clicking of their golden retriever's claws as he paces back and forth on the shiny, reddish-brown hardwood kitchen floor. *I need to take Murphy in for grooming on Saturday if I don't forget again.*

The day's calendar runs through her mind one patient at a time, until she pushes it back, thinking, *Yeah! It's finally Friday.* She climbs out of bed and grabs her robe, hanging from a hook on the center of the bathroom door. She raises both arms before slipping it over her body and tying the belt loosely in front. She catches another whiff, this time of bacon, and decides to follow the smell. She listens to her stomach growl with every other step, before peeking around the corner to see Sandra sitting in one of the kitchen chairs, watching her dad flip pancakes.

Rachael gazes over at Jack and is reminded more of a fireman than an accountant, based solely on his physique and good looks. She is tempted to walk over and run her fingers through his thick, blond hair when she hears her daughter ask if she could have another glass of orange juice. Rachael makes the *psst* sound while stepping out from behind the wall and is met with a happy, ear-piercing scream of "Mommy!" followed by "I've missed you."

Sandra's light blue eyes were one of Jack's greatest gifts to her and complement her dark hair and light brown skin perfectly. *She's already beautiful at six. I can't imagine what she'll look like when she's a teenager.*

"Good morning, Dr. Livingston," Jack says, standing over the griddle with spatula in hand.

"Are you wearing my apron?" she asks, laughing.

"I am. Sandra begged me to. So I made a deal with her."

"Okay. What deal was that?"

"If she would work on her multiplication tables with me while I cooked, I would wear your apron. Besides, she keeps telling me how handsome I look in it."

"I agree," Rachel says, leaning over the island, meeting him halfway for a kiss. "The pancakes smell really good."

"Wait until you taste the bacon. I decided to go with the thicker smoked-maple flavor," he says, placing the dirty frying pan in the dishwasher.

"I can't wait."

"Your breakfast is in the microwave, keeping warm. A pot of French vanilla coffee is ready, and I need to jump in the shower so I can drop off Sandra at school on my way to work. What time is your first appointment?"

"Not until 9:00, but I'm planning on going in a little early today to glance over some paperwork."

Jack takes Sandra's plate and heads toward the dishwasher. "Sweetheart, please go get dressed for school, and let's give Mommy a few minutes to eat in peace."

"Okay, Daddy," she answers back, before turning around and skipping away, yelling, "*pan-cakes, pan-cakes.*"

"Sugar's kicked in. I guess I didn't think this one through. Sorry about that."

"No problem," Rachel says softly, watching as he takes off her apron.

"I'm glad to see you didn't have to work as late last night. I've been worried about you. The last couple of weeks have really seemed to wear you down."

"It's been hard. I don't like getting home after Sandra's already in bed. I've missed not having as much time to spend with both of you. So I've decided to scale back next week and have already begun lightening the schedule of patients."

Jack smiles, feeling a small sense of relief.

"One thing while I'm thinking of it," she says, her voice changing to concern. "I've tried calling Judy several times to see if she's interested in coming back to work starting on Monday, but she hasn't returned any of my calls. I tried her one last time before I left the office last night and received a message that her phone was no longer in service."

"I'm confused. I thought you were thinking about getting rid of her."

"I was, but I feel she deserves a second chance. I'm really starting to worry. I've never known her to flat-out not return any of my calls. Maybe I'll try and swing by her place later today to make sure she's okay."

"That's a good idea. Face to face would probably mean more to her than receiving a phone call anyway."

"I agree. Thanks again for taking care of everything. It means a lot to me, and I swear I'll be back to normal on Monday."

"Take your time. We're doing just fine." He reaches over and places his hands on her shoulders, rubbing out some of the stiffness, before heading toward the master bedroom.

Rachael takes her breakfast out of the microwave and sits down at the table, admiring how wonderful everything looks. She's startled by Jack's voice calling out to Sandra, asking if she's almost ready.

"For heaven sakes, Jack," she mumbles, "It's been less than two minutes."

Looking down, she notices her plate is empty except for a tiny piece of fat from the bacon sitting next to her crumpled paper napkin.

"What's going on?"

Looking up she sees that Jack is walking straight for her. He's fully dressed in slacks and a dress shirt. His face is cleanly shaven, and his hair has been blow-dried. He leans over her, hovering long enough to receive several kisses before stating, "I'll see you tonight."

She can smell his aftershave and remembers it was a Father's Day gift from Sandra last year.

"You smell great," she mumbles, half out of it.

"Are you okay?"

"I'm fine. Thanks for breakfast. It was really good." *I think.*

Jack smiles and nods as Sandra emerges from the hall wearing her plaid skirt and white-collared shirt, ready for school.

"Say good-bye to Mommy."

She runs up and gives Rachel a hug before planting a big kiss on her lips. She then grabs her backpack and takes her dad's hand as they both head for the garage.

Rachael continues to sit in her chair, trying to figure out what happened. *It's obvious I've eaten.* Her stomach is full and she can taste the syrup from the pancakes, along with the smoky flavor of bacon. Her husband has a very dry sense of humor, so most likely he's not pulling a practical joke. *Then what's going on?* She walks around the house, searching for a clue. *This must be what Calvin feels like most of the time.*

Unable to find anything missing or out of the ordinary, she makes her way to her bedroom to get ready for work. After her shower, she dresses, puts on her makeup in front of the mirror while rambling to herself, "I refuse to accept that I might be going crazy."

Almost an hour has passed without any additional blackouts, and she's beginning to wonder if maybe this is still part of the backlash of being overly tired. *I'll catch up on my rest over the weekend and everything should be better.*

She grabs the key to her Mercedes from the top of the counter and, while engulfed in thought, clumsily drops it to the floor. She leans over to pick it up and hears a whisper.

"You must protect me."

She lets out a shriek before yelling, "Who are you? What do you want?"

With her key tightly clenched she frantically searches for the source when the whisper repeats, "You must protect me."

Unwilling to give in to the panic trumping all other emotions, she leans against the door leading to the garage. *There's no one here, which means it's all in my head.*

Her mind is immediately bombarded with questions, all of which point back to her sanity and how far removed it has become since her introduction to Calvin.

Is this related to Calvin in any way? I have to admit the timing is coincidental otherwise. There has to be an underlying issue, which I'm reluctant to believe has anything to do with hysteria or the power of suggestion. Then what else can it be? I have no mental illness on either side of the family.

Realizing she needs to calm down, she stays in the same position for almost five minutes, taking deep breaths in through her nose and releasing slowly through her mouth. She rationalizes her fears until her muscles relax, beginning with her neck. She opens the door and sticks her head out into the garage, wide-eyed and alert but incapable of shaking the feeling she's not alone.

Finally, she builds up enough courage to scurry through the garage, unwilling to look back. She quickly gets into her Mercedes and locks the doors before starting her engine. She debates cancelling her appointments and resting for the day but knows there are too many people counting on her. *Besides, someone else's problems might distract me from my own.* Backing out into the alley she fixates on the events of the morning, replaying each moment over in her head, hoping she's overlooked something.

The entire fifteen-minute drive to work is a blur as she's lost in deep thought that she's only able to snap out of the moment she parks in her designated spot. She sits in her car for a few minutes, mapping out a full plan, and is confident she can put this morning's occurrences aside. *I need to focus all of my attention on my patients today.*

She waves to a couple of familiar faces while stepping out of her car and unlocking the door to her suite. One of the first things on her agenda is to check her answering machine messages. She makes her way over to a table next to the receptionist's chair and pushes the button displaying a red number two on the answering machine. Turning up the volume to the highest level she laughs at how outdated it is. *Oh well. No one has mentioned anything about it so far. Besides, as long as it continues working, there's no point in switching to a service.*

As she's walking to her office, she hears an automated voice sound out, "First message received at 7:30 p.m., Thursday, June 11."

She settles in behind her desk, listening through the wall, grabs her mouse and wiggles her wrist from side to side until sleep mode disappears. As she pulls up the calendar, a familiar voice echoes throughout the empty office space.

"Hi, Dr. Livingston, this is Pamela Collins. I need to cancel my 9:00 appointment for tomorrow morning. I'm really sorry for the short notice and hope I don't get charged. I know I cancel a lot, but I really do think I'm making progress and hope you'll continue to see me."

Not surprised by the message, she mumbles, "No, Pamela, I won't charge you." Dr. Livingston taps away at the keyboard, knowing there isn't anyone around to bother. She opens up the timeslot to cancel but is interrupted by the automated voice stating, "Second message…received at 11:22 p.m., Thursday, June 11."

Jeff Jergen's voice rings out, instantly sending chills over her body. "Dr. Livingston, I really need to set up an emergency meeting for tomorrow, if at all possible. I've done something." She notices that his Southern twang is much stronger, reminding her more of a Texas accent than the Georgian one from their first session. His voice goes quiet, and the deafening silence consumes the office for several seconds until the only noise she hears is his heavy breathing coming through the phone. A muffled sound takes over as he covers his mouthpiece and whispers something unintelligible.

She's startled as he bellows, "I think I lost time tonight, and don't understand. I can go into more details later. Let's just say that it's important I meet with you as soon as possible. I'll even go online and pay up front if you send me the invoice."

Dr. Livingston swiftly walks to the receptionist area and plays the message a second time while hovering over the speaker, unable to decipher the whispers. She replays the message several times and also focuses on the change in his accent. *Something doesn't add up.*

She heads back to her office a little more sluggishly this time. She finishes typing a note on the calendar for Cindy to call and verify with Mrs. Collins that her appointment has been cancelled and she will not be charged.

Dr. Livingston could tell there was a distinctive sense of urgency in Jeff's voice, but his erratic behavior has her feeling anxious. The tiny voice of reason enters into her thoughts, reminding her that this is someone in need. Someone she has already agreed to see as a patient. She types a second note for Cindy to also notify Mr. Jergens that a 9:00 appointment is available.

Opening the bottom drawer to her desk, she pulls out her purse, and hastily unzips it. She reaches in and immediately starts taking large, bulky items out, beginning with her makeup bag. She reaches in one of the inner compartments and pulls out a key. She jumps up, speed-walks over to the oil painting of the blue water canals surrounded by cottages, and pulls the left side of the painting outward, revealing a hidden wall safe.

She puts the key in and turns it while lifting up on the handle. Swinging open the door, she sees several paper documents, including her will and testament, and a registered handgun sitting on top. She remembers back to when she and Jack had taken the safety courses together. Neither was extremely comfortable with the idea of owning a gun, but she felt it was a necessary evil in her line of work.

Pulling out the pistol she checks to make sure it's still loaded and the safety is on before opening her middle desk drawer and lightly placing it on its side for the time being. *I'll lock it back up once he is gone. He seems too unstable for now. Maybe as we make progress, I'll feel more comfortable.*

Dr. Livingston looks down at the clock on her computer to see 8:15 a.m. when the buzzer sounds. Cindy calls out, "Good morning!" as she places her purse under the front desk and heads for the refrigerator to put in her lunch. Dr. Livingston talks briefly through the wall before going over her notes from Jeff's previous session. The buzzing of the front door alerts her they have a visitor. She looks at her watch and is surprised to see it's almost 9:00. Eager to dive into someone else's problems she quickly makes her way to the front.

"Good morning, Jeff," she says, noticing his hair seems a brighter red than yesterday.

"Good morning, Dr. Livingston."

"Let's head down to my office."

Entering, she pauses to let Jeff pass through, and then closes the door. She takes her seat and watches as he casually walks around the room, taking a particular interest in her diplomas hanging on the wall.

"I was surprised you wanted to see me again so quickly after yesterday's session. There seemed to be a sense of urgency in your voice message last night. Is everything okay?"

"It's started again," he mumbles, unwilling to make eye contact.

"What's started again?"

"The beacon."

"I don't understand. What exactly is the beacon?"

"The beacon is what I call the bright light that acts as my guide. It was gone for roughly three years, and I thought maybe that part of my life was behind me, but now it's back. Whenever it shows up, I've always followed it without question, and it always takes me to my…" He keeps his focus on the floor.

Dr. Livingston pauses, fearing the worst. She senses she should ease him into confession rather than force the issue and risk a potential shutdown.

"Will you please tell me about the light?"

"Yes, ma'am. It's a bright light that shows up in the sky, like a beacon that I'm supposed to follow to a target."

"It happened last night?"

"Yes, ma'am."

"Do you think this is a man-made light of some kind?"

"No, ma'am. I'm not sure what it is or where it comes from, but I know it ain't made by a human. I can tell you it doesn't make much sense. When I looked at it straight on, it was an equal mixture of red and silver. But as soon as I tilted my head to the left, the red overpowered the silver."

"What happened when you looked at it with your head tilted to the right?"

"Then it's more silver than red. Pretty weird, but I've never been in a position to question...only to follow."

"Once you make it to your destination, then what happens?"

"My next kill," he says, incapable of looking up.

"Did you kill someone last night?" she asks, trying to refrain from displaying any emotions.

"Two people actually."

He buries his head in his hands and begins to cry loudly from the shame. Dr. Livingston says nothing, allowing him a chance to collect his thoughts. Her mind is racing. She notices her hand trembling slightly at the thought of a potential killer sitting only a few feet away.

Jeff removes his hands from his face, showing a big smile, before stating, "Gotcha...and the Academy Award for best actor goes to...wait for it."

Dr. Livingston interrupts. "This is a joke? My time means nothing to you? How am I supposed to help you? Or better yet, how are you supposed to help yourself unless you are willing to change?"

"What makes you think I'm capable of change?"

"Faith."

"In what? God? I stopped believing in him the moment he stopped believing in me. I think I was nine, walking down—"

"No. Faith in yourself. So why bother seeking help if you're unwilling to try and make a difference? Why waste our time and your money?"

"I don't care about the money," he snorts. "I'm supposed to be here with you in this office. I don't know why, but every fiber of my being is telling me here is where I belong...with you. I noticed yesterday I felt better than I have in a long time. Therefore, I apologize if you feel I'm wasting your time, but let me remind you that I have bought and paid for this time in full."

Dr. Livingston's voice shakes with frustration at his attitude and his unwillingness to try. "I'm confused. What you're telling me is that you didn't kill anyone last night?"

Jeff sits motionless, refusing to answer.

"I think we should be honest with each other. I don't believe you have a photographic memory. Were you lying?"

"Yes."

"What about your accent? Is it a fake too? I noticed slight variations from your first session, to your voicemail, and even this morning. It seems to vary from day to day. And while we're on the subject, I've noticed inconsistencies regarding your ability to speak as well. In our first session, you had me believing you were uneducated and ignorant, to be blunt. However, I know that's not the case anymore. I think you are far more intelligent than you're letting on."

Jeff chimes in, "Two sessions. That's got to be a record. Man, you're good."

"Why put on the charade?" she asks irritably.

Jeff's accent drops, and his face turns stone cold. "The funny thing is, when you speak in an unintelligent way, people automatically write you off and think they are better than you. It doesn't matter to me what people think, as long as it leads them to underestimate me. This is all I really care about. You would be surprised at how easy it is to manipulate someone by padding their ego. It's amazing how willing they are to drop their defenses. It's really much easier than you would think." Jeff looks directly at her, waiting for her to make eye contact.

Dr. Livingston stops writing, detecting that her attention is needed, and looks up guardedly.

"You are a beautiful woman. I don't suppose you would go out with me on a date?"

Dr. Livingston doesn't dignify him with an answer.

Taking the hint, he says, "Oh well, you can't blame a guy for trying. Besides, you're much too smart for me anyway. It probably wouldn't work out."

Dr. Livingston tries hard to fight it, but against her better judgment decides to take the bait. "You don't believe that."

"Believe what?"

"That I'm smarter than you. You're padding my ego, as you mentioned earlier. But to what end? You know that even if I wanted to go out with you, I could never date a patient and that I would consider it to be highly unethical. Consequently, you are purposely antagonizing me for a reason. From years of related experience, I know you have something you've wanted to get off of your chest since our first encounter. Maybe it's time for you to stop playing games and be brave enough to say it," she says, pretending to be upset. *I sure hope this works.*

"Wow. You really are good."

"You're still padding," she snaps back.

"No, this one I mean," he says, smiling.

She places her notepad on her desk and leans forward, about to stand up, signifying the end of the session.

"Okay, fine. I'll stop playing games with you right after this. Has anyone ever told you that you're quite the pistol when you're angry?"

Dr. Livingston rises. "I guess we're done. You can call my office in a couple of days to get names and numbers of therapists in Plano. Please don't feel like you are being pushed aside. I consider each of the recommendations to be quite good and an excellent replacement for my services."

Jeff stands. "Please give me one more chance. You have my word I'll stop playing games and be more respectful."

She is skeptical at first, but remembers that Calvin said Jeff was still there when everyone else disappeared. She realizes he's connected and in some way maybe the key to helping her figure out her earlier experiences.

"Let me make something clear," she says sternly. "If you would like to continue to see me professionally, those types of comments stop now. Otherwise, I have no problem recommending you to another therapist."

"My apologies. I was way out of line. You're right, though. There's something I would like to get off of my chest. Quite a lot actually. I just have no idea where to start."

Dr. Livingston sits back down and signals to Jeff to do the same. "You seemed upset when you left the message last night. What happened?"

"I saw the beacon, and I followed it. Just like I always have in the past. I could tell I was getting close, because my adrenaline was pumping so hard I thought I was going to lose consciousness. There was a Baptist church that had a sign in the front for Alcoholics Anonymous meetings every Thursday at 7:00. Well, I'll go out on a limb and say it wasn't a fluke that I showed up just before 7:00 on a Thursday night. Keep in mind I had no idea the church even existed. So I ask you in all seriousness, how do you stop something you have no control over?"

"With time and lots of help from others."

"If only it were that simple. Besides, I don't get the impression time is on our side," he says as if he's hiding something.

"You'd mentioned your adrenaline was pumping when you realized you showed up on time for a meeting you didn't even know existed. What was going through your mind?"

"I had to get psyched up before getting into character."

"Which character was this?"

"My favorite one, an alcoholic Texan with an abusive father. I got up and spoke for a while. Even the pastor of the church, Mr. Smithers, seemed to enjoy my performance. I felt I was doing pretty well, until Kathy came in."

"Who's Kathy?"

"Some mousy chick that attends the weekly meetings at the Holy Temple Baptist Church." His tone switches to hatred. "She showed up late. Who shows up late to an AA meeting? She broke my concentration and pretty much messed up everything."

"Your body language is signaling that you like her."

"She's annoying and talks too much."

"I take that as a yes."

"How about we agree on a *maybe* and move on? Besides, I get the distinct impression I know her from somewhere else, but I can't quite place her."

"Do you consider yourself to be an alcoholic?"

"No. I rarely indulge. I never did acquire the taste for it."

"Let me get this straight. Your sole purpose in attending last night's meeting was to play a trick on everyone there and hope for the outcome of finding your target."

"Kind of. To clarify, I drove around following the beacon that led me to the meeting. I saw the number zero on each of the sisters' foreheads and heard the whisper, 'Zero days left.' Only then, at that exact moment, did I know I was going to kill them."

"Tell me about the numbers and the voices."

"It's been several years since I've come across either."

"How many people did you kill last night?"

"Two. I believe they were sisters. I even rode the fatter one like a cow for a few seconds before she fell to the ground. I was hoping for eight seconds, but I guess there's always disappointments around every corner."

Dr. Livingston is disgusted by his lack of remorse. "Do you plan on stopping?"

"I'm not sure that I can."

She takes a long pause before stating, "I will not be able to continue seeing you if you are going to kill people, whether it is premeditated or not. I would like to remind you that if I feel at any point that you are a danger to yourself or society, I am obligated to notify the authorities, and will do so regardless of the risk."

She gently slides out the middle drawer to her desk, verifying that the gun is still there.

"I see," he says, irritated. "Let me guess. Calvin's told you I'm dangerous and that you shouldn't see me anymore."

"Please don't try and divert this onto anyone else. This conversation is strictly between you and me."

"Fine. I will concentrate on you then."

She reaches in with her right hand, which is shaking almost uncontrollably as she wraps her fingers around the handle of her pistol. She removes the safety with a simple flick of her thumb and maintains eye contact, fearing he will stand and charge at any moment.

CHAPTER

15

JEFF SITS STRAIGHT up in his chair, staring at Dr. Livingston, trying to get a read on what she's thinking. He senses something is wrong and wonders why she hasn't removed her hand from inside the drawer. Realizing she's up to something, he decides to relax and sits back in his chair, slumps down slightly, then crosses his legs.

"Hmm. I guess this is where I outsmart you, Doctor. How do you suppose I'm a threat to society? Let me rephrase. What proof is there that I'm a threat to either myself or anyone else, for that matter?"

Dr. Livingston takes her time, realizing this could become very uncomfortable if she's not careful. "You admitted to me you killed two women last night and that you have no intention of stopping. I would say that qualifies as a threat to society."

"I would normally agree with you, but before you reach any rash conclusions I would suggest you take your time and do some investigating yourself."

"I don't need to—"

"Yes you do. You think I'm out running around killing innocent people. I assure you I'm not."

Slowing down the momentum, Dr. Livingston releases the gun and removes her hand from the drawer. She takes her time flipping through the pages of her notes and even circles a couple of different places, before saying, "You mentioned you attended an AA meeting at the Holy Temple Baptist Church around 7:00 last evening. Is this correct?"

"Yes."

"You also mentioned the pastor's last name was Smithers. Is this correct?"

"Yes. That too is correct," he states agitatedly, feeling his patience wearing thin.

"Were the two women you mentioned earlier present at this meeting?"

"Objection!" he shouts and uncrosses his legs. "Sorry," he says, laughing. "I felt like I was on trial for a minute. Besides, I've always wanted to do that. You know you won't find any record of either of these women attending the meeting last night."

"What do you mean?"

"From past experiences, my guess is they're no longer alive."

"Yes, because you killed them."

"Good Lord, it's like talking to a nine-year-old. I'm pretty sure they died long before last night. Probably about a year ago, if things haven't changed much. The point I'm trying to make is that they were never at the meeting. I made them up. I had to say that I killed someone to test your backbone. I wanted to make sure you're trustworthy and willing to stand behind your principles, regardless of the cost or sacrifice. I apologize if my methods were extreme."

Dr. Livingston's face hardens. "Let me make sure I understand what has just transpired. You tell me you were testing my backbone by lying to me and insulting me. Furthermore, you compare my intelligence to a nine year old, and then you apologize by saying, 'If my methods were extreme.' I'm not really sure you understand the seriousness of mistreating your therapist. You do realize that I'm on your side and here to help you work through your issues, correct?"

Jeff doesn't say a word, only listens and studies her mannerisms as she talks with both hands.

"It seems you have a lot on your mind that you need help sifting through in order to pull out the significant details and organize these thoughts. Once we're able to do this, I strongly believe your state of mind will be as good as it once was."

"That's disappointing. I'm not sure I want my state of mind as good as it once was. How about a fresh start?"

"How about I rephrase? We can build your state of mind to wherever you are most comfortable with. That part is entirely up to you, but I'm only prepared to help guide you through as long as you're willing to let me in. Oh, and just for the record, lying to someone and twisting the facts at your leisure to add confusion to the situation is not the same as outsmarting someone."

"My apologies again," he says, refusing to look her in the eyes.

She looks down at her watch and can't believe there's nearly twenty minutes left in their session. "I have never given up on a patient, but I have to admit you're really testing your boundaries with me today."

"I understand, and I'm ready to let you in," he says nervously. "I'm not used to trusting anyone, and to be honest I don't know how good I would feel talking about certain things. I'm afraid I might go too deep or say too much. I would like to put my trust in you, but you have to understand this is new territory for me. Is there a way you can help put me at ease? Have you ever had a patient with similar concerns?"

"I've had many patients with exactly these same concerns for reasons ranging from embarrassment to worries regarding legal issues. I'm willing to try something that I think may do the trick. It's a technique I've used in the past, which has proven to be quite effective. I will give you three verbal passes during today's session. If at any point you're unable to continue with our discussion, all you have to do is simply state that you would like to use a pass. We'll consider the topic closed for today without any additional questions, regardless of the nature. You can look at this as a safety net to be used only if needed—therefore allowing you to talk freely—and once you uncover a subject you're not willing to talk about, merely stop. Does that sound like something you think might help?"

"Yes, that sounds perfect," he says, taking a deep breath and
|easing it. "There's something important that I've been meaning to tell
)u, if you would like to hear it."

"Absolutely. Go ahead."

"You asked me about last night."

"Yes."

"I lost time somewhere around 10:00, during which I was able to see
nages of you in my head as if I were watching a movie about this
iorning. You were sitting down eating pancakes and bacon without any
xpression on your face, looking like some sort of a drone. It was really
:eepy. I felt like I was watching a show about zombies," he says,
ughing. He looks up and sees the harsh look on her face and realizes it
robably isn't as funny to her. *I need to stay in character.*

"Please continue."

"I also saw an old farmer standing very close to you during this time.
hortly after, the vision disappeared. I realized what had happened and
new the only thing to do was to call and leave you a message to
:hedule an emergency meeting."

Dr. Livingston stares at Jeff and says nothing. Her mind is spinning
iut of control while trying to process what was said. Her first reaction is
iaranoia. *How could Jeff possibly know what I ate for breakfast this morning unless
e's watching my house? Even so, how would he know about the farmer? How could
be farmer be standing next to me, and why? Am I in danger? Is my family in
!anger?* She grabs her pen and pad and begins writing down her thoughts.
ihe continues writing for nearly a minute before Jeff speaks out,
ireaking her concentration.

"Wow. I must have really hit a nerve. You've written almost a page
nd would still be going if I didn't interrupt. Is the farmer your father or
omething?"

"Would you please describe the farmer?" she says.

"Sure. He's older, wearing blue overalls and a dirty white undershirt."

"You stated he was standing next to me. What was he doing?"

"He was staring at you, watching you eat."

"Do you know why?"

"No. All I know is at some point he leaned over, and I swear he put his hand on your shoulder as he whispered something into your ear. I never saw you blink once the entire time this was going on."

An unnerving feeling consumes Dr. Livingston unsure what the farmer could have whispered. The more she thinks about it, though, the more she keeps coming back to "You must protect me." *It must have been the farmer who whispered to me. He needs my help, but how can I protect him…and from whom?*

Jeff disrupts Dr. Livingston's concentration. "You know the farmer, don't you?"

"Yes. You could say that," she replies, looking at the door and wondering if she could step away for a few minutes without Jeff knowing how much what he's said bothers her. *This guy is really freaking me out.*

"I don't suppose you know where he is?" he asks, using a strange tone.

"No. I'm sorry. Wait…you ask as if you're searching for him. Do you know the farmer?"

Jeff is caught off guard by the question and decides against telling a lie. "Yes, I've seen the farmer on many occasions."

"Thank you for telling the truth. I believe honesty is necessary for attaining our long-term goal. Where do you know him from?"

"Let's just say I've seen him around. I don't know how to say this without sounding weird, but have you felt a strong connection with me?"

"Mr. Jergens, please. We've already been through this. I don't date my—"

"You misunderstood what I was saying. I believe we're linked somehow, and I'm wondering if you feel it too."

"Yes. I feel the connection between us. That sort of thing seems to be running rampant lately."

"You're talking about Calvin now, aren't you?"

"I'm sorry. Forget I said anything. It was very careless of me."

"I take that as a yes. You know I get the feeling we're linked with Calvin too. Something about that crybaby has me baffled, though. I'm pretty sure he's the main player in all of this, but I haven't quite figured out how exactly. Although I can tell I'm getting ahead of myself now. I'm curious and would like to go back to talking about us being linked. Do you have any thoughts?" he asks, enjoying having the control, even if it only lasts for a few minutes.

"I admit there are many unanswered questions I've been struggling with since our meeting started. However, I need to know how you're acquainted with the farmer."

There went the control...that was short-lived, he thinks, starting to really enjoy this session, realizing she makes an excellent opponent. *Now it's time to have a little fun.* "He's one of many necessary keys to stopping..." He looks over at Dr. Livingston. "Let's just say you're not the only one with a mirror, Doctor. I would like to use one of my passes on this topic, if that's okay."

Dr. Livingston's mouth is already open, ready to spout off questions, but she is left feeling like a bomb just exploded. *Wow, I really walked right into that one.* "Of course. That's exactly how it's supposed to go. How about we change the subject? Let's talk about last night. Where were you when you had this vision of me?"

"I was in my house. I had just turned on the TV."

"Were you alone?"

"Yes."

"There was a brief moment during the voice message where you stopped talking, and it became extremely quiet. The only thing I could hear was your breathing. During this time, I swear I heard you whispering to someone. Whom were you talking to?"

Jeff fidgets in his chair. "Man, another tough question. I can't really tell you. Correction...I shouldn't tell you. I'm afraid it's too soon. I don't know that you can handle this type of responsibility yet."

"I'm intrigued. I want you to be completely comfortable. If you need to use another pass, please don't hesitate. That's what they're here for. Compare it to procrastination. Why discuss it today when we can push it off for another day?" she says with a smile.

"The only thing I can tell you is that I've only been linked with one other person before you, and that was roughly three years ago."

"Please continue."

"It didn't turn out so well for her."

"Sounds almost like a threat."

"Not from me. I'm guilty of a lot of things, but this was not my doing. It went well above my head."

"Please clarify. Is there a threat that you're aware of? If so, who wants to harm me?"

"I don't know."

"You mentioned that 'it went well above my head.' What did you mean by that?"

"I think there's a higher power that has been intervening in my life. I thought it was gone, until I saw it again yesterday. I don't even know where to begin in describing it. It's really blurry and hard to make out. I think this thing is controlling me somehow. I sound crazy, right?"

Dr. Livingston thinks of Figure X and instantly knows Jeff is far more involved than she earlier expected.

"No, I don't think you're crazy. No more than the rest of us, if secrets be told. What's the name of the woman who was linked to you who you said it didn't turn out so well for?"

"I would rather not say."

"Do I know her?"

"Yes and no. I believe you know *of* her." He pauses for several moments, his face showing signs of deep concentration. "It was Crybaby's wife. Or at least an image of her. I would like to use my second pass, if that's okay."

"Sure," she says, regretting that she brought up the idea. "How about we turn the control over to you for a while? Is there anything you would like to discuss?"

Jeff opens his mouth to answer, but before he has a chance to speak, Dr. Livingston vanishes in front of his eyes. He sits there staring at a blank chair, not believing the timing. He walks out to the receptionist area and notices Cindy is gone as well. He becomes extremely annoyed and yells up at the ceiling, "Seriously, Calvin, are you really that selfish? It was just getting interesting. Get it together, loser. You're cutting into my therapy time!"

CHAPTER

16

JEFF WANDERS AROUND the office for several minutes, taking in the quiet, and examining his surroundings. He rummages through the filing cabinets located in the corner of the receptionist area but quickly loses interest. He eventually makes his way back down the hall and over to Dr. Livingston's desk before opening the middle drawer, curious as to why she held her hand inside as long as she did. He picks up the weapon and nods with appreciation, understanding the fear she must have felt to hold a loaded gun during their session.

Wow. Dedicated much? I guess I've finally managed to stumble across the right person this time. Although I'm not convinced she has what it takes to pull the trigger. I guess only time will tell.

Jeff continues thinking about Dr. Livingston and the fact that after only one session she already felt the need to protect herself against him. *She seems much smarter than her predecessors.* An emptiness consumes him as he understands her fate and the inevitable role he must play. *Too bad she didn't shoot me when she had the chance. Now if she would only come back so we could finish the rest of my session, I would certainly be grateful.*

Bored and trying to keep himself entertained, he makes his way to the receptionist area and wraps his fingers around the handle of the mini refrigerator. *What's for lunch today? Let's see. We have your typical condiments, several Diet Cokes, two apples, and one neatly folded brown paper bag.* "Very exciting stuff," he mumbles. Reaching for the lunch, he hears a car door being shut. *I guess the mystery items contained inside this bag will have to remain that way.*

He strolls toward the front, taking his time, and as he's walking through the front entrance he's met by Calvin standing on the sidewalk.

"Mornin', sunshine," Jeff says, unable to contain a grin. "I was just saying nice things about you to Dr. Livingston, until she vanished because you're an idiot. Seriously, dude, you really need to get it under control. It's starting to become a real nuisance."

"How? I don't know what you're talking about."

"I can't imagine why it takes you so long to put two and two together. What a waste," Jeff mutters.

"What are you doing here? Shouldn't you be in prison somewhere?"

"Prison? What on Earth for?"

"I don't know. How about murder?"

"That's a little vague. Can you be more specific?" Jeff says, toying with him.

"Last night you broke the neck of a man wearing a Mountain Dew T-shirt and khaki shorts. Ring any bells now?"

"Oh, I believe it's starting to sound more familiar. However, I'm still a little cloudy on the details after this alleged murder. What happened next?"

Calvin shuts his mouth and glares back, refusing to say another word, knowing exactly how it will sound if spoken aloud.

"Go ahead and scream it from the rooftops." Jeff cups his hands around his mouth and yells, "The chubby man's body and his vehicle were swooped away by pretty white lights and disappeared into thin air."

"I don't like you."

"Who cares? I don't like you either."

"Why are you even here?" Calvin asks.

"I'm here for the same reason as you. In fact, I was talking about you earlier in my session and referred to you as a crybaby. Dr. Livingston thought it was really funny. She laughed every time I mentioned it. Although I can't say that I blame her. I wonder if she pictures you sucking on a pacifier, and that's why she finds it so amusing. I don't really know. You might want to ask her—if she ever comes back, that is."

Adrenaline rushes through Calvin as hate turns to fury. "You do realize I'm six foot three to your maybe five foot seven. Do you really want to do this?"

"You should try and channel some of your anger. I think you would be amazed at what you could accomplish."

"You're lucky I'm not a violent man."

"You're unlucky that I am," Jeff responds, and slips his right hand slowly into his pocket.

Calvin reaches over and grabs him by the front of his shirt with both hands and pins him against the door.

"I wonder, if I killed you right here and now would you be surrounded by lights and disappear."

"Go ahead. Let's find out. I'll be back in less than five years for my revenge."

"What?" Calvin asks, feeling like the wind has been knocked out of him, and releases his grip.

"I'm just messing with you." Jeff quickly recants, rubbing his chest. "I had to think of something—you were wrinkling my shirt."

Calvin, tired of his games, mutters, "I don't have anything else to say to you."

"That's a shame. I have a feeling there's quite a lot to discuss between the two of us. Maybe we save it for another time."

Calvin turns to walk away but stops and asks, "What's your problem?"

"If you only knew," Jeff states, and laughs an obnoxious laugh.

"I think it's best if we try and avoid each other as much as possible in the future."

"You seriously have no clue about anything. You can't possibly be as naïve as you're coming across. First of all, you're stuck with me whether you are smart enough to have figured it out by now or not. Secondly, I have a wealth of information regarding your situation, and quite frankly I'm surprised you're not nicer to me for this reason alone." Jeff looks to the right and stares at the corner of the building.

Calvin glances over and looks in disbelief as he sees Janice standing in the same spot as yesterday. She's wearing the same long-sleeve plaid shirt. She turns away, and with every step Calvin watches her jet-black hair bounce, until she vanishes from sight, escaping behind the back of the building.

"You can see her?" Calvin asks, unable to conceal his shock.

"Of course. Who do you think I was watching the day you came out and yelled 'One will go away soon'? That's where your nickname crybaby came from."

"Have you seen her before?" Calvin asks, ignoring the insult.

"Which version of her?"

"What do you mean? There's more than one? Are they ghostlike too?"

"Never mind. It's not important right now. Did you ever figure out what she meant?"

"No."

"How about I give you a clue?" Jeff snaps his fingers once before looking up at Calvin.

"I don't understand."

"Okay. Let's try it again. I sure am thirsty and wish I had a Mountain Dew," he says, snapping one more time.

A look of horror consumes Calvin's face as he's suddenly aware of Jeff's meaning.

"She was talking about the man in the khaki shorts and Mountain Dew shirt. He was the person she was talking about when she said one more will go away soon. Why would she tell me that in advance if there wasn't any way for me to have stopped it?"

"Are you sure she was telling you? If memory serves, I was also there."

"Yes, I'm positive she was telling me."

"If you say so." Jeff shakes his head, displaying skepticism. "That was the first time you saw the number and heard the voice, wasn't it?"

"No. The farmer was the first," Calvin replies, feeling his face becoming flush as his frustrations become more apparent. "I hate all the games. Janice was always the one good at solving puzzles."

"You can do it. Just take your time."

"Wait…you're intentionally stalling me so she can get away." He takes a step to follow her, mumbling, "I've got to find Janice."

Jeff immediately kicks out his leg, tripping Calvin and knocking him to the ground face first.

"Are you crazy?" Calvin says, turning over and sitting up.

"Most would say yes. However, I needed to get your attention. You can't follow her this time."

"But she's my wife. She's trying to tell me something."

"No, she's not. She's telling *me* something. It's my turn."

Jeff's level of intensity grows, while Calvin is lost in his soft green eyes. He's pulled into a trance by sheer panic. Images of people trickle inside his mind, disguised as his own thoughts as he feels himself slipping away to another place.

All of a sudden, he's yanked out of what feels like a daydream by Jeff yelling, "You've been away long enough. You need to bring everyone back before it's too late. You can trust me or not. It doesn't matter, as long as you do what I say, and do it now!"

Calvin remains on the ground, sensing a hidden agenda and unsure what to do. He feels his blood pressure rising as his heart pounds erratically. His head throbs, causing a ringing in his ears, while his mind races wildly with questions raised by doubt and uncertainty. *What if he's tricking me? What if I don't go after her and something bad happens because of it? Can I really trust him?*

CHAPTER

17

JEFF PACES BACK and forth, intentionally mumbling something too low to be heard. He rubs his fingers roughly through his bright red hair, pulling several strands out by the roots. He stops suddenly and turns, his face pale and his pupils dilated from unrestrained fear.

"Listen to me carefully. You're out of time. If you want us to die, then by all means continue to sit there like a moron and do nothing."

Calvin's confusion and concern linger over him like a low, drifting cloud.

"I have to follow my wife. What if it's important?"

"Then it will still be important another time."

"Why should I trust you? You've never given me one single reason to so far."

"Because I'm telling you the truth. You need to bring everyone back," Jeff yells loudly.

"I don't know how!" Calvin screams, overwhelmed by the pressure.

"Yes, you do! Concentrate!"

Calvin thinks about the previous times, and a spark of remembrance glimmers in his eyes. Willing himself to be calm, he says, "If you answer one question honestly, I'll stop this right here and now. Do we have a deal?"

"Yes. Anything."

"Just a moment ago I felt like I was losing myself in you. As if we were merging into one. I saw images of people, some of whom I recognized and others I did not. How did you do that?"

"I didn't. It was you."

"You're lying!" Calvin shouts, feeling like he's being tricked.

"No. It's true. I promise. Listen to your inner voice, and you should be able to hear things you have no business knowing. Almost like secrets hidden deep inside." Jeff pauses briefly before pleading, "I did my part; now bring everyone back. Please."

Without another word, Calvin places his face inside his hands and fills his mind with thoughts of Janice's kindness and Daniel's innocence. He does so for several moments while taking in and releasing long, deep breaths in one steady rhythm. His shoulders drop, and as relaxation approaches it brings welcome sounds of dogs barking off in the distance and the whining of hydraulics from a sanitation truck preparing to lift a Dumpster. Road noise echoes from the busy parking lot as impatient people drive recklessly in search of open spaces.

"Nice going," Jeff says, reaching his hand in Calvin's direction and helping him to his feet.

A forest-green, four-door Buick pulls out from one of the spots several rows over and drives by slowly. Jeff glances up and whispers, "Kathy," locking eyes with her as she passes. *What's Mousy Chick doing here?*

Calvin clears his throat to get Jeff's attention. "You know something about me, don't you?"

He just smiles, refusing to give any more information away. Instead, he points over to the corner. "Go get her."

Calvin looks in the direction of where they last saw Janice but has a sinking feeling in the pit of his stomach. "I'm pretty sure she's gone."

"I'm pretty sure you'll see that version of her again."

"You seem to know a lot about my situation. Would you be willing to answer some questions?"

"No. Maybe another time," Jeff responds hastily. "You realize what almost happened, don't you?"

"I have no clue."

"What a waste."

Jeff turns and heads for the doorway of Dr. Livingston's suite.

"Hey!" Calvin shouts. "Why won't you help me?"

Jeff stops for a second and turns around to face him. "Why should I? Have you ever considered it's not in my best interest?"

"There's something familiar about you. We've spoken before, but it was a long time ago. I can only vaguely remember."

"You must be mistaken. The first time I saw you was the day you were chasing the ghost of your wife. I have an eidetic memory and should know better than you," Jeff says smugly, knowing it's a lie.

The door opens, and Dr. Livingston is standing on the other side. She had been watching Jeff through the glass but is shocked to see Calvin.

"What are both of you doing out here?"

Jeff speaks up. "Calvin had another blackout sometime during our session, so I didn't get to finish."

She has a blank look on her face and says nothing. She glances around, uncomfortable about discussing this topic outside, where anyone could overhear.

"You didn't know," Jeff states. "You thought we finished our entire session without interruption. That's amazing." He turns back to Calvin and says, "Did you know time would keep going without us in it?"

"Yes, unfortunately that one I knew."

"I would be curious to know what we talked about during the rest of the session while I was on autopilot," Jeff says, looking directly at Dr. Livingston. "Any chance you can spare some time to go over this with me?"

"Gentlemen, please," she says, looking down at her watch and realizing it's 11:20. Let's step inside, where it's more private. Jeff, I can meet with you for a few minutes to discuss in more detail. Calvin, I have a quick errand to run during the latter part of my lunch, but I'm willing to go over our normal scheduled time by half an hour. This should almost ensure that you receive the full amount of time, if that's okay. We should end around 12:30."

"That would be great," Calvin replies.

All three file into the waiting area, one after the other. Jeff and Dr. Livingston make their way to her office, while Calvin stops by the neatly arranged magazines stacked on top of the table.

"Okay, let's see. Do you recall the last thing we discussed before I disappeared?" Dr. Livingston asks on her way to her desk.

"Yes. You had just given me control."

She scans her notes and looks somewhat disturbed. "The remainder of the session was spent talking about Kathy, or as you referred to her, Mousy Chick. I'm not usually one to make judgments about matters that don't pertain to me, but I'm not too sure she would appreciate the nickname you've assigned her."

Jeff sits quietly. Why would I talk about her?

"You also mentioned you've known her for many years. Is this true? Or is it true you met her last night for the first time at the AA meeting? I only ask because you made two different, contradicting statements during the session."

That's impossible. Was I still in character when I said these things, and why would I? She has nothing to do with anything I'm aware of. Why was she in the parking lot? Is she following me?

"I guess I've heard enough," Jeff says, puzzled.

"I know I mentioned I wasn't willing to give discounts for emergency sessions. However, in light of recent events, I've had a change of mind. I've been thinking and believe you were correct in stating we're somehow connected. I have a strong feeling this connection goes much deeper than just you and I. That being the case, there seems to be a mutual interest in helping you resolve your issues sooner rather than later. How would you feel about switching to daily sessions starting as early as Monday, if I have a timeslot available? Is this something you might be interested in?"

"I think that would be best."

"Great. I'll speak to Cindy and have her reach out to you once she's had a chance to work out the schedule."

"Thanks, Doctor," Jeff says, unable to clear Kathy from his mind.

"You're welcome. Have a good weekend."

"Thanks again. See you on Monday…hopefully."

Jeff walks into the waiting area, reaching for his pack of cigarettes, and says only one word as he passes Calvin: "Next."

Calvin nods before heading in the direction of Dr. Livingston, who surprisingly is smiling.

"You seem like you're in a good mood this morning."

"I am," she says while heading for her office, with Calvin following close behind. "It's Friday, and I'm looking forward to resting over the weekend."

"I appreciate your being flexible with your schedule. There's still so much going on, it's hard to keep track of everything."

"I agree," she says, also feeling the stress weighing heavily on her mind. She takes a seat behind her desk, pulls Calvin's folder from one of her drawers, and grabs the notes from yesterday's session. She picks up her red-framed reading glasses and uses both hands to tilt them in different directions while examining them.

"Sorry," she says, distracted. "I've been having issues with the nosepiece pinching my skin. I've been trying to avoid wearing them until I have time to take them in to be fixed. Unfortunately, I've been getting headaches recently, which I think are due to me straining my eyes when I read over my notes. What a vicious cycle. It's hard to figure which of the two is the lesser evil." She lets out a laugh before slipping the glasses on carefully. "What would you like to talk about this morning?"

"I had a reoccurring dream again last night. This is the third time within a couple of weeks, and I'm wondering if there's any significance to it. Do you mind discussing and maybe walking me through it?"

"Of course," she replies without hesitation.

"It started off with me lying in a bed in some sort of a hospital room. I'm sleeping lightly and can hear background noises all around me. There are two women arguing about my chart, but I can't remember what was said…sorry."

"That's quite all right. Try and remember as much as you can."

"They were hovering above me, doing something like putting an IV in my arm, but I'm not exactly sure. I swear I felt pressure whenever they would touch me, as if it were really happening. Strangely, I'm pretty sure one of the voices is Cindy, your new receptionist, but have no idea why she would be there since I don't know her very well."

"Are you able to describe your surroundings?"

"Yes and no. My eyes are closed in the dream, yet somehow there's a strange familiarity about the place, as if I'd seen the room on many occasions either as a long-term patient or a frequent visitor. As you enter through the door, there's a bathroom on your right. Beyond that is my bed, then a couple of chairs next to a window. The room is pretty small, with white walls and a linoleum floor. The whole time I was dreaming, the smell of cafeteria food was overpowering, and I even felt my stomach grumbling from hunger pains when I awoke."

"Interesting. It's pretty common to have a dream where you smell food and wake up hungry. On the flip side, it's equally common to have dreamed you've eaten a big meal and wake up full. It's truly amazing what our minds are capable of. Could you tell if the setting was current?"

"I don't really know for sure. I can't see myself, but I have the feeling I'm much older and weaker."

"What else can you tell me?" she asks, adjusting her glasses and massaging the bridge of her nose.

Calvin closes his eyes, taking in every detail of the dream as if he were reliving each moment. "I can hear the sound of a broken wheel on a cart echoing down the hall as it clunks its way in my direction. I've counted, and I'm the third and final stop on this side. I'm pretty sure there are three other rooms on the opposite side of the hall as well." Calvin opens his eyes and watches as Dr. Livingston focuses on his every word. "Do you think this means anything?"

"It's hard to tell. I get the distinct feeling your mind is trying to reveal something, but I don't think it's going to be easy to solve. Have you been involved in any life-changing events or tragedies within the last few years?"

"No," Calvin replies, recognizing the question from an earlier session.

"Has anyone close to you had a long stay in a hospital room?"

He remains quiet and distant, his insides begin to ache, as his attention shifts around the room.

Picking up on his reluctance, she continues speaking. "The dream could be as simple as unbridled guilt surfacing, allowing you to see yourself through someone else's eyes." She flips to the beginning few pages of her notes, scrolls her index finger halfway down and stops. "Has anyone close to you passed away? Specifically, either of your parents?"

Calvin's eye twitches, and his body tenses at the thought of his father. *How does she know these things?* He refuses to look her way, eager to conceal his shock, and fumbles around, searching for the right way to avoid answering her question. He feels a sudden sense of relief as he discovers how to deflect back onto her while staying true to his previous lie. "Haven't you already asked me about my parents? I swear you have, and I told you my relationship was strong and that I speak to both on a regular basis. Am I wrong?"

"No. You are correct. I just didn't believe you were being completely honest at the time. I got the impression you were hiding something important. So, I figured I would revisit in today's discussion and maybe ask the question in a different manner. Looks like I may have struck a nerve, though."

Calvin stares back, stunned and somewhat agitated by her response. "I didn't think you were paying such close attention."

"I was," she says, smiling while treading carefully. "You could say it's a big part of my job criteria. Besides, I've always been fascinated and taken a strong interest in human behavior. It's one of the main reasons I decided to become a psychiatrist. Reading mannerisms and body language helps me differentiate between non-truths and truths." She senses his discomfort and decides on a different approach. "If you're not ready to discuss your parents, we can always change the subject."

"No need," he says softly. "I knew this day would come. I was just hoping it wasn't today." Calvin breathes deeply while focusing and arranging his thoughts. His nervousness surfaces and becomes apparent thanks to the excessive shakiness in his voice. "My father often spoke of aliens. He believed they were here among us, crossbreeding with humans in an attempt to eventually weed out every single person and take over our planet. In fact, he claimed to be a product of one himself. I spent the better part of my youth watching him down-spiral day after day, until he was eventually diagnosed and began treatment for schizophrenia."

Dr. Livingston stops writing in mid-sentence and looks up, catching a glimpse of pain emitting from his eyes. He turns his head, breaking their connection, unable to contain his embarrassment.

"He received plenty of medications, which he faithfully took on a regular basis for many years. He even participated in several outpatient programs. Unfortunately, over time his behaviors worsened, and a week before my twelfth birthday he was admitted into an out-of-state hospital which specialized in his condition. After a nine-month stay, he was finally released and able to come home. He was never the same after that. We saw improvements in his personality here and there, but the paranoia was too much for him to bear."

"What happened to him?" she asks in a concerned voice.

"It started off a normal school day. I was headed to the kitchen for breakfast when my father walked passed me down the hall, muttering the same words over and over."

"What was he saying?"

"'I can't fight them any longer.'" Calvin takes a deep breath and releases it slowly before continuing. "He walked into the spare bedroom and moments later I heard the gunshot. I rushed in and found him lying on the cream-colored carpet with a self-inflicted bullet wound to his chest."

"That's horrible."

"Yes. It was."

"Did your parents normally keep guns in the house?"

"No. Never. Not with his condition. Honestly, I have no idea where he got it from."

"That really is awful. No one should ever have to experience that kind of pain. How old were you when this happened?"

There is a long, uncomfortable pause. "Fifteen. But that's not the worse part. I was relieved more than horrified. The nightmare my father had created for me, my mother, and everyone else who knew us was finally over. I know that probably sounds terrible, but up until this point, my life was an emotional roller coaster. Especially considering he had made several attempts on several different occasions to take my life because…" Calvin's voice fades.

"You can do this. I'm here to help you in any way," she says sincerely. "If you're capable, please try and finish your sentence. Why would he have wanted to harm you?"

"Because…he felt he had no choice. Since he had been compromised himself and believed he was part alien, it stands to reason, so was I. And now with me seeing Figure X, it's all hitting a little too close to home."

"What if we ran blood work on you? Would that help remove any lingering doubts?"

"I don't know. My father had an explanation for just about anything you could imagine. Besides, we tried that with him already."

"And?"

"When the results came back normal, he was convinced it was because the body he was walking around in was no longer his own. He claims he was taken to their planet, where his soul was extracted and placed in a newly created body to match identically, one that at the root was alien, but looked and functioned like a human. Even had the capabilities of hiding any foreign DNA. He used to say their intelligence far exceeded ours." Calvin's face tightens as painful memories fill his head. "Would you like to hear the example he always used?"

"Of course," she says eagerly.

"Imagine you're trying to deceive a small child so you can take something he or she possesses. How difficult do you think it would be to lie and manipulate, to have him or her believe exactly what you want, and not be noticed?"

Dr. Livingston smiles. "Not very. I'm guessing in this scenario humans are the children, and the aliens are the deceivers with an agenda."

"Exactly."

"Do you feel there was any truth to what your father believed?"

"I didn't. Although I have no idea anymore. His example was simple, but the meaning behind it wasn't. I guess if I think about it deeply, I've always had traces of doubt in the back of my mind. If they are real and he was correct, then how would we ever know, unless they wanted us to? I've been plagued by that very question since the arrival of Figure X. I don't know. Maybe I'm as crazy as my father for even humoring the idea." He looks up with sadness and desperation in his eyes. "I wish you had seen Figure X in the broken mirror instead of the farmer. I would feel a lot better about myself."

She flashes back to Jeff's mention of the blurry figure and realizes she should say something to comfort him. "You're not alone in what you've seen recently. Someone else saw Figure X, but I can't reveal who or divulge any other information."

"I understand. It's okay."

"That's not it. Things have been happening to me as well since I saw the farmer. Things I can't explain. I'll save the details for another time, but what I'm trying to say is that I don't think you're crazy. And for what it's worth, I don't believe you and your father are the same."

"Thanks," he mumbles. His lip quivers, and a steady stream of tears glides down his cheek. His insides are overwhelmed by guilt and overpowered by grief. "Would it be okay if we changed subjects? I don't know how much more of this I can stand."

"Of course. Would you like a few minutes to collect yourself?"

"No. I'm fine," he says, sniffling quietly.

"I believe you've earned the right to select our next topic. What would you like to discuss?" she asks, handing him some tissues.

"Honestly, I would rather you stay in the lead."

"Sure. Let's talk about your seeing Figure X in the field next to the Shell station."

He wipes his cheeks, eyes, and nose with unsteady hands before answering. "All nine people were present, and Figure X was standing on one of the larger branches high up in an oak tree. I could feel an enormous amount of pressure in my head, as if he was trying to control my mind. He wanted me to do something, but I wouldn't give in to him."

"What was he trying to get you to do?" she interjects.

Calvin pauses and looks around the room with a nervous feeling. "He was trying to get me to kill the farmer. I've wanted to tell you this since it happened, but I was afraid of how you would react."

"Actually, I already knew."

"What? How's that possible?"

"We discussed it during the last twenty to twenty-five minutes of the session during the disappearance. I wanted to mention it before but could tell it was a touchy subject. I made a judgment call and decided I should let you bring it back up at your own pace, once you were ready." Calvin's demeanor changes, and she can tell he's upset. "Please describe what you are feeling right now."

"I'm irritated," he snaps. "I think it is really sneaky of you to have hidden this from me. Are you hiding anything else?"

"No. I apologize if you feel my methods are a bit extreme. Again, it was a judgment call that I deemed necessary for us to continue to make progress." Dr. Livingston's voice softens. "I am on your side and we are in this together, but you have to trust me."

Calvin hesitates before responding, "You're right. I do."

"Good. Then we should keep going. You were saying that you believe Figure X was trying to get you to kill the farmer. Is this correct?"

"Yes," he says, feeling himself calming down. "But I refused. As soon as he realized I wasn't going through with it, I saw an image appear inside my head as if he was trying to either show me something or threaten me with it. I'm not sure which."

"What was the image of?"

"My wife, Janice. She was lying on the concrete."

"Please be specific. What else did you see?"

"Blood. She was lying on her back in a pool of her own blood. Her shirt was drenched in it." His face turns pale, and his attention shifts. He enters a daze and mumbles, "Shirt."

"Are you okay?" Dr. Livingston asks, concerned about Calvin's sudden change in behavior.

"I think I may have uncovered something."

She looks up and watches his lips moving slightly but not making any sound.

CHAPTER

18

CALVIN SITS DISTURBINGLY still, calculating in his head while concentrating intensely, refusing to lose his train of thought. He breaks himself out of his stupor and is startled by the strong look of concern engrained on Dr. Livingston's face.

"What is it?" she asks impatiently.

"I can't believe I didn't realize this before," he mutters.

"What?"

"When Figure X showed me the image of Janice, she was wearing my long-sleeved, button-down plaid shirt with blue-jean shorts."

"I don't quite follow," she says, puzzled.

"In the last three months, I've seen a ghostlike vision of Janice on more than one occasion. In every instance, she was wearing my long-sleeved, button-down plaid shirt with blue-jean shorts."

"What do you think it means?"

"I have no idea, but I can't shake the feeling that it might be important. Maybe Figure X didn't intend the vision as some sort of threat. What if he's trying to help me, and there's a hidden message of importance? Like a future warning of some kind." Calvin slumps forward and runs his hands through his thick, dark brown hair, instantly gritting his teeth at the thought of sounding like his father. "I don't know. What if I'm making something out of nothing? It could be as simple as I'm losing my mind. Runs in the family, after all."

Dr. Livingston frowns with disappointment. "I'll say it again and again until it finally starts to sink in: I don't think you're crazy. No more than the rest of us anyway. We can't get wrapped up in self-doubt. Our attention should be on Janice right now. Can you do that?"

"Yes."

"When was the last time her image visited you?"

"Earlier today, when I was with Jeff."

Dr. Livingston's eyebrows arch, and her expression changes to a look of curiosity. "Could Jeff see Janice?"

"Yes."

"How does that make you feel?"

"Very confused. When I asked him questions, he refused to answer. He seems to think my wife was there to give him clues. There's something truly wrong with that guy…delusional perhaps."

To say the least, she thinks, unwilling to let on that she agrees.

"Did either you or Janice know Jeff before your encounter with him in the parking lot yesterday?"

"No. At least I don't think so. He kind of looked familiar earlier today while standing outside your office, but I have no idea from where. I'm planning on describing him to Janice to see if she has ever seen him."

"I would be curious to hear her response." Dr. Livingston removes her glasses and places them on the corner of her desk. "I'm sorry. I can't stand to wear them a second longer. They frustrate me beyond belief."

"It's okay. I don't know anything about glasses, but I don't mind taking a look."

"Thanks. Maybe another time," she says, sounding distant.

She reaches into her top drawer and pulls out a second folder before glancing over her notes. She rearranges some pages that she's torn out of the notepad and does so with a fierce look of concentration.

"I'm going to ask you a series of questions involving Jeff, but I want to be especially careful not to infringe on patient confidentially."

"It doesn't matter to me. I know you would never intentionally do or say anything against one of your patients. Honestly, I think Jeff is a total dirt bag, and it wouldn't hurt my feelings if you trampled all over his rights. He would do the same to us without a second thought."

Dr. Livingston listens to his words as they roll off his tongue but doesn't comment. Instead, she studies her notes one last time before making eye contact.

"How involved do you feel Jeff is in all of this?"

"Judging from some of the conversations we've had, I would say pretty deep."

"Do you trust him?"

"No. Not even a little. I saw a side of him today that was surprisingly helpful, until I figured out he was only stalling me. He even mentioned at one point that if I didn't hurry up and bring everyone back, it might be too late for us."

"What do you think he meant?"

"I think he was implying that we would die."

"Did you believe him?"

"Yes. He was very convincing. He knows too much about my situation, which bothers me immensely. He even knew I could break the disappearance and bring everyone back. He practically talked me through it."

"Do you think he's dangerous?"

"Absolutely. I saw him kill one of the original nine people in the field next to the Shell station."

"You're kidding. When was this?" she asks, feeling anxious.

"Yesterday. He snapped someone's neck without any remorse."

"Which person?" she asks, slowing her tempo, being careful not to display too much emotion.

"The overweight man in the Mountain Dew T-shirt and khaki shorts."

"Did you call the police?"

Calvin looks down, dreading his response. "No. I didn't."

"Why not?"

"Because the body eventually was surrounded by lights and disappeared, along with Figure X. Maybe if his Jetta had stayed behind—"

"What happened to his car?" Dr. Livingston interrupts, before mouthing, "Sorry."

"No problem. It disappeared right after his body. I have no pictures of him or any proof of his existence. I remember seeing his license plate was from New Mexico, but that's about all I know."

She stares blankly at a spot on the wall across the room while trying to wrap her head around what he's saying. "What was Jeff doing after he killed the man?"

"He had one foot on the dead body and was staring up at Figure X. Like the man was a sacrifice or offering. It was really creepy how proud he was."

"Do you get the impression Figure X is out to harm anyone?"

"I'm not sure."

"Will you text me all of the pictures you have of the group of nine, including any of their vehicles, when you have a chance? Also, do you mind taking more photos? I would like for you to include their license plates if possible. I have a friend who's a police officer here in Plano who might be able to help us track some of these people down."

"Sure. That's a great idea," he says excitedly. "After our session, I'm planning on going to the Shell station. Hopefully, I'll be able to get some good shots then, assuming anyone's there."

Dr. Livingston looks down at her watch and notices there are only a few minutes left. "Do you have any other topics or issues you would like to discuss today?"

"Just one more thing. I can't believe it's only been three days since I became your patient."

"Yes. That's true. I was looking at the calendar this morning and noticed as well."

"How do you think everything is going?" he asks with an unsure tone. "Please be honest."

"My professional opinion is that we're right on track and making excellent progress. I'm hopeful we'll start to uncover more answers in the near future. We just need to remain patient."

"Thanks, Doc," Calvin says, standing up. "I really do feel these sessions are helping."

"That's great to hear," she says, meeting him at the door. "If something comes up, please don't hesitate to call me."

"I won't. See you on Monday."

"Have a good weekend."

Dr. Livingston watches Calvin walk through the doorway and disappear into the hall. She remembers her pistol is still out and makes her way back to her desk to retrieve it. She carefully slides open the middle drawer and mumbles, "Oh my God." The wind is stripped from her lungs, leaving her gasping for breath. *That's impossible. Where is it? Who could have taken my gun? I only left my office for a minute.*

She glances around frantically, unable to stifle the horrifying thoughts running rampant in her mind. She shuffles through each of her drawers and removes all of the contents before finally giving up. *The wall safe. Maybe I put it back and just don't remember.* She hastily makes her way over and removes the oil painting from the wall. She places her key in the slot and pulls the door open, only to be greeted by more documents. *This can't be happening. Where is it?* She closes her eyes and examines everything that has happened since removing the weapon from the safe. "Jeff," she mumbles. *He would have had the perfect opportunity during the disappearance period at the end of this morning's session.*

She cringes, feeling like her privacy has been violated, as she imagines him walking around her office alone with unlimited access and freedom. Locking the safe she replaces the painting on the wall before heading to the front of her desk. She flips her laptop around and logs in with unsteady hands. Her mind is racing as she searches her list of contacts. Feeling lightheaded, she is unaware that she is taking short, shallow breaths. *I have to calm down and relax.* Closing her eyes she gradually regains control of her emotions before dialing his number.

"Come on. Please answer."

His voicemail picks up but is devoid of any message. Only silence greets her, then the long sound of the beep. Caught off guard, she stumbles around for the right words.

"Jeff, it's Dr. Livingston. Would you please call me immediately? There's something I need to discuss with you."

Hanging up, she grabs her purse, and reaches for her keys. She walks to the receptionist area and says to Cindy, "I'm heading over to Judy's to check on her. I can't get through to her on the phone and I'm starting to worry that something may have happened. I shouldn't be long and have my cell phone if something comes up."

"Okay. I'll hold down the fort," Cindy says with a smile.

Dr. Livingston takes a few steps and stops. Turning back, she says, "I would like to tell you how much I appreciate the job you've been doing here for me as her temporary replacement. Even though it's only been two days, I've already bragged to my husband about how positive the atmosphere has been since your arrival. I've been thinking I could use a second full-time person if you're interested."

Without hesitation, Cindy responds, "Yes, I accept. I was hoping you would offer me a job. I really like it here."

"That's great news. I look forward to working with you on a more regular basis. I'm kind of crunched for time right now. Do you mind if we go over the details later?"

"Not at all," Cindy responds, trying to curb her excitement.

Dr. Livingston walks to her reserved spot in the parking lot directly across from her suite. She opens the driver-side door of her silver Mercedes sedan and does a quick peek into the back seat before getting in. She pulls out a piece of paper with the address 3312 Cherry Blossom on it and keys the information into her navigation system, then pulls out. The closer she gets to Judy's neighborhood, the more she's unable to shake the uneasy feeling consuming her.

"Something's happened. I can feel it," she mumbles.

Driving up to Judy's house, she notices that the red brick, one-story home is older and in an established neighborhood. She has worked for me for almost three years, and this is the first time I've tried to spend any time with her outside of work.

Parking alongside the house, she makes her way to the front door and notices the sidewalk is riddled with cracks partially filled with a mixture of grass and weeds. She pulls on the handle of the storm door, only to realize it's locked. Reaching up she knocks on the glass before taking a couple of steps backwards.

A young man in his late teens answers the door wearing a Texas Rangers baseball cap. The dark black hair flaring out from both sides of his head overlaps the tops of his ears. He's slightly overweight and is chewing a mouthful of food. She hears a loud gulp as he swallows hard.

"May I help you?"

Dr. Livingston realizes she has caught him during lunch and apologizes for the intrusion. At first glance, he could be quite intimidating, with his broad shoulders and large stature, but the stories Judy has always told revealed a much gentler side. His IQ is slightly below average but not enough to prevent him from graduating from public high school a few weeks ago. His black eyes are beady and concentrate solely on her movements as she gently sways from side to side, trying to conceal her nervousness.

"Hi. May I speak with Judy please?"

There is a long pause, during which neither makes a sound, until he breaks the silence by clearing his throat.

"My mom's dead. She died over a year ago," he says, his voice cracking.

Dr. Livingston is speechless and unable to muster any strength. Instead, she stands facing him, wondering if he is attempting to be funny. The intensity in his face increases, forcing her to look away, unable to take the sadness radiating from his eyes. *This isn't a joke.* Her emotions almost surface unwittingly as her mind strays to another place, searching for an escape. The blistering heat of Texas in June catches up to her as the direct sunlight relentlessly burns through her shirt and onto her back.

"I'm really sorry for the intrusion," she states again, her voice quivering. "You look just like your mother. Are you Gary?"

"Yes."

"It's nice to finally put a face with the name. Your mother talks…please forgive me. Your mother talked about you often."

"We already met at the funeral. Are you okay?"

"No. Actually, I'm not sure that I am. I've been under the weather for several days and have mixed cold medicines by mistake. It has my head all cloudy," she says, hating to lie but not sure what else to say.

"Do you want to come in? I heated up a pizza and only ate part. It might be better if you have some food in your stomach. I don't mind sharing."

"No, thanks."

She's instantly reminded of when Judy would receive the occasional call from teachers just to let her know how much of a blessing her son was in their classroom.

"Your mom once told me you gave away your sandwich at school to another student. Is that true?"

"Yes," he answers proudly. "She forgot hers, and I didn't want her to go hungry."

Dr. Livingston's heart breaks at the thought of Gary not having his mother around any longer.

"But weren't you hungry?"

He looks down at his stomach protruding slightly over the top of his shorts and grabs a handful. "I'm doing okay. Are you sure you don't want any pizza? It's pepperoni."

She smiles at his generosity. "That does sound good, but I need to be getting back to work. Thanks for the offer. My condolences to you."

She turns around and swiftly moves to her vehicle, unwilling to look back until she hears the click of the front door closing and locking.

What's going on? The intensity of her pain grows with each step. She does her best to fight the inevitable flood of tears that has been building since Gary's first mention of his mother's death. Unwilling to lose control, she tries to clear her mind long enough to start her car and adjust the air conditioning to the coolest setting. She breathes deeply, trying not to give in to the overwhelming sense of sadness and disbelief as she clumsily types an e-mail to Cindy.

Would you please reschedule my one-thirty appointment?

Yes, ma'am. I'll do it now, she replies almost instantly. Is everything okay?

Yes. It's fine. I just need a little more time. I can explain once I'm back in the office.

She sits in her car, her body trembling, unable to steady her composure. A dull ache eats away at her insides as large tears free-fall down her cheeks and onto her pant legs. She struggles to understand the meaning of Gary's words "My mom's dead. She died over a year ago."

That's impossible. I just saw her on Wednesday. It hasn't even been two full days. She wipes her eyes and tries to regain her composure. A conversation with Jeff regarding their session, held less than two hours earlier, surfaces and lingers in the back of her mind. At first, she pushes the thoughts away, unwilling to dwell, only to have them reappear again and again. *Something about his confession of killing the two women from the AA meeting seemed genuine.* A repulsed look crosses her face as she rehears his words: "I even rode the fatter one like a cow." *Was he telling the truth when he told me he was only testing me? Or did he really kill both women without an ounce of remorse?* Her chest tightens, and her eyes turn cold as his previous insult comes sneaking in. "Good Lord, it's like talking to a nine-year-old. I'm pretty sure they died long before last night. Probably about a year ago, if things haven't changed much."

"A year ago," she mumbles with a hint of intrigue in her voice, feeling like she's on the verge of a discovery. *If what things haven't changed much?* Her jaw drops at the possible connection. *Jeff, what have you done?*

CHAPTER

19

CALVIN DRIVES DOWN the service road of US 75, headed north, astonished at how many people are out in the middle of the afternoon on a weekday. He can hear the voice of the local DJ in the background talking about hot spots for the weekend and listens for less than a minute before becoming tired of the incessant rambling. He turns down the volume to a low hum, deciding to concentrate on the road ahead.

The yellow and red sign in the shape of a shell floats high above the store, eerily welcoming him as he approaches. Pulling into the parking lot, he heads down his usual path and stays to the left of the building. As he passes the store, he notices Jeff's car parked next to the air and water machine. *What are you up to this time?*

He studies the long, black, four door sedan and startles when the driver's door is flung open and a large cloud of smoke drifts out. Calvin parks his Audi and takes his time studying the situation before leaving his vehicle.

"What are you doing?" he calls out, walking up to Jeff's car. "I figured you would be off killing an unarmed person somewhere."

"I was waiting for you."

"Me. Why?" The stench of cigarettes overwhelms Calvin more and more the closer he gets. "Wow. Did you smoke an entire carton while you waited? You know those things will kill you, right?"

"We'll all be dead long before the emphysema has a chance to catch up to me. I give us nine days at most. Some I give less than that," he says with a wink.

"Sometimes I think you say things for the shock value alone. Do you honestly think I'm going to believe we have no more than nine days before we all die?"

"I personally don't care what you believe. It doesn't change the outcome any."

"Sure it does," Calvin says with disdain in his voice. "You mentioned you were waiting for me. What do you want?"

"We have a dilemma on our hands. See the man in the suit standing in the middle of the field next to the long-haired motorcycle guy?"

"You mean the hippie? Yes. I see him. I also see the older woman, the grandson, and three teenage girls. What about them?"

Jeff looks around and ignores his comment. "I can't tell from here, but I know as of yesterday he had the number one on his forehead."

"I already knew that. I also heard the whispers. And?"

"Really?" Jeff rolls his eyes and shakes his head in disgust. "You have no clue, do you? It means he has the number zero today."

Calvin stares blankly, focusing on Jeff's words but not understanding where he's headed.

"Good Lord," Jeff says, frustrated. "It means he's supposed to die."

"Isn't that what you live for?"

"Pretty much." Jeff lets out a chuckle. "You would freak out if you only knew how true your comment is."

"Then why haven't you rushed out there? I didn't think you understood the definition of fear."

"I'm not afraid. I'm trying to do the right thing for once in my life. Even if that means I will cease to exist when everything completes."

"When everything completes?"

"Yes. We're on a specific course, and when it runs its cycle, let's just say nothing will be the same. If we're all still around, that is."

Calvin opens his mouth and starts to take the bait. Instead, he stands quietly, unwilling to hide his look of mistrust.

Jeff's demeanor changes, and agitation rings loudly in his voice. "Again, it doesn't matter what you think to be true. It only matters what is destined to be true, or in our case fated to repeat itself. Listen to me when I tell you this. I'm trying to do the right thing here. If you get nothing else from our conversation, you need to remember this. You have to protect what's left of the group. It's that simple. They're the key, and once they're gone..." Jeff is distracted by Kathy emerging from the dense wooded area. She stands in place, holding her hand up to her face, blocking the sun. She scans the entire parking lot before stopping at the two of them. She gives a small wave, then turns and heads back into the woods.

"What's Mousy Chick doing here?" Jeff says, looking around for her car.

"You call her Mousy Chick, and she hasn't killed you yet?"

"She doesn't know," Jeff says with a smirk. "Besides, she's not like me. And by the way, her name is Kathy, in case you're interested."

"Good to know. And how well do you know...Kathy?"

"I met her last night...I think."

"I'm confused. You did or didn't meet her last night?"

"That's correct," Jeff answers, purposely trying to complicate the situation.

"Seriously, you have to recognize you're a jerk, right?"

Jeff remains quiet and concentrates solely on the trees. "Why aren't you showing yourself?"

Fed up with the games and in need of a break, Calvin says, "I'm going to walk out into the middle of the field with the remaining seven to see if I can begin protecting them. One last thing, how do you propose I go about doing that? Especially if they creep me out to the point that I can't stand to be around them."

"That's your problem. I've already said too much."

Calvin remembers the request from Dr. Livingston and pulls out his phone. He flips to the camera application and zooms in before snapping several pictures of each person. He turns to the parking lot and captures their vehicles and license plates.

Kathy emerges from the thick of the woods a second time and makes her way over to the group of seven. They immediately chant at a much faster pace than usual while forming a circle around the man in the suit, who has dropped to his knees, awaiting his destiny. The chatter becomes extremely loud, as if each person is shouting. Calvin puts away his phone as Jeff joins him at the gate, and both stand motionless, unsure what they should do next.

"You don't think she's capable of anything crazy, do you?" Calvin asks with concern.

"I've already told you she's not like me."

"I don't know. It seems like she's about to..." Calvin's eyes widen.

Kathy pulls out a revolver and holds it stiffly down by her side, keeping the muzzle pointing at the ground. She makes her way over and signals to the group to open their circle and allow her access. She steps into the center and stands face to face with the man in the suit, encountering only emptiness. His dull, gray eyes shift and fixate on the ground. She lifts her foot and places it on his side before pushing him into the dirt face first with great force. She leans over, holds the revolver six inches from the back of his neck, and fires twice. The shots echo through the trees, scattering a murder of crows inhabiting the wooded area. Blood squirts from the bullet wounds in a rhythmic pattern while the man in the suit's last remaining heartbeats pulsate erratically. His body twitches momentarily as reflexes from his nerves gradually fade away.

"She killed him!" Calvin yells in disbelief, realizing he's incapable of moving, his body frozen from shock. His first thought is to run after her, but he realizes there's nothing he can do. The damage has already been done.

Lights surround the man in the suit. His lifeless body disappears, leaving behind the usual twinkles of light, until they too are gone. Calvin glances behind him at the parking lot and stares while the Jaguar vanishes in front of his eyes.

"What do we do?" he asks, searching the trees unsuccessfully for Figure X. "We can't overtake her. She has a gun."

"I have no idea. I guess she finally made her first kill," Jeff mutters with a glint of appreciation.

"Are you smiling?"

"No, I'm squinting. The sun is bothering my eyes."

Kathy lowers the gun down by her side as Calvin and Jeff watch, mesmerized by her actions. She keeps a close eye on the remaining six as they line up in single file, facing the trees. The older woman is first, followed by the grandson, the three teenagers, and the hippie last.

Kathy walks toward the gate roughly twenty feet away and slows down after a few steps. Her mind is racing, and her adrenaline is high. She does a quick turnaround and heads back to the remaining six, lining up directly behind the hippie.

"Is she going inside with them?" Calvin asks.

"I don't know. She shouldn't be. It's not in the plan," Jeff states, baffled.

"Why not? You did," Calvin says, watching the older woman and her grandson disappear behind the shrubbery lining the entrance.

"Because I was supposed to make the kill today, not her."

The three teenagers follow the lead of the older woman and grandson and are next to be consumed by the shelter of the wooded area. Kathy, following closely behind the hippie, lifts her gun, aims directly at the center of his back and fires three times. The sounds of the shots echo inside her ears, leaving a slight ringing noise, causing her to shake her head.

Total anger consumes Calvin as he clenches his fists and stares at the empty shell of a man falling to the ground.

"What is going on?" he screams, and rushes through the gate with Jeff close behind.

"I guess you decided against my advice to protect them. Good call," Jeff says obnoxiously. "Talk about a blind side. That was awesome."

The lights surround the hippie, and in a matter of seconds his body is gone. Moments later, all traces of his motorcycle vanish as well.

Kathy raises her revolver as they approach less than ten feet away and points it directly at Calvin's face.

"That's close enough," she calls out.

He says nothing, still completely stunned.

"You don't talk much this time, do you?" she says.

"This time?"

"You don't remember me either? Sometimes I feel like I'm the only one with a clue. Come here," she calls to Jeff, signaling him with her gun.

He walks over and is surprised when she leans over and kisses him on the lips.

"Hello, sweetheart. Remember me?"

"From last night?" he replies, confused by the turn of events.

"No, not from last night. Welcome back. I really missed you, but we need to go now. I can explain on the way."

"Okay," Jeff replies in a daze.

Kathy looks over at Calvin and asks, "Has Jeff mentioned he has a photographic memory?"

Calvin says nothing.

"Answer please," she says, waving her gun.

"Yes. He told me today, but I don't think he was being truthful."

"He wasn't. He's a habitual liar. You can't believe anything that comes out of his mouth. He likes to lie for shock value."

Calvin glares at Kathy, refusing to take his eyes off of her, hoping for an opportunity to snatch the gun.

"One more thing. Don't try and follow us or call the police. If you do, I will go against the order of things and come after you now instead of waiting."

Calvin remains quiet and stands in one spot as Jeff and Kathy head toward the Shell station. His head begins to throb as vivid images of his wife wearing the long-sleeved, button-down plaid shirt and blue-jean shorts appear inside his mind. He stands paralyzed, envisioning her lying on her back—lifeless and covered in her own blood. He focuses his attention on her pinky finger and startles when it twitches. A nervous feeling covers him like a blanket, leaving him anxious and afraid her image might be lost at any point. He watches as she struggles for a moment before finally sitting up. Her head is lowered, her shoulders slumped, and her awareness nonexistent.

"Janice," he whispers, scared for her safety and feeling powerless.

He sees shadows of people running in different directions, all in a panic. A sudden jolt of energy rushes through his body and has him gasping for air. Her head moves slightly, lifting upwards a little at a time, until he's able to see the dull gray of her eyes surrounded by her blood-soaked hair. She opens her mouth to speak but lets out a bloodcurdling scream that rips through him as if to steal tiny pieces of his soul.

CHAPTER

20

KATHY AND JEFF move quietly through the field, picking up their pace the closer they get to the front of the Shell station. Not one word is spoken between them. Jeff's mind is too distracted going over the details of what he just witnessed. Kathy glances back to confirm that Calvin is taking her threat seriously and realizes from his stance that he's preoccupied and in a far-away place.

"I can't believe it's happening again," she says, feeling her excitement grow.

"What's happening again?" he says, approaching the store.

One of the glass doors opens swiftly as Jeff looks back at Calvin, wondering if he's okay. Suddenly, a familiar voice makes him cringe. "Are you okay, Mrs. Kathy?"

Jeff looks up and is surprised to see Frank, the man from the AA meeting, standing in front of them wearing an employee name tag in the shape of a shell.

"I'm fine, Frank," Kathy replies. "We're still on track. A little ahead of schedule by one body, to be exact."

Frank's expression changes to concern. "What are the consequences?"

"I don't know. I've always followed exactly as I'm supposed to until today. I can't describe the feeling, but I knew I was supposed to take one more."

"Who did you take?"

"The long-haired motorcycle guy."

"Did he have a number?"

"No. He didn't, and I don't appreciate all of the questions, Frank," she responds, her voice agitated.

Without saying another word, Frank points in Jeff's direction.

"No. He doesn't remember either of us. Unfortunately, it's true. Once you die, you come back with very little memory of before."

"What a waste," Frank says as he turns around and heads back inside the store, upset with Kathy for her careless behavior.

Jeff has a puzzled look on his face as they make their way to her car. "I died?" he asks.

"Yes," she answers.

"When?"

"Almost three years ago."

"Why did you wait so long to meet back with me if we were close?"

"Because it wasn't time to start killing until now. We need to go before we miss our window. How about we talk on the way?" she asks, opening the driver-side door and climbing in. Once inside, she places her gun inside the glove compartment on a stack of fast-food napkins, and then slams it shut.

"Where are we headed?" Jeff asks.

"Our next target. Some chick named Alicia in Oklahoma. Hop in. We're running late."

"How do you know her name?"

"Wow. How do you not know her name? You really don't remember anything, do you? I thought at first you might be in character, since you love to act out scenes."

"I'm not acting. I really have no idea what is happening."

"Then you need to spend more time in the wooded area to help regenerate your memory. Tell you what, we have a little bit of time to kill. No pun intended," she says, pulling onto the service road. "So we can talk on the way. Can I still call you Horse Jockey?"

"Why does that name sound familiar?"

"Because that's my nickname for you. Just like you used to call me Mousy Chick."

"I still call you Mousy Chick," he spouts back.

"I like to call you Horse Jockey because of your height. I'm pretty sure you could have been one. Who knows, maybe you'll come back as one next time," she says with a laugh while heading north up the entrance ramp to US 75.

"Funny," he mumbles. "How well did you and I know each other?"

"Pretty well."

"Did we date?"

"You could call it that," she says with a smirk.

"I can't believe I don't remember anything. What happened to me?"

"I happened to you. Maybe this time around will be different, but you need to stay away from Calvin. You seem to be destined to repeat your same mistakes."

"Why did you pretend not to know me at the AA meeting?"

"At first I wanted to find out how much you remembered, in case you were holding a grudge. No sense in running full speed at you, yelling, 'Here I am.' Besides, I wanted to see if you were still capable of getting the job done."

"And?"

"You are. I realized that the second I saw you ride one of the sisters like an animal before you killed her. Cold-blooded," she says, smiling.

She turns on the radio, and for the next hour neither of them speaks. Kathy thinks of Jeff and how nice it is to have him back, while Jeff focuses on everything he recently saw and heard, doing his best to make sense of it.

"We're here," Kathy says.

She reaches over and turns down the radio as they pull up to a big, beautiful house with a water fountain in front.

"Wow. I guess Calvin's perception of them has changed this time around."

She looks over at Jeff, who is trying to understand the conversation, feeling like she is speaking another language.

"Kathy steps out of the car. "I call dibs on the woman, but you can have her family. Do you have a weapon?"

"I do," he says, chuckling. "Someone was careless and left one sitting out just for me."

"That was nice."

"Yes, it was. I'll have to thank Dr. Livingston next time I see her."

Minutes pass and then nothing but screams fill the empty silence, followed by a series of gunshots.

CHAPTER

21

CALVIN RAISES HIS head, realizing he's lying face down on the ground next to a quaint, white wooden farmhouse. *What happened? Where am I?* he thinks, brushing the dirt off of his shorts and shirt, sitting up. *The last thing I remember is standing in the field, seeing the vision of Janice and hearing her scream.*

He glances up at the freshly painted wrap-around porch and notices there are only two windows, separated by the front door, each one displaying thick curtains. He reaches over and, with a trembling hand, picks up his sunglasses. Standing, he turns and spots his car parked next to a "For Sale" sign at the edge of the property. Looking down at his watch, he's stunned to see it showing 3:43 p.m.

How's that possible? It should only be 1:30 at the latest. How could I have lost over two hours? Not being able to account for the missing time leaves him feeling uneasy, and his state of mind in disarray. He thinks of his father, William, and remembers a conversation that took place roughly nine months prior to his being diagnosed with schizophrenia. He can hear each word clearly inside his head, as if his father were speaking to him right now.

"Son, I want you to listen carefully to what I am about to tell you. Something isn't right inside me. It started before you were born and has progressed into something I can't explain. Over the course of my life, I have lost several hours here and there with no recollection of why or for what purpose. Every time it happens, I feel as though a piece of me was stolen, never to be recovered again. I have the distinct impression an alien force of some kind is responsible and using me for some sort of an experiment. An experiment to what end I am uncertain. Whatever happens, please know that I love you very much and would do whatever necessary to keep you and your mother safe."

Sadness radiates off of Calvin while several tears stream down his cheeks. I miss you and wish things could have been different between us. But you didn't protect me or Mom. Instead, you took your own life and left us alone.

Calvin's anxiety builds, and his emotions take a toll on his sanity as he frantically searches his body for any visible signs of abduction. The sun shines brightly, bringing with it a relentless heat bearing down on him. Unable to clear away thoughts of Figure X, he looks up at the cloudless sky and yells, "Are you real? What do you want from me?"

Closing his eyes, he focuses on his breathing. *There must be a reason I was brought here.* He walks around to the side of the house, surveying the property with each step, hoping to find a clue. He comes to a chain-link fence surrounding the back yard and rests his arms on top. He sees a white wooden shed, also recently painted, located in the far corner. Hearing a rustling noise coming from behind he is startled to see Janice standing near the front of the house. She's wearing the same long-sleeved plaid shirt, along with blue-jean shorts. Her long black hair gently sways in the breeze. Her face is pale, and her breathing is hard. She remains motionless, watching his every move.

"I know you're not real, and I don't care!" he shouts. "I love you, and I'm going to say it every time I see you. There are so many horrible images I keep being shown, and I don't know if you're going to live or die, but I can't imagine my life if you're not in it. The worst part is that I feel powerless against all of this. I can't..." He stops in midsentence to collect his thoughts. His eyes water, and his voice shakes. "Whatever you are here to tell me, please do it now, because I can't take much more today."

Calvin instantly sees vivid images of Jeff and Kathy standing face to face in his front yard next to his garage. She's holding a revolver and pointing it directly at Jeff, smiling and awaiting the command.

Jeff is acting strangely and doesn't seem to be afraid. Instead, he asks, "Aren't you at least curious to see what will happen?"

"No. Not at all," Kathy replies angrily.

"Just give it a chance. What's the worst thing that might come from stopping the cycle right now?"

"We could all die. You know we shouldn't break the pattern. Without it, everything changes. I'm not willing to risk my survival because you grew a conscience and, against my advice, started merging with Calvin. Your weakness at this moment disgusts me."

A third person walks up from across the street, but the image is too distorted to identify. A nod from this person is enough of a signal, and without showing any reluctance Kathy pulls the trigger. The bullet hits Jeff in the chest, puncturing his left lung. He falls to his knees and places his hands on the ground for balance, trying to speak but sputtering out blood instead. His light green eyes fade and lose their vibrancy. A long strand of reddish saliva drips from his mouth as his body falls to the ground. He wheezes loudly, trying to catch his breath, straining violently, before the last remaining pockets of air empty. His face loses color, and his lifeless body lies still on the red-stained grass.

"See you in five years," Kathy mumbles. "Maybe."

She takes a few steps toward the street, with the gun still clutched tightly in her hand, and is met by the third person.

"All nine are dead, and everything is almost complete. The doctor's family is dead, but not the doctor…Not yet anyway," Kathy says, turning and pointing to the house. "Our next move is to get rid of your family."

Calvin awakens from his trance, gasping for a breath. He flails his arms around in a panic as he desperately searches for any sense of normalcy to help regain his bearings. The first thing he hears is the clicking sound of his hazards blinking on and off. He glances around anxiously, taking in as much of his surroundings as possible, until he recognizes he's sitting inside his car, parked in the driveway outside of his house.

"That wasn't real," he mumbles, repeating it several times before the fear sets in. He quickly looks over to where Jeff and Kathy were standing in his vision and says with relief, "Oh, thank God. They're gone, and there's no blood on the grass. It wasn't real."

The time on his console reads 6:17 p.m., and Calvin wonders how he made it home. Realizing another two hours have elapsed, he puts his head down, uncertain what else to do. *I lost time again. That's twice in one day. The same thing that happened to my father is happening to me.*

Completely on edge, he's startled by the rumbling of the garage door opening. Janice is standing at the top of the steps, wearing a short-sleeved shirt and dark green shorts. He lets out a sigh of relief, knowing he's seeing his actual wife, and is thankful for her smile as he pulls into the garage.

"I love you," he mouths, keeping up his promise.

She responds in the same manner before being nudged by Daniel, who yells, "Daddy!" and rushes over to greet him. Calvin's day has suddenly gotten better. He stares at his beautiful wife while holding his son tightly in his arms. *The rest isn't worth worrying about right now.*

"Are you okay with pizza for dinner?" she asks, walking toward him.

"Sure. Anything is fine."

"That's great, since I've already ordered it," she says, laughing. She leans in and gives him a kiss. "I'm hoping it will be here soon."

"Sounds good. Have you checked the mail today?"

"No. Not yet."

He picks up Daniel, takes Janice by the hand, and all three walk to the mailbox together. The delivery driver turns onto their street. Calvin notices it's the youngest of the pizza shop owner's three sons and nods to him once he has come to a complete stop.

"Good evening, Mr. Johnston," the skinny young man calls out before hurrying to the passenger side to collect the pizzas.

"Hey, Vincent," Calvin replies. "How's your dad?"

"Good. Just as pushy as always," he says with a smirk. "Now that school's out for the summer, he switched me to full-time."

Janice smiles and steps closer.

"Hi, Mrs. Johnston."

"Hi, Vincent. Sorry to hear about the increase in hours."

"That's okay. I can use the extra money. Besides, I just like to complain about the old man every now and then. It always has a way of making me feel better."

Calvin laughs as he signs the receipt while Janice reaches out and takes the pizzas. She heads toward the front door, with Daniel leading the way, and wave's good-bye to Vincent before making her way inside their house.

Calvin holds out the receipt. "I know it's only been a couple of weeks since I've seen you last, but you look different to me. Have you changed anything about your appearance?"

"No, sir. I am just as handsome as always," the young man says playfully before heading back to his car. "You take care of yourself, and I'll see you again in a couple of weeks."

Calvin waves as he drives away but can't seem to shake the muddled feeling in his mind. He heads for the front door and it opens as he approaches.

Janice sticks her head out and asks, "Do you want a Coke with dinner or iced tea?"

"Coke with extra ice would be great."

Once inside, he makes his way to the half bath next to the kitchen and washes his hands before grabbing a couple slices of pizza. He takes a few bites and is instantly reminded why they will never order from anyone else. The perfect blend of spices and sauce makes for a pleasing taste with every mouthful. Calvin closes his eyes as he chews, taken in by the flavor for a brief moment, before hearing Janice saying something about Alicia.

"I'm sorry, honey, I wasn't paying attention. What did you say?"

Janice starts over. "I was thinking about driving to Oklahoma this weekend with Daniel to visit Alicia and her family's grave, if you would like to join us."

"What?" Calvin replies.

"Can you believe it has already been a year since their car accident?"

"What?" he repeats, unable to process how to react to the news.

"Are you okay?"

"I don't understand. We just saw her yesterday. She decided against spending the night because she wanted to plan for Brendon's birthday party tomorrow. You cooked tuna casserole for dinner because it's her favorite. Oh, and she was fighting with Dave, but they made up through an email."

He places his partially eaten slice of pizza on his paper plate, unable to stop his head from spinning.

"Everything you described is correct, but it happened last year, not yesterday."

"I don't understand."

His first thought is that he somehow has lost an entire year. In a panic, he pulls out his phone and verifies the date: Friday, June 12. Unsure of the year, he switches to his calendar application and is relieved to see 2015 in bold black numbers. *If I didn't lose time, then why does she think this happened a year ago?*

"When?" he mutters.

"Early June almost one year ago."

"How did it happen?" he asks, his voice shaky, deprived of any emotion.

"They died in a car accident. They were on vacation on their way to Colorado."

Calvin's eyes shift downward. "I can't believe they're dead. This can't be true."

"I'm really starting to worry about you. How do you not remember the death of one of our closest friends?"

"I guess I had pushed it out of my mind for so long I began to believe it wasn't true," he says, hoping his lie will be convincing enough for her.

"We haven't talked about Dr. Livingston lately. Do you think her therapy is still helping, or should we look for another doctor?"

"Honestly, I think her therapy is one of the few things keeping me sane. I still feel confident she's the right doctor. We just have to be patient for now."

Janice's tone switches to a caring one. She reaches over and gently rubs his hand. "You know you don't have to pretend to be strong for me, right? I'm sturdy enough you can lean on me anytime you need to."

"I know. I appreciate you always being there for me. You and Daniel are the most important part of my life. Without each of you, I would have given up long before now."

Calvin takes a few more bites and is disappointed to find the flavor bland and unappealing. "Maybe I should take a few minutes. I'm feeling really out of it right now."

"Sure. I wish there was something I could do to make you feel better."

He gets up, walks toward the hall, and stops. "I think I'll pass on visiting the cemetery this time. I don't know that I'll be up to it by tomorrow. I'm sorry."

CHAPTER
22

THE FAMILIAR HUM of the box fan drowns out the background noise of the kitchen as Rachael Livingston fights a losing battle for peace of mind. Her comforter is pulled over her head and blocks the rays of sunlight streaming in through the window next to the bathroom. She twitches her nose twice before reaching up to scratch the itch tormenting her.

"Judy," she whispers, reminded of the tragedy she's incapable of comprehending. The dark circles under her eyes are evidence of the sleepless night. All she could hear was Gary saying, "My mom's dead," his voice cracking with every word.

"I can't do this today," she mumbles. "I have to be strong."

She can instantly smell the familiar aroma of bacon for the second day in a row. She stretches out her arm and gently glides her hand across the cool, satin sheet, hoping to discover the warmth of her husband, Jack. Instead, she finds an indention in the mattress where he once lay. *Something isn't right,* she thinks, refusing to acknowledge the unnerving feeling creeping inside her head.

She glances around the room and focuses on the wall directly in front. Her vision is hazy at first, until an image of their antique, bronze-colored clock comes into view. *Seven-thirteen,* she thinks, feeling her frustrations build. *It's Saturday morning and earlier than I would have gotten up for work on a weekday. And why is he cooking bacon again?*

She throws back the covers in one sudden movement. Her eyes shift to a red bandana resting against her calf. An unsettling fear consumes her as she realizes it belongs to the farmer. She immediately sits up in bed, pulls her legs toward her chest, and frantically searches the room. *How would his bandana make it into my bed? Was the farmer under my covers at any point last night or this morning? What if he's still in our house somewhere?*

She reaches out to grab hold of the bandana and is dumbstruck by the appearance of numerous white lights fluttering around. Mesmerized by their beauty, she watches the lights surround the bandana, each with a specific placement. With her arm still extended, she feels her fingertips penetrate one of the lights, sending slight electrical pulses racing throughout her body. Multiple images flash into her mind instantaneously. A pulling sensation develops in the pit of her stomach and spreads to her chest. Afraid of what might be happening, she jerks her hand back and watches as the lights change to red, then disappear entirely, taking the bandana with them. A few small twinkling lights appear briefly, until they too vanish without a trace. She's reminded of an earlier session with Calvin and relates it to his mention of the disappearance of people and their vehicles also consumed by the lights.

Her thoughts are interrupted by the movement of a dark shadow gliding across the back wall and into the bathroom. She quickly turns her head but isn't fast enough to catch anything other than a glimpse. *What was that?* Incapable of doing anything else for the moment, she continues to sit in bed motionless, trying to rationalize what she has seen. *Maybe my eyes are playing tricks on me.*

Unsure what to do next, she opens her mouth to call Jack but realizes that without being able to prove any of this she's only going to end up sounding crazy. Unable to sit any longer, she makes her way to the master bathroom and studies every inch, making sure each item is in its proper place and undisturbed. Not finding anything out of the ordinary, she puts on her robe and splashes some cold water on her face, hoping it might help her relax. Glancing up into the mirror, she's frightened to see the farmer looking back at her. She shrieks and instantly turns, hoping Jack didn't hear.

She returns her focus to the mirror. "What do you want?"

He says nothing, only watches her intently without blinking. His face is old and sunken, his eyes dull gray and eerie.

"How did you leave the bandana in my bed?"

She sees his mouth moving but can't hear anything he's saying. She reaches up and places her hand gently on his image, feeling nothing other than the hard, cold surface of the mirror. She is startled when his words suddenly echo inside of her head. "Eight days."

"Eight days until what?" she asks.

Sandra's laugh reverberates off the walls and can be heard coming from the kitchen, diverting Rachael's attention. Turning back, she's disappointed to find the farmer gone. She washes her face a few more times, hoping for his return. Giving up, she switches the fan to off and heads to join her family.

Opening her bedroom door, she can hear the clicking of Murphy's toenails as he paces back and forth on the hardwood floor. As she approaches, she hears Sandra asking for another glass of orange juice and is reminded of yesterday.

"Mommy," she yells, and runs over to give her a big hug.

"Good morning, Dr. Livingston," Jack says, standing over the griddle with spatula in hand.

Rachael is overwhelmed by the strong sense of déjà vu but carefully collects her thoughts before speaking. "Didn't we just have pancakes and bacon yesterday?"

"No. Yesterday we had cereal," he answers. "I thought I would try something different for today. Wait until you taste the bacon. I decided to go with the thicker smoked-maple flavor."

Yes, I know. The same as yesterday.

"How do you like your apron on me? I made a deal with Sandra that if she works on her multiplication tables with me while I cook, I would put it on for her. Besides, she keeps telling me how handsome I look in it."

Rachael doesn't respond, knowing they've already had this conversation the day before.

"What day is this?"

"It's Saturday, sweetheart. Are you okay?"

"I'm sorry. I have a pounding headache, and I think I'm going to skip breakfast this morning."

"No problem. I wasn't sure when you would wake up, so I've already saved a plate for you in the microwave, if you change your mind."

As she walks away, she hears Jack asking Sandra to be quiet and let Mommy rest. Her heart breaks, knowing she's treating them unfairly. Closing her bedroom door behind her, she takes several steps and falls onto her bed, wondering why the morning repeated. She hears a buzzing noise coming from the nightstand and notices Calvin has sent her a text. Scrolling down, she reads, *"Sorry to bother you on a Saturday, but I had a pretty bad day yesterday. I could really use a therapist. Are you planning on going in today? If so, can we meet?"*

Feeling anxious and hoping this might be exactly what she needs, she responds almost immediately with *"Yes. How about 9:00 this morning?"*

"Sounds good. See you then."

She hurries and takes a quick shower, continuously checking the mirrors, concerned the farmer might reappear at any time. Drying off, she hears the bedroom door open as Jack makes his way over to her.

"How are you feeling?"

"Better. I have a patient I'm planning on meeting at the office at 9:00. I'm really sorry."

"It's okay. You seem to have quite a lot on your mind lately. Is there anything I can help with?"

"No. Thanks for the offer, though," she says, buttoning her shirt. "I think I may be having too much empathy for one of my patients, but nothing serious. I shouldn't be gone too long. Maybe the three of us can go out to dinner somewhere tonight."

"Sounds like a good idea. I can book a reservation at Landry's for 7:00 if you're in the mood for seafood," he says, leaning in for a kiss.

"Seafood would be perfect," she replies, brushing several strands of his hair away from his eyes.

She walks out into the hall and calls for Sandra, giving her an extra-long hug before heading to her car. As she's backing out of the garage, her phone rings.

"Dr. Livingston."

"Hi, this is Pastor Smithers returning your call from yesterday. I hope it's not too early for you."

"No. Not at all. I wanted to ask you about your Alcoholics Anonymous meetings you hold on Thursday nights."

"Yes, ma'am. Every Thursday night at 7:00 here at Holy Temple Baptist Church located at 1327 Sycamore Street. If you're interested in joining, you're more than welcome just to show up. We accept walk-ins and would never turn away a stranger in need."

Dr. Livingston smiles at his kindness. "I appreciate the offer, Pastor Smithers, but I'm more concerned about discussing the meeting you held Thursday evening."

"Sure. I don't see any harm in that."

"Specifically, I'm interested in two sisters that would have attended," she says, pulling up to a red light.

The phone goes quiet for several seconds, leaving her wondering if calling him might have been a mistake.

"No, ma'am. I didn't have any sisters attend Thursday's meeting."

"That's great to hear," she says, relieved. "Thank you for taking the time—"

"Hold on a second before you hang up," he interjects. "My apologies, but I just remembered something. I'm not sure if this pertains, but we did have two sisters that used to attend every Thursday meeting like clockwork. Unfortunately, they were both killed in a car accident around a year ago. It was a beautiful service. I had the opportunity to say a few words myself. Is this what you were looking for?"

"Um…I believe so," she says, her voice fading. "Thanks for returning my call."

"Anytime. Good-bye now."

"Good-bye."

She continues driving another fifteen minutes, focusing only on his words, lost in deep thought. She pulls into the empty parking lot of her office and heads straight for her designated spot. *This is too much.* Glancing over, she sees Calvin drive up and park in the space directly next to hers. He gives Dr. Livingston a quick wave and already has a sense of relief just from the sight of her. They walk in together and head straight to her office with few pleasantries other than a simple "Good morning."

Calvin is the first to break the silence as they enter her office. "I'm sorry again for the lack of notice this morning."

"It's not a problem. I needed to get out and clear my head anyway. Is everything okay?" she asks, trying to pretend all is normal.

"I don't really think so anymore. I'm not even sure I know where to begin."

"How about starting from the time you left my office after our appointment yesterday?"

"Sure. I had a strong feeling and drove straight to the Shell station. When I got there, Jeff was in his car waiting for me."

"That's odd. Why was he there?"

"He told me he knew the guy in the suit had a zero on his forehead, and he was afraid if he went any closer he would be the one who killed him. He also mentioned the reason he was trying so hard was that he had made a promise to you."

"Obviously, with Jeff also being a patient of mine, I shouldn't comment, but please keep going."

"Jeff was very adamant about me protecting the remaining seven. He said they're the key, and something about once they're gone. I can't remember the rest, because some woman named Kathy showed up and killed the man in the suit, along with the hippie, in a matter of minutes. It was crazy. I've never seen anything like it before. I believe Jeff called her Mousy Chick. Have you heard of her?"

Dr. Livingston pauses before answering, "Yes. I've heard of her, but do not know her personally. Were both bodies taken by the lights?" she asks, flashing back to the bandana in her bed.

"Yes."

"Did you actually see Kathy kill both of these people?"

"Yes. She walked right up and without any hesitation shot them both. I'm not intimidated very easily, but I had a hard time controlling my fear when she was around. All I could feel was an insane amount of distress. She's not a good person. At one point she held a gun to me and asked if I remembered her. I didn't say anything at the time, but the funny thing is I know we've crossed paths before. I'm almost positive this wasn't the first time she's held a gun to me. I feel as though..." Calvin stares into Dr. Livingston's dark brown eyes.

"What is it?" she asks. "Did you remember something else?"

Calvin hesitates, choosing his words wisely before stating, "I feel as though she's inside of me. Or at least inside my head somehow. I don't know how else to explain it. As if she's a part of me, but I know that doesn't make sense."

"Did she mention anything to Jeff?"

"Yes. She called him 'sweetheart,' kissed him and said, 'Welcome back.' She went out of her way to make certain I didn't trust him and to discredit anything he has told me in the past. It seemed really weird, like it was overkill."

"She must be afraid he has told you something he wasn't supposed to. Do you know what that could be?"

"I'm not sure. There are so many things in my head right now...I'm sorry."

"No need to be. You mentioned she said, 'Welcome back' to Jeff as if he had been gone for an extended period of time. What do you think she meant?"

Calvin's face lights up as he states, "Dead. I think he was dead. Jeff had slipped and told me that it didn't matter if I killed him that he would be back in less than five years."

"You are doing really well. Is there anything else she might have mentioned? Please take your time."

"Before they left, she told me not to call the police and threatened me."

"What was her threat?"

"Something about going against the order of things and killing me next. Although I didn't believe her. Everything else she told me had an extreme sincerity, except for this part. I think she wants me to call the police. It felt almost like a dare or a challenge."

"Why would she want you to call the police?"

"She knows there's nothing they can do. Maybe she wants to keep me occupied and away from the remaining five."

The scratching sound of the pen against paper distracts Calvin as Dr. Livingston writes down several notes.

"One other thing…" Calvin hesitates briefly. "I've been thinking about the original nine, and something doesn't add up. It's like they're not real."

"What makes you say that?"

"First of all, why don't any of them fight back if they know they are about to be killed? I thought our will to live is supposed to kick in. Besides, I've been up close with each of them. They're not there anymore. Only empty shells of people walking around without a purpose. As if they're completely hollow on the inside, and most of the time show very little emotion. They remind me of someone under a spell of some sort."

"That's interesting. Do you believe in witches and spells?"

"No. But then again I don't really believe in half the things I've seen over the last few months."

"I understand entirely. I guess my question would be, if they aren't real, then what are they?"

"I have no idea. I was hoping this is one of the areas we may be able to figure out together."

"Did you remember to take the pictures I asked you about on Friday?"

"Yes, I did."

"Great. Can I see them?"

"Absolutely," he says and texts a total of eleven pictures to her phone.

She scans through and is instantly reminded of the farmer that morning.

"Everyone appears to be wearing the same clothes in these pictures as they wore in the ones you sent during the disappearing period."

"That's correct. No one has changed even a shirt since my first encounter on Wednesday."

"It's been four days, and no one has changed their clothes," she mumbles, pausing on the picture of the three teenage girls. "You mentioned the farmer would have been the first to disappear if he had been killed. Is this correct?"

"Yes. Instead, I escorted him to his truck. The man wearing the Mountain Dew T-shirt and khaki shorts was actually the first to disappear."

"You also mentioned that yesterday the man in the suit and the man you call the hippie were killed. That puts my count at only five remaining people. Is this correct?"

"Yes."

Dr. Livingston continues searching through all eleven pictures but keeps coming back to one. "Something doesn't add up. Why isn't anyone missing any of these people, especially the three teenage girls? They look to be high school age. I find it hard to believe no one has filed a missing person's report in four days."

"Unless they're not real," Calvin states.

"What can you tell me about these girls?"

"The dark-haired girl drives the black BMW with a bumper sticker from Plano West Lacrosse."

"So they live here in Plano, or at least one of them does," she says. "My police officer friend whom I've known since high school works for Plano. Are you okay with me calling him to do a search on the license plates? I could send him these pictures to use as a reference."

"That would be great."

"If Kathy truly does want the police involved, she must have a reason. However, if we take this slow and careful, hopefully it will be useful. I can have him run a check on missing persons as well."

"Would you like for me to meet with him too?"

Dr. Livingston pauses for a moment. "I don't think that will be necessary. I don't want to raise too many suspicions. He's pretty good about not asking questions if he knows patient confidentiality is involved." Dr. Livingston flips back to a page she folded under and says,

"I think we may have gotten off track a little. I would like to circle back to the man in the suit and the hippie. What happened to their bodies?"

"The lights came and they eventually disappeared."

Dr. Livingston is about to speak but stops herself before any words can leave her lips.

"Is there something you want to say?" Calvin asks.

She sits in her chair, motionless and with an anxious look, unsure if she should divulge any personal information to one of her patients. He senses her hesitation and can tell by her body language that it's serious.

"It's okay, Doc. You can say it out loud. I promise I have no intention on judging you."

Dr. Livingston clears her throat while stalling momentarily. "I've never discussed my personal life with a patient in my seven years of practice, but I'm really struggling right now. I know when I'm out of my element, and I passed that point yesterday with news about Judy." She pauses for a breath, shakes her head as if to dismiss her own comments, then blurts out, "I saw the lights in my house this morning."

Calvin remains quiet and shoots a look of confusion in her direction.

"I woke up in my bed and found the farmer's bandana..." She stares at Calvin in disbelief. His eyes turn dull and fixate on the wall behind her. His face loses all expression, while his mouth hangs slightly open.

"Calvin!" she yells, trying to get his attention. He continues to stare blankly, reminding her of how he described the original nine. She wonders what could be going through his mind.

"Oh my God," she mutters as hundreds of lights appear.

She rushes over to him, as they slowly descend, landing on top of him one at a time. She brushes a few of the lights away with her hand, only to watch them return to the same spot almost instantly.

"Calvin, please wake up. You can stop this. I know you can."

Her panic increases at the realization that only a few remaining stragglers have yet to settle. She forces her hands through the lights and shakes Calvin vigorously.

"Please hurry and wake up!" she yells. "What if you end up like the farmer?"

CHAPTER

23

DR. LIVINGSTON EXHALES deeply before mumbling, "Please don't leave."

Her anguish builds with the thought of Calvin's disappearance and the uncertainty of his return. She tightens her grip and violently shakes him in a final attempt to awaken him from his trance, nearly pulling him off his chair. She is unaware that a small group of lights has formed on each of her hands. She lets out a high-pitched shriek as tingling in her fingertips turns to electrical pulses before racing down her arms. A pulling sensation from the inside out induces immediate visions engrained with vivid detail. Strong vibrations take over, forcing her to release her grip.

"No!" she yells loudly, without effect.

In an instant Calvin is gone, and all that remains are several smaller twinkling lights glimmering above the seat of his chair. Dr. Livingston stands alone, hunched and aching for understanding, fearing for his safety. *What should I do now? How do I get in touch with him?* She grabs her phone, tries to steady her hands while slowly typing, *"Where are you?"*

She sits behind her desk for what seems like an eternity, unable to take her eyes off of the screen, eagerly awaiting his response. Extremely anxious and tired of feeling helpless, she rushes out of her office, heads down the hall and peers through the glass entrance door with wide eyes. She gasps as she sees that his car is missing from the lot. The sting of reality sets in all at once as she imagines the worst possible scenario, her mind relentlessly telling her he's gone for good.

Looking down at her watch, she's surprised that it's already a little after 10:00. *He's been gone for over fifteen minutes.* Suddenly her hand vibrates, catching her off guard. A sense of relief blankets her the moment she realizes Calvin has replied to her text.

"I'm fine. I'm at the Shell station. That was really freaky. Don't want to say any more until we're in person. Can we meet?"

"*Of course,*" she types as fast as her fingers will allow. "*I'll be waiting for you at the office.*"

"I'm about twenty minutes out. See you then."

Dr. Livingston paces back and forth for longer than that, unable to stifle her impatience, the whole time debating whether or not to call when she sees his car drive past. Fighting the urge to meet him in the parking lot, she watches as he finds a spot close to hers. As soon as he's safely inside her suite, she wraps her arms around him tightly, and for this brief moment is able to ignore the many emotions fighting within, desperately trying to emerge. He holds on to her, relieved that everything is normal once again, and senses she must have been a nervous wreck.

"Welcome back," she says, releasing her grasp. "Let's head to my office."

They both walk down the hall, their minds swimming with questions.

As they approach Dr. Livingston's office, she blurts out, "What happened to you?"

Calvin looks surprisingly refreshed, his body language more relaxed than during any of his earlier visits. He takes a seat and even crosses his legs as he stretches out.

"I'm not a hundred percent sure. We were talking, and I could tell there was something you wanted to share but seemed skeptical about revealing. I felt my mind drifting to when the diesel truck had thrown the water over the guardrail onto my car. I remembered vivid details that seemed important at the time but seem insignificant now."

"Please be specific."

"Like the size of the raindrops as they hit my windshield. Or the strong gust of wind that carried pieces of trash through the air. Both images seemed wrong and out of place."

"That's interesting," she mumbles.

"While I was watching these images in my mind, I was reliving every moment of the accident, including every emotion possible. The more I watched, the more I was being drawn in and exposed to a new level of fear. It was nothing I had ever experienced before. At one point I even heard my wife's panicked voice calling out as the car spun around in circles."

Dr. Livingston chimes in, "I'm confused. Was your wife with you?"

"No. I was alone in the car."

"Why do you think you would hear her voice during this critical time?"

"I'm not sure."

"What was she saying?"

"She told me she loved me. Only I could sense she was telling me primarily because she was afraid."

Dr. Livingston clears her throat, following his every word closely. "What happened next?"

"As soon as the accident was over, my attention switched to the fact that everyone had disappeared and all of the water from the rain was gone. I was faced with an unbearable number of questions but somehow found a small place inside my mind that I could slip away to unnoticed. It was there that I experienced peace and quiet. I felt a strong force inside taking over and telling me to relax for a while." Calvin stops and watches Dr. Livingston staring blankly. "I can tell by your expression that I'm not explaining this as well as I had hoped. Does any of this make sense?"

"Not entirely. Put another way, would you say that while you were watching the images you figured out a way to make them stop by relinquishing control to this strong force? And by doing so you were able to find peace?"

"Not exactly, but close enough," Calvin replies, fidgeting with his hands, refusing to make eye contact.

Dr. Livingston shifts to the edge of her chair. "There's more to this that you're keeping from me. Is this true?"

Without hesitation, Calvin responds, barely above a whisper. "Yes…I saw my father, William, during this time."

Dr. Livingston concentrates, studying each movement. "Was he the strong force you were feeling?"

"No. He came to me during the peace-and-quiet time."

"What was he doing?"

"Talking to me as if he were trapped inside my head with me somehow."

"What did he say?"

"He told me he was sorry and that he has been watching over me. He explained how important it was for me to know his body had been replaced before I was born. He showed me a vision of when his soul was extracted for the first time."

Dr. Livingston places her pen on her pad. "I'm confused. Supposing I believe a soul could be extracted and put into another body, how could it happen more than once?"

Calvin glances upward, his expression hard, his voice shaky. "The first time was before I was born, and the second was with his suicide."

She grimaces. "You're talking about his belief in aliens switching his body with an exact replica for the reason of crossbreeding with humans."

"Yes, I am," he replies, his eyes darting around the room, embarrassed to hear the words spoken out loud. "I watched streams of different-colored lights exiting his body. The weird thing is—"

"Some were colors you've never seen before. Also, there was something familiar about the streams of lights, as if you'd experienced them first hand somehow."

Calvin shudders. His expression changes to shock. "That's impossible. How would you know what I was thinking?"

"I'm not sure. I feel as though we're linked somehow. I've felt a strong connection with you on and off since our first meeting but was afraid to say anything until now."

"How long have you been able to read my mind?"

"This was the first time."

"Can you tell me what I'm thinking now?"

Dr. Livingston closes her eyes and concentrates before whispering disappointedly, "No. I guess it's gone."

"Why do you think you were able to read my mind?"

"I'm not sure. I was holding on to you the whole time the lights were consuming your body. Maybe that connected us somehow or strengthened our bond in some way. Were you aware that the white lights appeared and surrounded you?"

"Yes and no. I couldn't see them, but I knew they were there. I believe I'm the one who made it happen."

"What do you mean?"

"Once I was able to block the images and my mind was clear, I'm pretty sure I was able to call on them or will them to come to me. It's really hard to explain, but I could tell they were there because I wanted them to be."

"Were you able to control their placement on your body?"

"No. I could feel slight electrical pulses only in concentrated areas in the beginning. But once they were in position, the pulsating switched to an extreme amount of energy, combined with a strong vibration. I felt like I was being pulled from the inside out, but not in a painful way."

"I felt the exact same things while I was holding on to you."

Calvin ignores her comments and maintains his focus. "It was during this time that I diverted all my attention to the Shell gas station, which is why I'm guessing I ended up there. Again, I don't know if I am making sense. I feel really weird saying this out loud."

"You're making perfect sense. I think you and I have passed the place where we should worry about how things sound, especially since I can relate to most of what you're saying."

"Really?"

Dr. Livingston places her notes on her desk and sits back in her chair. "I saw the lights today on two separate occasions. The first was in my bed this morning, and the other was with you. This is what I was trying to tell you earlier, before your disappearance. We can go into more details later, but for now I would like to stay focused on you. Can you call on the lights again?"

"I don't think so. Should I try?"

"No!" she responds in a panic, her face hard and sincere. Realizing how that must have sounded, she lets out a laugh. Her voice softens. "Maybe another time. I think my heart is at its limit for the day. Do you remember anything about traveling with the lights?"

"I don't. I've tried to remember several times while I was driving back but haven't been successful."

"That's too bad. Describe what happened after you arrived at the gas station."

"I woke up in my car where I would normally park. None of the remaining five were there. In fact, no one was. I didn't see one car the whole time. As soon as I regained my composure, I saw you had texted me, so I sent my response." He sits up. "I'm curious about what you saw and felt. Do you mind discussing what it was like from your side?"

"Very traumatic, to say the least. I thought you were going to disappear and end up either dead or in a mirror somewhere. You were in a catatonic state. I tried everything I could think of, hoping to snap you out of it. Your condition reminded me of how you had described the original nine. You mentioned earlier that you suspected they were either not real or under some sort of spell. I believe it may be the latter of the two."

"That's interesting. Based on what?" he asks curiously.

"You exhibited the exact same behaviors that you mentioned. Basically, you were an empty shell incapable of showing emotion. I shook you several times while yelling directly at you and received no response. Instead, you continued to stare at the wall behind my desk with a blank expression."

"It sounds exactly like them," Calvin says, confused.

"I believe Jeff was telling the truth about them being the key. We need to make sure and protect as many as we can."

"I agree. I'm planning on heading over to the gas station after we're done here. Do you want to meet me there? Otherwise, I can always text you and let you know what I find."

"Being able to experience this first hand sounds like a good idea. Hopefully, it will lead to a better understanding." Her body stiffens.

"There's something I've been meaning to tell you, but I'm not really sure how to approach the subject."

Calvin concentrates, giving her his full attention.

"I saw a vision while I was holding on to you earlier. I'm not sure how to say this, but I'm going to describe a woman, and I need you tell me if it's who I think it is."

"Sure," he answers, intrigued.

"Pale skin, long jet-black hair, with a small scar on the bridge of her nose. She's really quite beautiful."

"Janice," he mumbles. "You saw an image of my wife?"

"I believe so. She was wearing a long-sleeved plaid shirt and blue-jean shorts. Does your wife have a scar?"

"She does, but it's so faint I hardly ever notice it anymore. Was she alive?"

"Yes. She was completely surrounded by thousands of the lights. They were all around her. It was truly amazing to see."

"Was she in any danger?"

"No. She was smiling and had a calm way about her similar to when you came back to my office after disappearing. She gave me a message, but I'm pretty sure it was meant for you."

"What did she say?" Calvin asks.

"She told me, 'It's almost time.'"

"Time for what? Do you know what she meant?"

"No, I'm sorry," she says sympathetically.

"Do you think it was real?"

"I'm not sure, but it certainly seemed so."

"Where do we go from here?" Calvin asks.

"How about we circle back to when I saw the lights for the first time this morning?" Dr. Livingston says.

"Sure."

"The short version is that I found a red bandana in my bed under the covers, and I feel strongly that it belonged to the farmer. I was going to grab it to get a closer look, when the lights appeared out of nowhere. Several of them landed on my hand, and I felt the same electrical pulses as earlier. I even had the pulling in my stomach, although not nearly to the point that you described. During this time I had the distinct impression that if more had landed on me, I would have been invited to go with them."

"Really?"

"Yes. Although, I'm not sure where I would have been taken. I ended up panicking and pulling my hand away, but before I did I had a vision of Figure X, or a blurred version of him anyway."

"What did he do?"

"He referred to me as Laerton. Does this mean anything to you?"

Calvin shakes his head. "I can't say that it does."

He also showed me images of almost everyone I know and quite a few people I don't and referred to them as Laerton. My first thought was it must be a name. I Googled it and came up with zero persons in the US and Canada, which leads me to believe either it's not a name or it's not in English."

"Maybe it's Figure X's name," Calvin states.

"I wondered that too, but I don't think so. I get the impression it's important somehow, and it really bothers me that I can't figure it out. Just before he disappeared, I heard a phrase inside my head. I even saw images of it. I'm hoping you will know what it means."

Dr. Livingston pulls out her phone and clicks on the notes application, bringing up the page with the phrase "*Er'ouy lla Deknil Ot Nivlac.*" She hands the phone to Calvin, who reads over it several times before saying, "How did you ever remember to type that in? Are you sure you spelled it correctly?"

"Yes. It kept flooding into my head as if it were my own thought. This was happening so frequently it was difficult to think of anything else, until I captured it in my notes application. Oddly enough, as soon as it was typed and saved, the thought went away and hasn't been back since."

"Have you had a chance to research the phrase?"

"I have. Unfortunately, the only information I could find was on Deknil. This word pulled up a link to a Columbian college, which turned out to be nothing. I thought it might be German or French like your phrases, but I'm not sure."

Calvin nods and cringes at the thought of how frustrated he was by the two phrases he'd been given.

"Shortly after the images faded, I saw a shadow of some sort move across my wall and into the master bath. Have you ever seen anything like that before?"

"No. How big was the shadow?"

"It went by so fast, but I'm pretty sure it was the size and shape of a person," she says reluctantly. "Unfortunately, that's not the worst part. I ended up seeing the farmer shortly after in my mirror in the same bathroom. He told me, 'Eight days.' Does this mean anything to you?"

Calvin's expression changes to a look of shock. "Till we die."

"What do you mean?"

"I was talking to Jeff yesterday, and I thought he was telling me things for shock value. He mentioned in one of our conversations that we only had nine days left to live. That was yesterday. Which means today it would be eight. It seems like an awfully big coincidence to not be related. I wonder if this is one of the things Kathy was afraid Jeff had told me."

"Maybe. But how could it be true?"

"I have no idea. How can any of this be true?"

Dr. Livingston nods before admitting, "I'm in way over my head."

"Me too. But what can we do about it?"

"I guess continue talking for now. Hopefully, we'll stumble across some information that will shed some light on our situations. Is there anything you can think of that we haven't already discussed that could be important?"

"I heard some news last night that I don't understand and was hoping you might be able to help me sort out in my head. It's about my wife's best friend, Alicia, who we've known for years. She came over a few days ago—Thursday to be exact—and last night Janice mentioned that Alicia and her family had all been killed in a car crash over a year ago. At first I thought I lost time again, but the more we spoke, the more I realized that somehow my wife's memory had been changed and tricked into believing this lie."

Calvin looks up and notices a tear run down Dr. Livingston's cheek.

"Are you feeling okay, Doc?"

"I'm sorry. The exact same thing happened to Judy, and I haven't fully adjusted to it yet. In my vision while holding on to you earlier, I also saw Judy being killed by a woman I suspect to be Kathy. During this time, I heard 'Laerton' whispered again. It was as if I was supposed to know what Figure X was trying to tell me."

"I'm feeling a little lost. Who is Judy?"

"She was the receptionist who was rude to you on Wednesday. I had a conversation with her that night and made her take Thursday and Friday off to regenerate. I feel like I'm to blame for her being gone, and the guilt is eating me up inside. If she had been here at work instead of home, she might still be alive," she says, unable to control the tears. "Excuse me. I'm sorry, but I need a minute."

Dr. Livingston rushes to the restroom. Closing the door behind her, she turns on the water full blast. *You lost it in front of a patient. What's wrong with you?*

Calvin sits in his chair feeling really uncomfortable, wondering if he should sneak out. He is overcome with guilt thinking, *If I hadn't complained about Judy Wednesday night, maybe she would still be alive.* His guilt worsens as he remembers leaving early that night and telling Dr. Livingston she should have time for the talk with Judy as he rushed out of her office.

She comes back in and apologizes for the outburst. "I'm feeling really emotional right now. Could be my hormones," she says, half serious.

Calvin only smiles, unsure how to respond. "Would you like to continue this another time?"

"No, I'm fine now. I think I needed a good cry. It's all been really hard for me to take lately, and the guilt over Judy was the last straw."

"So you think she died by Kathy's hand? That doesn't surprise me in the least."

"Actually, my vision from Figure X showed she was killed by Kathy, but Judy's son, Gary, told me she died in a car crash. He even said I was at the funeral."

"My wife pretty much said the same thing about Alicia and her family. By the way, it was also supposedly a car crash."

Dr. Livingston concentrates deeply. "This seems to be the complete opposite of your car accident."

"What do you mean?"

"You thought you wrecked your car but never actually suffered any of the damage or consequences of being in a true crash. On the other hand, Judy, along with your friend Alicia and her family, were never actually in a car crash, yet everyone is made to believe that's exactly how they died. I think we're onto a huge piece of the puzzle, but I don't know how it relates. Normally, two separate instances wouldn't be enough proof for something this complicated. However, I may have a third. Have you heard the name Pastor Smithers?"

"No, it doesn't sound familiar at all. Should I know him?"

"I wouldn't think so but figured I would check just in case. I have a strong hunch two sisters that attended an Alcoholics Anonymous meeting on Thursday at his church may have been murdered. Without going into too many specifics, I called Pastor Smithers, and he stated that both sisters were killed in a car accident over a year ago."

"That's interesting."

"I thought so too," she says, feeling like they're starting to make headway. "Not only do I think the two sisters are connected to this in some way, but we may have the proof we need to establish a timeline, based on several of the related deaths. We should start with the last day I saw Judy alive, which would have been Wednesday night. Her son mentioned she had been dead for roughly a year. The last time you saw Alicia alive would have been Thursday, and your wife gave you basically the same news about her, correct?"

"Yes, she said a little over a year."

"Lastly, the sisters I believe would have been killed on Thursday, and Pastor Smithers believes it was also over a year ago. I have so many questions in my head, but the one I keep coming back to is, why so many car accidents?"

"That's exactly what I was thinking."

"One variable I'm uncertain of is how the numbers relate."

"How do you mean?" Calvin asks.

"I have it on pretty good authority that the sisters would have had a number. However, I have no idea about Judy or Alicia. Did you ever see a number on Alicia's forehead or hear a whisper?"

"No, I didn't."

"So I should write this down, and we can come back to it if we ever have more proof. While I'm thinking of it, how is it that once these people are killed everyone else remembers their deaths as occurring roughly a year before? Who could be capable of brainwashing that many people at one time into believing that to be true?"

"Figure X," they both say at the same time without thinking.

"Have you ever seen a number or heard a whisper?" Calvin asks.

"Not yet."

"I wonder why your memory didn't default to thinking Judy had died over a year ago."

"I don't know. I spoke to my husband on the same day I found out and nonchalantly brought up the subject of Judy's funeral. He mentioned it was a nice service."

"What did you say to that?"

"I told him I agreed and switched the subject."

"This is crazy," Calvin mumbles.

"Do you think the number on the victims' foreheads could be related to some sort of pecking order?" Dr. Livingston asks.

"Absolutely."

"You sound confident. How about you let me in on the secret?"

"I had a vision of Kathy and Jeff in my front yard arguing about something. Kathy had a gun and was pointing it at Jeff. He wanted to know why she wasn't curious about what would happen if they stopped right now."

"Stopped what?" Dr. Livingston asks.

"It sounded like Jeff wanted to stop killing, but Kathy was afraid to break the pattern."

"Did she mention why?"

"Yes. She was afraid that if the pattern was broken, everyone would die."

"That doesn't make sense. Why would everyone die if they stopped killing?"

"I wish I knew. A third person walked up and gave a signal to Kathy."

"Then what happened?"

"Kathy shot and killed Jeff. She told him she would see him in five years. But then she said, 'Maybe,' as if she didn't know how this was going to end."

"Which means," Dr. Livingston says, her excitement building, "there's still a possibility we can influence the outcome."

"Exactly," he states with confidence.

"You mentioned you weren't able to identify the third person. Why is that? Was the figure blurred out like Figure X?"

"No. All I could see of the third person was more like a shadow of a person with no distinguishable characteristics. One thing I feel I should mention about Kathy: she was smiling when she killed Jeff. There's something really wrong with her. Once she received the signal, she never even hesitated to pull the trigger."

"Why do you think she's taking orders from this person?" Dr. Livingston asks.

"I don't know, but the next part is really disturbing and involves you. Are you sure you want me to continue?"

"I think you have to. What if it's important to helping us find answers?"

Calvin hesitates. "I've replayed the words from Kathy's lips in my head many times, trying to make sense out of any of it. She told the third person that 'All nine were dead, and everything is almost complete.' She then said, 'The doctor's family is dead, but not the doctor…Not yet anyway.'"

Calvin looks over at Dr. Livingston and is relieved that she's taking the news well so far.

"What else?" she asks, her voice sounding as if she is trying to distance herself from the details of the conversation.

"She turned to the front of my house and pointed, while saying, 'Our next move is to get rid of your family.' Shortly after, I woke up in my car, sitting in my driveway and staring at the same spot my vision had taken place. Everything from the vision was gone. I'm not sure if it was supposed to be a warning for the future or if it has already taken place in the past. Or maybe it doesn't mean anything at all." Calvin looks up and notices Dr. Livingston losing focus. "Are you okay, Doc?"

"Yes, I'm fine."

"Kathy never specifically mentioned your name. She only stated the doctor and the doctor's family. I don't get the impression she was talking about you and your family. It feels like something that happened in the past rather than what will happen in the future."

"Do you know if you are the third person?"

"I thought so at first but could never be certain."

"What do you mean?"

"At first I assumed she was talking to me, but let's pretend that Janice was the third person. Wouldn't Kathy's words, 'Our next move is to get rid of your family,' still be true? Not that I think Janice would ever hurt me or Daniel, but it works both ways."

Dr. Livingston's attention diverts to her family's safety. She continues taking notes for a moment, then says, "I think this is a good place to stop for today."

"Sure," Calvin responds. "If nothing is happening at the Shell station, I won't bother you with a text."

"Actually, it's no bother. I would prefer to know either way so I'm not just sitting around wondering."

"Makes sense," Calvin says while getting to his feet. "Are you sure you're okay? You seem distant and cut off all of a sudden. I shouldn't have told you what Kathy said in my vision."

"I disagree. Please don't ever hide anything if there's a chance it might be related. Especially something as important as this. I'm planning on checking in with my husband in just a few minutes. I'm sure everything's fine."

"I'm sure it is too. I'll text you in about twenty minutes."

Dr. Livingston nods as Calvin slowly turns and heads for the hall, feeling guilty, wondering if he may have said too much. She impatiently waits for the buzzer of the front door to echo off the walls before frantically dialing her husband. Her anticipation builds with each ring as she firmly presses the phone tightly against her ear.

"Come on, Jack, pick up," she mumbles. The series of unanswered rings continues, until her heart almost stops at the sound of his voice. "Hi, this is Jack. I'm not able to answer..." She lowers her phone down by her side, refusing to hang up, and listens to the thud as it slips through her fingers and falls to the floor.

CHAPTER

24

OVER TWENTY MINUTES have passed since Calvin's session with Dr. Livingston. His mind drifts in and out of deep thought as he nervously drives down the service road a couple hundred feet from the Shell station. Without warning, he imagines blurred, faceless people and unfamiliar screams of panic fill his head.

"Please stop," he mumbles, consumed with fear.

"You caused this," his inner voice whispers.

"What? No, I didn't," Calvin says angrily to an empty car, snapping back to reality.

He immediately yanks the wheel. His tires squeal as he makes the quick right turn into the parking lot and comes to a complete stop.

His heart pounds, and his hands shake. He closes his eyes, desperately trying to clear his mind. After a few deep breaths, he scans the area, looking for signs of life, and spots the older woman's Honda Accord beside the first set of gas pumps closest to him. Farther in the distance, he sees the black BMW belonging to one of the teenagers parked in front of the store. *Okay. I found their cars. Now where are the remaining five people?* He removes his foot from the brake, heads down the left side of the building and parks in his usual spot next to the water and air machine. An eerie feeling hovers over him, causing him to shudder. He grabs his phone and scrolls through a list of contacts before sending a text to Dr. Livingston. *"Both cars are here at the Shell station, but I haven't found any of the people yet. Are you still coming?"*

"Yes. I'll be leaving the office shortly. I have a couple of things I want to finish first."

"Sounds good. How's the family?"

"They're fine. I finally got ahold of my husband after three attempts. Apparently, he had left his phone in the car while he and my daughter were at the park. I swear I'm going to duct-tape his phone to his hand the next time I see him."

"Lol…I'm glad they're okay. Someone in a forest-green Buick just pulled in behind me. Does this vehicle sound familiar?"

"No. Sorry."

Calvin tosses his phone in the passenger seat and watches intently through his rearview mirror, cringing as he recognizes Kathy behind the wheel. Jeff opens the passenger door and, while making his way to the front of the Buick, gestures hello with a simple wave.

"Seriously?" Calvin mumbles. *What, are we buddies now?*

Kathy strolls around the car, refusing to take her eyes off of Calvin, displaying a crooked smile, sending shivers all the way down his spine. She joins Jeff at the front of her car and leans against the hood, where they stay quietly chain-smoking for nearly thirty minutes.

Calvin sighs in relief when he spots Dr. Livingston's Mercedes driving up behind Kathy's car.

Jeff grinds the butt of a half-smoked cigarette into the cement and rushes over to meet with her. She shuts her door behind her and is surprised at how much he reeks of cigarettes as he approaches.

Jeff places his index finger up to his mouth with a look of guilt. "Shh, don't say a word. I have something for you." He uses his body as a shield and nonchalantly places the gun in her hands. "This needs to be a secret just between us. I was going to wait until our next appointment to return it, but this is as good a place as any, I suppose. You might not want to let Kathy see you with it, unless you're looking for a fight."

His bright red hair blows gently in the wind as the heat from the sunlight overhead is unbearable. *Something is mesmerizing about his light green eyes,* Dr. Livingston thinks, feeling herself slipping away to another place. She studies his movements and breaks the trance, noticing a smirk forming in the corner of his mouth.

"Thanks for letting me borrow your gun."

Dr. Livingston feels her blood pressure rising. "I want us to be perfectly clear on the facts. You stole it from me. You did not borrow it, and I don't appreciate your breaking our trust." The disdain in her voice rings out loudly.

Jeff looks away, mumbling, "You'll understand later, I promise."

"Did you use it?"

He looks back, his expression stone cold. "Would it matter?"

"It would to me."

"Not if you knew what I know."

"Then tell me," she commands, trying to bait him into a confession. "I think you owe me at least that much. Did you kill anyone with it?"

"No need to worry, Doctor. Even if I did, nothing could ever be traced back to you."

"So you say. What if you're wrong?"

"I'm not," he blurts out, losing interest. His attention diverts to a figure walking up to Kathy. "Frank's here. I gotta go. Make sure that gun stays hidden. It's important."

"Fine. I'll put it in my car."

"No. You have to keep it on you. Trust me," Jeff says sharply before jogging over to Kathy.

Dr. Livingston places the pistol in her shorts pocket, using her hand to block the bulge. *He must know something, and he's trying to protect me. Otherwise, why would he want me to bring my gun?* She glances up and feels her heart flutter as Calvin walks past Kathy's car, all three glaring at him with every step. His body's rigid, and his movements are carefully calculated. She senses his nervousness and unknowingly holds her breath as her apprehension builds. Calvin's demeanor softens and his confidence returns the closer he gets to Dr. Livingston.

As he approaches, she lets out a deep breath, feeling her fear weaken, and with a steady hand points over to Kathy's car. "Do you know who Frank is?"

"No. I've never seen him before. I have a weird feeling, Doc."

"I know. Me too."

Kathy, Frank, and Jeff in unison turn and follow the worn dirt path leading up to the gate and make their way through the field. They stop ten feet from the entrance to the wooded area.

Dr. Livingston follows them with her eyes before asking Calvin with uncertainty, "Should we follow them?"

"Yes. As long as we're careful and keep our distance. I don't trust Kathy, and I know for a fact she's dangerous, but I couldn't imagine she would do anything with both of us here. Besides, I get the impression Jeff is coming around."

"I wouldn't be too sure about that. He seems to be a better actor than he is a person."

Calvin laughs, caught off guard. "Nicely put."

"Sorry. I was out of line. Please forget I said anything."

"No problem. If it makes you feel any better, I agree with you a hundred percent."

Dr. Livingston's dark brown eyes sparkle as a smile crosses her face. "I would feel better if I knew for sure what was about to happen."

"Me too."

Although neither says so, they both realize what must be done. Calvin takes the lead, with Dr. Livingston following behind in sync with each step, until they are roughly twenty feet away from the wooded area. The three teenagers, the older woman, and her grandson file out from the seclusion of the flowery bushes and dark green shrubbery. They maintain an even pace and stop abruptly after only a few steps.

Dr. Livingston is taken aback by the appearance of each of the remaining five. Her stomach immediately knots when she glances over and sees the number zero etched into all three girls' foreheads. She turns to Calvin and hears a whisper, "Zero days left."

"Do you see the number zero on the teenagers?" Calvin asks.

"Yes."

"Did you hear the—"

"Yes."

"Something must have changed," Calvin says, intrigued. "Last time I saw them, there weren't numbers on their foreheads."

Jeff turns away from Kathy and Frank and walks toward Calvin and Dr. Livingston.

"How do you feel now that you've seen the numbers?" Calvin asks.

Dr. Livingston takes a breath, feeling her face become flush with uneasiness. "A certain part of me is exhilarated, but in a morbid-curiosity kind of way."

"What about the rest of you?"

"Anxious and petrified with fear," she says without hesitation. "Do you really think they won't do anything as long as we're here?"

"Yes."

"I hope not. You were right in your description of the remaining five. They don't seem to know their surroundings or have any emotions. I haven't been able to look away yet. I can't believe they're still wearing the same clothes. Isn't this the fourth day in a row?"

"As far as I know. I saw them on Wednesday for the first time, and all five are still wearing the same thing. How come?"

"I'm not sure, just curious more than anything else. I sent an e-mail to my police officer friend, Robert, with the picture attachments before I drove here. Hopefully, he will be able to find something out sooner than later. I'll let you know once I hear any news."

"Thanks, Doc," Calvin says, glaring at Jeff as he walks up.

"I'm sorry, I can't let either of you go any farther," Jeff says with a snarl.

"Do you realize if anything happens to any of those people and you allow it, you're just as guilty?" Dr. Livingston asks.

"It's okay, Doctor, this is meant to happen this way," Jeff says.

Calvin chimes in, "As I've said before, I'm not a violent man, but if you try and stop us from passing you will be forcing my hand."

Dr. Livingston reaches out and rests her arm across Calvin's chest before turning back toward Jeff. "Please, can you give me this one?"

"Fine," Jeff replies. "But you owe me. Oh, and you better hurry."

Calvin bumps Jeff with his shoulder while passing, fed up with his attitude and hoping he will make a move. Dr. Livingston focuses on Frank and Kathy and is overcome with panic when she notices the three teenagers are now kneeling in front of them. Calvin instantly realizes what's about to happen and can hear the chanting of the older woman. He yells, "Stop!" as Kathy and Frank both pull out guns and point them at the girls. Shots ring out, sending all three teenagers falling face forward onto the dirt and grass as each of their lives is stolen away.

Dr. Livingston grabs hold of her pistol but decides against revealing it, realizing it would be certain death for her and most likely for Calvin. Instead, she yells out, "Why?" over and over, until Kathy is finally fed up and shouts, "Shut up! You're ruining this for me."

The lights appear and surround the bodies, and as they disappear, Dr. Livingston screams, "Do you realize these were only young girls who had their entire lives ahead of them? You have robbed them of the luxury of growing old. What gives you the right?"

"I do," Kathy spouts back. "I have chosen this right for myself and will exercise it as often as I please."

"Someone has to stop you before you hurt anyone else."

"Let me guess. You're that person?"

Dr. Livingston stays quiet for a moment, realizing there's no point in trying to reason with her, then says, "I guess nothing I say to you will make a difference. What if I try and appeal to your caring side?"

"My what? Okay, Doctor, you need to stop talking now before it's too late."

Calvin moves toward Kathy, prompting her to raise her gun. "Don't be stupid."

Jeff makes his way past him and stands over by Frank and Kathy. "Only two left. I can't believe we're so close to completing this stage."

"No thanks to you," Frank replies.

Dr. Livingston studies Kathy's face. "I've seen you in a vision."

"Good for you. I've seen you too, Dr. Livingston."

"How?"

"Long story. However, I expect you and I will be seeing each other in the near future under much different circumstances," she says in a tantalizing voice.

"Are you trying to frighten me?"

"Not in the slightest."

"Then explain what you meant." Dr. Livingston keeps her tone firm, hoping this will pressure her into answering.

"Maybe later. You look better than the last time."

"You seem like you have answers," Dr. Livingston states without acknowledging Kathy's response. "I have questions. Can I persuade you to meet me at my office for a free session?"

Kathy bursts into uncontrollable laughter, allowing a couple of snorts to escape on purpose. "I'm not sure you're ready for what I have to tell you."

"Did you kill Judy?" Dr. Livingston blurts out.

"Don't look at it as a killing. Look at it as setting her free."

"What about her eighteen-year-old son, who you've left motherless. I suppose you set him free as well?"

"Actually, I did," Kathy says proudly with a slight chuckle. "Shortly after you visited their house yesterday, to be exact. Sweet boy. He even thanked me in his last remaining breaths."

Dr. Livingston's eyes water, and she can feel the fury rising from deep inside. Moments before she loses it, Jeff yells, "Kathy, stop! What's wrong with you?"

"Stop what? And what is wrong with you? Why aren't you joining in? You were supposed to make the kill today. In fact, you were supposed to have done a lot of things that you seem to be slithering away from. You're becoming extremely predictable. All because you let this doctor lady get inside your head. I thought you would have learned from the last time. You're a disgrace."

Jeff says nothing, feeling Kathy's anger intensifying. He can barely contain his excitement, knowing he has crossed the line, and certain that only he can predict the outcome. Concerned he may be about to give away his plan, he looks down, pretending to be embarrassed, and mutters, "Sorry" as if his pride is wounded.

"I'm not letting this go," Kathy growls. "What do you have to say in your defense?"

"Nothing," he replies, fighting back a smile.

"That's too bad. You're no longer worth the effort." She turns to Frank and says with a scowl, "He's converted to their side. Kill him."

Without hesitation Frank reaches into the back of his pants and pulls out a revolver. Before he has a chance to pull the trigger, Calvin grabs him by the throat, knocks the gun out of his hand, and wrestles him to the ground. They continue struggling, trying their best to gain possession of the weapon and overpower each other. Frank manages to get the upper hand by bending Calvin's wrist backwards to the point of almost breaking, causing him to shriek with pain. Frank grabs hold of the gun and points it directly at Calvin's face.

Frank growls, "You should have minded your own business and let me kill Jeff."

The entire area goes quiet just seconds before one single gunshot rings out.

CHAPTER

25

THE COLOR IN Frank's face fades and he slumps forward. Dr. Livingston stands still, both arms extended, with her fingers tightly gripping her pistol. She lowers her trembling hands, mumbling *"Re'ew lla Nivlac"* several times, unaware of the meaning. Her expression is blank as the shock of killing someone for the first time sets in.

Calvin pushes Frank's lifeless body off of him. He wipes the blood staining his hands onto the grass before standing to his feet.

"What have you done?" Kathy asks, staring directly at Dr. Livingston.

"I don't know. Everything happened so fast. I was afraid Frank was going to hurt Calvin, and I couldn't let that happen. The next thing I remember is pulling the trigger and hearing the shot."

"It's okay, Doc. You did the right thing in protecting me," Calvin says, reaching down for Frank's firearm.

"No!" Kathy yells, and backs him up by waving around her gun. "Leave it. I want it to be taken with him. Yours too," she says, pointing the muzzle at Dr. Livingston, who is staring down at Frank, still in a daze.

Jeff clears his throat, hoping to break her trance.

Kathy becomes angrier and shouts, "Dr. Livingston, I swear to God if you don't put your weapon down next to Frank, I will shoot you regardless of the order we are supposed to follow."

Calvin slowly moves over and stands in front of Dr. Livingston, separating her from Kathy, hoping to divert some of the attention onto him. Dr. Livingston takes a few steps toward Frank and does exactly as told, knowing she will most likely regret this decision.

The lights appear out of thin air and immediately surround Frank's dead body. Within an instant, he and both weapons have disappeared, leaving behind several groups of tiny white lights. Calvin reaches toward a cluster, but Jeff stops him. "These are just the leftovers. You can't touch them. I've tried many times."

Calvin pulls back his hand and watches as they vanish one by one.

Jeff makes his way over to Kathy in an attempt to show loyalty and get back into her good graces now that Frank is gone.

Trying her best to keep her composure, Dr. Livingston pushes any thoughts of Frank out of her head. Instead, she focuses on the opportunity in front of her, seeing a chance to gather information.

"I'm sorry I shot Frank," she says with sincerity. "I feel really guilty and wish I hadn't."

"It doesn't matter," Kathy responds harshly. "I personally didn't think he was going to make it the full eight days anyway. You just managed to take him sooner rather than later. I'm surprised you had it in you. The fact that you brought a gun with you proves you are much smarter than you were last time. You might have even earned a little respect from me today."

"Last time?"

"Yes. I'm the one who killed you."

"How did I—?"

"Come back? It's all part of the repeating cycle."

Dr. Livingston immediately flashes to her earlier conversation with Jeff. *Did he know we were going to need protection?* She moves back behind Calvin and, while using him as a shield, mouths, "Thank you" to Jeff as he turns, pretending not to notice.

"Maybe I will have that conversation with you at some point after all," Kathy says, starting to walk away.

"How about now? I don't need an office."

Kathy hesitates, feeling up for a challenge. "Convince me why I should."

"Because you're not afraid of divulging information, especially to someone who means so little to you. Consider this your one chance at bragging rights, knowing there will be zero consequences."

Kathy is intrigued realizing it could be fun. "You have three minutes. Better make them count."

Dr. Livingston wastes no time. "Have you ever been in Calvin's front yard?"

"Yes."

"Were you arguing with Jeff at the time?"

"How would you know that?" Kathy asks with an inquisitive look.

"I take that as a yes. Did you shoot him in the middle of Calvin's yard?"

"So what? That was nearly three years ago, and he's back now."

"Is three years the normal span of time for someone to come back?"

"No. It's always been five until now. Something has changed."

"Who was the third person?"

"It was Calvin. Or at least a version of him."

"I don't understand."

"You will in eight days. Patience is a virtue, Doctor."

"Do I die in eight days?"

"You would die right now if I had a choice in the matter," Kathy responds coldly.

"You didn't answer my question."

"Yes. Everyone is supposed to die in a maximum of eight days. However, I give you less than that."

Dr. Livingston switches her technique, hoping to take some of the focus off of herself. "Something significant must have happened for you to have such a deep hatred for people. Who made you this way?"

Kathy glances over at Jeff before locking eyes with Calvin. "I guess in a roundabout way he did," she says, pointing at Calvin.

"Why would Calvin have anything to do with how you turned out?"

"He just does. I suggest you move on to the next question."

"Is there a pecking order you have to follow?"

"Yes."

"Does this include the original nine?"

"The original what?"

"The nine people counting the three teenagers you and Frank just killed."

"Yes. It includes the original nine. Other than Calvin, they are the most important."

"Are they real people?"

"They were. Although it's been a while now. You have one minute left."

"What happens if you go out of order?"

"Everything changes, and certain people may not come back."

"You're talking about yourself?"

"Yes. Among others."

"Do you mean me?"

"You're iffy regardless. No offense, Doctor, but no one cares about you."

Shrugging off her comment, she asks, "Then do you mean Calvin?"

"No. Calvin needs to be one of the last and will always come back. Time's up," Kathy says as she smiles at Jeff, before turning away and walking toward the wooded area.

Dr. Livingston desperately wants more answers but senses Kathy is not the person to continue interrogating. She waits until the timing is right and says to Jeff, "I don't really approve of you stealing my gun, but I do appreciate you giving it back to me when you did. I think you might have saved our lives."

"No problem. You're changing me into a better person, I can feel it. I don't think I would have made it this far without you," he says, trying to conceal his smirk with his hand while pretending to cough.

Dr. Livingston recognizes the insincerity in his tone and follows his body language as the words are spoken. "You're not telling the truth."

Jeff ignores her, wondering how long it will take her to figure out his plan.

Dr. Livingston starts to speak but remembers something Jeff said in yesterday's discussion. "Calvin, do you mind if I talk to Jeff alone? I'm planning on going over a previous session, which falls under patient privilege."

Before he has a chance to answer, Jeff responds, "I don't mind, Doctor. Let him hear. There's a good chance some of what we say will include him anyway."

Dr. Livingston is hesitant at first, feeling a little skeptical about revealing patient information, but understands these are not normal circumstances. She looks at Jeff. "I'll continue, with your consent, as long as Calvin also agrees."

"Are you kidding? Of course I agree," he replies instantly.

Staring into Jeff's eyes, she says, "You mentioned in yesterday's session how easy it is to pad someone's ego. Are you trying to manipulate me, hoping I will let down my defenses?"

Jeff smiles, refusing to speak, watching Kathy disappear into the dense cover of the wooded area.

Dr. Livingston continues, "I think you're not telling me the whole truth when you say I'm helping change you into a better person. The only thing I think I may have done is place you in higher standing with Kathy. Is this why you took my gun? When did you begin planning to have Frank killed?"

"I'm confused. What are you talking about?" Calvin asks.

Jeff ignores him, feeling the tension in her voice rising. "It's been in the making since I saw Frank at the AA meeting. However, I didn't realize how close he and Kathy were until I mentioned how much I wanted him dead on the way back from Oklahoma."

Calvin shouts, "What? Why did you go to Oklahoma? Did you kill Alicia and her family?"

"I don't know anyone by the name of Alicia. Maybe you should describe her to me," Jeff answers, using a tantalizing tone, hoping for further irritation.

Calvin lunges toward Jeff but is only able to take one step before Dr. Livingston wedges herself between them.

She whispers to Calvin, "Please stop. This isn't helping."

Calvin takes a step back, keeping Jeff in full view. "We're not finished. Consequences or not, I am the one who will kill you when the timing is right."

Jeff says nothing, only winks at Calvin, trying to increase his agitation.

Dr. Livingston's patience is wearing thin, but she remains composed, knowing this could easily get out of hand.

"Please continue, Jeff," she says in a calming voice.

"Kathy made it perfectly clear that if I touch Frank, I die, which is what I'm guessing happened almost three years back. So the moment you pulled up, I knew I had a better way of getting rid of him. Not to mention bringing me and Kathy closer."

Dr. Livingston's expression changes as his words ring loudly in her head. She can feel the rage building but refuses to let it surface.

"How did you know Kathy would order Frank to kill you?"

"Let's just say she and I haven't been getting along lately."

"Kathy mentioned you were supposed to have killed the three teenagers today. Is that true?"

"Yes."

"Instead, you decided to hang back in the field and not commit the murders as originally planned because you knew it would not only make Kathy angry but also give us the impression you had changed. You gave just enough resistance before letting us pass to prevent us from saving the girls, but also to put on a show for the others."

"Don't forget I also managed to earn a favor from you in the process," Jeff says, laughing, enjoying their conversation. "I told you we were in tune. One might even say we are the same."

Dr. Livingston disregards his comment. "Please keep going."

He reaches in his pocket, pulls out a half-empty pack of Marlboros, and fumbles around, searching for his lighter. With the flick of his thumb, the flame engulfs the tip of the cigarette. He takes a long, deep drags and releases a thick cloud of smoke in Calvin's direction.

"Seriously?" Calvin mumbles.

Jeff smiles, then looks at Dr. Livingston. "I took your side when you and Kathy were arguing because I knew it would send her over the edge. She actually mentioned I was predictable," he says, shaking his head. "Talk about not having a clue. I'm the puppeteer pulling all the strings, not her."

"I understand now," Dr. Livingston says. "You knew Kathy would order Frank to kill you in front of us to show her dominance as the leader."

"Yes. I also knew Calvin would try and stop it, even if it meant saving little ole me. Another extremely predictable person, by the way," he says, looking at Calvin and mouthing, "Thank you."

"Which is where I came in," she mutters. "I shot Frank with my own gun that you handed me as soon as I got out of my car. I actually thought you were trying to help me. How naïve I must look in your eyes. I never stood a chance."

"Because you underestimated me."

"No. That's not correct. Because I trusted you. Don't confuse the two," Dr. Livingston snaps back. "By killing Frank I thought I was protecting Calvin, but in a sense I was protecting you both. You masterminded this whole plan, and we all played our parts."

Jeff takes a final drag before grinding the half cigarette into the dirt. Unable to contain his excitement, he claps several times, grinning widely.

"Last man standing wins or is at least guaranteed a spot back anyway."

"Spot back where?"

"Here. To have another chance to live again. We're coming up on the end, so I'm doing what I have to in order to guarantee I'm not left out again."

"Something you said a few moments ago stands out in my mind. Why do you think we are the same? Because I fell for your trap and killed Frank? You knowingly turned me into a murderer, but that doesn't make us the same."

"You don't understand what I'm trying to tell you," Jeff says, taking a step closer. "You and I are merging. *Re'ew lla Nivlac.*"

"What does that mean?" she asks.

"Did you see the zeros and hear the voices?"

"Yes."

"Then you are just as much a part of this as the rest of us. The last stages have begun. Surely you know your involvement is much more than a coincidence by now."

"If we are truly merging as you say, then help me find answers. What's the order of sequence Kathy referred to?"

"I can't tell you."

"Yes, you can. Stop thinking for just this once. If we're linked, then I need to know."

Jeff looks around and stares off into the trees for a few seconds. "Once the nine are gone, you are fair game."

"What about Calvin?"

"He must be one of the last. The cycle restarts with him."

"Restart what cycle?" Calvin asks, completely confused. "Why me?"

"I've said too much already. I should go."

Dr. Livingston, realizing they're not getting anywhere, decides to stroke Jeff's ego in a final attempt to keep him answering more questions. "What's your favor?"

Jeff doesn't say anything, only stares back blankly.

"You said I would owe you one. What do you want?"

A smile crosses his face. "Not a thing. You've already given me so much more than I could have ever asked for by killing Frank. What do you say we call it even?"

Kathy reappears from inside the thick covering of the wooded area. She pulls the leaves off of several flowering bushes and dark green shrubs while staring across the field at Jeff.

Feeling like he's being beckoned, he turns his body only partially toward her and gives her a short wave.

"She's making her presence known. I gotta go. I don't want the woman who thinks she's in charge to get suspicious."

"Wait," Dr. Livingston calls out. "What do you do while you're in the woods?"

"It's a place we go and reconnect. I would invite you in, but I'm afraid it's a little too soon."

"Reconnect with whom?" Dr. Livingston asks.

"Sometimes each other, but mostly ourselves."

"How?"

"It's easy. You just have to know how to listen." Jeff turns his back to Dr. Livingston before jogging the entire way, putting forth the extra effort for Kathy's benefit.

I'm a psychiatrist. Surely I know how to listen.

"Thanks for saving me, Doc," Calvin says, interrupting her train of thought.

"Of course."

"He really is slimy. I almost feel dirty."

Dr. Livingston laughs before giving in to the sickening feeling gnawing away at her conscience. *I can't believe he got the best of me.*

A gust of wind blows several leaves and branches, concentrating on a specific area midway up one of the larger oak trees. Calvin is overcome by an anxious feeling, knowing what is coming.

"Keep watching over there," he says, pointing to a group of trees. "I think we're about to be visited by Figure X."

Lights appear, and within seconds the blurred figure is standing on the oak branch with a bright glow around his right ankle. Calvin and Dr. Livingston simultaneously grab their heads as the pressure builds. They fight with every ounce of energy until the pain subsides. Calvin notices Dr. Livingston hunched over and places his hand on her back for reassurance. Suddenly, he can hear all her thoughts and feels the deep concern she has for Frank.

It's okay. You did what you had to.

Dr. Livingston stands and takes a few steps away, breaking contact. "What just happened? I was reading your mind again."

"I think so," he replies. "Only this time I could read yours as well."

They both turn, knowing Figure X is responsible, and startle when they notice he is now at the base of one of the trees, less than ten feet away.

Dr. Livingston lets out a screech and takes a step back. Her body stiffens, and her fear becomes unmanageable, causing her body to shake erratically as if consumed by chilling temperatures. Her eyes stay fixated, incapable of straying from the blurry shape of Figure X. She focuses on her breathing and slows her heart rate, allowing a calming sensation to blanket her. She feels a nudge on the side of her arm from Calvin as they watch in awe as Figure X approaches.

"What do you want from us?" she calls out unsteadily.

A deep, booming voice responds, "I am here only as a guide. You have nothing to fear in me."

She feels her thoughts slipping away and being replaced with images. The further her mind drifts, the more vivid the details become. She feels a slight tingling sensation as Calvin reaches out and interlaces his fingers with hers, filling their heads once again with each other's thoughts.

"Why can't we see you?" she asks.

The second the words leave her lips, the blurriness of Figure X begins fading one section at a time, starting with his chest and moving downwards. The figure is fully clothed in a short-sleeved, charcoal-gray uniform. His skin is golden brown, extremely smooth, and absent of hair. A connection forms among the three of them, and both Dr. Livingston and Calvin are instantly overcome with a strong feeling of peace and tranquility, relieving their minds of all afflictions.

This is wonderful, Dr. Livingston thinks.

Calvin concentrates on Figure X's face, but the blurriness remains. "Protect the three" echoes inside his head. *Protect which three?* Immediately, he's shown a series of images, starting with the farmer. The older woman and her grandson are next and have the number two on their foreheads. The images weaken, and without warning Figure X is surrounded by lights and vanishes.

Calvin and Dr. Livingston stand motionless for several moments, processing what has just taken place.

"How do we find the farmer to protect him?" she asks.

"I have no idea. We could always start with the mirror in your master bathroom."

Dr. Livingston cringes and releases her grip from his hand, finding his joke more harsh than funny. "Would you like to talk about what we just saw?"

"I don't think it's necessary. What are you planning on doing now?"

She looks at her watch and is relieved that it is only a little after 1:00. "I think I'm going to head home and spend time with my family," she says, pushing the thought of Frank as far out of her mind as possible.

"That sounds nice."

Calvin stares into her dark brown eyes and is overcome with nervousness. His heart begins to pound inside his chest. He wipes away small beads of sweat from his face. *This can't be happening. Please be a mistake.*

"Your body language changed. Are you okay?"

"I'm fine. I think I'm just worn out. It's been a long day." He leans over and gives her a side hug, afraid to break eye contact. "I'll see you on Monday. Thanks again for being there for me. I believe I owe you my life."

"Not a problem. Besides, with everything going on, maybe you can return the favor some time," she says with a partial smile.

Dr. Livingston turns toward her car, losing the eye contact Calvin had tried so hard to maintain. He reaches up and covers his ears but he can't block out the whispers, "Three days left."

CHAPTER

26

"WAIT," CALVIN CALLS OUT. "There's something I should tell you."

Dr. Livingston stops midstride. She slowly turns, fearing the worst, and as he approaches, she sees the worry written all over his face.

"I have something to tell you as well," Dr. Livingston says.

Calvin panics and says without thinking, "You first."

She pauses briefly, sensing his reluctance to share, but dismisses it quickly. "I believe I saw your dad."

"What do you mean? When?"

"While we were connected with Figure X."

"How old was he?"

"I'm terrible at guessing people's ages, but I would say late twenties, give or take."

"How do you know he was my dad?"

"Because he told me."

Calvin's face turns sullen. "Can you describe him?"

"He looked a lot like you. He was tall and thin, with dark hair and light brown eyes, not to mention you both have the same chin."

"Did he say what he wanted?"

Dr. Livingston hesitates, unsure how he will take the news. "He wanted me to tell you your time is almost finished here."

Calvin opens his mouth, and as the words are about to leave his lips he decides it isn't worth discussing. A flash of light several hundred feet in the air diverts their attention.

"What is that?" he asks, relieved for a reason to avoid telling her she is going to die in three days.

Dr. Livingston studies the object, admiring the combination of red and silver. She flashes back to yesterday's session with Jeff. "I know what this is."

"Yeah, what is it?"

"It's a beacon. Or at least that's how someone described it to me."

"I bet it was Jeff," he mumbles, not expecting a reply. "What is a beacon?"

"I'm not exactly sure, but I have a feeling we're supposed to follow it. Would you like to ride with me so we don't have to take separate cars?"

"Sure. That's a great idea," he says, watching as Dr. Livingston tilts her head to the left.

"What are you doing?"

"I'm checking my information to see if it's true. The colors are supposed to change, depending on how you view the object."

"Really?"

"If what I was told is accurate, then yes."

Calvin bends down placing his hands on his knees. "Wow, that's pretty cool. They really did change right in front of my eyes. Now it's more red than silver."

Dr. Livingston starts her car by remote, hoping to cool down the dark leather interior that has been baking in the Texas heat. She cups her hands around her eyes and stares up into the sky. "Looks like it might be somewhere in the northeast part of Allen. What do you think?"

"Judging by the distance, I would say that sounds about right," he replies, opening the passenger-side door.

Dr. Livingston takes her time getting into the car, adjusts the air, then switches the gear shift into drive. As they pass Kathy's car, Calvin is tempted to suggest flattening her tires but decides against it, fearing retaliation.

They head north on US 75 for a couple of minutes before Calvin breaks the silence. "I don't know that I would have ever guessed that my psychiatrist and I would be heading down the highway together after only four sessions. Please don't take offense, but it seems like I've known you much longer than that."

Dr. Livingston laughs while agreeing.

"Come to think of it, I've only missed three days of work so far."

"Have you decided how long you're planning on taking off?"

"Not really. I figure I will play it by ear."

"Probably a wise decision, considering everything that's been going on. Oh, I almost forgot. You mentioned there was something you wanted to tell me before we were distracted."

"I'm okay now. I think it would be better left unsaid for a while."

"That's fine. I'm here if you change your mind."

"Thanks," he says, feeling guilty.

Her concentration deepens as she focuses on aligning her car with the beacon. "It looks like I should take the next exit."

"I agree," he answers. "This thing is really weird. The longer I stare at it, the more blurry my focus becomes, and I still can't detect a shape."

"Me either," she says. "I was hoping it wasn't just me."

"It's not," he mutters, staring out the window. He reads the road sign up ahead: "Stacy Road Exit 37."

"I think I might know where we're headed."

Intrigued, Dr. Livingston asks, "Really? Where?"

"There's an old farmhouse not too far from here. I woke up on the ground next to the steps after my first blackout."

"That must have been unnerving. Was this recent?"

"Yes."

"About how many blackouts have you had to date?"

"Only two so far. Although both happened yesterday after our session and they were nearly back to back."

"That's a terrible way to start a Friday night. Why didn't you mention it this morning when we met at my office?"

"I don't think we ever made it that far. Besides, things started taking a turn for the worse, so I figured I would catch you up another time."

"Makes sense, and I appreciate that. Looks like we have a little time now, if you're up for it."

"Sure. Where do you want to start?"

"How about your blackout periods? Is there a common denominator that you can think of?"

"I saw a vision each time before they occurred."

"Were they the same images?"

"No. The first was of Janice covered in her own blood, screaming."

"That's horrible," she replies, driving down Stacy Road, heading east toward some construction.

"Yes, it was. The second happened at the farmhouse when I saw the vision of Kathy and Jeff arguing in my front yard. I eventually woke up sitting in my car, facing the exact spot where Kathy had killed Jeff," Calvin says, looking out ahead of them. "There's going to be a street up over the hill on the right side you might want to take. It looks like we will still be in line with the object if you do."

"Okay. Thanks. What do you think is special about the farmhouse? Did it look familiar in any way?"

"No. Not really. It's just a normal white wooded home with a little bit of acreage and a For Sale sign in front."

Dr. Livingston carefully turns onto a dirt road and instantly tenses, tightening her grip on the steering wheel, as rocks are kicked up from her tires, pinging the side and undercarriage of her Mercedes. Calvin watches her facial features change with each pebble.

"There's the house," he says, pointing to the left.

She switches on her signal out of habit as she passes the For Sale sign and turns into the driveway before placing her car in park.

"Sorry about your car, Doc."

"It's okay. I know I'm being silly. I've been told on more than one occasion by my husband that I'm oversensitive about scratches and dings."

"I'm the same way, so I completely understand."

Both look up through her sunroof at the beacon, which is directly in line with them.

"I guess this is the right place," Calvin says.

They sit without speaking for several moments, staring out at the farmhouse, waiting for something to happen. Dr. Livingston studies the front of the house, admiring how clean and fresh the white paint looks.

She glances around the manicured lawn before stating, "I like the wrap-around porch. Although I personally think either the previous owner or the realtor should have added a swing for the full effect."

Calvin smiles. "Are you in the market for a farmhouse, Doc?"

"No," she replies, laughing.

A shadow passes in front of the window and stops.

"I wonder if it's the owner of the house," he says. "I'm going to see if we can get a tour. Maybe there's a clue inside as to why we ended up here."

Calvin leaves the vehicle, walks up the two steps onto the porch, and knocks on the front door. The shadow moves away, vanishing inside the house. He pushes the doorbell, hoping this might do the trick, but is disappointed when it too goes unanswered. Slightly irritated, he walks to the left side of the porch and peeks in through a crack in the curtains. He sees a lethargic-seeming man standing there. He is portly, in his early sixties, and wearing a John Deere hat and black suspenders. His blue jeans are tight and pulled up well above his waist. Calvin signals to Dr. Livingston to join him, hoping together they might be able to persuade him to answer the door.

Walking up the steps, she continues scoping out the property and mumbles softly, nodding with approval. She comes up on Calvin, who is still peeking through the curtains.

"I know this person."

"You do? From where?" she asks.

"I don't know, but I have definitely seen him somewhere before."

"Maybe you should try and talk to him."

He clears his throat before calling out, "Excuse me, sir. I'm sorry to bother you, but my realtor and I were in the neighborhood. We really like this house and would like to take a tour, if at all possible. Are you the owner?"

"I don't know," the man replies.

Calvin is a little confused. "Do you need some help?"

Again the reply is "I don't know."

"Do you know who you are?" Dr. Livingston asks.

"I don't know. I've got to save them. Everyone is dying."

They look at each other.

She whispers, "We need to help him."

Calvin turns back to speak to the man and is shocked to find he is gone. The creak of the front door catches their attention as it opens slightly.

"Okay. That's a little spooky," Calvin says, pushing the door open in one swift motion, surprised that no one is around. "Well, that's not good. Did you see any shadows pass the window?"

Dr. Livingston shakes her head. An eerie silence has them both debating whether to continue.

"Maybe we should just leave," she says nervously.

"We were meant to show up to this particular house for a specific reason, and I want to know what it is," Calvin says, taking a step through the doorway. He calls out as soon as his foot hits the hardwood floor. "Is anyone in here?"

"Maybe we should call the police," Dr. Livingston says. "I would rather not be picked up for breaking and entering."

"And say what exactly?"

"I don't know? This feels all wrong."

He glances toward the kitchen and notices no one is there. "I admit this is really creepy, but we both know there is a beacon directly over this house. I'm guessing it's related somehow to the disappearance of this man. I don't have a strong feeling we are supposed to involve the police right now. Besides, if we don't find anyone within the next few minutes, we can leave, and I promise I'll lock the door behind us. What do you think?"

Dr. Livingston is reluctant but finally agrees. "That's fine, but I'm planning on staying right here at the doorway. I'm not comfortable walking around inside uninvited, even if it is a vacant home."

"I understand," he says, and calls out again, "Is anyone in here? Please answer. We have no intention of hurting you. We only want to help." Calvin glances in the direction of the living room and is surprised to find it empty as well. He spots a hallway and says, "Looks like this house only has two bedrooms. I'm going to check them out."

"Do it fast," she replies, feeling anxious.

He heads down the hall and enters the room located on his left, while she stands next to the front door with her hand tightly clenched around the knob. She peeks inside and stares in disbelief at a shadow swiftly moving across the top of the living room wall, next to the ceiling, heading in the direction of the hallway. "Calvin, watch out!"

He comes rushing out of the room and is met face to face by the portly man. He yells out, startled by his appearance. The entrance into the living room is now blocked by the stranger. Calvin stares into his light blue eyes, then studies the details of his rounded face.

"Please forgive me," the stranger whispers.

Calvin takes a couple of steps back. "Forgive you for what?" he asks curiously.

The man says nothing, only stares back with a blank expression.

Calvin's eyebrows arch, and an inquisitive look crosses his face. "You look really familiar to me. Do I know you?"

Without acknowledging Calvin's question, the stranger turns and faces Dr. Livingston, continuing to block off the living room. A bead of sweat trickles down the side of her face as she watches nervously.

Calvin, concerned she may be in danger, bulldozes past the man, and at the exact moment their bodies collide, images consume both Dr. Livingston and Calvin. They are unable to control the amount of thoughts flooding into their minds—visions of people with blurry faces scrambling around frantically. There are screams inside their heads as they see an image of the stranger running from person to person, asking if anyone needs help. The man in the suit is on his knees, leaning over a man wearing a leather jacket performing CPR. There are pieces of debris scattered all along the road. Only the back portion of a motorcycle remains intact. They immediately recognize this person, and as soon as Calvin whispers, "The motorcycle guy," the image disappears, and everything goes black. He opens his eyes and is alarmed to be sitting inside a car.

"Where am I?" he mumbles, looking around.

Next to him, slumped over in the driver's seat, is Dr. Livingston. He reaches over, shakes her and calls her name until she awakens.

"What's going on?" she asks. "Where are we?"

Calvin looks over, sees his car, and realizes it is still sitting in the same spot. "I think we're in your car back in the parking lot of the Shell station."

"How did we end up here? I don't remember driving."

"I don't think you did," he replies, looking down at the console, which shows 4:34 p.m. I think we lost time."

"Are you kidding?" Dr. Livingston asks while looking at her watch. "How is that possible? I wonder what triggered it. Do you think you are controlling these as well?"

"I don't think so. Looks like we are missing about three hours." Calvin glances around and realizes Kathy's car is gone. "I wonder where they went."

Dr. Livingston picks up her phone and notices she has one missed call, along with one voice message.

"Robert called," she says, before turning toward Calvin. "He's my police officer friend who I was telling you about. He works here in Plano. Do you mind if I listen over the speakers?"

"Not at all. That's one of my most favorite features of my car."

Dr. Livingston hits Play and hears, "Hi, Rachael. It's Robert returning your call. I found out some information on the plates you asked me to run a check on." The car goes quiet as he searches for the right words. "It's pretty strange. I hope it makes more sense to you than it did to me when I first discovered it. Anyway, I'm patrolling and will be driving around all day today, so if you have a chance, give me a call back. Talk to you soon."

A couple clicks are heard and then nothing but silence. Dr. Livingston, anxious to hear the news, calls him back immediately.

"Hello, this is Robert."

"Hi, Robert, it's Rachael. How are you?"

"I'm doing great. I'm guessing you're calling about the message I left you."

"I am. However, before you say anything I would like to let you know I have another person in the car listening to our conversation. He is directly involved, but I want to make sure you are okay with this before we continue."

"That's fine with me. Hi, my name is Robert to whoever is listening in," he says with a chuckle.

"Hi, Robert. My name is Calvin Johnston. Thanks for taking the time to help out."

"No problem."

Dr. Livingston chimes in, unable to contain herself. "So by your voice message, it seemed you have some interesting information for us. What did you find out?"

"Well, I ran the specialized plates 'SWEET P' and confirmed that they did in fact belong with a black BMW that matches the picture. However, this vehicle was involved in a fatal accident, killing all three teenagers inside. The multicar collision happened on the northbound side of US 75 at approximately 1:30 in the afternoon, according to the files."

"Let me guess. This happened one year ago, give or take," Dr. Livingston says.

"Actually, add two and you have a winner," he replies. "June 21 will mark the third anniversary. So basically, eight days from today."

"Eight days," she mouths to Calvin. "What else did you find out?"

"The yellow Honda Accord was a match to a car belonging to an older woman who was also killed in this accident."

"Was there a young boy with her?" Dr. Livingston asks.

"Let's see," Robert mumbles as he types on his keyboard. "Here it is. The older woman's name was Vera Langston, but I show no record of there being a boy with her."

"Do you have the cross streets of the accident?" Calvin asks.

"Yes. Let me give you the full information. I show northbound US 75 between Parker Road and Spring Creek Parkway."

Dr. Livingston asks, "Was anyone on a motorcycle killed?"

"Yes. A solitary man on a Harley. Would you like for me to try and pull his name as well?"

"No. That's okay."

"The pictures of some of the license plates you sent me didn't register in my system at all. I don't show any trace they ever existed."

"That's strange," she replies.

"I took the liberty of doing additional research for the final victim and came up with a name that didn't match any of the information you provided. Oh, wait," he mumbles. "I think I might have just realized something. Calvin, you mentioned your last name is Johnston."

"Yes, that's correct."

"There was a Johnston—"

Robert is interrupted by a tapping on his driver's-side window.

"Rachael, could you hold on for a few seconds," he says, placing his phone down next to him in the front seat of his patrol car. "Can I help you?"

"Yes, sir. Are you Officer Robert Blankenship?"

Dr. Livingston turns up the volume. "The sound is a little muffled, but the voice sounds really familiar."

"Please call me Robert."

"Robert, my name is Jeff Jergens, and I own a specialty plant store a few miles down from here. Well, actually it belongs to my fiancée, Kathy, as well."

"Hi, Robert. It's nice to meet you," Kathy says loud enough for Calvin and Dr. Livingston to hear plainly.

"Hello, ma'am."

Jeff takes Kathy's hand and says, "I would like to talk to you about a break-in that occurred three nights ago."

Dr. Livingston can feel her heart drop into her stomach as the realization sets in. She immediately yells, "Robert, they are dangerous! Don't talk to them!"

Jeff can hear a noise coming from the officer's front seat and asks, "Sounds like you might be on the phone. If this is your break time, we can come back."

"Not at all. My apologies," he responds and picks up the phone, saying quickly, "Rachael, I'll call you right back then hangs up."

Dr. Livingston, unsure what to do next, yells in a panic, "I just got Robert killed!"

Calvin, trying to console her, says, "Maybe not. Let's try him again."

She immediately hits Redial and feels her eyes water as the rings are unanswered and eventually go to voicemail.

"He's not answering," she says with a shaky voice. "What have I done?"

CHAPTER

27

DR. LIVINGSTON CLOSES her eyes and takes several deep breaths, hoping to calm her nerves. She says with uncertainty, "Maybe it's not too late for Robert. The last time I tried to contact Judy, I remember receiving a recording that her phone was no longer in service."

Calvin looks over, unable to make the connection between the two.

She shifts in her seat while holding on to the steering wheel for support. "At least Robert's voicemail picked up, which means his phone is still working. Therefore, it hasn't happened yet."

He nods for reassurance and watches as she fumbles around clumsily with shaky hands, trying to dial his number again. Without warning, the phone vibrates, causing her to shriek. Her heart beats faster the instant she realizes it's a text from Jeff. She positions the phone so that Calvin can also read it and mouths, *"We are at an impasse, Doctor. I have persuaded Kathy to leave this one alone. However, she wants something in return, which means you have a choice. Are you willing to suffer the consequences as a trade?"*

Without hesitation she types, *"Yes."*

"That's good news for Robert, but I'm not sure you're going to like the cost. One last thing, tell Crybaby to man up and tell you what you need to know…tick tock."

Dr. Livingston breathes a sigh of relief for Robert but is unable to relinquish the fear for her own well-being. She glances over at Calvin and notices that he looks nervous.

"You know something you're not sharing with me."

He looks down, unable to maintain eye contact and stop the dull ache from growing inside. *How could Jeff have figured this out?*

"What does he mean by 'tick tock'?"

"I'm sorry," Calvin says softly. "I wanted to say something sooner but wasn't sure how to approach the subject."

She falls into deep thought for several moments before looking into her rearview mirror and staring at the center of her light brown forehead. "Even though I can't see or feel anything, you might as well tell me what my number is. There's no point in prolonging the inevitable. Besides, I would much rather find out from you than Jeff."

Calvin responds anxiously, "When did you figure it out?"

"I didn't," she says disappointedly. "I was just guessing and hoping I was wrong."

He stares into her eyes and feels the concern radiating from them. "You have three days. I'm really sorry."

"Maybe it's not final yet," she says with desperation in her voice. "Did you hear the whispers?"

"Yes," he answers, refusing to break eye contact.

"When?"

"Right before we saw the beacon."

"We need to make a pact. You have to promise you will never keep pertinent information from me again."

Calvin looks away and glances into the parking lot of the Shell station where his car is parked.

"Please," she says. "I need to know that I can count on you if anything else happens."

"I promise."

"And I promise too."

"What are we going to do now?" he asks.

She takes one final deep breath and exhales quickly. "I don't know, but I'm not ready to die, so we're going to have to figure out a way around it. I don't suppose there was an actual time to go along with the day?"

Calvin senses she's trying hard to hide her feelings and gives a warm smile for emotional support. Suddenly, the ringing of her phone sounds from each of the speakers, catching them both off guard.

Dr. Livingston's entire persona changes. "Hey, Robert. Is everything okay?"

"Yeah, I'm sorry for the interruption. I had a couple approach my car inquiring about what to do about a break-in. Between us, they were really weird, constantly arguing back and forth. Chalk one up for the men versus the women, though. It looks like he might have won this round," Robert says with a chuckle, not realizing how close he'd almost come to dying.

Dr. Livingston weighs the consequences of telling him the truth and taking a chance on warning him, but she is fearful he may not be spared a second time.

Robert clears his throat. "Anyway, I'm free now, if you want to finish our conversation."

"Hi, Robert, it's Calvin Johnston again. You mentioned the last name of the final victim was also Johnston. Do you have the first name?"

Robert searches for a few seconds before coming back. "Rachael, this next part gets a little rough. I'm guessing you're on some sort of a fact-find, and I'm trying not to pry. But are you sure you wouldn't rather carry on this conversation with just the two of us?"

Dr. Livingston senses the stress in his voice and looks over at Calvin, who is vigorously shaking his head while mouthing, "No."

"I appreciate your concern, Robert, but I feel it's essential that Calvin be a participant in this conversation. I know this probably seems unorthodox, but under the circumstances I assure you it is necessary. You're just going to have to trust me."

Calvin's eyes widen as he hangs on every word, ready to join in and plead his side if needed.

"It's up to you," Robert says, his voice showing concern. "I can continue if that's what you feel is best. I'm just trying to look out for the guy."

"And we appreciate that," Dr. Livingston replies. "The fact that you actually care about other people as much as you do is one of the reasons we are so close."

Robert's radio crackles in the background, and the voice of dispatch can be heard echoing over her speakers.

"Is that for you?" she asks.

"No. Not this time, thankfully."

"That's good. So are you okay with Calvin staying on the call?"

"I guess so," he grumbles. "I'm not sure how else to say this, so I'm going to stick mainly to the report. Janice Johnston is the name of the last victim in the multicar collision that occurred on the northbound side of US 75."

Calvin's jaw drops as each word hits him like a slap in the face. How can that be? He has to be talking about a different woman with the same name.

Dr. Livingston places her hand on Calvin's and asks, "Is there any additional detail you could give us? We want to be sure we are speaking about the correct person."

"Of course," Robert replies. "Let's see. There was a police report filed on the 21st of June—so approximately three years ago. It shows Janice Johnston was pronounced dead at the scene after several attempts to revive her by the EMTs."

"Do you have the make, model, and year of the car?" she asks.

"I only have the make and year, listed as a black 2011 Acura."

"That's Janice's car," Calvin mumbles.

"I also have information that Calvin Johnston was the driver of this vehicle and was rushed to the hospital after sustaining several lacerations to the upper body and face. The cause of the crash, according to several eye-witnesses, was a wave of water thrown over the barrier wall separating the northbound traffic from the south, forcing more than one vehicle to lose control and skid uncontrollably." Robert stops talking and listens to the uncomfortable silence that follows. "Would you like for me to continue?"

Dr. Livingston tries to contain her confusion and stammers before finally blurting out, "Um, I don't know." She looks at Calvin, who is slumped over in his seat with very little coloring left in his face, and tries to imagine what could be going through his mind. "I think we've probably heard enough for now, unless you have any additional information you feel might be important."

"I don't believe so. Just more of the same."

"Thanks for all of your help. Once again, you have exceeded my expectations. I appreciate you taking time to research this for us."

"Sure. Anytime. I'll talk to you later." He hangs up.

Calvin stares blankly out the window, unable to speak, trying to digest every word that was just spoken.

CHAPTER

28

THE CLOCK ON the console changes to 5:54 p.m. Half an hour has passed and Calvin is still stuck in a daze. He sits motionless, glaring out the passenger-side window of Dr. Livingston's Mercedes into the empty field by the wooded area. Cold air blows wildly from both vents pointed directly at him.

Caught up in a moment of grief, she has fallen into deep concentration, imagining life without her in it. *My family,* she thinks, feeling her eyes water as she imagines the future. *Would Jack remarry? Would Sandra eventually replace me and call her Mom?* A sickening feeling in the pit of her stomach develops and worsens with each thought. *I can't get sucked into self-pity.*

Without warning, she slams her hand down onto the cool, dark leather of the driver's seat, causing her fingers to tingle on impact. Calvin slowly shifts his body until he's facing her and, without saying a word, lowers his head, before turning back.

The anger inside her builds as she yells, "That's enough. What is wrong with both of us? We need to snap out of it."

He continues sitting motionless, with his face sullen, giving off the appearance of someone ready to quit.

Dr. Livingston places her hand on his shoulder for reassurance and asks calmly, "Have you tried calling Janice?"

"Yes. Several times, and I've also sent five separate text messages."

"And?"

Calvin hesitates, not wanting to hear the words spoken out loud. He looks over and, while grimacing, he mutters, "Her phone is no longer in service."

Dr. Livingston, shocked at his response, carefully studies his mannerisms before choosing her next words. "We don't know anything for sure. When was the last time you spoke to her?"

"Sometime around 7:00 this morning. She and Daniel left for Oklahoma City to visit Alicia and her family's graves at the cemetery. Janice and I discussed it last night over pizza, but I explained to her I wasn't up for the trip."

She gently pats his shoulder, desperately wanting to be his friend rather than his therapist, but loses out to her instincts. "What are you thinking right at this moment?"

He hesitates, then answers, with regret in his voice, "I should have gone with them today instead of letting them make the trip alone. After that, I would say I'm pretty much numb. I don't know what to think or where to focus my thoughts."

"This is not your fault. You must—"

"I disagree. One way or another, I'm quite certain I am to blame."

Dr. Livingston removes her hand and senses he's slipping away. She watches as his frustrations build with each sent text. Realizing this may be her only chance, she distracts him by asking, "What time do you expect them back?"

Calvin lets out a long, deep sigh, slightly annoyed by the interruption. "If they come back, it shouldn't be until tomorrow, late afternoon. They were planning on spending the night and breaking the trip into two separate driving days."

"Maybe something's happened to her phone, and she hasn't realized it yet."

"I appreciate your efforts, Doc. Don't give up on me."

"Never."

He shifts in his seat until he is facing her. "Something just doesn't make sense. When can the dead come back as if nothing ever happened?"

"I don't know. But I'm pretty sure we both believe Jeff has figured out a way to do it. I think our best option would be to find him so we can get answers."

Dr. Livingston's phone vibrates, causing her to jump. Looking down, she realizes the text is from Robert.

FOR YOUR EYES ONLY.

Dr. Livingston nonchalantly turns her phone to where the screen is facing only her and reads, "I was doing a little extra research to make sure I hadn't missed anything important and stumbled onto something I wish I hadn't. I debated not telling you but didn't feel right withholding crucial information for Calvin's therapy. Will you call me as soon as you are alone?"

"Of course. Just give me a couple of minutes," she texts back before looking over at Calvin. "I have to make a quick phone call."

"Do you need me to wait outside?"

"No, you should stay in here, where it's cool. I'm not expecting it to last long."

Dr. Livingston steps out of the car with her phone in hand and immediately has her breath taken away by the high humidity. She looks back at her car with remorse, wishing she had thought this one through. After dialing Robert's number, she feels her anticipation growing with each unanswered ring.

"Hello, this is Robert."

"Hey, Robert, it's Rachael," she says, pacing back and forth a few feet from her car.

Sitting inside, Calvin listens as the hands-free feature blasts their conversation over the car speakers. He reaches over and turns down the volume, debating whether or not to alert them of his presence on the call. Dr. Livingston focuses only on the ground, keeping her back toward him.

"Sorry to bother you again, but I found additional information that I felt you should know. Can Calvin hear our conversation?"

"No. I stepped out of the car. What do you have for me?"

"It turns out Janice was pregnant the day of the accident."

"Are you sure? How did you confirm this?"

"I didn't realize the coroner's report was part of the file until I read the last page. By then it was too late, and I had already hung up. According to the information, she had just passed her first trimester, but it doesn't list how many months exactly. It really broke my heart to find out, on top of everything else, this was going to be their first child."

"I'm really confused. Maybe you can help clear up something for me."

"Sure. I'll do my best."

"You're saying that both Janice and the unborn child were killed in this accident?"

"That's correct."

"You also mentioned that this was going to be their first child."

"According to the obituaries, yes."

"That doesn't make sense. Calvin and Janice have a boy named Daniel around three years of age."

"Not according to the information I pulled. Do you think he could be adopted?"

"I'm not sure of anything anymore," she says, her voice fading.

"Would you like for me to continue digging?"

"No. I don't think that will be necessary."

"I'm sorry to bring additional bad news. I hope everything goes well. At least we know he's in good hands."

Dr. Livingston smiles briefly then says, "Good-bye."

She turns around and notices the horrified look on Calvin's face as he steps out of the car. He slams the door shut, and she wonders if he has somehow overheard bits and pieces.

"Please tell me you didn't hear any part of my conversation."

"Daniel isn't adopted," Calvin shouts out. "I am his biological father."

"How did you—"

"Your hands-free picked up."

"That's impossible. That's not how that feature is supposed to work."

"Well then, it's broken. Maybe Figure X had something to do with it. Besides, who cares? That's not really the point. So now I'm to believe my son doesn't exist?" Calvin stops and looks Dr. Livingston directly in the eyes, standing less than three feet from her. He notices that several beads of sweat have formed on her upper lip. "Robert specifically said Daniel was never born. So that makes you a hypocrite," he says, pointing his index finger at her, feeling his temper rising. "You weren't going to tell me."

"How do you know? You never gave me a chance," she says back abruptly.

She can feel her emotions running rampant and takes a couple of steps backwards, allowing for more room between them. She recognizes she is too involved and must distance herself as quickly as possible. "I understand you are in a delicate situation, and I want you to know I am here to help you through it." She takes in a quick, deep breath and exhales, thinking, *If I can change the focal point, maybe I can help calm him down.* "You mentioned Daniel is almost three. When is his birthday?"

"June 21."

Her eyes widen, and her eyebrows raise as the expression on her face changes to confusion. "My car is still running. Let's get in where it's cooler," she says, motioning with her hands.

Calvin makes his way to the passenger's side.

"Do you realize the importance of that date?" she asks

"No. I have no idea. My head is spinning right now, and I can hardly complete a thought."

"June 21 marks the anniversary of your wife's and unborn child's deaths."

He feels lightheaded and is unable to decipher the many questions rushing into his mind.

"What's happening?" he mutters. "Are you and Robert playing some kind of sick game with me?"

"No. I promise. I would never do that to anyone, especially you."

"How do I know you are not conspiring to make me think I'm crazy?"

"I understand you're upset, and I swear I'm on your side. If you were thinking clearly, you would know this to be true. We need to stick together in order to figure this out."

Calvin, incapable of hearing anything at this point, opens his door and stumbles out of the car, refusing to shut it behind him. He follows the worn dirt path leading to the field and stops just before the gate, his face beet red with anger. He focuses on the large oak trees at the opening of the wooded area and yells at the top of his lungs, "What do you want from me?"

A strong gust of wind blows a section of oak trees, violently ripping green leaves from their branches and sucking them up into the air. A whirlwind of lights forms at the base of the trees. Without hesitating, he heads straight for them, running full speed.

Dr. Livingston yells, "Calvin, stop! Not like this."

CHAPTER

29

THE CHIRPING FROM a cricket is the only noise within earshot. Calvin slowly opens his eyes and blinks a few times, trying to focus. He can feel the warmth from the earth rising through the dirt as he places his hand on a patch of grass and sits up. A slight breeze gently blows the leaves of nearby plants, allowing him to peek through a small break in the brush. He spots the Shell station off in the distance and notices that the passenger door to Dr. Livingston's Mercedes is still ajar. An overwhelming feeling of sadness and confusion settles in as thoughts of Janice and Daniel flood his mind.

He hears a groan coming from behind several large bushes and makes his way over, spotting Dr. Livingston lying on her side on top of a grouping of yellow and white flowers.

"Are you okay?" he asks, reaching out his hand and helping her up.

Her eyes dart around, trying to get a bearing on where she might be. "I'm fine. Just a little...confused."

"I'm sorry for my behavior earlier."

"Don't worry about it. I completely understand. Where are we?"

"I believe it's the wooded area."

"How?"

"I don't know. The last thing I remember was running and screaming toward Figure X."

She looks around, curious as to what significance this place holds before reaching into her pocket and pulling out her phone. A feeling of panic arises as she notices it's almost 7:00. *My dinner plans with Jack and Sandra,* she thinks while reading his text: *"Are we still on for seafood tonight?"*

She shakes her head in disbelief; unable to fight off the shame of knowing it will be the third time this month if she cancels. *I can't do this to him again, but I really need to stay. I refuse to die in three days.*

She looks over at Calvin. "How long are you planning on being here tonight?"

"As long as it takes. I have no one waiting for me at home. How come?"

"I'm debating cancelling my dinner plans with my husband and daughter, but before I do I want to make sure you weren't planning on leaving right away."

"Nope. I'll be here."

Dr. Livingston feels the sting of guilt with every word as she types, "I'm really sorry, but it doesn't look like I'll be able to join you tonight. I promise to make it up to you and Sandra."

"I kind of figured this much when I hadn't heard from you. Is everything okay?" Jack asks.

"Yes. Doing field research...I feel like I'm close to uncovering something important with one of my patients."

"How about brunch tomorrow at Max's Grill instead? You could have your usual mimosas and cinnamon rolls after sleeping in."

Dr. Livingston smiles, reminded of how understanding he has been. *"Sounds perfect.*

Good luck, and I love you."

"I love you too," Dr. Livingston responds and glances at Calvin fumbling with his phone. "I just cancelled my plans. I guess you're stuck with me for a while."

"I hope it's worth it."

"Me too."

While surveying the area for Figure X, Calvin trips over a small mound of dirt and almost falls. "What a way to spend our Saturday night—in the woods looking for aliens and answers. Should get interesting once it's dark."

Dr. Livingston nods while letting out a slight chuckle. "Have you heard from your wife yet?"

"No," he responds disappointedly. His shoulders slump, and his head lowers. "I'm getting the feeling…" Calvin's mouth hangs open as their eyes lock.

"What?" she asks eagerly.

Calvin's excitement grows. "I can't believe it."

"Your number…it's vanishing."

Feeling like a huge weight is being lifted off her shoulders, she blurts out, "Are you serious?"

He concentrates his focus solely on her light brown forehead, grinning happily as the number disappears, leaving no trace. "I can't believe it. Your number is completely gone. Congratulations!"

She takes a step back for a different perspective and looks around anxiously. "I wonder what changed." Feeling skeptical, she pulls out her phone and quickly scrolls through her text contacts. "Here it is," she says, pointing to a message. Jeff specifically stated, 'Are you willing to suffer the consequences as a trade?' But this isn't a consequence. We're missing something."

"Maybe you passed some sort of bravery test, and now they're rewarding you."

Dr. Livingston tilts her head slightly to the side and drops her shoulders in disbelief. "There's no way it would be that simple. Kathy really seems to have it out for me."

"Then maybe Figure X had something to do with it. Who cares? You should be ecstatic."

"I don't know. I would feel a lot better if I understood why."

Calvin's face hardens, and his stomach turns as he's overcome with nausea. "Come on!" he yells, flailing his arms in the air. "You've got to be kidding me."

Dr. Livingston, overcome with panic, looks behind her, wondering if someone is sneaking up on them. "What now?" she asks, her heart racing.

He immediately turns away, closing his eyes tightly, refusing to believe this could be happening again when he hears the whisper, "One day left." His fingers twitch, and the hairs on his arms stand as chills consume his body.

"What is it?"

Calvin turns to face her and says in a disheartening tone, "Your number didn't disappear after all. It only changed."

"Changed to what?"

"One," he sputters, unable to make eye contact. "I'm sorry. I'll do everything in my power to stop this from happening."

"How can I only have one more day to live?"

Calvin takes several steps backwards and turns, making his way deeper into the woods, mumbling, "This is my fault. I need to fix it somehow." His attention quickly diverts to an object moving in the thick part of the brush up ahead.

Dr. Livingston, unwilling to accept her altered fate, becomes angry to the point that her veins protrude from her forehead.

"I'm not going to let them get away with this," she calls out.

She gradually makes her way over to Calvin, who is pointing to an area farther in. She spots Figure X, motionless and camouflaged by the surroundings, standing less than ten feet from them. Startled, she lets out a scream. Her first impulse is to run, but her desire to find answers is much stronger. She remembers the peacefulness she felt last time and opens her mind, willing to let him in once again.

The blurriness surrounding Figure X begins to fade, starting with his head, revealing a face narrow and almost twice as long as theirs. His eyes are white as snow and shine through his translucent eyelids with each blink.

Dr. Livingston's concerns lessen as her fascination increases. She stares in awe, mesmerized by his image, presenting itself one section at a time. At first glance, his charcoal-gray uniform appears to be normal, revealing a single diamond-shaped badge on the left side of his chest. She focuses on the silky material and gasps as it changes colors with each of his movements, until blending in with all elements of the woods.

His golden-brown skin is smooth, devoid of any hair. A beam of sunlight pierces through the branches, uncovering a silver tint to his skin, undetectable without the presence of the sun.

Calvin whispers, "He looks almost human, doesn't he?"

"He is truly amazing," she replies as if hypnotized. "I wonder what other hidden abilities he must possess. I can't believe how much he towers over both of us. How tall are you?"

"Six foot three," Calvin answers. "Why?"

"I was trying to gain a perspective on his height. I'm guessing he must be several inches over seven feet tall. What do you think?"

Calvin, unsure why her comment has managed to hit a nerve, grumbles back, "I have no idea how tall he is."

She senses the frustration in his voice. "Last time we touched, we were able to read each other's mind. Do you think it would be possible again?"

"I hope so," Calvin replies, moving his hand toward hers.

The instant their fingers unite, they are inundated with each other's thoughts and overcome with peace as the connection among the three of them forms once again. Calvin closes his eyes and concentrates, unsure if Figure X will respond. *Do you have answers to my questions?*

The word "yes" comes rushing back.

Can you stop Dr. Livingston from dying in one day?

The word "no" enters his thoughts.

"Why not?" Calvin asks out loud, unwilling to accept that reply.

Figure X takes several steps in their direction. "It has to happen as part of a break in the cycle...Your cycle," a deep voice with a pleasing tone responds.

"Will she come back?"

"Nothing is certain at this point. One of the remaining three must be protected to break this cycle. Only then will your true path be revealed."

Calvin's hands shake as he shouts, "She has to die so that I can know which path will be chosen?"

Dr. Livingston keeps her eyes on Figure X, studying his human qualities from the upper and lower torso down to his five functioning fingers attached to each hand.

Sensing she needs to intervene, she asks, "What is your purpose here?"

"I am only meant to observe Calvin's behavior. To help shape some of his decisions with the ultimate goal of breaking the cycle."

"Then what?"

"I am hoping to persuade him to travel with me to my planet."

Calvin chimes in, "How about my family, or Dr. Livingston and her family? Are all of us welcome?"

"No. This invitation is meant solely for you."

Calvin's voice rises an octave as his temper flares. "Why not? That doesn't make sense. I don't know where you're from, but here on planet Earth we don't take people away from their families and friends. So just in case you're unclear, I am never going with you."

Dr. Livingston tugs at Calvin's hand, hoping to help him realize he is acting foolish. "What would he do on your planet?"

"He would live there permanently."

"When will we know which path has been chosen?"

"Soon."

"Any chance I can talk you into extending my life for more than just one day?" she asks him.

"Your path has already been decided and cannot be changed. *Uoy lliw eunitnoc ot evil edisni Nivlac.*"

Calvin leans over and whispers, "We'll figure something out. I promise."

Dr. Livingston, ignoring his comment, asks, "What does that mean?"

Figure X doesn't respond. Lights begin to appear and form from the ground up.

"Wait. I feel like I've lost my family," Calvin says, watching as Figure X responds by waving away the lights. Calvin clears his throat, trying to stall long enough to shake the anxiety eating away at him. "Did the accident involving the death of my wife and unborn child really happen?"

"Yes."

"Did they both die?"

"Yes."

"When?"

"Many years ago."

"I don't understand," Calvin replies. "What about my son? Did I ever have any children?"

"No."

"That's impossible. I have a son named Daniel who is three. I have held him in my arms many times and kissed him good night even more. He and my wife are what make my life worth living. How can you tell me these things?"

Figure X remains silent for several moments. "It is the truth."

With a shaky voice, Calvin asks, "Are they coming back to me?"

"No."

"Ever?"

"No. Not if the cycle can be broken."

Calvin releases Dr. Livingston's hand and takes several steps, until he is standing directly in front of Figure X. Breathing heavily, he stares into his glowing white eyes and says angrily, "Then I guess the cycle will complete. I have too much to lose otherwise."

Lights surround Figure X while Dr. Livingston frantically searches for one last question. "Is it true Calvin's father was also part of your research?"

Yes, it is true floods both their minds.

Figure X vanishes, leaving behind several small, twinkling lights in his place. Calvin reaches over and brushes his fingertips against a small grouping that has formed near him and feels a jolt of energy rushing through his body, knocking him to the ground. He looks up and sees Dr. Livingston standing quietly, concerned for his safety. *I hope he's not hurt* enters his thoughts.

Can you hear me? he thinks.

Yes.

How are we still reading each other's minds? Figure X is gone, and we're no longer touching.

I'm not sure, she thinks.

Without warning, they are both overcome by an image of Jeff and Kathy driving down the highway. The sound of Kathy's voice echoes inside of their heads as she carries on a conversation with Jeff.

"I can't wait to see the number one on Dr. Livingston's forehead," Kathy says with a laugh. "I wonder if she knows I'm the one who's going to kill her."

"I think she might have an idea. You haven't exactly been subtle," Jeff replies.

Calvin, completely baffled, mouths the words, "Can you hear them?"

Dr. Livingston quickly nods and holds her index finger up to her lips as she continues watching the images and listening closely.

Jeff's voice rings out, "I'm more excited about staring into her eyes and hearing the whispers 'One day left.'"

Kathy smiles, feeling her excitement build. "The old woman's and her grandson's time runs out tomorrow. When do you want to take care of them?"

"I'm not sure. I may have something going on."

Kathy pauses. "I was planning on sleeping in, but we can meet at the Shell station around 11:00 tomorrow morning, if that works for you."

"I don't know," Jeff replies hesitantly. "I have a certain pastor from our AA meeting that I was planning on paying a visit to before his Sunday morning service."

"Why? Pastor Smithers is insignificant in helping us complete the cycle. Don't you think you should stay focused?"

"I know. I just want to watch him squirm and beg for his life."

"Whatever. We can plan to take care of the old woman and her grandson at 2:00 tomorrow then, if that fits into your schedule," Kathy says sarcastically.

"I can live with that," Jeff snaps back. "Too bad Pastor Smithers won't be able to. Do you want to watch?"

"Of course," she replies, laughing. "Have you found the farmer yet?"

"No. He seems to have vanished without a trace."

"You realize it doesn't work without him, right? If we don't kill the remaining three, I'm not sure we will make it back. Pay attention when I tell you how important it is for us to kill all nine members before the cycle can be completed."

"I know. You have already reminded me about 100 times. Maybe we can locate him tonight when we listen inside the woods."

"I hope so," Kathy says, tapping on the brakes of her forest-green Buick as she slowly turns into the parking lot of the Shell station.

Driving down the left side of the building, Jeff scoots up to the edge of the passenger seat the instant he notices Dr. Livingston's Mercedes parked on the side.

"Now why would *you* be here on a Saturday night at 8:00?" he mumbles. "Do you see her anywhere?"

Kathy shakes her head. "Nope. But it looks like Calvin is here somewhere too."

She creeps up behind his Audi and turns off her car.

Jeff opens the glove compartment, grabs the revolver sitting on top of a stack of napkins, and checks each of the chambers, making sure it's loaded. "They must have been in a hurry. Her passenger door isn't shut."

Kathy scans the area thoroughly, and then gets out. "You don't think they figured out the secrets of the woods, do you?"

"No way. That would mean…"

"It would mean they're not only watching us right now but listening to every word we're saying."

"We should check it out just in case."

Jeff opens his door and, while stepping out of the car, secures the gun behind his back, halfway into his pants. Kathy leads with Jeff closely behind as they follow the dirt trail and head through the gate, picking up speed as they go.

"This is way too fast," Kathy says in a panic. "If they're already inside, we're much closer to the end than I thought. It's not supposed to happen like this."

"I know. So much for eight days left. There's no way anyone will last that long at this rate. Can all four of us occupy the woods at the same time?"

"I have no idea," she replies, trying to catch her breath. "I'm not sure what will…"

Both are suddenly stopped twenty feet from the edge of the woods.

"What's happening?" Jeff asks.

An enormous amount of pressure fills their heads, bringing both to their knees in an instant. They shut their eyes tightly and hold their hands up to their ears, screaming out from the intense pain.

Calvin looks at Dr. Livingston. "Now's our chance. We need to leave before it's too late."

They quickly emerge out of the woods and, as they approach Kathy and Jeff, Calvin shields Dr. Livingston with his body.

"We're not giving them the satisfaction of seeing your number or locking eyes with you this time."

With a straining voice, Kathy calls out as they pass, "You can't hide her from me for long. You have one day before I kill you. See you tomorrow, Dr. Livingston."

CHAPTER

30

CALVIN CONTINUES ESCORTING Dr. Livingston through the field with his arm draped around her shoulders. His pace increases the closer they get to the gate, until the realization sets in that his adrenaline is the driving force behind their speed. He quickly releases his hold, glancing backwards, unsure if they are being followed. He spots Kathy and Jeff crouched down on the ground and feels a sense of relief.

Dr. Livingston concentrates on slowing her breathing, interlacing her fingers, and placing them on top of her head. She gradually walks the last few remaining steps, taking in and pushing out several deep breaths, then settles in behind the wheel of her car. Calvin shuts the passenger door while keeping an eye on her, concerned by her slumped demeanor.

"Are you okay, Doc?" he asks, walking around to the driver's side.

She grinds her teeth, unsure if she will be able to suppress her emotions, and conscientiously fights the urge to shout, "I'm going to die tomorrow!" Instead, she forces a smile, starts her car and rolls down the window, unaware her hands are trembling.

"Try not to let Kathy get to you. We'll figure something out," he says, concealing the doubt in his voice. "We still have plenty of time.

Besides, if what they said is true, they still have to kill the older woman, the grandson, and the farmer, before coming after you."

She watches his mouth move but isn't able to comprehend any of his meanings. Instead, all of her attention is consumed by the thought of dying.

"I think I should go home and spend what time I have left with my family."

"That's a good idea. Why don't I come back tomorrow before 2:00? I can get the older woman and her grandson to safety by myself. You should rest."

"I can't," she snaps back. "Not knowing what I know. Besides, we would have a much better chance of protecting them together than apart."

Calvin's face softens, and his tone switches to concern. "I agree, but I'm worried what might happen if you get too close to Kathy. My advice would be to stay as far away from her as possible."

She nods, incapable of speaking. He can tell her spirit is broken and wishes he had never brought her into all of this. He stares into her saddened eyes, sensing she is trying to be strong purely for his benefit.

She turns toward the dashboard and adjusts the temperature of the air to a cooler setting, refusing to cry in front of him. She tries to maintain her composure, but to no avail. Her heart flutters when a tear trickles down her cheek and lands on her leg.

He places his hand on her shoulder and whispers, "Take care of yourself, Doc."

She reaches up and pats his hand, not able to face him, as more tears stream down her cheeks.

Calvin takes a few steps backwards and is consumed with emptiness when she drives away, afraid he will never see her again. An overwhelming feeling of despair seizes his thoughts as the realization that he is alone sinks in. He focuses on his family and dwells on the statement from Figure X that his son never existed. *That's impossible. How can that be?* he thinks, ignoring the dull pain eating away at his subconscious. "I have no one," he whispers to an empty parking lot.

He turns in the direction of the wooded area and is awestruck momentarily by the fluorescent glow of orange from the sun illuminating the sky above the treetops, signaling dusk. He cringes and feels his body tighten when both Jeff and Kathy sluggishly rise to their feet and stare in his direction. *I wonder if I were to kill them right now, would all of this end?*

Kathy blows him a kiss, then turns and faces Jeff. "We should talk about our options."

"I was just thinking the same thing," Jeff says, concentrating on wiping off the clumps of dirt stuck to his hands and legs. He violently shakes his arms, hoping to circulate the blood and remove the numbness from his fingers. "That was really weird. I couldn't move any part of my body for several minutes. What do you think happened?"

"Calvin happened," she replies, feeling her strength returning. "He's getting stronger and doesn't even realize it."

"Has anything like that ever happened to you before?"

"Never," Kathy says back quickly.

"I guess all four of us can't occupy the woods at the same time. That's good to know. You don't think they were watching us while they were in there, do you?"

"Of course they were."

"I bet you're right. That would explain how Calvin knew to hide Dr. Livingston's face as they passed." He replays the entire scenario and nods. "How much do you think they know?"

"More than they should at this point," Kathy responds. We need to assume they know everything. This reminds me of when you first came back. You had very little memory of the past or our purpose, until I introduced you to the wooded area."

"Yeah, but it took many trips until I was fully exposed. I must have entered at least three times before I was able to see the images and hear the conversations."

"That's true. But to be on the safe side, we should still probably kill the old woman and her grandson sooner."

Jeff acknowledges this by a quick nod and watches Calvin gradually walk to his car. "I wonder if they've figured out that they could kill either of us at any time without consequences."

"It doesn't matter. I don't think they have it in them."

"I disagree. Who knows what anyone is capable of when their life depends on it? Besides, you forget about Frank. Dr. Livingston didn't even hesitate before pulling the trigger."

Kathy remains silent and can almost feel fumes radiating as her anger increases. "There'll be one less irritation tomorrow," she mumbles.

Jeff realizes he hit a nerve and turns away briefly to hide his smile. "I'm just saying we should probably be careful with them, in case they decide to try something." He lights a cigarette and takes several deep drags, studying Calvin from a distance. "Why do you think everything is moving faster this time?"

Her expression becomes sullen. "Because we screwed up. We were supposed to make sure the farmer was the first to die. Instead, he is roaming around who knows where."

"He won't be a problem anymore," Jeff states with sincerity. "I'll focus on finding his whereabouts tonight as soon as we head into the woods."

"You'd better. Otherwise, these could be our last days indefinitely."

"I understand. I'll get it handled. What do we do about our plans?"

"Most likely they know about you wanting to kill Pastor Smithers tomorrow morning before his sermon."

"And?"

"You should push it off for now. It's too risky."

"Fine," Jeff states agitatedly. "What about the old woman and her grandson?"

"We should move them up."

"To when?"

"I'm not sure. I was thinking a few hours earlier."

He shakes his head. "That's too easy to figure out. How about midnight?"

"Why?"

"Because 12:00 marks the beginning of a new day. If what I'm thinking is correct, then their numbers should switch to zero, making them available for the picking."

Kathy laughs. "That's an excellent idea. I doubt Calvin or Dr. Livingston would be expecting it. All we need to do now is find out where the old woman and her grandson will be at that time. Are you ready for the woods?"

Jeff's attention is drawn away as he hears Calvin's Audi heading toward the service road. He watches the blinker flash several times, as Calvin makes the turn. Glancing back to her, he says, "I like it better that they may know everything. It kind of evens the playing field."

"You won't if the cycle doesn't repeat."

Kathy reaches over and takes the cigarette from Jeff's fingers and places it up to her lips before inhaling.

"Point taken." *Only four hours to midnight.* "Now that Calvin's gone, I'm ready for the woods. One thing before we go. You do realize the sun has almost set, right? Are you sure you're up for a stakeout in the dark?"

She nods, letting the cigarette slip out from between her fingers and onto the ground, then grinding the butt into the dirt. She blows out smoke in one steady stream and watches as a light breeze carries it away.

"I'm not afraid of the dark," she mumbles, before turning and taking the lead.

Approaching the wooded area, she pushes a few smaller branches back and feels several tickles from the leaves of a large fern brushing against her legs. Jeff stops briefly at the entrance, overwhelmed by an anxious feeling. *I'm not sure I'm ever going to get used to being in here.*

The covering of the trees blocks out most of the remaining light, forcing him to use the flashlight application on his phone. He walks several paces with it above his head, scanning the area cautiously, making his way in the direction of a grass path, dodging left to right to avoid being stabbed by branches spilling over into the trail. He travels in the opposite direction of the entrance, trying to put distance between him and Kathy.

Approaching an area dense with trees and bushes, he mutters with confidence, "This is the right place."

He closes his eyes and focuses on the farmer, hoping to discover his hidden location. After forty minutes of unsuccessful attempts, he allows his frustration to take over, causing him to pick up a dead branch and slam it against a neighboring tree.

The stress of knowing he is blowing his chance to prove himself has him rattled. *I need to clear my head.* He removes his revolver from the back of his pants and leans over and stretches out his stiffening lower back. His arms dangle helplessly in front for several seconds before he stands upright again.

He shoves the gun into the back of his pants and closes his eyes, channeling all of his frustrations onto Calvin. An image appears inside his mind. He watches the metallic gray Audi idling in Calvin's driveway inches away from the closed garage door. The headlights reflect off of the glossy aluminum, casting unstructured shadows several feet across the yard. Calvin stares blankly through the driver-side window and remembers his vision of Kathy killing Jeff.

Suddenly, Calvin panics and gasps for air. His eyesight fades, and his breathing turns shallow. He can feel a sharp pain in the exact spot on his chest where Jeff was shot. *Help me,* he thinks, wondering if this is the moment he is supposed to die. The increasing pain surpasses anything he has ever felt before, and just as it breaches the point of being unbearable it disappears, leaving him panting profusely. Feeling slightly disoriented, he stumbles out of his car and slowly makes his way over to the grassy area. He stands motionless for several minutes, surrounded only by shadows.

Jeff immediately flashes back to the day he was shot almost three years ago. The memories fill his mind, and the left side of his chest begins to tingle. He remembers being tricked and manipulated by Kathy, until the sound of single gunshot rings out in his mind. His anger becomes overpowering, devouring every thought. He places his hands out in front of him. *I need to calm down. It's too soon. Bide your time for your revenge.*

Calvin mimics the very words Jeff is thinking: "Bide your time for your revenge."

Jeff panics and breaks contact by clearing his mind. He abandons his entire thought process, unsure why this is happening. He hears a loud rustling noise charging toward him at full speed and is overcome with fear. He turns the face of his phone, lighting up the entire area, and grasps the handle of his revolver.

"Calvin. Is that you?" he asks, his voice trembling.

Kathy yells from ten feet back, "Turn it off. You're blinding me."

Jeff immediately releases his grip and changes the direction of the light.

"What's wrong with you?" she screams.

His breathing is erratic, his entire body shaking uncontrollably. "I'm freaking out. Calvin just entered my thoughts without my permission."

"It's really happening. It must only be days now. *Uoy era gnimoceb Nivlac*," she chants.

"What does that mean?"

"You are becoming Calvin," she answers in a monotone voice.

Everything goes quiet, and the whole area turns pitch black as his flashlight application suddenly shuts off.

"Now what's happening?"

He can hear dead leaves crunching and the snapping of small twigs with every footstep as the noises become closer and closer, until they suddenly stop. The silence is deafening. Feeling like his head is about to explode, he tries to focus, but his eyes haven't adjusted to the dark yet. He shakes his phone and tries several times to turn it on, without any luck. He reaches his hand out in front of his face, hoping to make contact.

"Hello," Jeff calls out, his voice shaky and raised an octave as his heart pounds inside his chest.

"I'm behind you," a voice whispers back.

Jeff jumps, startled by the warmth of Kathy's breath across his ear.

"This is about the time you tried to cross me."

He slowly reaches his hand behind his back, going for his gun, until he feels the tapping of the barrel of her revolver against his thigh.

"Don't think I won't kill you again if you are suddenly overcome with any illusions of grandeur. You do not control any of this. Stay within our boundaries."

Jeff realizes this is only a threat and lowers his hand back down to his side. He tries his phone again and this time is blinded as the light shines directly into his eyes. He repositions it behind him and is struck with an unnerving feeling, realizing she is no longer there. *I never heard her leave.* He stands in one place and spins in a complete circle with his light glaring, until a voice bellows out from the darkness, "I'm over here, and yes, it really happened. Nothing personal. I'm just protecting my interests. No hard feelings?"

Jeff mumbles, "Whatever" under his breath, still trying to understand how she managed to walk away without him knowing. He stands in one spot for nearly an hour, trying to make sense of everything, before giving up and channeling Calvin once more. *This time I need to stay focused and make sure he doesn't get inside my head.* He sees an image of him in his house, pacing back and forth in the kitchen with his cell phone in hand.

"What if he wants me to return to work?" Calvin mumbles, placing the phone down on the table and pressing Play before switching to speaker.

"Calvin, it's Darrel, your boss. I was just checking on you to see how you are doing. I know it's only been three workdays since you've taken your leave, but everyone at the office is concerned. It's just not the same without you. Anyway, I hope you are doing well. This is only a courtesy call. Please don't feel obligated to call me back."

He reaches for his phone as soon as the message stops and freezes, with his arm stretched outwards. An eerie feeling of being watched sneaks up on him, causing goose bumps to form all over his body. Closing his eyes he concentrates, and imagines he is in the wooded area with blackness all around. He visualizes an image of himself instead of Jeff standing there alone. His mind is inundated with Jeff's memories, almost to the point that it is too much too fast. He takes in every thought and every image before realizing what is happening.

I'm absorbing you, Calvin thinks, knowing Jeff is listening. I can feel us becoming one. You should stop pretending you know more than you do. In case you're interested, I'm the one who's going to kill you this time around, not Kathy. I saw the image earlier, and I can see it in your thoughts now.

Without hesitation, Jeff screams, "Get out of my head!" and falls to his knees.

Kathy rushes over and collides with Jeff, knocking him to the ground. "You need to leave the wooded area now! Calvin is too strong for you."

Jeff doesn't move. Instead, he lies on his back with his phone turned face down in the dirt.

"You are going to screw this up. Get out!"

He reaches over and picks up his phone, then hastily finds his way to the edge of the field by following the grass path.

What just happened? I lost my edge. Kathy's going to kill me.

He reaches behind himself and pulls out his revolver, unable to fight off the weird feeling that he needs to check his gun. He slowly opens the cylinder and can feel the pounding of each heartbeat inside his head. "There's no bullets," he whispers. *How could she have taken them?*

Kathy emerges from the wooded area and enters the field in full stride, her gun gripped firmly in her hand.

"Why are you checking for bullets? The older woman and her grandson aren't here yet. I've summoned them both just minutes ago. What happened with the farmer?"

Jeff takes several steps backwards, increasing the space between them. "I don't know. I can't find him anywhere."

"I can't believe you are the weak link twice in a row. I warned you to stay within the boundaries."

"I'm on your side. I looked for my bullets because you've gone a little crazy over the last hour, but we're fine now. Let's get the job done so we can move on."

She raises her gun and points it directly at his face, aiming very carefully and closing one eye. She takes several steps closer as Jeff takes several steps back.

A trickle of sweat rolls down the side of his face. "You're not the one who kills me this time!" he yells out, flushed with panic.

Kathy stops. "What did you say?"

"If I die, it isn't going to be by your hand."

She lowers her revolver. "How do you know this?"

"Calvin told me a few minutes ago."

"Is he listening now?"

"How could he? We're not inside the woods."

"Go home. I'll take care of the older woman and her grandson by myself and meet up with you later. You are compromising everything. *Uoy era gnimoceb Nivlac. Ew lla era.*"

"You keep saying phrases you know I don't understand. Tell me how to interpret them and I'll leave."

The words are backwards. *Uoy* is backwards for the word 'you.' *Era* is backwards for the word 'are.' Do you understand now?"

Jeff pauses and is trying to digest everything she is telling him when Kathy yells, "Do you understand or not? Hurry. We don't have much time. The older woman and grandson should be here any minute."

"I get it. It means, 'You are becoming Calvin. We all are.' But why would you say that?"

"Because we're losing. Now get out of here, in case he is listening through you."

CHAPTER

31

KATHY WAVES HER hands quickly, shooing Jeff away like a pesky fly, before turning into the wooded area and disappearing into the brush.

Jeff cups his hands and calls out, "I'll be back for you later."

He takes off, running full speed in the direction of the gate, accompanied only by darkness. Nearly fifty feet away, the light from the parking lot of the Shell station spills over onto the field as Jeff heads straight for it. His breaths are shallow, and his fists are clenched tightly. He tries to shake the unsettling questions rattling around in his brain, each one stepping over the other. *What is going on? Am I merging with Calvin? Can he really absorb me? What happens to me after?*

His footsteps are light and quick at first, until the weight of exhaustion begins to take its toll. He stops suddenly, inches away from the gate. Wheezing and hacking, he somehow musters enough strength to scream out, "Seriously?"

Turning around, he faces the woods, growling with anger. He shouts to Kathy, "How am I supposed to go anywhere without your car keys?"

Placing his hands on his knees, he tries to remember the last time he purposely ran anywhere and shakes his head in disbelief at his fatigued state. Uncontrollable deep coughs take over for several minutes as he contemplates smoking another cigarette, knowing it will probably finish him off for good. He glances up, hoping Kathy has emerged, but knows it's impossible to tell without the assistance of light. The entire area is devoid of sound.

"Are you listening to me?" He waits intently for any response.

An uneasy feeling arises as he stares out across the field into a blanket of never-ending blackness. The words "I'm absorbing you" devour his thoughts and infect his mind. He rests for a moment before turning on his light and using it to guide his way as he leisurely heads back to the cluster of trees. The closer he gets, the more defined the shape of each tree becomes. *I'm not usually scared of the dark, but there seems to be something really spooky about tonight.* He looks up and watches the leaves sway back and forth in the light breeze.

With the entrance of the woods less than ten feet away, he nervously reaches behind his back and pulls out his revolver while slowing down his strides. "Useless," he mumbles. *What point does an empty gun serve?* He stops and turns his head, glancing off in the distance toward the store, before noticing the soft glow of the shell-shaped sign next to the service road.

With a flick of the wrist, he pops open the cylinder of his gun and stares at each of the chambers in disbelief. *What is going on?* His left eye twitches nervously. *How are the bullets back? And how did—?*

His thoughts are interrupted by headlights reflecting off the trees, as a car pulls into the Shell station. He instantly recognizes the yellow Honda Accord passing under one of the streetlamps. Immediately, he changes the direction of his light to shine it on his watch for a second before turning it off. *Eleven fifty-seven. Right on cue.*

Hidden by darkness and feeling like a hunter stalking its prey, Jeff feels his excitement build with each passing second as she makes her way down the left side of the store. *Patience,* he thinks, taking a deep breath, desperately trying to slow down his pulse.

Kathy surfaces from within the depth of the wooded area, walking confidently with her head held high, still gripping her revolver tightly.

She walks up to Jeff, who is deeply focused, caught up by the prospect of another kill and unable to take his eyes off the car.

"What are you doing here? I told you to leave."

Kathy's shrill voice pierces through him like several sharp knives cutting down to the bone. Startled, he snaps his head around and is instantly put on defense.

"Really? It's hard to drive anywhere without keys."

"They're in the car under the driver's seat."

Jeff stares back, unwilling to contain the snarl on his face. "You could have mentioned that before I took off running."

"I always leave my keys under the seat. How do you not know this by now?"

They are disrupted by the faint sound of car doors shutting. The older woman and her grandson grab hold of each other's hands. They stand motionless next to her car for several moments before heading toward the woods and stopping at the gate. Kathy and Jeff immediately realize it must be midnight and move quickly to meet them. As they approach the gate, she notices that the area is lit up by the overflow lighting of the parking lot and tries to hide her enthusiasm. His reality comes crashing in around him the second he sees the innocence of the grandson's face. *I can't do this. He's just a child.*

The grandmother lines up with Kathy, while the grandson stands directly in front of Jeff. Guilt over what he knows must happen next eats at his conscience.

"I thought we were going to have to kill them in the dark. How exciting is this?" Kathy screeches. "Which one do you want?"

Jeff remains disturbingly still, unable to speak. What is happening to me? Something doesn't feel right.

"Hey. I'm talking to you. Which one do you want to kill?"

"I don't care," he sputters back.

"Fine. Then I have dibs on the kid."

She takes a step in front of him and lifts her gun to the face of the boy standing not much taller than three feet.

"Man, I may have to lean down for this one."

She notices their hands are still tightly clasping and stops.

"Do you think they will let go after I shoot him, or do you think she will keep hold of him up until he vanishes?" she asks before going on a rant. "I still can't believe we have light. That's awesome. Much better than I expected."

Jeff ignores almost everything Kathy is spewing out and can only concentrate on one thing. *Calvin, you are trying to turn me into something I'm not. I appreciate the effort, but it won't work. I know you are in my head. Say something, you coward.* His focus is broken by Kathy waving her arms. Glancing over, he senses he has been asked a direct question and nods.

She tightens her grip around the handle of her gun, eager to take the child first. With the barrel pointed at the ground, she stares at the grandson's black hair and lets out a squeal at the sight of the zero on his forehead. She turns and stares in the direction of the older woman, confirming the zero on her forehead as well.

"Why don't you just kick back and relax? I've got this."

Turning back to the grandson, she hears the whisper, "Zero days left."

Her eyes are gleaming at the prospect of standing over her kill as she raises her gun.

Feeling like his chest is up in his throat, Jeff closes his eyes, and before he knows what has happened, he yells, "Stop!" Opening his eyes, he continues, "I can't let you do it. Not like this."

He pushes her aside and wedges his way in between them.

"What's your problem? You know we have to kill both of them."

"Not by shooting him. He's, like, four or five years old."

"What do you care?"

"Because he's a child. Where's your decency?"

Jeff realizes, as the words leave his lips, that he is flirting with death. He should know better than to blatantly pick a fight with Kathy, yet there is a force inside him willing to fight for the survival of this boy. *Calvin, if you stay quiet, the boy dies.*

"Quit going soft," Kathy states angrily. "You know he's not real, right?"

"What do you mean?"

"None of the nine people are."

He looks down at the child and stares deeply into his brown eyes. The color is dull and seems to be lacking the vibrancy he is certain they once held. *Must be the poor lighting.*

Glancing back to Kathy, he says, "I remember you mentioned that to Calvin and Dr. Livingston yesterday, standing in this very field, but I thought you were only messing with them. You know, to keep them confused, so we don't lose our edge. How about you explain this to me? Because I don't understand."

"All nine people are some sort of twisted set of Calvin's memories. None of them are real. Not even this precious little boy with his cute little chubby cheeks."

"If that's the case, then how can we see them? Does it have something to do with that thing they call Figure X?"

"Sure. Let's go with that," she says, laughing.

Kathy takes a step in Jeff's direction and is eye to eye with him, her temper rising rapidly. "You really don't know much, do you? Get out of the way."

She nudges him until he is no longer in front, and lifts her arm, aiming her gun at the grandson from only inches away. She places the muzzle onto his forehead, grinning widely.

Jeff reaches up and moves the gun to his own chest instead. "I've already told you once, I am not going to let you shoot him just because you say he is not real."

"Stop playing around, you moron."

"I'm not. I don't believe you. If you can prove it to me, then he's all yours."

"Fine," Kathy says, fed up with his stupidity. "How about the fact that he has no emotions?"

"Again, he's four or five. How do you know he's not scared to death and afraid to move?"

"You deal with him then. I'm washing my hands of both of you as of right now." She shifts her weight to her left leg and is quiet for a few seconds. "But just so we are clear, if this child, his grandmother, and the farmer are not killed very soon, the cycle that has looped for several years will not repeat. This means we do not come back...period...end of story. Got it?"

"Yeah, I got it." Jeff is shocked at his own blatant disregard for Kathy and lowers his head in defeat. "You're right. I'm sorry."

She takes a couple of steps, lines up with the grandmother, and raises her gun, saying, "See you in the next life."

Three shots ring out. The grandmother instantly drops to the ground. Kathy stands over her body, waiting for her to disappear, but is disappointed when nothing changes.

"Where are the lights?" She looks around, confused. "Why is the body still here?"

The noise of the gunshots scares Jeff back to reality. He is surprised that the boy never even flinched. Jeff extends his arm, reaching toward the grandson, his hand suspended in midair. Within seconds, the boy's tiny digits have curled around his index finger, gripping it securely.

"You look real enough to me," Jeff says hoping to receive some sort of indication of the boy's free will. Instead, he is met only with an empty glare, as if something has left him hollowed out inside. *I guess that's proof enough for me.* He lowers to one knee and reaches over, placing one hand over the child's mouth and nose, cutting off all airflow. He brushes back several strands of his hair with his other hand and whispers, "It will be over soon. I'm sorry."

No! Stop! comes rushing into his thoughts as Calvin breaks through. Jeff feels his concentration slipping away as it becomes apparent that Calvin is truly in his head. The hairs on his arms stand straight up. *It's too late. You had your chance. Besides, this is the way it is supposed to be. Go away!*

Please show mercy, Calvin begs. He's just a child.

You and I both know he isn't real.

I need him. Don't forget you are the true leader, not Kathy.

I'm sorry. You know we have to do this. Now get out of my head, or I'll kill Dr. Livingston's family as well.

Unsure of everything at this point, Calvin screams out of desperation from his kitchen, "He's one of the last reminders I have of my wife. Please don't take that away from me."

Uninterested, Jeff concentrates on blocking Calvin and resists any future persuasion he might have, before changing his focus. He watches as the boy closes his eyes and lays his head helplessly on Jeff's chest. Jeff refuses him the air supply he needs to live and without any sort of struggle it is over. The tiny, lifeless body lies limp in Jeff's arms as he continues to smother him long after he has passed.

He glances over and sees Kathy pacing back and forth by the older woman's body, mumbling something too low-key for him to understand.

She stops and with concern ringing loudly in each word asks, "Is it done?"

"Yes," he whispers, unable to look up.

"The old woman is still here. What if she doesn't disappear?"

Jeff says nothing. Instead, he silently carries the grandson and lays him in his grandmother's arms. Closing the boy's eyes he rubs his soft jet-black hair one last time before muttering, "Good-bye." He is consumed with shame, knowing he is responsible, and is overcome with emptiness, which demolishes his insides. He takes a few steps backwards as the lights appear, and within an instant they are gone.

Kathy cheers, "Oh thank God, she finally disappeared. I thought I did something wrong."

With hate in his eyes, Jeff opens his mouth to say something, but he changes his mind at the last second. Instead, he lowers his head and walks quietly next to Kathy all the way to her car. *My heart has broken over a stupid child who has no importance to me whatsoever. What has Calvin done to me?*

CHAPTER

32

THE TIME ON the microwave changes to 1:07 a.m. Calvin sits hunched over in one of the six chairs surrounding his kitchen table, his face buried in both hands. He silently counts to ten while slightly moving his lips, hoping to rid Jeff from his mind and free himself up for sleep. He tenses as he hears Kathy talking in the background, his body reflexively cringing the louder her voice becomes. He is stunned by the amount of hatred bottled up within one person. Her uncaring tone fills his head, releasing a deep-seated fear he wasn't aware existed. His heart pounds with dread as he hears her say, "I found the farmer."

They must be in the wooded area.

Unexpectedly, the talking stops, and everything goes deathly quiet, as if they were listening to his thoughts. The pace of Calvin's breathing increases while he reflects upon the deaths of the older woman and her grandson. Flashes of images reveal themselves as he remembers witnessing everything through Jeff's eyes and questions his own emotions. *Why would it excite me that they both disappeared? What am I missing?* A rogue thought relating to the deaths lingers, causing him to be consumed by an anxious feeling. He nervously taps his fingers on the kitchen table.

Calvin knows the only way to figure this out is to replay the entire scenario. Reluctantly, he revisits each grueling detail, and as he vividly remembers Kathy cheering at the disappearance of both bodies, his heart flutters. He returns to the scene over and over, each time feeling increased eagerness building inside of him as if he had been there celebrating alongside her.

Why would this thrill me? He concentrates deeply, going over every aspect. "That's it," he calls out, pushing away from the table in one fluent motion, then rising to his feet. *It wasn't Jeff. I must have switched over to you at some point after the murders.*

Congratulations! I was wondering how long it was going to take you to figure it out.

What are you doing in my head, Kathy? You have no reason to be here.

I should be the one asking you. I've felt you loitering in my mind ever since Jeff took care of the grandson. Did you enjoy the show from my point of view?

Ignoring her question, Calvin thinks, *Am I absorbing you too?*

Not if I have anything to say about it.

You don't. At least I don't think you do. Now get out of my head!

A noise coming from the living room diverts his attention. Refusing to give up hope for the return of his family, Calvin mumbles "Janice" and rushes over. He bumps the sofa table, moving it several inches as he hurriedly makes his way around the couch. He imagines his wife and son walking through the front door as if nothing has changed, all the while knowing, deep down inside, that Janice is dead and Daniel was never born. He makes his way past the textured wall blocking his view and fumbles over an end table, barely catching the lamp before it hits the floor. As he reaches the living room, his face is gleaming and his eyes are wide with the expectation of seeing them standing in the doorway.

Instead of being greeted with open arms and laughter, he is met only by darkness and emptiness. He stands in one place, looking around for several moments. He is engulfed in the misery of reliving his loss again and again. He lowers his head and fights back tears as his eyes water uncontrollably. *You win.* He wonders if Jeff and Kathy are still listening. *I'm tired, and it's no longer worth it. Here's your one and only chance to kill me without a fight.*

He glances over at the couch; feeling exhausted, he grabs both decorative pillows and stacks them neatly against the corner of the couch. Falling into them face first, he drifts off to sleep within minutes of lying down but tosses and turns the entire night.

He hears the familiar clanking of a broken wheel as the sound of a cart makes its way toward him. He opens his eyes barely past a slit and sees two blurred shapes lurking over him.

"It shouldn't be too much longer now," a female voice whispers.

Overwhelmed with the possibility of Jeff and Kathy taking him up on his offer of surrender, he sits up abruptly, swinging his arms wildly and yelling "No!" at the top of his lungs. He looks around frantically, before realizing it was nothing other than his reoccurring dream taking a stab at his sanity one more time.

Still wearing the same clothes from last night, he decides against kicking off his shoes and sluggishly heads toward the kitchen to make a pot of coffee. Several minutes pass, and as he is pouring his first cup, he glances at the clock on the microwave showing 10:17 a.m.

"Wow. I guess I really needed some sleep."

He yawns at the thought of the word "sleep" and takes a small sip. Walking toward the living room with coffee cup in hand, he searches for the television remote. Lights appear within a few feet in front of where he is standing, only inches away from his sixty-inch plasma. He watches in confusion at the arrival of Figure X inside his house. Fear sets in, forcing him to take several steps backwards and scan the room for a weapon. Within seconds, he is overcome with a peaceful feeling as the outline of Figure X becomes clearer. Calvin's heart rate is racing even though he knows there is no danger.

The tall, slender figure stands over seven feet tall, wearing the identical charcoal-gray uniform as before, revealing the same diamond-shaped badge. Calvin nonchalantly looks down at the golden-brown hands and is relieved to see, again, five full fingers on each. The hairless creature moves his elongated face bit by bit until he is staring directly at Calvin. His beady eyes are set deeply into his face, leaving a hollowness surrounding the sockets and deepening the effect of the white glow. Calvin tries to contain his feelings but his anger rushes forth.

"I blame you for everything! Why aren't you stopping any of these bad things from happening?"

"It is not my job," a deep, soothing voice replies. "This is something you must work out on your own."

"Then why are you…. Oh that's right, I remember now. You are here to observe and to take me to your planet."

"Yes. Most importantly, we are also here to help guide you toward the right path, to not only break the cycle, but to end it for good."

"I overheard Jeff and Kathy talking about the nine people being memories of mine. Is this true?"

"Yes."

"I think Kathy and Jeff may still be in my head. Is there any way to block them?"

"The power to beckon or to block is already within you. It has always been there."

"Please tell me how."

"Trust that you are strong enough and it will happen."

Calvin closes his eyes and focuses on the one thing he knows to find strength. He imagines his wife standing in front of him with the long curls of her jet-black hair resting slightly past her shoulders. Her skin appears to be more pale than usual against her black shorts. Remembering his promise, he whispers, "I love you," at first glance not caring that the image isn't real. The longer he focuses, the more he can feel his muscles relax and the tension in his neck decrease. Knowing the pressure has lifted, he smiles and clears his mind of any unwanted intruders.

"Why is all of this happening to me?"

Several moments pass before Figure X speaks. "I can start from the beginning and show you many keys to help you unlock the answers to each of your questions."

"Why not just come out and tell me what I need to know?"

"It is better if you find the answers you seek."

"Based on what?"

"Long-term experience in working your case."

"How many years has it been?"

"Forty-one."

Calvin looks away in disbelief. "I'm forty-three. You're telling me this started when I was two?"

"That is incorrect."

"I don't understand. Will you explain it to me?"

"You were one of many scheduled to die the day of your accident. A colleague of mine had been researching your background information for several months, until it was decided by our council that you were no longer a person of interest."

"Council?"

"Yes. We have many different types of citizens on my planet, including humans. The council is responsible for the well-being and safety of each one. There are sixteen members, presiding over different regions. The closest I can come to explaining would be to compare them to your politicians, only without the corruption."

Calvin chuckles, before realizing that Figure X was not kidding. "What about the humans. How were they chosen?"

"All of our human habitants started out the very same way we approached you."

"How's that?"

"We followed a process that had been put in place and improved on for centuries. A monthly list is handed down from our council, revealing potential human candidates."

"Where does the list come from?"

"It is put together through studies, research, and on occasion we receive recommendations from other humans living within our communities. My colleague received your name as part of his list three months before you were scheduled to die."

The realization hits him hard like a slap in the face. "Oh my God." His voice quivers as he struggles to comprehend what he is being told. "Am I...*dead?*"

CHAPTER

33

A SILENCE FALLS in the room so devastating that Calvin can hear each shallow breath as he slowly exhales. Damaging images and thoughts run rampant throughout his head, exposing him to a whole new level of concern. He questions everything he knows to be true, inviting doubt to creep inside his mind and bits of reality to escape. Fear takes up residency as he repeats one more time, "Am I dead?"

A booming voice fills the room, echoing off the walls. "No. You are very much alive."

"Are you lying?"

"No. Your death never occurred."

Calvin sighs in relief, sensing that what he is hearing is the truth. *Okay. I need to calm down now.* "How is it you know when we are supposed to die? Are you or your colleagues responsible for human deaths?"

"No. We merely observe and offer our invitation, if selected."

"Why would I be on the list?"

"You were a potential candidate chosen from a select few worldwide."

"I was selected because of my father, wasn't I?"

"Yes. On many levels your father did help influence this decision, but your connection to us goes far deeper than you realize. After you were selected, my colleague would have been obligated to research your background information in great detail. Much time in preparation would have been spent collecting key parts before presenting his findings to the council."

"And?"

"You were not selected. Instead, another was taken in your place."

Calvin's face saddens. "It's because they realized I'm just an ordinary guy who was about to lose his wife and unborn son in a car accident."

"That is incorrect. You were supposed to die that day alongside your wife. Several of my coworkers were present and witnessed the miracle of your unexplained survival. Because of this, you became a person of interest within our council once again. Special permission was received to pursue you further and was granted with the understanding that you were only to be observed. You are the first recorded to have escaped death while having a representative as a witness, and so far the last. Because of this, an entire team three times the size of any other was assembled and dedicated specifically for you, starting that day. You state you are ordinary. In the eyes of all that are involved, you are nothing of the kind. I have quoted this exact statement, defending the extension of our involvement countless times."

"I'm confused. Your involvement has been extended countless times?"

"Yes. Every five years."

"And the extension was approved every time?"

"Yes."

"Based on what? Has something else happened?"

"A great deal of things."

"Like what?"

"We were able to determine from your memories that you saw my colleague the day of the accident. He also admits that you have seen him on more than one occasion without his consent. We are never and have never been seen, unless it is our intention. Except by you."

"I don't remember him or much about that day."

"It doesn't matter. With my guidance, I believe you will. All I ask is that you trust and follow my lead wherever it might take you. Is this agreeable?"

Calvin's mind races, filling up with question stacked upon question. He grimaces at the thought of never being able to filter through them all. "I don't know anything about you or where you're from. What you are asking from me is almost impossible to accept."

"This may be true, but if anyone is capable, we believe it to be you. At this moment, we are closer than we have ever been to breaking the cycle. With your trust, I am confident it will put you back on the right path and perhaps lead you to your final destiny."

Calvin's feelings are running wild, with skepticism highest on the list. "If what you are saying is true, then I am obligated to give you at least one chance. I am willing to trust you, but only until I have a reason not to. And if that day ever comes, you will lose me for good. That is the best I can do for now, with one remaining condition. I would like to find out more about you and your background. Do we have a deal?"

"I am not accustomed to speaking so freely about my life or the lives of my team members, especially to a case study. Once again I am faced with another first when dealing with you. This is a very critical moment, but I believe you are within your boundaries to make such a request. In an attempt to show you how serious we are, I will make the effort. This is also the best I can do for now. Is this agreeable?"

"I'm not going to be expected to go to your planet, am I?"

"You have received an open-ended invitation, redeemable after you have passed on."

"Hopefully, that won't be for a long time," Calvin says, laughing.

Figure X remains quiet, refusing to acknowledge or respond. Instead, he waits patiently until he hears the answer he desperately wants to hear.

"Yes, I agree," Calvin says, wondering what he is getting himself into.

"Then we will begin. When is the first time you saw me?"

"Wednesday of this week. I was headed to speak with Dr. Livingston as a new patient. I swear I had an accident on the way to my appointment, but I guess my mind was replaying bits and pieces of the actual wreck. As I left the Shell station and entered the ramp for US 75, I saw an image leaning against a green and white highway sign."

"What did the image look like?"

"I'm not really sure, because everything was all blurred out, except for something glowing on the right ankle."

Figure X nods in approval. "That matches the report filed. However, it was not me you saw. It was my colleague, Дми́трий Фома."

Calvin stares in amazement, realizing this must be Figure X's attempt at making the effort he promised only moments ago. "I think I recognize the language, but it sounds a little different coming from you. Is that Russian?"

"Yes. His name translates into 'Loves the Earth and Twin.' It was bestowed upon him by the council, signifying the completion of training for this mission. The name given to each member is unique, permanent, and always taken from our assigned regions."

Calvin shakes his head as he attempts to pronounce it. "It's never going to happen," he says, smiling. "Do you think he would be offended if I call him by a nickname?"

"He would be honored. This will be something that he and I will share as brothers."

Calvin's expression changes to inquisitive as his eyebrows arch upwards. "Brothers?"

"That is correct. My chosen name is Коля Фома, which is also Russian, and translates to 'Victor of the People and Twin.' It was recently changed."

"I'm confused. I thought you just said the names were permanent."

"There was a one-time exception to this rule because of the following I have had since my involvement in your case. Your success over the years has become my success."

"That seems like good news. Any chance you can give me examples or details?"

"This is where I am going to test your trust. Please forgive me, but I cannot continue any further at this time."

Calvin puts his frustrations on hold and says calmly, "I understand. How about we get back to the nickname for your brother?" He clears his head before thinking of Dr. Livingston and knows of only one name that would be fitting under these circumstances. "Since we refer to you as Figure X, how about we call your brother Figure Y? What do you think? Solve for X and Y? Too corny?" he asks, with doubt lingering in the air.

"That name suits him perfectly. He will be very pleased."

Calvin senses they are bonding and is beginning to feel more comfortable. "So that wasn't you in the oak tree either?"

"No. It would have been Figure Y. Do you remember the phrases he used on you?"

"Yes. Like it was yesterday. Both phrases are pretty much burned into my memory. *Peux-tu m'entendre?* Which I later found out from Dr. Livingston means, 'Can you hear me?' And *Du gehörst mir*, which means 'You belong to me.'"

"Do you understand what was happening?"

"I believe he was making some sort of contact with me."

"That's correct. This is when he established connection, which opened up a bridge allowing my team to communicate and extract data from your mind."

"Data?"

"Everything you think and feel from one side, while being able to implant our own thoughts and visions from the other."

Calvin grinds his teeth, not liking what he is hearing. Taking a deep breath, hoping to contain his anger, he asks, "You violated my thoughts? What gives you the right?"

"This was an extreme measure rarely ever performed to this extent. It was decided by the council and used primarily for your protection."

Figure X looks down quickly before slowly raising his gaze to meet Calvin's.

"What? Why did you look away? What are you not telling me?"

"I misstated. I used the word 'rarely.' What I should have said is that only one person has ever received as much attention from any one team, and that person is you."

"Seems like a lot of trouble just for me. Whom do I need protection from that warrants this much devotion? Let me guess…Jeff and Kathy?" He pauses briefly, trying to think of any other names, and pulls one more, just before giving up. "I almost forgot about Frank. Surely there were other ways to have sheltered me against the three of them."

"That is incorrect."

"Then who?"

"From yourself."

Calvin tenses and his body becomes rigid as he stares down Figure X for several minutes, watching and wondering what he is thinking.

"I'm not sure what to say to that. You know I don't understand, and I'm guessing from your silence you are not willing to tell me. So where does that leave us?"

Figure X remains quiet, only returns the stare, showing true concern in his eyes.

Calvin decides to let it go. "Why the different languages? Why not just speak English to me?"

"We had recently lost our bridge, and our attempts with English were no longer working. You weren't responding, and our connection had to be reestablished before the window of opportunity was lost. In a last-minute attempt, Figure Y used the languages spoken in the region he is most comfortable with. The timing turned out to be perfect, and the mystery kept your mind intrigued, which resulted in our success."

"Was he responsible for the fake car accident? Or the people disappearing right after?"

"No. You were the one in control. There is still much that needs to be discussed, but it is time to guide you in a different direction. Your focus should switch to what you remember about the day leading up to the accident that killed your wife."

Calvin shifts his weight from one leg to the other, feeling uncomfortable with the adjustment in discussion, and decides to take a seat on the couch. "I hope you don't mind if I sit. There's a chair behind you, if you're interested."

Calvin squirms around uncontrollably, trying to relax but unable to shake the uneasy feeling that is settling in. "You know I think I may have blocked these memories for a reason. Are you sure this is what we are supposed to talk about?"

Figure X remains standing, refusing to break eye contact. His stares pierce through Calvin, as if he is trying to find a way into his soul. "This is where you are supposed to be. There isn't much time left."

Overwhelmed by the amount of detail flooding into his thoughts, Calvin realizes there must be truth to what he is saying and decides to quit stalling.

"It was a cloudy and rainy Thursday. To be honest, it was completely dismal, and a great day to stay at home in bed. Instead, we had an appointment with her gynecologist at noon. Janice was scheduled to receive an amniocentesis test, since she was thirty-nine and a little over four months pregnant. At first, we were completely against the entire notion, concerned for the safety of her and the baby, until we found out it is recommended for pregnant women over the age of thirty-five. It determines not only the sex but also checks the baby's chromosomes, identifying any potential genetic problems. As you can imagine, neither of us slept very much Wednesday night." Calvin stops. "Am I talking too much?"

"What you are saying is exactly what needs to be said in order for you to continue heading down the correct path. You should go wherever your mind takes you."

Calvin rubs his hands together nervously before combing them through his hair. He looks up and says, "But we managed to get through this by leaning on each other, just like always. People used to joke all the time, saying that together we made one perfect person."

Figure X takes a step forward. A beam of light sneaks in from the living room window and shines directly onto the silky fabric of his uniform, changing the charcoal gray to a variety of colors blending in with the surroundings.

Feeling a little uneasy, Calvin asks, "Why did you move closer?"

Figure X blinks twice but says nothing.

Calvin senses he is up to something but can't quite figure out what. The onslaught of memories overwhelms him as they barrel their way into his mind. Enthralled at the level of detail, he ignores everything else and picks up where he left off.

"I had gone in to work for half a day on Thursday and met Janice at the house around quarter after 11. It had been raining heavily all morning long and continued throughout the entire drive to the doctor's office. Without warning the rain stopped, and the sun finally came out right before we pulled into the parking lot. The timing was incredible. I even whispered to Janice, 'This must be a sign of good luck.' Our nerves were on high alert, and after parking, neither of us spoke a word for what seemed like an eternity. Instead, we just sat there quietly, staring into each other's eyes, wondering what the other was thinking. Finally, a few minutes before our appointment, we decided to head in. We held hands from the moment we met at the front of the car to the point of entering through the glass door of the doctor's office located on the third floor."

Calvin feels his excitement build briefly, then fade away once reality sets in. "This is the day we found out we were having a son. I was so proud; I was speechless for the rest of the visit. All I could think about was teaching him how to play sports, fly kites in the open area behind our house, and about a thousand other things. My head was swimming from that point on. As we were leaving, one of the nurses handed us one of those fake cigars made out of bubble gum with 'It's a Boy' inscribed on the wrapper. It is truly baffling how a simple gift such as this can impact one's life."

Calvin turns his head slowly and finds a focal point on the wall across the room and stares blankly. He chuckles, thinking about Janice discussing the many places she wanted to eat lunch from the time they left the office until opening the car door.

"She kept having these crazy food cravings pretty much the entire four months of her pregnancy. The worst I can remember was one morning she ate scrambled eggs and mashed potatoes mixed together. I watched in awe as she scarfed them down. I'm not even sure she stopped to take a breath." He looks over toward Figure X, hoping to get a reaction, but is disappointed by the lack of response. "Let me tell you, in case you do not know what that is, that is gross!" he says, laughing.

Calvin is feeling fully relaxed. *So far so good.* He ignores the emptiness creeping up inside him and is overcome with the desire to talk about everything.

"I'm sorry I'm rambling on. This isn't like me at all."

Figure X thinks for a moment before saying, "Keep on this path. You are opening new avenues with uncharted results."

Calvin feels a sense of accomplishment as he clears his throat. "Anyway, she finally narrowed it down to three choices before deciding on Mexican food. I really lucked out, although a part of me thinks she only chose it because she knew it was what I wanted. We drove about ten minutes, and I gave her a hard time about wearing my long-sleeved plaid shirt in the middle of June. She told me it was her favorite, and she only wore it because she loved the way I look at her with it on."

He slams his fist down onto the couch. "I should have stopped the conversation right then and told her how much I loved her, because that was exactly what I was thinking. I should have screamed how beautiful she was and that I never imagined I would be lucky enough to spend my life with someone like her." He grimaces, and his face turns cold. "Instead, I said nothing of the kind." He grabs one of the cushions and squeezes it tightly with a shaky hand, until the muscles in his arm tire, forcing him to let go. "I guess it doesn't really matter anymore. All those years we tried to have children, and when the time finally came it turns out it was for nothing." He buries his face in his hands and mutters something unrecognizable. He stays in this position for several minutes, taking in and releasing deep breaths, until surfacing with an expression of panic.

"The outfit she was wearing the day of the accident is the same as in every one of my visions. My mind has been trying to tell me something for quite a while, but I haven't been listening. I know that now. Only…I'm afraid it may be too late for me. Will you help me?"

Figure X takes another step toward Calvin. "Our help has been here for the last forty-one years and will remain until it is no longer needed."

"Thanks," Calvin says with a partial smile. "Forty-one years? Can you explain this to me now?"

"This is something that should be explained, but at a later time. For now you must concentrate on continuing before it is too late."

"I can't," he mumbles, choked up.

"You must."

"I don't want to!" His words reverberate off the walls as he closes his eyes, trying to shut out the world around him. He can feel the presence of Figure X less than two feet away. He can also feel the pressure of knowing he must continue or suffer whatever consequences lie before him. "She removed her seat belt, and I did nothing to stop her."

A long, uncomfortable silence fills the air.

"Looking back, I can't believe I was driving down the highway in the fast lane after hours of torrential downpours, and she takes off her seat belt." Calvin shakes his head before opening his eyes and glancing up at Figure X. "Did you hear me? I didn't try and stop her. Instead, I placed two hands on the steering wheel and slowed down a little, as if that was all that was required to protect the safety of my family. We were going to be blessed with having a healthy baby boy. Because of this, I completely ignored common sense and let myself get carried away in the moment."

Figure X's voice booms. "There was a decision made at precisely this moment. What was it?"

"We had agreed to call our son Daniel."

Figure X remains quiet, feeling the pain radiating off of Calvin as his expression intensifies.

"Do you know why she took off her seat belt?" Calvin's chest tightens as he answers his own question. "She took it off to grab her purse so that she could hold that stupid fake cigar in her hands one more time. She said it somehow confirmed that her pregnancy was no longer just an idea or a dream but in fact our reality. The words 'our reality' haunt me to this day. I wake up screaming, knowing I will never hold my wife in my arms again. I wake up screaming Daniel's name, knowing I will never get to know what a wonderful person he would have turned out to be. She read the inscription 'It's a Boy' over and over until I couldn't help myself and joined in. This was the very last time she would ever speak those words." Calvin bites his lip, wanting to scream out profanities to help erase the pain, but refrains, knowing it would be of no use. This never-ending agony is permanent, and no amount of obscenities or anything else will ever make it go away. There is an emptiness deep inside he knows will never be filled.

Calvin wipes away a single tear as it glides down his face. "Funny thing is…she would have been a great mother." He reaches for one of the decorative couch pillows and throws it down the hall, knocking several pictures off the wall. "I feel responsible. I know in my heart I let her down." He uses every ounce of strength within him not to lose control in front of Figure X. "A split-second decision against switching lanes and our entire lives…" He lowers his head in shame. "I was careless, and it cost us everything."

Figure X takes one final step toward Calvin and reaches out, taking hold of his hand. "You are ready to face your darkness, your fears, and all that you have been hiding behind for so long. It is time to visit the details of the car accident, the death of your wife and unborn child."

Calvin is hesitant at first but knows deep inside that Figure X is right. He looks at how far he has come and the progress he has made, and can't help but wonder if this is the last chance he might have to find himself.

His voice cracks as he says softly, "Seconds after she unbuckled her seat belt, I saw a diesel on the other side of the divider wall, and moments later a large wave of water. After that, it's pretty fuzzy but seemed like a lifetime, until I figured out what had happened."

"What do you remember?"

"There was lots of panic, lots of loud crashing sounds, and lots of blood." Calvin pushes on his temple with his free hand and rubs in a circular motion.

"You can't stop," Figure X says, squeezing tighter.

"My body is numb, and whatever I was supposed to work through I believe I have."

"You haven't. You must continue."

Calvin grits his teeth, wishing this misery would end. "I remember standing outside of the car, wondering if I had been knocked unconscious or lost time. All I could think about was my wife. The passenger-side window was busted, and she had vanished into thin air. A horror came over me as I realized she must have been thrown from the car. I couldn't think clearly and therefore couldn't figure out when or where. I called out her name several times, but there was so much chaos around, no one was paying attention to me. I went searching for her, but it was too hazy from the smoke coming off the cars to see more than a couple feet out in front. A small gust of wind came and left an open path, which I followed. The first person I saw was the farmer running in slow motion, meeting up with the man in khakis and Mountain Dew T-shirt. The man in the suit joined them shortly after and pointed in several directions, looking like maybe he was trying to come up with a plan, before they each took off running separately. I walked aimlessly around, confused and aching from every inch on my body. I refused to give up and continued screaming out her name until my throat was raw and my voice raspy."

"You are getting closer. What happened next?"

"I heard the cries of the three teenagers from the black BMW. The girls were screaming something, but there was too much commotion, and I couldn't understand what they were saying. I realized their car was burning, and as I took a step in their direction, it exploded, scattering debris and fire over everything around it. My ears were ringing as I continued walking through all the damaged vehicles as if I were in a maze. I waved the smoke away from my face, revealing pieces of the Harley spread all over the highway. I looked around, and next to one of the largest pieces of the frame is where I saw his lifeless body lying face down on the road."

Calvin stops talking briefly and gasps for air as if he is drowning. "This is absolutely terrifying. I feel like someone is ripping out my insides."

CHAPTER

34

THE HORROR ON Calvin's face reveals signs of true heartache as his memories continue to make their presence known without regard for his mental health. He glances up to see the illuminating white glow of Figure X's eyes as they immediately shut out all anguish and relieve his pain. There is a tunnel of safety he is able to slip inside just before falling into a deep trancelike state. He relinquishes himself fully and is met with warmth and comfort as if they were a blanket wrapping themselves tightly around him. His mind drifts to another place far from the suffering currently surrounding him. The feeling of agony has been lifted, and the thoughts of death and sorrow removed. His breathing slows, and his body calms. He closes his eyes and imagines himself in a field overflowing with tiny white lights hovering in place. He places his hand on the trunk of the only tree in sight and is surprised to find it soft and spongy. The leaves are also soft and unlike anything he has ever seen. He watches in wonder as a light breeze changes their color from silver to red. He takes a step and discovers the ground is a thick white sand that turns to red with each movement. Glancing around, he is taken by surprise by the dark, orange color of the cloudless sky. "This is truly amazing."

The lights begin to move and gradually make their way toward him in a never-ending stream, until he is engulfed in a sea of lights waist-deep. The energy level is high, adrenaline coursing through his veins.

He reaches out as several of the lights float upward, landing in his cupped hands. They rest gently, before a tingling sensation moves across his palm, giving off the illusion that all of this is real. One by one, as the lights pass by they start to dim, letting him know this is only a glimpse into a future he could call his own, a destiny he has been told is there for his taking. A flood of disappointment consumes him when he realizes this temporary escape is coming to an end, leaving him with the undying burden of his reality once again.

"That was incredible. How did you do that?"

"You needed a break, and I was able to provide one for you."

"Was that your planet?"

"It was a memory of a very small piece."

"Thank you for sharing this with me. It was truly amazing."

"It is one of many mysteries of where I am from. I look forward to having you experience it on your own someday. One visit to this spot will change your life forever."

Calvin continues to sit on the couch, wondering if this is part of the plan to convince him to someday leave Earth permanently.

"Are you ready to start again?"

He senses the impatience in Figure X's words and is shocked by the amount of heat radiating off of his hand. He realizes it is also much clammier than he first knew. He opens his mouth, but decides against saying anything, afraid it may be interpreted as an insult. Instead, he relaxes, surprised at how calm he is feeling.

"I came up to the yellow Honda Accord and remember seeing the driver's side was completely smashed in and the older woman was crushed and hunched over, already dead. The grandson was in the backseat crying loudly for her but reaching his hands out for me. The window had been shattered, so I yelled for him to shut his eyes and look away as I pulled open the door. There was a loud scraping noise of metal on metal, which sent shivers down my spine. I leaned in and was able to tell blood had soaked into the fabric of his seat. There was a thin layer of glass covering everything, including the floorboard. I kept telling him it was going to be okay, even though I had a strong feeling it wasn't. The coloring in his face was changing rapidly, and I knew he must be bleeding out from somewhere on or inside his body. I frantically searched for a paramedic, and when I couldn't find one I panicked. I pushed the button releasing his seat belt and picked him up without hesitation. I know better than to move someone before their injuries have been assessed, but I was scared and wasn't thinking clearly."

Calvin glances over toward the hall and notices that one of the family pictures he had knocked off the wall earlier has disappeared.

Figure X squeezes his hand briefly. "Don't stop."

"I pulled him into my arms and realized that a small piece of metal must have been wedged into his side somewhere out of sight. The moment I lifted him from the backseat he squealed with pain, and his crying became inconsolable. The second our eyes met, I could see fear. Fear from not understanding, and perhaps even fear of death. He was thrashing around uncontrollably as if he was looking for something. He pointed to an area on the other side of the car, but because I was more concerned with reassuring him I didn't pay much attention. I've told myself since that day that there could have been a number of reasons why he was pointing to that specific area. What I want to believe was that he had connected with my wife somehow before her passing and needed to be near her so neither would be alone in their final moments. I can't be certain of anything, although I do take comfort in this idea. I know it's a far reach, but when you lose everything in a matter of moments, sometimes that's all you have. And you hold on to that feeling, even if it means an eternity of misery."

Calvin clears his throat, trying not to let himself get sucked into an emotional downfall. "Either way, it doesn't matter anymore. The flailing stopped suddenly, and his body fell limp. I continued holding him tightly, telling myself he was quiet because he was in the safety of my arms. In those few fleeting seconds, I felt like a father—something I had been longing to be for quite some time, a feeling I was about to realize would be stolen from me. My body may have survived the car accident, but I assure you most of me died that day."

Figure X watches in silence as Calvin's emotions fluctuate unpredictably.

"I'm guessing you already know this, but the reason the grandson stopped crying had nothing to do with being in the safety of my arms. He stopped because he died while I was holding him and telling him everything is going to be okay."

His lip quivers uncontrollably. He stops to catch his breath. "I handed his body off to a paramedic. I went in the direction the boy had pointed and found Janice lying on her back, alone in a pool of her own blood. As I was rushing over and yelling her name, I saw an overweight man running from person to person, trying to help. He kept apologizing, taking the bulk of responsibility onto himself as if he didn't know I was the first car and the most to blame. I might have prevented all of this from happening if only I had paid attention. We crossed paths for a brief moment, but neither of us acknowledged the other."

Calvin concentrates for a few seconds, wondering why he seems so familiar. "There's something about this guy I am supposed to know, but for some reason I can't place him." He dismisses the thought and continues. "Her body was twisted and broken. A paramedic found her about the same time, but I knew it was too late. All of her color had already left before we arrived. Her eyes were wide but dull, staring blankly into space as if she were an empty shell. I held her hand while the paramedic tried to revive her, knowing full well his attempts were in vain. But it didn't matter. As long as he was willing to try, I would be there with him every step of the way. I relied on hope and faith, knowing neither could bring her back to me."

Calvin stops and lets the tears quietly stream down his cheeks. He can feel an ache in the back of his throat, worsening with each second. He turns away slowly, wheezing with each deep breath. He blinks several times, concentrating deeply.

"Figure Y was there, along with one or two others, standing behind a tree over by me and Janice, watching us. I remember the glow of his right ankle through the thick fog of smoke."

"What else can you tell me?"

"I think I may have figured out something about the pecking order of the nine, but I'm not exactly sure."

"This is the correct path. You are doing well."

"It seems like the first person I saw at the accident was the farmer. Then I remembered he was the first in line to be killed. I thought it was only a coincidence, until I put more thought into it. The next on the scene was the guy in the Mountain Dew shirt, followed by the man in the suit. Everyone in the exact sequence as when they were supposed to be killed, except the motorcycle guy and the three teenagers. It's as if they switched places for some reason, but I can't figure out why. Am I making sense?"

"Yes. You are correct. This was Kathy's mistake. She blatantly disregarded the sequence and in doing so has put the continuation of the cycle at risk. We strongly believe there are consequences to her killing the man on the motorcycle out of order."

"Like what?"

"They are no longer going to be as successful in killing your memories of the nine. Even with only the farmer remaining, they have given you the edge you need to defeat them. Your memory is restoring itself, and as you absorb Jeff and Kathy the reverse should also be true."

"What do you mean?"

"There is an opposite effect. As your memory improves, theirs will worsen."

Calvin chimes in excitedly, "I think you're right. It's hard for me to explain, but when I was in their heads I could tell they were already thinking something wasn't right. And you feel it's all because Kathy didn't follow the rules?"

"Not exactly. We are in agreement that it is a major contributing factor, but not the only one. We feel there are many other variables which led us to where we are now."

Calvin is relieved, knowing what is being said is true. "Why was I asked to kill the farmer?"

"We are unsure. This was also a first."

"So the command wasn't yours?"

"No. This came from a voice hidden deep inside you."

"There's something that has been bothering me for a while now. I didn't go through with killing the farmer, yet I, along with Dr. Livingston, have seen him inside mirrors. Did you or Figure Y do this?"

Figure X says nothing, only shakes his head.

"Do you know where he is now? It seems like Kathy may have already found him, and I want to make sure he is protected, just in case."

"He is only a memory. This is something you must work out for yourself."

Calvin's face turns pale as he is overcome with an anxious feeling. "The overweight man at the accident who was trying to help everyone, I know why he was there. He was the driver of the diesel truck that started this whole mess, wasn't he?"

"Yes."

"What a pair we make together," he grumbles. "I saw him, or at least the ghost of him, at the farmhouse with Dr. Livingston yesterday." Calvin looks toward the hall again and realizes another picture is missing.

Figure X's voice carries throughout the house. "You must hurry."

Calvin's nerves are scattered as he searches for the right words. "He was pacing back and forth inside the farmhouse, mumbling how sorry he was. I got the impression he was the owner of the house. Is this true?"

"Yes."

The pressure is too much for Calvin to withstand. His frustrations break free, causing him to snap. "Why are you only giving me one-word answers? I know there is more to this than you are saying. So, either you tell me what you know about him and his house, or I swear to God I'm done." He releases his grip and forces his hand free, wiping the sweat on the front of his shorts.

Figure X takes several steps back, trying not to crowd him. "What you have said so far matches with my reports. The driver of the diesel hit the standing water, which caused the accident. By the time he realized what was happening, it was too late to prevent the chain of events. He turned around and went back to the scene of the accident and tried to render aid."

Calvin attempts to massage away a headache he can sense is coming on with full force. "I feel a strong desire to go back to the farmhouse. How am I connected?"

"I am sorry I must disappoint you here. Please trust that I cannot continue for your own good. This is the most I can say for now."

"Unbelievable," Calvin growls.

As his temper flares, he remembers his promise of trust. He concentrates intensely on controlling his anger, until he is able to push it aside. Thoughts flood his mind, causing him to rise and shout with excitement, "I know where the farmer is, and I know how to protect him!"

He looks around and is alarmed that all of the pictures, including the ones of Daniel on the mantel, are now gone. He glances down at his hand to see that his wedding ring is also missing. Calvin does a spot check around the room but can't find any evidence his wife or son ever existed.

"What is happening to me?"

"This is the closest you have ever been to breaking the cycle. Your memory is coming back but cannot fully be restored without completing the second piece."

"What do I need to do?"

"There are still forces working against you."

"Jeff and Kathy," Calvin grumbles. "How do I beat them?"

"You must complete this next part on your own."

"You're abandoning me?" he asks, his voice showing concern. "If I'm as close as you say, then please help me, and we can defeat them together."

"I am truly sorry."

Figure X closes his eyes and summons the white lights. They fill the living room right on cue and take their places before hovering. The colors change to red, and within seconds Figure X has vanished, leaving behind only brief traces of lights, until they too have disappeared.

Calvin is startled by an image of a small child standing and watching him from the opposite end of the hall.

"Hello," he calls out, his voice echoing off the walls. "Who are you? Daniel…is that you?"

As the figure approaches, Calvin is left speechless. Chills consume his body, causing his insides to ache.

"What are you doing here?" he asks, unable to stop his eyes from filling with tears.

The boy remains quiet, only stares blankly at him. "Dad?" He raises his arms as if to suggest he wants to be held.

"No, kid, it's me. The man from the accident. I tried to save you but ended up taking your life instead. I'm really sorry. I made a mistake. I should have never moved you from your grandmother's car. Please forgive—"

He is interrupted by an enormous amount of pressure inside his head, squeezing so intensely he falls to the ground screaming and begging for it to stop.

CHAPTER

35

CALVIN AWAKENS TO a gentle whisper of his name. He is lying on his stomach with his arms spread out over a mixture of grass and dirt. He slowly raises his head and notices the steps leading to the farmhouse. *Why do I keep losing time?* He tries to clear away the images of the grandson, but the harder he pushes, the more they appear. Confusion gnaws away at the remaining pieces of his sanity. He questions why he is plagued with so many horrifying thoughts and memories, but the only answer he is able to accept is grief and unrestrained guilt. He places his hands on his face and tries to subdue his emotions while gently rubbing his eyes, wishing the end were finally here.

He sits up realizing his body is stiff and his self-esteem low. I can't do this any longer. How could I ever face two killers and expect to survive? Especially two that seem to know me better than I know myself.

His mind drifts further away from reality, with blame and surrender entwined with each passing thought. The realization of his death seems imminent. Unknowingly, he lets down his guard as his frustrations build, allowing the feeling of helplessness to creep in and take control. *Why don't I just give up and let Jeff and Kathy win? At least then this whole thing will finally end.*

Engulfed in deep concentration, he feels the tug of awareness as a light wind carrying the aroma of steaks being grilled passes through him. Calvin grabs a handful of dirt and throws it toward the house. A cloud of dust lingers briefly before dissipating. Tiny pebbles bounce off the wood railing and scatter along the porch. He rises and notices the heat from the sun isn't as direct as he would expect. *How much time did I lose?*

Pulling out his phone he is relieved to see it is still Sunday, but is overcome with panic, mumbling the words, "I lost almost eight hours. I can't believe it's 7:21." He repeats "7:21" over and over, half expecting the time to reverse back to earlier that morning. A fear ignites at the thought of Dr. Livingston, and he wonders if she is still alive.

Turning around he spots his car parked over by the "For Sale" sign on the edge of the grass, next to the entrance of the gravel driveway. He is surprised to see "Contract Pending," and is rattled when it comforts him.

He hears a loud noise coming from inside the house. *I'm pretty sure this is the reason I'm here. I might as well check it out and see if I'm right.* Walking toward the front door he makes his way up the first of three steps leading to the wrap-around porch, stopping abruptly when mental alarms sound. *Why don't I let Jeff and Kathy win?* His face livens, and his eyes gleam wildly. *This can't really be an option...can it?* His hands tremble as the reality of his idea sets in. *Why not? If what I understand is true, then my entire life will start over, and I will have my family back. I can always worry about what to do after I come back again. Besides, there are no guarantees that Jeff and Kathy will even be an issue next time.* Calvin takes another step toward the house, exhaling a deep breath. *This is crazy, but I could see how it might actually work.*

His passion for his family inspires him to come up with a plan. *What if I examine each detail from every angle, and if I'm missing something, then I'll find it? If not, I'll have my answer.* His concern grows as he realizes his judgment may have already been clouded. He pushes the thought out of his mind and starts with the negatives first. *If I let them win, then I'm pretty sure that means they would have to kill me. Do I have enough faith that I would come back to let that happen?*

Calvin sits on the top step facing toward the front yard, having a sense of déjà vu, when the warmth of the fresh summer breeze passes through him. Panic nestles in as his mind is inundated with thoughts and questions, filling his head with doubt. *What if I die and don't come back? Then what? I have no idea what will happen to me. I may also run the risk of Figure X abandoning me and lose my opportunity to go with him to his planet.* Calvin clears his head for the moment and listens to the slight hum of a lawnmower off in the distance. *Honestly, I wasn't planning on joining him anyway, so nothing would really change if he did leave.*

He continues weighing his options for several more minutes, never straying far from the thought of being united with his family. *It's a huge gamble, but if Figure X is right, then I have completed many cycles and have always come back. What makes this time any different?*

His body relaxes at the possibility of starting over and knowing there is very little that will change his mind at this point. *So on to the positives...I don't have to understand or even try hard to make it happen. Seems like I'm already on a course, with the outcome preset.* He rubs his hands together. *What else? I have always said I would give anything to see my wife and son again. Here's my chance to prove it. There's no reason why starting over every few years has to be a bad thing. Especially with so much to gain. Who knows, maybe I could eventually figure out a way of increasing the cycle and extending the time.*

Calvin pushes out a steady stream of air, trying to slow his excitement, before continuing. *Not to mention Dr. Livingston wouldn't have to die. If I can protect her, then she should come back in the next cycle.* He closes his eyes and imagines Daniel and Janice holding hands. *I love you both and can't wait to see you.* He finds relief in knowing his decision could unite him with his family for at least one more cycle. His smile changes as a thought of disapproval enters his mind. *I can't let Dr. Livingston find out. I bet she would try and talk me out of it.*

Hearing footsteps closing in he turns his head quickly and rises before walking across the porch, watching the shadows cross in front of the window. He tries to peek in, but the shades are drawn tight, concealing whoever is inside.

He calls out to the farmer, "I know you're in there. I placed you there myself this morning to protect you from Jeff and Kathy. I want you to know I am setting you free. You don't have to hide any longer. It doesn't matter anymore."

Calvin notices movement in the curtains. "Also, to the owner of the house, I know you were the driver of the diesel responsible for the death of eight people, including my wife and unborn son. I accept that you made a mistake, and I know it was an accident. I forgive and hold no ill will toward you."

The door unlatches and squeaks as it gradually opens a few inches at a time. Taking this as a sign, Calvin heads over and gently nudges his way through. His eyes widen, and he feels like the wind has been knocked out of him. He stands motionless, unable to look away from Alicia and her family. The four of them stand together, huddled in their own group. Alicia smiles, waiting for Calvin to make the first move.

"What are you doing here?" he asks.

His question is answered only by silence. She takes a couple steps toward him, with her arms held open wide. "Hey, stranger, I've missed you."

Without hesitating, he rushes over and grabs her tightly, lifting her off the floor. "I can't believe you're alive. You have no idea how alone I've been. I thought…" Calvin's face shows skepticism. The reality comes crashing down around him, forcing him to release his hold. "You're not real. Jeff and Kathy killed you at your home in Oklahoma. Your entire family was murdered."

Alicia's eyes dull as she loses her smile. "That's not true. If it were, then why are we here?"

"I'm not sure, but I'm thinking it has something to do with Kathy breaking the rules. You are only a memory."

Alicia takes a couple steps back to her original spot and rejoins her family. The four of them stare blankly at Calvin without speaking, as if waiting for something to change.

"I'm guessing Figure X was right. Jeff and Kathy must be losing control. I love all of you and wish you could stay, but it's time for you to leave. You shouldn't be here any longer."

The images of all four fade a little at a time, until they are gone. Calvin wipes the tears from his eyes and is overcome with a strange feeling, accompanied with distorted memories filling his head.

Not understanding, he pushes them away while spotting Frank over by the window. "You shouldn't be here either. Dr. Livingston shot you in the field next to the Shell station. I watched you die. It's time for you to leave now."

Frank closes his eyes, and his image disappears. Calvin is surprised to see members of the original nine walking into the living room from the hallway. There are several more people lining up behind them, but he is unable to make out any faces. He glances over and sees the first receptionist from Dr. Livingston's office holding hands with a younger man wearing a Texas Rangers baseball cap. Suddenly, the room is overrun with images that can't possibly be real. Knowing he must take action, he clears his throat before saying, "None of you belong here anymore. I'll see you again shortly." He is briefly taken aback by the warmth of the friendly faces staring at him. "It's time for all of you to leave. Please go now."

Calvin watches closely, feeling pieces of him returning with the disappearance of each person. His memory grows, and his mind is no longer weakened by the demoralizing torment of unrepressed guilt. Relief replaces stress and pressure as he feels a large weight being lifted off his shoulders. Only loneliness remains, until he is reminded of his plan. *I can't believe I'm really going through with it.* He sticks out his chest and yells to an empty house, "I choose my family."

He imagines himself driving far away from here and wonders if time would eventually run out, forcing the cycle to start over as some sort of default. *Then I wouldn't have to die.* Suddenly, he is inundated with thoughts of Dr. Livingston being hunted down and killed all alone. *I can't abandon her, especially in her time of need.*

A whisper inside his head eventually turns into a conversation. Calvin walks toward his car and hears Kathy saying to Jeff, "I don't understand why we can't kill the doctor now. I don't feel like waiting."

Jeff's frustration level rises. "Because we need to handle the farmer first. Why can't you follow the rules?"

Her difficulties are becoming more apparent as she struggles with her memory. *I can't even remember why I'm so angry with Dr. Livingston, but I know I want her dead. What is happening to me?* She focuses, trying not to show weakness, afraid of how Jeff might respond. "I understand how it all works," she says firmly. "My point is that we lost the farmer and have no idea where he is."

Calvin continues to make his way to his car, not letting on that he is listening to their conversation. He quietly opens his door before climbing in and devoting his full attention to them. He concentrates and is able to see an image of both completely surrounded by bushes and trees.

"Everyone is off the grid except for Dr. Livingston. So again I say we go take care of her now before we lose her too."

Jeff shakes his head in disgust. "I don't know. I haven't felt right since you killed the guy on the motorcycle out of turn, and it seems to be getting a lot worse." He grimaces as he grumbles, "That was really dumb, by the way. But if you kill Dr. Livingston before her time, it will be your second stupid move and will most likely break the cycle, sealing our fate. I'm not sure we should take that chance."

Kathy remains silent, feeling like she is losing her edge. She knows he's right, but there is a driving force raging from deep inside wanting Dr. Livingston dead. She realizes she may be slipping but knows they're close enough to finish it. Fed up with the resistance, she takes control of the conversation and states, "With or without you, I am going to kill her as soon as I find her. I don't need your help."

"Fine. This is a mistake, but whatever."

Calvin panics and focuses on his family and clears his head, removing all traces of Jeff and Kathy. He reaches for his phone, debating if he should warn Dr. Livingston, but decides to try something else instead. He closes his eyes and concentrates, repeating her name over and over until he is able to see her image. She is sitting inside a restaurant at a corner table with a long, white cloth tablecloth draped over the sides. Her daughter is to her right, while her husband is directly across from them both. All three are dressed nicely for this occasion.

She thinks this is her last day alive. *I need to tell her she doesn't have to die.*

The sounds of silverware clanking against plates mixed with a light rumble of chatter fill the air. All the while Calvin is only able to keep his attention fixated on her and notices she is only midway through her meal.

Can you hear me?

Dr. Livingston is talking to her daughter and doesn't acknowledge him.

He tries again. This time he channels all of his energy into one purpose. *Hey, Doc, can you hear me?*

Dr. Livingston stops talking and puts down her fork before rubbing her temples. *I can hear you. Are you in the wooded area?*

No.

Then how are you able to communicate with me?

A lot has changed since we were together yesterday. It's important that I speak with you as soon as possible.

Where are you?

I'm in my car at the farmhouse. Shouldn't you be at home with your doors locked?

I refuse to hide. Besides, I figured if it were truly my last day alive, I should eat at my favorite restaurant with my family one more time.

There's been a change of plans. Long story short, you should probably leave there sooner than later.

Calvin watches as Dr. Livingston takes the napkin from her lap and wipes her mouth. She is startled when she looks up to see the farmer standing at the edge of their table. Her husband and daughter stop moving, mesmerized by the surprise guest, and watch silently as he stares into Dr. Livingston's eyes before saying, "You must die. It is the correct path."

Everyone stops eating and stares. In a matter of seconds the entire restaurant is deathly quiet. The waiters are no longer taking orders, and the hostess has stopped midway to her destination. Guests stand motionless behind her. All the attention is on Dr. Livingston, every pair of eyes watching and waiting for something to happen.

"Mom," Sandra says with a look of terror, "I'm scared."

"It's okay, sweetheart."

What is going on? Calvin thinks.

I'm not sure, but I'm frightened. Am I going to die now? In front of my family?

I don't know.

The farmer turns and rushes toward the front door. Dr. Livingston releases her breath, unaware she has been holding it. Feeling like she must keep him in her sight, she rises too quickly, causing her chair to fall backwards, making a loud clatter.

"Wait," she calls out in a panic but he continues heading in the direction of the front door and exits without slowing his pace.

She leaves the chair on the floor and takes several steps away from the table, stopping abruptly. A gut-wrenching pain turns her stomach the moment she glances back to her husband and daughter. She screams their names as their images slowly fade away.

"What is happening?" Calvin mutters as he watches everyone inside the restaurant disappear one at a time, leaving him with extreme dizziness. He is forced to grab hold of his steering wheel for balance, unable to control the light-headedness. Memories from earlier life cycles find their way into his thoughts as he desperately tries to sort through them. His mind is distorted, and nothing is clear.

"I no longer know what is real," he mutters, clawing at his head.

Dr. Livingston quickly makes her way to the door and hurries through it, frantically searching for the farmer.

"Where are you?"

The street is empty and the parking lot holds only one car—her silver Mercedes.

"Where is my family?"

She takes several breaths, attempting to collect herself. *Why is this happening?* She is surrounded by deafening silence. Her panic increases as she awaits an answer. Several moments pass with no response.

"Why is this happening?"

I don't know, Calvin answers, afraid to say anything else. The image of the grandson appears, along with peace of mind, and he knows all is forgiven. The boy smiles and waves good-bye.

Dr. Livingston interrupts, causing his vision to disappear. *Do you know where my family is?*

No, I'm sorry.

Calvin, are you telling me the truth?

Yes. I am really confused right now, and I promise I don't know anything for sure.

You mentioned a change in plans. I think now would be a good time to include me.

Last I knew, Jeff and Kathy were tracking you from the wooded area, and they may already be on their way. She wants to kill you now instead of waiting. Kathy is no longer planning on following the rules or worried about consequences.

What about the older woman and her grandson?

They're both already dead. I'm concerned about you and need to make sure you are protected. Do you have a weapon?

No. Kathy made me toss my gun next to Frank's body before he disappeared. My husband has one locked up in our safe at home.

Can you get to it?

Yes.

Do you want to meet after? I think our smartest move at this point would be to stay together.

I agree. I'll run by the house, grab the gun and change clothes, and then head to my office. I should be there in about forty minutes. Does this work?

That's perfect. I'll see you then.

Dr. Livingston can feel a rush of adrenaline coursing through her body. Her mind races as she tries to understand the disappearance of her family. *What does this have to do with me?*

She stares, baffled, out into the empty parking lot next to the restaurant, thinking, *Less than an hour ago, there was barely a spot available.*

The streets are vacant, and the hum of the stoplight has her mesmerized. Her mind is unable to cope, and for the moment she is dumbstruck. Unwilling to move, she continues standing and staring into the lonely streets, thinking about her husband and daughter. *Why me?* She falls into deep thought, no longer worried about Jeff and Kathy or her potential fate. Her main focus now is only on her family when she discovers, *I can't move*. She closes her eyes briefly and blocks out all concerns and fears.

Calvin's loud scream fills her head. "You need to run! Now!"

CHAPTER

36

DR. LIVINGSTON YELLS as the words echo inside her head, snapping her out of her daze. She reaches down and removes her heels, then sprints toward her car. Her heart is pounding. She wonders if this is the moment she is destined to die. Twenty feet away from her car, still running full speed, she reaches into her purse and pulls out her keys. One of her shoes falls to the ground and bounces several times, scraping against the asphalt before stopping heel-side up. She briefly glances back but never stops.

She unlocks her car when she's less than five-feet away and throws the other shoe aside, flinging open the driver-side door. Gasping for air, she tosses her purse onto the passenger seat and jumps behind the steering wheel. She takes off quickly without strapping on her seat belt and squeals the tires as she makes a sharp turn. Her makeup spills out of her purse and scatters along the floorboard. *I need to calm down.*

Are you okay, Doc?

I don't know. Are Jeff and Kathy close?

Not anymore. You're fine.

She breathes a sigh of relief. Please don't take this personally, but I really need to be alone in my thoughts right now.

Of course, I completely understand. I'll explain the rest once we meet up.

Calvin clears his mind, then starts his car and takes his time driving to her office. He sits in the parking lot, waiting and trying to connect the disappearances with the appearance of his new memories. He is startled by the flicker of streetlamps turning on signaling dusk is approaching. The white beam of Dr. Livingston's headlights bounces off the building as her car turns in. He can barely control his excitement when she passes by her designated spot and pulls in next to him. He quickly makes his way out of his car and rushes over. As he gets closer, his breath is taken away at the sight of the number zero on her forehead. She looks up and makes eye contact while smiling only partially. He immediately senses and understands her sadness. He smiles back before realizing what is coming next. Looking down he cringes, as he hears the whispers, "Zero days left."

He leans over, hiding his emotions, and hugs her softly before she has a chance to close the car door behind her. "I'm sorry. I'm feeling like we only have each other right now, and it's really great to see you."

She hugs him back, tearing up, and mumbles, "I know what you mean. It's great to see you too."

Calvin walks beside her, keeping guard the entire way to the front door.

"Do you have a gun?" she asks.

"No. I don't need a weapon."

"Why's that?"

"I'll explain once we're inside. We just need to focus on making sure you stay safe."

Dr. Livingston closes the door behind them and locks the deadbolt. It makes a loud click as it latches firmly. Calvin watches through the glass and tenses when another set of headlights reflects off the building. He watches Kathy's Buick slowly turn in and is unable to stop his fear from taking over. Dr. Livingston places her cell phone on speaker and dials

911. Neither of them says a word. Instead, they listen to ring after ring while watching her car pull into a spot next to theirs and park.

Dr. Livingston hangs up and tries again. "Why isn't anyone answering?"

"I don't think they're there."

"Why wouldn't they be? Isn't that their job?"

"I get the feeling they're probably in the same place as everyone else right now."

"What do you mean? Did you make everyone vanish?"

"I don't think so. Not on purpose anyway."

Jeff knocks, before cupping his hands around the glass door and peeking in. Calvin and Dr. Livingston rush back to her office and close the door. She pulls out her gun and confirms that it's still loaded for the sixth time since leaving her house.

The buzzer sounds, echoing loudly with the opening of the entrance door.

"How did they get in so fast?" Dr. Livingston says. "You saw me lock the door."

Calvin blurts out, "I don't think you're real. None of this is, but I can't figure out how to make it stop. I have decided to repeat another cycle, and I need you to stay alive so that you can come back too."

Dr. Livingston's hands shake as she feels the beginnings of a panic attack. Her face loses color as disbelief holds her sanity hostage. "Are you serious?"

"Yes. How else would you explain it?"

"How much do you trust Figure X?"

"Why?"

"When I saw the farmer in the restaurant earlier, he specifically said I must die. It is the correct path."

"Yeah, I was watching and I heard him. Where are you going with this?"

"That sounds exactly like something Figure X would say. Right? So maybe he's playing a much larger role than we first imagined."

Calvin shakes his head, discrediting everything she is saying. "That's not correct. I know the truth."

"Do you have any proof?"

"Not yet," he replies quickly.

"What do you mean?"

Dr. Livingston screams as Jeff pounds on the office door.

"Is anyone in there? I think we should talk."

Jeff gently opens the door, turning the knob slowly. He peeks in and says in a cocky voice, "There you are. We've been looking all over the place for you."

Dr. Livingston stands behind her desk, pointing her gun at him, hoping she doesn't have to use it. "What do you want from us?"

"You," Kathy says as she emerges fearlessly from the hall. "I want you...*dead*." Her heart races the moment she sees the number zero on Dr. Livingston's forehead. She closes her eyes to soak in the whispers "Zero days left," which bring on a smile of pure satisfaction.

Dr. Livingston switches her aim to Kathy.

Jeff chimes in completely off subject. "Your full name is stenciled on the entrance door. I guess I never paid any attention. Do you mind if I call you Rachael?"

Dr. Livingston gives back a confused look. "I don't care. What do you want with me?"

Calvin walks over and positions himself between Kathy and Dr. Livingston, making sure neither has a clean shot. The tension is thick enough to drown in, as all three weapons are drawn and pointing at someone different.

"I guess we all know why I called this meeting," Jeff says jokingly.

Calvin looks at him and Kathy before shouting with confidence, "Neither of you belongs here anymore. It is time for you to leave now. Go away!"

Jeff opens his mouth, and then stops, realizing something isn't right. He looks at Kathy. His face turns pale, and his expression switches to shock. "How did he figure it out?"

Kathy's demeanor becomes rigid as panic sets in. She lowers her gun and is unable to speak.

Jeff stares at Kathy, and as his eyes water he whispers, "Good-bye. I was hoping it would have ended differently. I love..." Jeff stops speaking the instant their eyes meet. A hush falls over the room. He winks at her before they both erupt into uncontrollable laughter. After catching his breath, he looks over at Calvin. "Thanks, dude. I really needed a good laugh. That was crazy funny." Jeff stands on his tippy-toes and in a mocking voice says, "It is time for you to leave now. Go away!"

The laughter roars even louder, lasting for several moments, until Jeff is finally able to catch his breath again. "You think we are memories and you can talk or wish us away?"

"I was hoping," Calvin mumbles, quietly feeling stupid. He fidgets with his hands, trying to calm his nerves, before looking over at Dr. Livingston. "You are no longer needed. You may leave and join your family."

She glances back at him, extremely confused and distracted by the laughter growing stronger by the second. "Please tell me you're kidding."

"I'm trying to save you. I don't understand why no one is disappearing. I know that none of this is real." His face turns bright red as he wishes he had brought a weapon. "I'm very confused right now."

"Was this really your big plan?" Dr. Livingston asks angrily.

Calvin turns away, avoiding eye contact. "I'm not sure my being honest at this moment will give you much comfort. Do you really want me to answer?"

"You just did," she says disappointedly.

Calvin's frustration and embarrassment become apparent in his voice as he tries to reason. "This doesn't make sense. It worked at the farmhouse. How do you explain everyone disappearing at the restaurant?" Calvin looks over to Jeff. "Why isn't it working now?"

"Because we're not your memories."

"Then what are you?"

"All I am willing to say right now is that we are a part of you. All three of us. The rest you will have to wait for."

Dr. Livingston changes her focus. "Jeff, look at me...please. You don't have to do this. You have made great progress. Don't ruin it now."

"But that's my job. If we fail, it could mean the end for me, and I'm not willing to take that chance."

"Just kill her, for Christ sakes," Kathy calls out. "Stop being weak for once, and do what you were put here to do."

Jeff grinds his teeth. His mood darkens. He turns toward Kathy, pointing his gun at her.

"What are you doing? Kill her!"

"Shut up! All of this is getting out of hand because of you. You screwed up, not me. But instead of admitting it and trying to course correct, you continue on the path of destruction. You know we are not supposed to kill Dr. Livingston before the farmer, yet you insist on it, as if you have any say. On top of everything else, you have the nerve to push it onto me so that I suffer the brunt of the consequences. Do you honestly think I was going to let you risk everything? For what? Your pride? Because she killed Frank? Personally, I never liked the guy and hope he doesn't return."

Kathy's face flushes. "I don't under—""Stop talking," Jeff says. "Now that I'm getting everything off of my chest you need to know that I'm tired of taking instructions from you. I've been biding my time, and it has finally arrived. Looks like I will be giving the orders from now on. So, put your gun away. No one is dying tonight."

Refusing to lower her arm, Kathy mutters, "Fine. You win. We'll wait until we find the farmer. Then I will kill her."

Jeff fires three times, hitting Kathy in the chest twice and once in the left side of her cheek. She falls backwards into the wall before hitting the floor face first with a thud. Blood trickles from her cheek, dripping onto the carpet. A pool of blood forms underneath her body and continues to grow, drenching the carpet around her.

Calvin starts toward Jeff, hoping to wrestle the gun away from him. His head is pounding, his ears ringing loudly.

Jeff points at Calvin. "*Don't!*"

Calvin stops and changes direction, making his way next to Dr. Livingston. Lights appear and hover in their designated places around Kathy's lifeless body before taking her away. Calvin grabs his head, trying to stop the pressure from building as more memories flood his thoughts. He focuses and is able to recognize them from prior cycles. He squeezes his eyes shut and is only able to concentrate on one image. He watches as the grandson blows him a kiss.

Calvin looks over at Dr. Livingston, who is holding her ears and trembling uncontrollably. "Are you okay?"

She refuses to answer or even look up. Unable to diminish her terror, she turns to Calvin and whispers, "I'm scared."

Before he has a chance to respond, three more shots ring out, piercing Dr. Livingston's side and neck. Shock consumes them both.

Calvin yells and throws his arms outward, trying to break her fall. He catches her and gently lowers her body to the floor, refusing to let go. "Please don't die. I need you here."

She coughs up blood as her vital signs fade. The desperation in Calvin's voice is evident as he searches for any inspiration, hoping she'll fight for life.

"You have a six-year-old daughter named Sandra. I saw her at the restaurant earlier eating dinner with you and your husband. She is incredibly beautiful and needs her mother. Don't forget about her. Giving up means you will never see her again." Calvin releases his grip from her blood-soaked body and watches as the zero disappears. "No!" he screams, unable to fight back the tears.

Her eyes are open, but her life has been taken. His fingers shake as he softly closes her eyelids. He looks over at Jeff with extreme hatred. "What have you done?"

"What I had to," he scoffs back. "Otherwise, you would have never done it yourself. Consider it a gift. Enjoy your freedom."

"I don't want freedom. I want to see my family again. It wasn't supposed to end like this. Dr. Livingston wasn't supposed to die. What if she doesn't come back now?" Anger and rage devour his mind, leaving little doubt regarding what has to be done. The thought of his family comes and goes as he fights within himself, deciding whether to kill Jeff out of revenge. He reaches over and grabs Dr. Livingston's gun and points it at Jeff's face.

"There's only one more piece to this puzzle," Jeff states confidently.

He knows all six shots have been fired and the chambers are empty but lifts his revolver and aims it directly at Calvin. *We've already lost. I might as well go out with a bang.* He makes his hands shake, as if he is troubled by the events that have transpired, and calls out, "You know I have to kill you now?"

Calvin says nothing and refuses to wipe the tears streaming down his cheeks.

Jeff pulls back the hammer, making the clicking sound for more dramatic effect. "The moment of truth. I always wanted to have a showdown." He places his gun inside his belt. "Kinda like the Wild West. We could draw for it."

Calvin says nothing. His finger is antsy and already on the trigger. He fights with every ounce of restraint he has not to pull it.

"I won't kill you. I want to come back and be with my family."

"It's too late for that now. That ship has already sailed. You have no choice in the matter. Good luck with the next stage of your life."

Calvin dismisses his comments, unsure if he is telling the truth.

Jeff's mind flashes back to the wooded area, and he remembers his bullets disappeared and reappeared without reason. He wonders whether, if it were to happen again, that would be his saving grace. He decides against looking, realizing that the uncertainty is far more exciting than the actuality of knowing for sure.

Jeff draws his gun from inside his belt, lifting his arm toward Calvin in what seems like slow motion. Calvin closes his eyes, awaiting the sting of pain to consume his body, and imagines the family reunion he is sure to be having in a matter of seconds. Silence is replaced by the clicking noises of Jeff's empty gun as he continuously pulls the trigger without stopping.

Calvin panics, and before he understands what is happening, his reflexes take over, and he fires. Jeff drops to the floor with a single gunshot wound to his forehead.

"No!" Calvin yells out. "You had plenty of time to kill me—why didn't you?"

Jeff falls back against the wall and slides down to the floor. Calvin looks at the pistol he is still gripping firmly and wonders, if he were to take his own life, if that would bring him back to his family.

Twinkling white lights appear, surround both Jeff and Dr. Livingston and in a matter of moments have vanished. Calvin is all alone once again and unable to complete a thought. His mind is scattered, and his hopes are gone.

Dr. Livingston's desk slowly fades, along with both chairs. Her paintings and diplomas hanging on the white, textured walls are next to follow. The sounds of crumbling are faint at first but grow louder with each moment.

"Someone please help me!" But his cry goes unheard.

Walls collapse, and chunks of ceiling drop all around, forcing his gaze upward. In a split second, he throws his arms over his head for protection as the ceiling comes crashing down on top of him.

CHAPTER

37

CALVIN AWAKENS SLUGGISHLY in a white-walled room, lying on his back and staring at the ceiling. His body is weak, and his mind disoriented. He shifts his weight and hears the familiar creaking of a hospital bed with each movement. Rays of sunlight escape from around the edges of the blinds as the aroma of cafeteria food fills the air. He watches particles of dust illuminated by the light linger in midair for several moments before settling on the windowsill. A whiteboard hanging on the wall at the foot of his bed displays the name "Cindy" written in pink marker next to the words "Day Nurse." Under her name are the initials "R. L." for "Doctor on Call." Above the whiteboard is a twenty-seven-inch black-box television set mounted just below the ceiling.

The sound of a clanking cart with one bad wheel has Calvin cringing as it slowly makes its way down the hall. The closer it gets, the more apparent it becomes that this is the moment his reoccurring dream is to come true. The noise increases intermittently, until hitting its loudest point just before coming to a stop outside his door.

A voice calls out to the room across the hall, "Are you ready for lunch, Mrs. Evans? I believe you have the chicken today."

Calvin chuckles nervously as he realizes his mind has been showing him glimpses of his own reality. He tries to move his arms, but both are tucked away, snug under the covers. He strains at breaking free a few more times before realizing his attempts are futile, forcing him to give up.

A shadow of a figure passes by his door.

"Excuse me, Miss," he calls, wondering why his voice sounds different. "Can you please help me?"

The woman stops and steps back, making her way into his room. She walks into his bathroom and emerges with a hand mirror. Her paisley scrubs are neatly pressed and look brand new. She places the mirror on the stand next to his bed, then checks the stats of his machines.

With her back still facing him, she asks, "You sound like yourself today. Do you know your name?"

"Yes. My name is Calvin Johnston."

The nurse turns around, smiling softly. "That's wonderful. I was hoping it would be you. How are you feeling this morning, Mr. Johnston?"

"What? What do you mean?"

She fumbles before stating, "I'm sorry, Mr. Johnston. I shouldn't have said anything. Your doctor should be here shortly and I'm sure she would prefer to be the one to explain this."

Calvin looks around confused. "I don't understand. Where am I?"

"Sounds like you might be having another spell," she says softly. "These seem to be occurring more and more lately, you poor thing."

She heads over to the window and in one swift motion pulls on the cord opening the blinds, allowing sunlight to spill in.

"There…That's much better. It was way too dark and gloomy before. Maybe your day will be much brighter now," she says, grinning happily.

Calvin glances up and is shocked as he recognizes the blond, curly locks and the bright, clear blue eyes staring back at him. "I know you."

"Of course…I'm your nurse, Mr. Johnston."

"No. That's not true. Your name is Cindy, and you work at the front desk behind the sliding-glass window in Dr. Livingston's office. You were filling in for Judy."

"I'm afraid I don't know anyone by the name of Judy. I'm sorry. Although I do know Dr. Livingston." Cindy looks down at her watch. "Actually, she should be making an appearance around noon."

"What do you mean? Dr. Livingston is dead. I watched her get shot. She died in my arms, because I couldn't stop it from happening," Calvin says with a shaky voice.

He concentrates on the initials R. L. listed on the whiteboard next to "Doctor on Call." *Dr. Rachael Livingston.* His excitement builds as he wonders if Cindy's memory loss is caused by the restarting of the cycle. *Did my plan work after all? If so, that means I kept my memory this time.* "Janice," he calls out. "Are you here?"

Cindy walks over to the intercom and presses the red button connecting her to the nurses' station. "Kathleen, are you there? It's Cindy."

"I'm here, Cindy. What do you need?"

"Would you please bring a fork to Mrs. Dickerson when you have a chance? Mr. Johnston is in need of additional attention after his morning nap, and I'm planning on being in here for a few more minutes."

"Sure thing. I'll take it right to her."

"Thank you."

Cindy picks up the hand mirror from his stand, before making her way over to Calvin. She pulls back the covers, freeing his arms, and pats his shoulder gently. He notices that his skin is riddled with age spots and is instantly overcome with confusion, coupled with anxiety. She places the mirror in his hands and gradually helps lift it to his face. In a panic, he immediately closes his eyes, afraid of what he might see.

"Here you go, sweetie. This usually helps," she says, using a caring tone.

It takes both hands and Cindy's help for him to hold the mirror in front of his face.

"It's okay. Take your time, and when you're ready, I'll be here with you."

Calvin senses her kindness and is eventually coaxed to give in. His hands are trembling as he opens his eyes barely past a slit to see a much different reflection than expected. His breathing increases as a sudden taste of fear presents itself, preventing him from looking away.

Stunned beyond belief, he asks, "What is this? Why am I so old?" He instantly remembers having to rush out of Dr. Livingston's office on his first visit after seeing this exact reflection. *Is this my life now? Has it always been my life? How many clues did my mind give me?*

Tiring out, he releases his grip and lets his hands fall against the bed. Cindy continues holding the mirror for a few more moments as Calvin stares at the old man spattered with age spots and topped by glowing white hair. He notices a long scar stretching down the side of his face and remembers the conversation where Robert mentioned the several lacerations he had sustained during the accident. A scar that has faded over time and been consumed by wrinkles. He pulls the fat of his cheek upwards and releases, watching it fall back into place.

Cindy laughs, saying, "You do that every time."

Calvin fidgets with his hands while collecting his thoughts. "You mentioned that Dr. Livingston is alive," he says, his voice showing skepticism.

"Yes. Alive and well. In fact, she is scheduled to meet with you directly following your lunch. She should be able to answer all of your questions and have you feeling less anxious in no time."

He glances over at a wall clock displaying 11:37. There is a knock at the door.

"Speaking of lunch," she says excitedly. "What are we having today, Clarence?"

"Salisbury steak for Mr. Johnston," a deep, raspy voice answers back.

Dr. Livingston pokes her head in through the doorway. She is wearing a long white coat with her name stenciled on the chest pocket.

"I heard from the nurses' station you are in need of additional attention this morning. Are you feeling okay?"

Calvin's eyes water at the sight of her. "It really is you. I can't believe you look exactly the same."

She watches and waits next to the bathroom as Clarence raises Calvin's bed to an upright position before moving the stand and placing his lunch tray on top. Dr. Livingston smiles with approval while Clarence nods, before leaving the room.

"Looks like you're having another bad day. Unfortunately, it seems to be normal for you lately. I'm planning on coming back after you've had a chance to enjoy your lunch. I just wanted to stop in before starting my rounds."

"Please don't go. I would rather talk to you than eat. I really miss our conversations. Having you around always makes me feel better."

Dr. Livingston looks toward Cindy and says, "It's really hard to say no to someone so sweet."

Cindy smiles as Dr. Livingston makes her way over to his bed.

"Tell you what. I'll come back in a few minutes to talk, if you promise to eat every bite."

Calvin grabs a fork, eager to please, but struggles briefly with maintaining his grip.

"Would you like some help with your lunch?"

"No, thanks," he mutters, fighting back his frustrations.

"I need to run to my office downstairs and pick up some notes before we begin. I'm planning on taking Cindy away for now so she can enjoy her lunch as well. In the meantime, go ahead and start eating and I'll be back shortly."

"See you later, Mr. Johnston," Cindy says, giving him a quick wave.

"Good-bye, Cindy. It was great to see you again. I'm really glad you were the first person I saw. Thanks for being so nice to me."

Dr. Livingston and Cindy walk out of the room together and head toward the nurses' station.

Halfway there, Cindy asks, "Do you think he's going to be okay?"

"I'm not sure. His health has rapidly declined over the last few months, and I'm not liking the direction he is heading."

"Did he ever change his mind about choosing not to be resuscitated?"

"No. It's still against his wishes. Unfortunately, as of this moment his DNR stands."

"That's a shame. I sure would miss our time together if he were gone. He's probably the sweetest patient we have, not to mention my favorite by far."

"I know what you mean. There's something about him that really stays with you. A familiarity that's hard to shake. I haven't received any text messages lately. Are you still teaching him how to text on your iPhone?"

"Oh, he's mastered that," she says proudly. "Over the last couple of weeks, I've even showed him how to take pictures and search the Internet. He's discovered YouTube and loves to watch videos of the Mercedes C-Class and the Audi A6."

Dr. Livingston nods, signaling approval. "He has nice taste."

"Yes, he does," Cindy says, stopping at the end of the hall. Her eyebrows arch as her expression becomes puzzled. "If he were to die, a part of me is hoping for today. Is that wrong?"

Dr. Livingston stops, turns, and faces her. "It depends on the reasoning behind your statement. I think I already know the answer, but I'm going to ask the question anyway. Why today?"

"Because of the love he still has for his wife. He always says his life starts and ends with her. It would…"

Dr. Livingston says, "Keep going. It's okay."

"It would seem almost poetic. A perfect way to end eighty-four years."

Dr. Livingston smiles softly. "I completely understand. It's a nice thought." She turns and heads for the elevators as Cindy makes her way behind the nurses' station and pulls up a chair behind the main desk.

A few minutes later, the ding of the elevator sounds. There is a slight pause before the doors open, and Dr. Livingston emerges with briefcase in hand. She heads for Calvin's room, the clip-clop of her heels echoing with each quick step, until stopping at the entrance of his doorway.

"Are you still in the mood for catching up?"

She gives him a thumbs-up as she realizes he is well on his way to honoring his part of the bargain, having already eaten a little less than half of his lunch.

"Of course. I'm looking forward to it."

"Wow. This is the most you have eaten in a while. How is it?"

"Not too bad. The best Salisbury steak I can ever remember eating."

Dr. Livingston chuckles at first, then shoots him an inquisitive look. She scoots a chair across the room and rests it against the side of his bed. She places her briefcase in it before walking over and sliding a second chair in front of the first. She sits while grabbing the notepad from her briefcase and immediately begins flipping through the pages.

"What are you doing?" Calvin asks.

"I have put together a list of questions and answers as an aid over the years. It helps guide me through your inquiries." She laughs softly. "As you can tell, we've done this a few times. Do you have specific questions for me?"

Without hesitating he states, "Yes, I have several. Cindy mentioned she was glad it was me when she first entered my room. What did she mean? Who else would it have been?"

Dr. Livingston takes his hand and begins stroking it gently. "That is an excellent question. It's the one I've had the most trouble answering over the years. I should start out by saying you have had some difficulty defining who you are as a person. It is something you have struggled with on and off for quite a while now."

"What do you mean?"

"Sometimes in your mind you become someone else. It's as if you take over their entire personality as your own."

"Are you saying I have multiple personalities?"

"Not in the traditional sense. To give you an example, a few weeks back early in the morning you were convinced you were me."

"You?" Calvin asks, trying to comprehend.

"Yes, and it was a little unnerving to say the least," she says warmly. "Actually, you were quite good. Much better than I expected."

"Nothing makes sense," Calvin mutters. "I can't believe this is my life."

Dr. Livingston senses his frustration and asks, "If you need a break we can always talk about something else and come back to this conversation at another time."

"How many personalities in total are there?" he asks.

She hesitates then decides against answering, instead trying to get a read on his stability.

"I'm fine, Doc. You can answer. It's okay."

"There have been many. You would often hold conversations as if they were here in the room with you."

"So I'm crazy."

"Confused would be a more appropriate description."

"Did you ever witness any of the conversations?"

"Yes, quite a few. They were fascinating to say the least."

"What did I discuss?"

"You talked to your wife often. You had somehow created an entirely new lifestyle away from this reality. One that seemed almost perfect. Until…"

"Until what?" Calvin asks eagerly.

"The most recent conversation was with a Jeff and a Kathy. It appeared as if you were reaching closure."

"You know about Jeff and Kathy?"

"Yes, I heard you speaking to them. I have to say both Jeff and Kathy were the least desirable by far."

Calvin's face softens as he stares caringly at Dr. Livingston. "Who else have I become?"

"My absolute favorite has to be Figure X."

Stunned, he sputters out, "You know about Figure X too?" But before she has a chance to answer, he pulls his arm out of Dr. Livingston's grip. His expression saddens at the realization that Figure X is only in his imagination. "You were right. I do need a break from this conversation. Can we talk about something else?"

"Of course. Your choice. Anything you like."

"Where are we?"

"You are a resident of Lakeside Assisted Care Living."

Lakeside. So the park wasn't real either. "How long have I been here?"

"A little over eight years."

"My room looks like I'm in a hospital. How come?"

"You are in the Alzheimer's ward."

Calvin's shoulders slump in defeat. "I have Alzheimer's too?"

"Not exactly. You have severe memory loss that has been working in conjunction with each additional personality. This ward was just a close fit. Although, after today's conversation, you do seem to be much clearer than ever before."

"You were right about the closure. I don't get the impression we have to worry about any future memory loss or any of my personalities coming back. I believe from this point on you are stuck with only me." Calvin grins while shifting his body so that he is leaning more toward Dr. Livingston. "Something inside my body doesn't feel right. What's happening to me?"

"Over time your illnesses have degraded your quality of life, including your ability to walk and, until today, your appetite."

"I feel like I'm on my deathbed. Am I going to die soon?" Calvin lets out a shallow breath, unable to accomplish anything deeper. "Please. Just the truth."

"There's no way to know for sure. The latest declines would suggest that unless something changes, there's a possibility of sooner rather than later."

"Thank you for being honest. How about my wife? Is she still dead from the accident, or was the whole thing only a dream?"

"You remember the car accident?"

"Yes. I was driving the day she and my unborn son were killed. This all happened in June 2010."

Doctor Livingston grimaces.

"What's the matter, Doc? You have that disapproving look on your face again."

"Nothing serious. Your timeline is a little off, and some of your information seems to be incorrect. Nothing we can't straighten out in a matter of minutes."

"What do you mean?"

"Do you know what today is?"

"No."

"It's Sunday, June 21."

Calvin closes his eyes. The dream version of Dr. Livingston was killed on Sunday, June 14. I lost exactly one week somehow.

"Do you know your age?"

"From my last experience, I would say forty-three. However, judging from the amount of age spots stacked on top of wrinkles, I'm guessing much older."

"We celebrated your eighty-fourth birthday back on March 13. Are you sure you want me to continue? Some of what I have to tell you is going to be painful, and at this point it might not matter to you any longer."

"I have to know, Doc. Why wouldn't my life matter to me?"

"That didn't come out right. My apologies for sounding inconsiderate to your feelings. Of course it matters. What I meant to say was that I would like to spare you as much grief as possible. I have witnessed from past experiences the toll and anguish hearing about your life seems to take on you each time. Your mental health is equally important to me as your physical health. I just want to prepare you, if you decide to continue."

"I have been confused for so long, I no longer know what's true."

Dr. Livingston reaches back into her briefcase and pulls out additional notes, including a police report she received from Robert. "There was a fatal car accident in which you were the driver, and your wife was killed. You are correct about that. But the date was June 21, 1973. Today marks the fortieth anniversary of your wife's and son's deaths."

Calvin slowly raises his head, trying unsuccessfully to sit up further. Shock takes over, leaving him in a daze as he slowly sits back and rests his head on his pillow.

"Your son was five at the time, not unborn."

"I had a son?"

"Yes. His name was Daniel. You had thrown out all of your pictures the first week you moved in, but I rescued them from the trash, if you would like to see him."

"Of course...please."

She stands and reaches over, placing a Polaroid in his hand. "Do you recognize the person in this photo?"

"Yes. He is one of the victims of the car accident. I don't know his name, but I referred to him as 'the grandson.' He is the one I pulled out of his grandmother's yellow Honda Accord. I think I may have been partially responsible for her death."

Dr. Livingston tenses, fearing his condition may be worsening.

"Mr. Johnston, I'm not sure you understand. The picture you are holding in your hand is of your son, Daniel. He was five years old when he died in the back seat of your wife's car after the accident." She flips through several pages of notes before reaching back into her bag. "I have the report here, and you are correct about an older woman. However, she was alone that day. No other people were in her car. In fact, there were no other children involved other than your son, Daniel."

"Did I move him from the car?"

"No. He died on scene in the back seat. There appears to have been something metal that pierced his kidney."

Tears trickle down Calvin's face as he stares into the dark brown eyes of Dr. Livingston. "Thank you. That was news worth hearing."

"I want to talk to you about the DNR you have on file. Do you know what that means?"

"Yes. Do not resuscitate."

"That's correct. Are you still in agreement with this?"

"Yes. I have nothing else to live for," he says, his voice weakening. "Can I have some time to myself? I would like to be alone for now."

"Of course. I'll check back in later."

Calvin lies quietly in his bed with nothing but thoughts of his life coming to an end. He struggles briefly with staying awake, trying to prolong the inevitable. His mind is telling him his body is tired and needs some rest. *Maybe another dream to see my wife and son one more time. I hope to see you soon, sweetheart.* A single tear runs down his cheek as he whispers, "I love you. I'm sorry I never got to say good-bye."

CHAPTER

38

OVER TWO HOURS have slipped away as the sound of Calvin's snoring rings out loudly, reverberating off the walls, ending with one final snort. Unexpectedly, everything goes quiet, leaving behind a peace in the air of unusual proportions. He opens his eyes and waits for the surrounding walls to come into focus before glancing around an empty room and discovering nothing has changed. He is still old and still alone. A slight wheezing escapes from his mouth as he takes what he expects to be one of his last breaths. His mouth is dry, and his body weak. His instincts for survival are tucked away, hiding in the fog of his mind with little chance of emerging. Knowing there is nothing else left, he is comforted the most by thoughts of drifting off to a permanent sleep. He fights this urge by blinking several times, but it's of no use. His eyelids are heavy, and their weight is too much to bear as his eyes slowly close a little at a time, until nothing but darkness prevails.

One by one, tiny white lights appear, twinkling wildly, as Figure X makes his entrance. He is standing tall and staring in Calvin's direction, with his white beady eyes gleaming brightly. He watches Calvin's chest rise and fall with every shallow breath before lowering his hand and draping his long, bony fingers gently onto his face. Calvin stirs a little while traces of heat begin to penetrate his skin, soaking into his mind and clearing away his thoughts.

"Please leave me alone," he grumbles. "I've had enough. Everything aches on my body, and I've lost the only things I've ever cared about. I just want to die, along with my self-pity, and put it behind me for good."

"It is not time for you to give up. Open your eyes," a deep, soothing voice commands.

A sense of panic suddenly consumes Calvin as he realizes this is not a nurse. "What are you doing to me?" he growls. "Wait…Figure X? Is that you?"

"Yes."

"Is this a dream?"

"No."

"I didn't think you were real. What are you doing here?"

"I made a promise, and I'm prepared to stand by my word."

"What promise?"

"The one where I vowed to remain by your side until my help was no longer needed. There is no reason for someone like you to ever die alone."

Figure X releases his grip that cradled Calvin's face and now takes hold of his hand.

Calvin sucks in shallow breaths, feeling like his lungs are working against him. "You say that like we're there," he states softly. "Is this the end?"

"Do you want it to be?"

"Yes. Very much so."

"Even now with so many unfulfilled questions, knowing I have the answers?"

Calvin absorbs the heat rushing through his veins as it escapes from Figure X's hand. A slight tingling sensation pulsates through his body, increasing his energy level only mildly, but enough to pique his interest.

"I was wrong. I want to know the truth, regardless of how painful it might be."

"Then you should ask your first question."

"I keep picturing images of the farmhouse. Why is it important?"

"After the deaths of your wife and son, it was deemed an accident and no charges were ever filed against the truck driver. He owned the farmhouse you are referring to. It was not far from where the accident occurred. You would often sit outside his house for hours at a time, thinking about Janice and Daniel, remembering better times and feeling overwhelmed with guilt and hatred. You blamed the truck driver as much as you did yourself for taking everything away from you. This turned into an obsession and eventually took control of your life. From that moment on, you were never the same."

Calvin moves his head slowly in the direction opposite from Figure X as the memories trickle in with each word spoken. "I remember this. I wanted to ruin his life the way I thought he had ruined mine. I needed to blame someone for robbing me of my family, hoping to lessen my guilt and my pain. I knew I was out of control, but I was blinded by my rage and refused to believe the truth. The simple God's honest truth..." Calvin says, his voice changing to a whisper. "It was merely a freak accident, completely out of our control. It wasn't anyone's fault."

His mind begins to wander. His body begins to shake lightly as he is consumed by an uneasy feeling. "When you mentioned the truck driver, you said he owned the house in past tense. I didn't do anything to him, did I?"

"No. It was never in your nature to be violent. Only to mourn for the loss of your wife and son."

Calvin feels a sense of relief and releases the self-sustaining burden that has overcome him since the accident. "What happened next?"

"Seven years later, he died from complications of heart disease. You had a contract pending the first week the house was listed on the market and lived there miserably for many years. Your mind had already begun experiencing lapses in time and started creating an alternate life cycle in your dreams. You were slowly drifting outside your realm of reality a small piece at a time. Your condition eventually worsened until you were unable to care for yourself and were forced to make other living arrangements."

"I remember. There were a total of three nursing homes, including here. Each one had a distinct smell, of which I wanted no part. They reeked of death and rotting souls. I missed my family more than I could comprehend and wanted them back so badly I could taste it. They were my passion and only reason for living."

"Your mind started to deteriorate, and the idea of creating your own world flourished. The memory loss and the ability to separate from everyday life by becoming someone else were all that were needed to complete the transition. You were finally going to be able to live permanently in a place you'd only ever been allowed to visit."

"This is when my first cycle began. I had no memory that I was reliving each moment of my life over again."

"Yes. You were sixty-one at the time, although in your world you were only thirty-eight, celebrating the birth of Daniel while standing alongside your wife in the delivery room. Your seemingly perfect life progressively took a change for the worse with each cycle. You were trapped in an infinite loop inside your mind, created to stifle your guilt and pain. The loss of your family and all of the lives taken the day of the accident was something you couldn't overcome, even in a fantasy you had created yourself."

Calvin clears his throat, trying to fight the dryness turning into a tickle. He is unsure what Figure X is doing but senses it is working. The ache in his body is slowly leaving as his thoughts and memories are becoming clearer.

"I spoke to you about my son before the cycle ended. I specifically asked if I ever had any children, and you said no. Why did you lie to me?"

"I had no choice. It would have only caused unnecessary confusion."

"What do you mean?"

"Imagine the consequences if I had told you the grandson never existed. That in fact that same five-year-old boy was actually your son. Everything you knew to be true would have started to unravel the moment it sank in. I would have put you in a dangerous position. There were specific steps and precise sequences to be followed in order to maintain the illusion. I did not feel the timing was right and was afraid you were not ready to hear the truth. I'm sorry I lied to you, but it was my decision to make, and I did so with your best interest in mind."

"I understand. No hard feelings. Please keep going."

"We have monitored you over the course of forty-one years. During this time, we have come across situations where the incorrect details were challenged by us in order to right the information. This only added chaos and was later self-corrected in your mind. We have tried using many methods to help guide you to a conclusion, with the ultimate goal of self-forgiveness and closure. We were confident those were the key elements needed to release you from your restraints and free you from your imaginary world permanently. The most effective way to do so has always been the mystery, which you had to solve to find the answers yourself. We learned from experience that the direction your mind chose was the path we must also follow without dispute."

"I don't understand."

"Think of the world your mind created specifically for you as comparable to a dream state. You are not only the main participant but the puppeteer who manipulates and controls as the need arises."

"If that's true, then how were you able to enter my thoughts?"

"This is something that took a decade to master. We have always been able to read your mind once the bridge was established. However, by the third cycle, when you would have been seventy-one, we were able to successfully implant into your dream world and became actual participants. The ability to not only monitor but to be partakers had never been achieved with anyone until you. This was quite an accomplishment and received lots of positive attention. Our council's fascination guaranteed me and my team approval to observe you full-time for the rest of your life. It was at that moment we proclaimed our commitment to remain by your side until the end. During all of the years, not one member of my group ever resigned from this assignment. We have all remained true to our word."

Calvin takes comfort in these words, knowing that at the worst moments in his life there was still someone interested in watching over him. He is startled by high concentrations of energy coursing through his body, with the release of endorphins, and lets out a slight shriek. The heat radiating from Figure X's hand is at its highest level and starting to become uncomfortable. Calvin can feel beads of sweat glide down the palm of his hand but does his best to push the discomfort out of his mind, knowing it is well worth it.

"What else can you tell me?"

"We believe this was to be your last cycle, regardless of the outcome."

"Do you know this for sure, or are you guessing?"

"This is based on our calculation."

Calvin takes a deep breath and does so several times while watching Figure X, intent on hearing every last word of what he has to say.

"I should mention that every cycle except the last has always been repeated after five years."

"Five years?" Calvin asks, his voice filled with doubt.

"That's correct."

"How many does that add up to?"

"There were a total of five cycles. Each one started with the birth of your son and lasted until a few weeks after the deaths of your wife and son. My team has done extensive research, and according to our calculations, we believe we have the answer."

"What are you saying? What calculations?"

"We believe this last cycle was cut down to three years based on the amount of time you had left in your life. This is the only scenario that makes sense. You were right on schedule until everything drastically moved up in time. The actual dates you were living in your mind did not coincide with the real world until the last week, starting with Wednesday, June 10, 2015. This was the day your mind recreated a version of Dr. Livingston in order for your first therapy session to take place."

"Why do you think she was added?"

"A drastic change had transpired, and you needed a way to cope. Since you were already familiar with Dr. Livingston and were not only fond of her, but trusted her implicitly, she became a reality inside as well as outside. She was the strength and guidance you needed to complete the final cycle."

"You're right. I did need her. That explains why she didn't vanish when I asked her to," he mumbles. Calvin glances over at Figure X. "I'm sorry. I got distracted. What were you saying about calculations?"

"According to our calculations, we do not think your body was going to last the full five years, as previously planned. As soon as it was realized, a new timetable was added and details changed."

"Like what?"

"This is when your mind took away the three-year-old Daniel and had you believe you never had children."

"And you reinforced the idea, making sure it would stick."

"Yes. We felt it was the best course of action. Even with the correction, we believe there was still a void that the creation of the five-year-old grandson was necessary to fill."

"I was standing in my hall and saw an image of the grandson. He reached his hands out for me and called me 'Daddy.' I didn't understand at the time," Calvin says, getting choked up. A look of confusion comes over his face.

"You have stated before that I avoided death the day of the accident. Is this true?"

"Yes."

"Then how do you know I won't do it again?"

"Your body is slowly shutting down and giving all the signs. We believe it is your intention, whether consciously or subconsciously, to die today on the forty-year anniversary of the death of your wife and son."

A smile crosses Calvin's face. *What a perfect ending.*

"We thought you might agree."

"I do. I can definitely live with that decision." He laughs, realizing what he said. "Correction...I mean I'm okay with dying on their anniversary. I wouldn't have it any other way, honestly. Do you know what time it's supposed to happen?"

"Yes. To the exact moment," Figure X states as he releases his grip.

"Based on your watch or mine?" Calvin says, trying to laugh, but ending up coughing deeply. After catching his breath, he states, "I believe you are right. My entire body aches and I can feel the end getting closer."

"Then it's time to face the last of your demons. What do you remember about Jeff, Kathy, and Frank?"

Calvin pauses briefly. "My mind had it wrong. Especially about Frank. He wasn't a killer. He was a good man. An innocent bystander caught in a situation that should have never happened."

"So you remember?"

"Yes." Calvin's expression turns cold. "Jeff and Kathy were in love but not in the traditional sense. They enjoyed creating pain for other people and thrived on taking the lives of the innocent. Their relationship was built on it."

Calvin closes his eyes and focuses before speaking. "Fifteen years to the day that Janice and Daniel were killed I started receiving newspaper clippings on my front porch. The first few were about a robbery turned to murder at a Shell station off of US 75. At first glance, I immediately realized similarities. I even made a list."

"What did it show you?"

"The location of the Shell station was a few miles away from my accident."

"What else?"

"The robbery and my accident were both on the same day and happened only a couple hours apart. It seemed too perfectly aligned to be a coincidence, but I could never piece together the details until one day I received several different papers all at once. They contained many articles including the obits for every person killed in the Shell station robbery and the car accident. There was a note written in blue sharpie duct-taped to the paper that was on top. It read, 'Truth or Ignorance. Stay ignorant or find out the truth—meet me—Shell Station, 1:30 p.m.' It was signed by Jeff Jergens. At the time I didn't know anything about this man. All I knew was someone appeared to have answers to my many questions." Calvin stops for a moment to catch his breath and notices his hands are trembling again.

"Please, don't stop. It is crucial that—"

"I brought a gun with me." Calvin keeps his focus strong. "I wasn't sure what I was going to find and I wanted to make certain I was protected. Although, looking back, I wish I hadn't." Calvin looks deeply into the beady white eyes and sees compassion. "I'm sorry I interrupted you."

"There is no need to apologize," Figure X states. "This is your moment to cleanse your soul."

Calvin hesitates briefly but knows he is right. "I made it to the Shell station about fifteen minutes early and as I pulled into the parking lot I immediately felt saddened. The store was run down and looked to be closed for some time, judging from the amount of rust on the pumps and the overgrown grass surrounding the building. My heart started pounding the moment a long, black, four door sedan pulled in. I watched him blow smoke rings through the few-inch opening in the driver's-side window for a couple of minutes and I wondered if I had made a mistake. He finally finished smoking and, while stepping out of his car, he flicked his lit cigarette toward the pumps. He was small in stature, maybe 5'6" or so, but I could tell by the way he walked that he was extremely arrogant and had something to prove. He wasted no time bragging about how he and his girlfriend Kathy had robbed and killed everyone at the Shell station. With every description, I remembered back to each of their articles and felt as if I knew them. The pain and suffering they must have felt, not to mention the unbearable fear."

"Do you remember how many people?"

"Nine. Frank was the first to die. He was working as an attendant behind the counter. Jeff shot and killed him for no reason other than for staring at Kathy for too long. The next victims were a mother and son by the name of Judy and Gary. From the articles, I knew that Gary suffered from a slight case of autism and that he and his mother had stopped for candy on the way to a doctor's appointment. He was wearing his favorite Texas Rangers baseball cap at the time." Calvin stops and sighs in disgust. "The Kearman sisters were next. Jeff was most excited to tell this story. He vividly described their deaths up to when he chased one of the sisters down and jumped on her back. He rode her like an animal before breaking her neck with his bare hands." He stares blankly at the wall feeling mentally exhausted and completely overrun with emotions. "This is making me sick, I'm not sure I can finish."

"Yes, you can. You must."

Fighting the urge to quit, he decides to keep going. "The last to die were a family of four killed in the parking lot: Alicia, Dave, Brian, and Brendon."

"This is the family whom you seemed quite fond of."

"That's correct. However, I didn't really know them except the made-up version my mind had created. They were close to our age and seemed like people we would have gotten along with pretty well. I guess I needed someone I could bond with and call a friend."

"Who was responsible for their deaths?"

"According to Jeff, Kathy shot all four in cold blood. Their youngest was about Daniel's age and died from a single gunshot wound to the head." Calvin's eye twitches as he fights to continue. "Jeff stated he was responsible for one more death, but I wasn't sure who he was talking about until he pointed to the station. The owner's name was James Smithers. He was a recovering alcoholic who used to hold AA meetings free of charge at a local church. After the murders the Shell station never reopened and James eventually killed himself. I guess if you count his death, then I misstated earlier when I said the count was nine. James would have been number ten." Calvin's voice cracks. "I didn't understand why he was telling me all of this until he described what came next. He claimed responsibility for the accident. He talked about how it had been raining heavily off and on all day and how after they left the Shell station they headed north on 75. They drove through some ponding in the fast lane of the highway and watched in amazement as a small wave of water shot barely over the wall into oncoming traffic. They both immediately realized the potential and knew what their next move would be. So, they drove up and down the highway for over two hours before finding an unsuspecting truck driver who they badgered and coerced into the left lane. They knew that the second he hit the standing water the size and force of the wave shooting over the barrier would almost certainly cause disaster for every driver in its path. The rest we already know."

Calvin slowly raises his hand to his face and gently rubs the faded scar on his cheek. "I can't believe they drove for almost two hours to find someone. And because of this all those people died, including my wife and son. I had blamed the truck driver for so long that I was completely blown away to find out someone else was behind it. I had never met anyone with such little regard for human lives. Listening to Jeff tell his version of what happened that day made me so mad I couldn't think straight. Before I realized what I was doing I had already pulled out my gun and aimed it at his face. My arm was shaking so badly I had to stabilize the gun by using both hands. He kept taunting me by telling me to do it. I felt my trigger finger twitching from an unquenchable ache deep inside. I kept thinking all I had to do was kill him and drag his body to the wooded area behind the store. There wasn't anything that would link me to him." Calvin turns away from Figure X to catch his breath. "Even after everything he put me and many others through, I was still weak and he knew it. He laughed at me and even called me a cry baby as I ran away like a coward. I let everyone down and I was haunted by it every day from that point on."

"You were right not to kill him."

"I know. I also know something inside of me broke that day."

Calvin looks over at the door and panics. "What if one of my nurses comes in? It just dawned on me my doors have been open the whole time you've been here. Aren't you worried about someone walking in and seeing you?"

"It's not necessary to worry. Do you remember when I told you that you were the only person to ever see either me or my colleagues without their sanctioning it?"

"Yes."

"That wasn't exactly true. There have been a total of three people in my lifetime to have seen either me or my colleagues without permission."

"Let me guess. Do I know them?"

"Yes. Very well."

Calvin thinks for a few moments. "My father and my son were the other two."

Figure X, surprised by his answer, looks directly into his eyes and Calvin can sense the sincerity in his voice. "You are correct."

Calvin grunts, feeling the life being drained from his body. His eyes water as the pain inside worsens.

"Please make it stop. It hurts," he whispers surprised to see two of Figure X's colleagues appear. "Why are they here?"

"This is the time I ask you if you would like to live amongst us on our planet. If you say no, they will disappear, leaving you to die in peace."

"What about you?"

Figure X takes hold of his hand one last time. "I am here to relieve as much pain as possible, regardless of your decision. I have no intention of leaving you until you have passed. As I stated earlier, there is no reason for someone like you to die alone, but I need your answer before it is too late."

"I want to get some things off my chest first."

"Of course."

"I'm really embarrassed at how my life turned out," he says, his voice cracking. Tears stream down his cheeks as he feels the last half of his life was a bitter disappointment.

"There is no disgrace in loving your family and devoting your entire existence to their memory. I have lived many years and have never come across anyone who has ever done it as well as you. You should be proud, not ashamed. Everyone familiar with this case has told me on more than one occasion that you have honored their memory to the fullest. They feel privileged to have been a part of this and to have known you."

Calvin smiles as his eyes close gently. "The pain doesn't hurt as much anymore. Thank you for taking that away for me." His strength diminishes to the point of almost disappearing completely. *I can tell my death is close now. Thank you for being so loyal. I'm not sure I deserve it but I'm certainly grateful.*

"It has been a pleasure," Figure X responds softly.

Calvin hears the beeping of a monitor in the background growing louder and wonders if it is for him as he feels his pulse weaken. "I appreciate the offer but think I should stick to my original decision and respectfully decline. I've lived many years with heartache as my companion. I think I've finally had my fill."

He glances behind Figure X and sees the arrival of many more colleagues now.

"What are they doing? I thought you said they would leave after I said no. Why have more joined?"

Figure X's voice quivers, humbled by their actions. "Every single member of my group has shown up to pay their respects. Something I have never witnessed before, but I feel is well deserved. Rest in peace, old friend."

Calvin's pulse slows even more as he loses his ability to speak. His mind wanders, and he begins to drift in and out of consciousness. He sees a large variety of lights, ranging in colors, some of which he is unable to identify. They are glittering wildly, reaching from the floor and extending through the ceiling. *They're so beautiful. Why do they look familiar?*

"Because you have witnessed them before."

I don't understand. Please explain.

"The day your father took his own life, we were there to collect him. We were also there to collect your wife and son on the day of their passing."

What are you saying? Is my family on your planet?

"Yes. In the beginning all three members were.

What do you mean were?

We ran into unforeseeable complications while on my planet. Unfortunately, only one of your family members were able to successfully complete the full transition."

Which one?

"I cannot say. I have been sworn to secrecy."

Why are you doing all of this? Why take humans?

"It is important to our survival."

Why me?

"We believe you are the key." Figure X leans in closer and whispers, "Come with me. There are things you need to experience. A whole new life is available, but you have to give permission."

I can't. I'm too afraid.

"Then we have misjudged you greatly."

Please tell me which person is waiting for me? Is it my father?

"I'm sorry. You are out of time and we can't take you after you've passed."

Seconds feel like minutes until Calvin finally realizes there is only one choice he must make. *I accept*, he thinks, before feeling a crushing weight on his chest as the lights turn out and his life comes to an end.

Dr. Livingston rushes into the room and is immediately greeted by the solid green flat line gliding across the screen of the heart monitor. Cindy is standing at the foot of his bed, wishing there were something they could do to revoke the DNR, but she realizes it's too late. She is holding three single red roses, with tears streaming uncontrollably down her cheek. Her heart is aching as she lightly places each rose down at his feet one at a time.

"These are for you, your wife, and your son. I hope you're finally together now."

She turns away, surprised to see that each of the attending nurses has gathered to say their good-byes as well. Not an eye in the room is dry as she walks toward the door and out into the hall, knowing she will never hold his hand again, never teach him another trick on her phone and, most importantly, never regret the amount of time she was able to spend with him. *I wish someone had been with you to comfort you during your time of need. It breaks my heart you died alone but at least I can take comfort in knowing it happened on the anniversary of the deaths of your wife and son. You will be missed more than you could have ever imagined.*

CHRIS LAMKIN lives in Texas with his wife of twenty years and two teenage daughters. He took a year off from his career in accounting to write his first novel, "Zero Days Left" and is currently working on the sequel.

WWW.ZERODAYSLEFT.COM

Made in the USA
Las Vegas, NV
30 July 2021

27253623R00184